D1053377

The Big Exit

BY THE SAME AUTHOR

Knife Music

The Big Exit

DAVID CARNOY

THE OVERLOOK PRESS
NEW YORK, NY

This edition first published in hardcover in the United States in 2012 by
The Overlook Press, Peter Mayer Publishers, Inc.

NEW YORK
141 Wooster Street
New York, NY 10012
www.overlookpress.com
For bulk and special sales, please contact sales@overlookny.com

Cataloging-in-Publication Data is available from the Library of Congress

Book Design and typeformatting by Bernard Schleifer
Manufactured in the United States of America
2 4 6 8 10 9 7 5 3 1
ISBN 978-1-59020-515-0

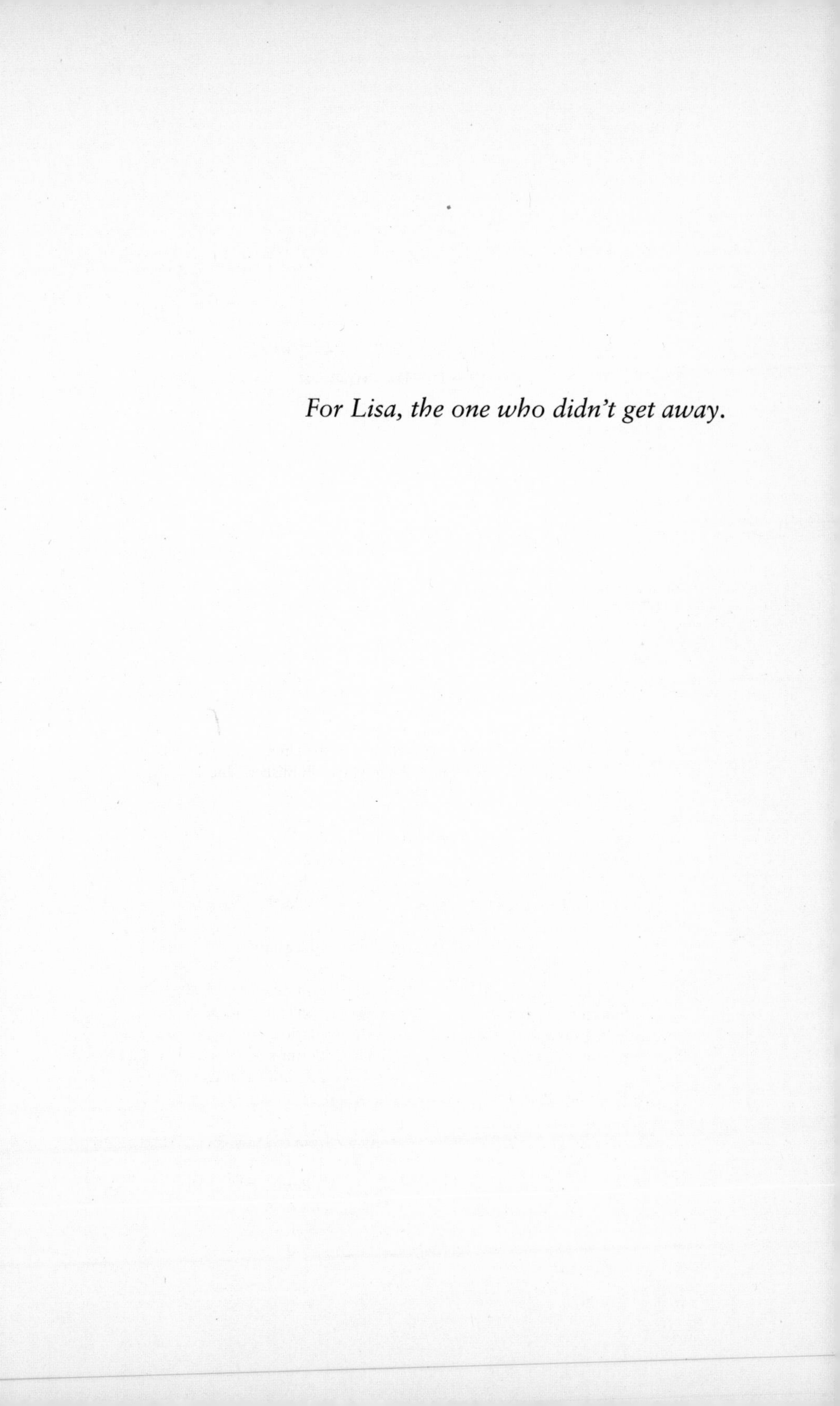

For Lisa, the one who didn't get away.

Don't get even, get mad.
—Frank Sinatra

0 / PROLOGUE

911 dispatcher: 911, state your emergency.

Hill: It's my husband.

911 dispatcher: Yes, go ahead.

Hill: Please get someone here. (Incoherent).

911 dispatcher: Miss, I can't hear you. Can you please speak into the phone?

Hill: My husband's dead. Someone's killed my husband.

911 dispatcher: Okay. Are you certain he's dead?

Hill: He didn't have a pulse. There's blood everywhere. Oh my God.

911 dispatcher: Ma'am, can you please tell me your name?

Hill: Beth Hill.

911 dispatcher: Are you in your home?

Hill: No, I'm outside. Please get someone here quickly. [redacted] Robert S Drive. I'm afraid he's still here.

911 dispatcher: Who's still there?

Hill: Whoever did this. My God. I can't breathe.

911 dispatcher: Ma'am, are you in a safe room? Are you in a room where the door can be locked?

Hill: No, I'm outside near the garage.

911 dispatcher: But the phone you're on, it's cordless?

Hill: It's my cell phone. I'm going inside now.

911 dispatcher: Is there anybody else in the house?

Hill: No.

911 dispatcher: Do you have children?

Hill: No. (Sound of door opening). Okay, I'm in the den. I'm shutting the door.

911 dispatcher: Good. Okay. Someone will be right over. A police officer will be there shortly. And I'll stay on the phone until he comes. My name is Susan. Can you tell me, where in the house did you find your husband?

Hill: He wasn't in the house. He was in the garage.

911 dispatcher: And you said there was a lot of blood. Did someone shoot him?

Hill: I don't know. I don't think so. There was so much blood it was hard to tell. I didn't think it was Mark. I kept saying, it's not him. It couldn't be. But I saw his watch. He wears a Rolex.

911 dispatcher: And you said you touched him?

Hill: I touched his wrist to feel his pulse.

911 dispatcher: And you couldn't feel anything?

Hill: I knew it. As soon as I saw him. I knew he was dead.

911 dispatcher: Can you tell me how you found him?

Hill: I came home. I went to pull the car in the garage and there he was. I saw him in my headlights. He was on the floor of the garage.

911 dispatcher: His car was in the garage?

Hill: No, just outside. Well, the one car—the one he was driving—was outside the garage and the other was inside. He has two cars.

911 dispatcher: Was the garage door open?

Hill: Yes.

911 dispatcher: The lights are off, though? The car wasn't running?

Hill: No, the car wasn't running.

911 dispatcher: Beth, the police should be there any minute. So hang on, okay?

Hill: (Incoherent).

911 dispatcher: If you want to say anything, you just go right ahead.

Hill: I can't believe this is happening.

911 dispatcher: Beth, can you tell me whether you saw anything unusual? Was there a car you didn't know parked down the street?

Hill: No. I didn't see anything.

911 dispatcher: And do you know when your husband came home? Did he tell you when he was coming home?

Hill: Not exactly. He BlackBerry'd me around four to say that he was leaving the office early today and that he wouldn't be late. But I don't know when he left.

911 dispatcher: And how long does it take him to get home?

Hill: Around twenty minutes, depending on the traffic.

911 dispatcher: So you think somewhere around—(Beeping noise). Is someone trying to call?

Hill: (pause) It's my neighbor.

911 dispatcher: You see the number in caller ID?

Hill: Yes. They must have heard me screaming.

911 dispatcher: Do you want to put me on hold and speak with them?

Hill: No. Wait, I hear something.

911 dispatcher: Is someone in the house? (pause) Beth, do you hear someone in the house?

Hill: It's outside. I think they're here.

911 dispatcher: Is there a window in the room you're in?

Hill: (pause) Yes, there's a police car outside.

911 dispatcher: Okay, Beth. I'm going to stay on the phone until you let them in. They're aware of the situation.

Hill: Thank you. Thank you for your help. I'm sorry. I'm so sorry you had to deal with this.

911 dispatcher: It's all right. It's quite all right.

END OF CALL

PART 1

1/ THE PERFECT CANDIDATE

A MONTH BEFORE BETH HILL MADE HER 911 CALL, RICHIE FORMAN saw the job posted on Craigslist.

Case assistant. Exoneration Foundation.

He'd been looking for weeks, but this was the first listing that really jumped out at him, truly suited him, and that he thought he had a shot at.

"Candidates must have strong analytic skills, attention to detail, commitment to social justice," the ad read. "Interest in criminal justice issues, collegial and collaborative work style are a must, candidates should be skilled in writing and presenting information clearly and succinctly and dealing with emotionally charged situations professionally."

Check, check, and check.

So there he was ten days later sitting on a worn black leather sofa, wearing a navy pinstripe suit that he'd picked up at a thrift shop. It hung off him a little loosely. He'd walked from his apartment. He was downtown, in SoMa—South of Market—on Third Street, in a small, cheerless reception area that didn't look so different from the waiting areas of the state and city agencies he'd been obliged to visit in recent months.

The Exoneration Foundation.

He'd known about the place before he saw the ad. Some called it the "court of last resort," but the foundation preferred a different, less dramatic description. It was a nonprofit, pro-bono legal clinic that represented prisoners whose wrongful convictions might be overturned through biological evidence, the kind that was overlooked, misinterpreted, or botched in one way or another.

The founder was an attorney named Marty Lowenstein, a preeminent DNA expert. To prison inmates he was simply known as the DNA Dude. That's what they called him. "Get the DNA Dude on it," was their mantra for every guy who claimed he was actually innocent. "Dial that mofo up. He'll get your actual ass off." Fucking idiots. No one believed it.

Marty Lowenstein was a do-gooder. An actual one. The poor, the forgotten, the innocent schmuck on death row, the royally screwed were his meat. The irony was that he owed his reputation to representing a handful of rich pricks in high-profile cases that got big spreads in *Vanity Fair*. Those people you didn't always exonerate. You got them off. You created reasonable doubt. But you didn't get to walk a guy out of prison after twenty-two years for a crime the evidence clearly showed he didn't commit and maybe even someone else had copped to in the meantime. That was exoneration. Lowenstein got off on it.

Richie Forman looked around. His suit fit right in. There was something a decade or two passé about the décor, a little off, a little tired. The furniture had obviously once served in another office, probably a corporate law firm.

Smack at ten, the receptionist, a young black woman with straightened hair, said the case director was coming out, she'd see him now. That got his heart going. *You're going to crush this*, he thought. *This one's yours.*

A moment later, a heavyset Hispanic woman with a pleasant face came out and greeted him. Her name was Lourdes Hinojosa, and after she shook his hand, she walked him back to her office. She looked fairly young, early forties, but she had a pair of reading glasses on a chain around her neck that made her look older, especially when she put them on to scan his résumé.

He sat there anxiously watching her. As she read, she nodded a couple of times but made no comment. The silence made him nervous. He crossed, then uncrossed his legs. Finally, she took off her glasses and looked at him with a renewed intensity.

"Richard—"

"Rick," he said. "You can call me Rick."

"Okay, sorry. Rick. I see you were in marketing at a dot-com."

"Yes."

"I suppose you're looking for a more noble calling. You understand, though, that the case assistant position is an entry-level position."

She obviously had seen his type before—or at least the type she thought he was.

"Yes, I know. But—"

"We get a lot of people applying for this who are right out of college, including schools back East," she said, referencing his résumé. "You'll be doing a lot of grunt work. When was the last time you did grunt work?"

He almost said "yesterday," but he held his tongue. He was prepared for this, the not-so-subtle age discrimination. He looked good for thirty-seven—but not that good.

"You might want to look again, Ms. Hinojosa. I *was* in marketing—but a long time ago."

She put her glasses back on and looked at the sheet.

"Oh," she said, reading the dates more carefully. "Wow. Seven years." She looked at him again. "What have you been doing since then?"

"Time," he said.

Her eyes opened wide.

"Out in gold country," he added. "Mule Creek."

"You've been in prison?"

"Yes."

He noticed her eyes zeroing in on the long scar on the right upper side of his forehead. He could have hidden the blemish better, but he kept his dark hair slicked back and parted to the other side—the left. The style was a little short to be a true pompadour, but it was longer on top and had some wave to it. She'd noticed the scar when he was in the outer office but probably thought it was some sort of athletic injury. Now it seemed to take on new meaning for her.

"If you don't mind my asking, what did you do?"

"Technically speaking, in the eyes of the court, I was responsible for the death of a twenty-four-year-old woman. Felony vehicular manslaughter with gross negligence."

"Oh."

"But there were extenuating circumstances."

He reached in his bag and pulled out a small sheaf of papers that he'd stapled together. They were mostly news clips, but he also had a couple reference letters thrown in at the end, both of them from the owners of restaurants where he'd worked recently.

He handed the packet to her. "In the interest of full disclosure, I thought you should have this."

She leafed through the clips, starting with the *San Francisco Chronicle* piece that would forever label the post-bachelor party accident the "Bachelor Disaster," then moved on to the *San Jose Mercury News*'s similarly provocative headline, TRADING PLACES, with the subhead, "Bachelor Party Boy Says He Wasn't Behind Wheel, Friend Switched Seats After Accident." There were pieces from the local papers, too, covering the trial and subsequent civil lawsuit.

"I vaguely remember this," she murmured, her eyes betraying conflicting emotions: she seemed partly empathetic, partly perturbed.

"As you might imagine," he said, "I feel uniquely qualified for the position. How many recent college graduates do you know who can say they have a corporate background and the kind of personal experience I have with this foundation's potential clients?"

She didn't seem to know quite how to respond. Perhaps she expected him to smile after he made his declaration, inject it with a little humor, but he didn't. He said it with a straight face, deadly serious.

For good measure, he added: "I also have a keen understanding of what it's like to be in a place where you don't think you should be."

She looked at his scar again. Then, touching the side of her forehead in the same spot, she asked:

"Did you get that in prison?"

"Yes." He pointed to a smaller scar just under his left eyebrow. "This one, too. But on the basketball court."

Before he was sent away, he'd been in decent shape. He ran twice a week and played some pickup games at the Jewish Community Center in Palo Alto. In the joint, though, he'd gotten ripped. He was putting up close to three hundred on the bench, which, for a guy his size—five-eleven, one seventy-five—was serious. And since getting out, he'd mostly kept up his workout regimen. The fact that he could wear the Boss suit, a size fifty, was a testament to that. Before he went up, he was two sizes smaller.

"I had six bad months behind bars, Ms. Hinojosa," he said. "The rest wasn't cake. But it was manageable. I helped some guys. I wrote some of the letters you probably received at one time or another. I have, as your ad says, an understanding of criminal justice issues."

She nodded.

"And you also understand that the starting salary for the job is twenty-seven thousand dollars?"

"That's better than I thought."

"How much were you making before you went to prison?"

"In a good year, counting stock and bonus, multiply by ten."

Now he did smile. And she did, too.

"Long gone," he said. "Whatever wasn't taken up in legal fees went to the accident victims' families."

Seeing her confusion, he quickly added: "A second woman was injured. Her roommate."

"Not your fault, though. You were innocent?"

"I didn't say that. There were extenuating circumstances."

With that, she looked at his résumé again.

"Well, Mr. Forman," she said. "You certainly meet the qualifications. But ultimately, I have to run this past a few other people. We have two case coordinators, one of whom isn't here today, and a second case assistant who you'd share an office with."

"I'll tell you what," he said. "I'll volunteer for a couple of weeks. You keep interviewing all the recent college grads you want. You're not going to find anybody more grateful to do grunt work. In that folder, I've included my parole officer's info, as well as the manager at a restaurant in Sacramento where I worked. I encourage you to talk to them."

She considered his request.

"We wouldn't be able to pay you."

"That's okay. I work nights. I have an income."

"What do you do?"

"I sing. Mostly at parties. Corporate gatherings. Sometimes at the wax museum at Fisherman's Wharf. Did a Bar Mitzvah last week."

"What do you sing?"

"Sinatra."

"What else?"

"Just Sinatra."

She raised an eyebrow, not quite believing him.

"I'm a Sinatra impersonator."

She laughed, and then looked down at his résumé again, stalling.

"Ms. Hinojosa," he went on, "you know damn well how hard it is for a guy like me to get a corporate job, even a low-paying one. Eventually, I want to start my own company. But today I'm just looking to get back in the game somewhere. If I have to start from the bottom, I at least want to do it at a place like this, where I'm personally invested in the mission."

She stared at him for a moment before her mouth gradually broke into a smile.

"I suppose you'd be willing to start Monday."

"Or now," he said.

"Monday's okay."

He stood up and shook her hand. The interview was over. He'd crushed it.

"Monday it is then," he said.

2 / MATH FOR THE REPRODUCTIVELY CHALLANGED

CAROLYN DUPUY STANDS IN HER BATHROOM, STARING DOWN AT A capped syringe filled with clear fluid lying on the counter next to the sink. Blood doesn't bother her, not even puddles of it. The inside of a human body isn't a problem either. But needles are. Having someone poke her with a syringe makes her queasy. And it's worse if she's having her blood drawn. The sight of the dark burgundy liquid rising slowly in the nurse's syringe makes her want to retch.

This isn't about that, though. Nothing's coming out, it's going in. All she has to do is pull the cap off the syringe, pinch a little skin next her belly button, and jab the layer of fat between her fingers with the short needle. She's done it two nights in a row (the first night she'd had some help from a friend), but it isn't getting any easier. For the first time in her life, she wishes she weren't as thin as she is. At forty, she's not the stick she once was, but when she pinches the skin between her fingers, what she gets doesn't feel substantial enough—there isn't enough meat there—and she's worried that if she doesn't make the jab just right, she might come in at the wrong angle and that instead of getting buried in her skin, the needle will end up poking out the other side.

She looks in the mirror and takes a deep breath. It's just after nine and she's already in her pajamas, a pink flannel set that's entirely—and absurdly—covered with lipstick-colored kisses. Her nieces gave her the pajamas for her last birthday, and with her fine dark hair pulled back in a ponytail, she notes how girlish she looks. Her olive skin and brown eyes have always lent her a Mediterranean appearance, and there's something mildly and comfortably exotic about her. She's never been someone who's had to put a lot of work into how she looks, and while she's never considered herself beautiful, she does think she's naturally pretty and likes how her face is able show a range of expressions. So many women are pretty—but pretty in a dull way. And she knows that men find it exciting that on the one hand she comes off as restrained and sophisticated (or even downright aloof), she is also capable of exhibiting a more playful and combative side that tends to be enhanced with a drink or two.

Yes, the years of failing to respect the sun have begun to take their toll. The moons under her eyes are present and accounted for, the crow's-feet impossible to miss. But for a fleeting instant, she believes her eternally optimistic, touch-me-and-I-breed sister is right. Sure, on paper she's forty, but all the exercise and good eating have to count for something. Maybe it's true. Maybe she really does have the reproductive system of a thirty-five-year-old.

Three months ago she was laid off from her job at Clark, Kirshner, and Dupuy. That's what she's been telling people anyway, even though it's not entirely accurate. Technically, you haven't been laid off when you're still on the company's healthcare plan and your name's still on the company stationery. But her fellow partners at the firm strongly encouraged her to take some time off.

"We're not forcing you out, Carolyn," Steve Clark insisted.

"Last I checked, Steve, 'unpaid leave of absence' was wussy for bye-bye. I didn't know you spoke that language."

He said he knew she was upset, but it was for her own good. She needed to get her shit together. Never mind that she'd become completely unreliable, coming and going as she pleased. But you just couldn't have criminal defense attorneys pulling DUIs.

"It doesn't work, Carolyn," he said. "You're better than this."

"I didn't get a DUI."

"You should have."

He was right about that.

Now, three months later, here she is, still at home. The time off had only hardened her resolve to become a mom. She'd met three times with a fertility doctor, done countless hours of research about

IVF on the Internet, and filed the requisite paperwork at the donor bank.

Fuck them, she thinks. *Fuck them all.*

She reaches down and picks up the syringe from the counter, which she's carefully sterilized with rubbing alcohol, not once, but twice, and pulls the cap off, exposing the short needle. She holds the syringe upright and flicks it with her right index finger until a few tiny air bubbles float to the top. Then she pushes up a little on the plunger until a drop of the Ganirelix concoction appears at the tip of the needle.

Ten, she says to herself. Ten eggs are all she's asking for. Fifteen would be better, of course. But ten she can live with. Ten will give her a decent shot at getting three to five quality embryos, maybe even a couple more if she's lucky. That's the new math she's mastering. Math for the reproductively challenged.

With her left hand, she pinches the skin on her stomach and takes another deep breath.

"Don't be a pussy, DP," she says out loud, calling herself by her nickname. "This is nothing."

This is just a subcutaneous injection. Back in the day, this was the practice round, the confidence builder. You first injected yourself with drugs that tricked your ovaries into producing several eggs instead of one. Then, after the extraction (which required more drugs), you pumped yourself up with progesterone to make your womb cozy and "sticky" and primed to host an embryo or two—or three. The only problem was the progesterone was mixed with sesame oil and you had to inject it intramuscularly with a 1.5-inch needle. Just right for a horse.

She remembers her friend Susan, years ago, showing her the discolored marks on her butt and thighs. They looked like serious insect bites. Her friend said that sometimes the oil would ooze out of the hole after her husband pulled the needle out. Often she'd cry afterwards.

Carolyn almost cried listening to her. She could never imagine having to do IVF, no way. But now here she is.

What the fuck happened? Circumstances changed, that's what the fuck happened. And so, fortunately, did the science. Now you can get all the progesterone you need through a suppository and not some big-ass needle. The hard part has been eliminated. *Now if they could just eliminate the easy part*, she thinks.

"You can do this," she says aloud, reciting the mantra that has gotten her through the last three nights. "You can fucking do this."

But just as she's about to make the jab, her cell phone, sitting on the counter on the opposite side of the sink, rings. In the caller ID window, there is a number she doesn't recognize. Her first impulse is to ignore it, but then she thinks better of it, welcoming the intrusion.

She holds the syringe upright and puts the phone to her ear.

"Hello," she says.

"Carolyn?"

"Yes."

"This is Beth. Beth Hill. From the club. I'm sorry to bother you so late."

She knows who it is, but it doesn't make sense that Beth Hill—the one she knows, the one who hates her—would be calling. Years ago, as an assistant DA, she'd prosecuted Hill's fiancé, Richie Forman, in a vehicular manslaughter case. She wonders how she got her cell number.

"Oh, yes. How are you?"

"Not so good. Which is why I'm calling. My husband's been murdered."

She says it so matter-of-factly, Carolyn doesn't know if she's heard her correctly.

"Excuse me?"

"Someone killed my husband."

"My God," Carolyn says. "Are you sure?"

"Yes. It's just horrible. I don't know what to do. The police are here and I think they suspect I had something to do with it. They want to take me to the station house. I need to speak with someone."

By someone, she doesn't mean just anyone.

"You need an attorney?"

"Yes. I didn't know who else to call. One of the detectives here gave me your cell-phone number. I know you have your own firm now, that you defend people. I read about you and that doctor a few years back."

For a second Carolyn can't accept what's happening. This has to be a practical joke. *Someone's punking me*, she thinks. But instead of calling out her caller, her first reflex is to brush her off.

"I'm sorry but I'm—"

Not with my firm anymore. That's what she wants to say. But at the last second some synapse trips and she realizes she's about to do something incredibly stupid. And just like that, checked-out Carolyn checks back in.

"When did this happen, Beth?"

"About two hours ago. I found him in the garage. There was blood everywhere. It was just horrible. I can't believe it. It doesn't seem real. Now I just can't think straight. I don't know what to do. Please, I need to talk to someone."

She can hear hysteria building in Beth's voice. She wants to bring her back to the place she was before.

"Okay, Beth. Has anybody read you your rights?"

"No, I don't think so. I just don't know what to do. Whether I should go or not."

"Don't do anything. Don't answer any questions. I'm coming right now. Just let the police know I'm coming. They won't let me through otherwise. Can you do that?"

She tells her where she lives, then starts to give her more detailed instructions on how to get there. But Carolyn cuts her off, saying she knows the street.

"I'm sorry to call so late," Beth says again, her voice quavering.

"It's okay." A beat, then: "Beth?"

"What?"

"Who was the detective who gave you my cell number?"

"The older guy. Madden. He knew Mark from the accident. He thinks I had something to do with this. And that Richie is involved."

"Did he say that?"

"No. I can just tell from his questions. And see it in his eyes. Oh God, I can't believe this is happening."

"Beth, do me a favor."

"What?"

"Take a deep breath. Try to remain calm. Count to five for me."

She hit the speakerphone button and laid the phone down on the sink.

"I'm okay," she hears Beth's voice kick in over the speaker.

Readying herself, Carolyn pinches the skin on her stomach.

"Just count. Slowly."

"One . . . two . . . three . . ."

On five, she makes a quick jab with the needle, stabbing her skin. When the needle's set, she exhales hard as she pushes the plunger down gradually, slowly injecting herself.

After a few seconds of silence, Beth gets concerned. "Carolyn? You still there?"

"Yeah," she says. Her hand trembles slightly as she removes the needle and caps it for disposal. "I'm on my way."

3 / NOT FADE AWAY

THE OLDER GUY'S FULL NAME IS HANK MADDEN. DETECTIVE SERGEANT Hank Madden, tall and thin, with a neatly trimmed moustache and a head of receding gray hair that he's recently taken to cropping very short, stands in the kitchen just down the hall from the family room, where Beth Hill is talking on the phone. It's not Beth's kitchen, but her neighbors', and Madden has his eye on the family-room door, which is only open a crack, making it hard to see anything. All he catches are fleeting glimpses of Beth as she paces back and forth in front of the small opening.

"Lululemon."

Madden looks over. Jeff Billings, the junior detective on their small four-person team has made himself right at home and poured himself a glass of water from a fancy ceramic carafe that's sitting on the island in the middle of the kitchen. He's standing there with his thumbs in his belt loops, striking what his fellow officers mockingly refer to as his "cowboy" pose. Billings should have been in the movies; he has the look for it, the strong jaw, small nose, bright blue eyes, and longish straight hair he keeps thoughtfully unkempt. He's also short. Five-seven tops, and he's always trying to make up for his lack of stature with some sort of macho pose.

"What?"

"The outfit she's wearing," Billings says. "It's Lululemon."

"What's that got to do with anything?"

"Lot of blood in that garage, Hank. Hard to picture a Lululemon hottie like her doing that kind of damage on her own. I'm just sayin'."

He's right. It is hard to picture. But Madden isn't thinking about that. He's going over in his mind exactly what he said to Hill just before she asked for a lawyer. He doesn't think he pressured her. A few years ago he'd been shocked to learn that she'd married Mark McGregor. As much as he now wanted to ask her how that happened, he held back, inquiring simply how long she'd been married. He mentioned the accident, but only in passing, remarking that he didn't recognize her right away because she'd changed her hair since the trial.

At this early juncture all he wanted her to do was tell him what she'd seen and heard, and when. She seemed genuinely distraught. He gave her that. But as soon as he mentioned the possibility of her coming down to the station house, she grew agitated. He didn't push her; it was more of a gentle prodding. He just said it was important for them to get everything down—record everything—as soon as possible, while it was fresh in her mind.

For some reason she wasn't buying it. She said, "You think I had something to do with this, don't you?"

The truth was he didn't know what to think. If a Belle Haven *cholo* with an attitude and a couple of priors got stabbed multiple times, the easy money was on Drug Deal Gone Bad or Guy Who Stuck His Dick in the Wrong Place. But when a hotshot Internet entrepreneur with a $5 million spread and a bumpy past bought it like this, there weren't any favorites to bet.

He didn't tell her that, though. He just shook his head and said, "I'm not sure what gives you that impression."

She nodded, appearing to accept his response. But after mulling it over for a few seconds, she put her hand to her forehead and sat down on the couch. She appeared to be dizzy.

"I'm sorry. I'm just having trouble thinking straight. My head's spinning. Maybe it would be best if I speak to someone."

"Do you want to speak to a counselor? We have people we can put you in touch with."

"Do you know Carolyn Dupuy?" she asked. "I know she has her own practice now."

He glanced over at Billings, who flashed a wary return look. They both thought she was looking for psychological, not legal assistance.

"I know her well," he said.

"Do you have a number where I can reach her?"

Now, thanks to his munificence, Beth Hill is on the phone talking to Carolyn Dupuy. Looking at the family-room door, Madden thinks, *Lawyering up after thirty minutes of questioning. You think that's so smart? What kind of message do you think that sends?*

"Stay here," he tells Billings. "Keep an eye on her. Don't let her go anywhere. And call me when Carolyn shows."

"Where are you going?"

"To see if Lyons has anything for us."

"Great. So I just gotta stand here?"

"Sit if you want," he says, walking out. "Just don't eat their food."

Madden is more than twenty-five years Billings's senior. In law-enforcement years, he's ancient, a relic at sixty-two. After his promotion to detective sergeant last year, he retired the gold wire-framed, oversized glasses that his colleagues liked to suggest could be carbon-dated back to somewhere between the Disco and New Wave eras. They've been replaced by a more stylish half-rim, gunmetal variety that helps make him look a little younger. When he's stationary, he can pass for someone in his early to midfifties. But he's got a limp, so when he moves, people perceive him differently. He looks older, he thinks.

On his right foot he wears a thick-soled orthopedic shoe. As a young boy he'd contracted polio, one of the last known cases in the United States, the result of which was a drop foot. His handicap was the topic of a few local newspaper articles over the years, and more recently, after he'd shot and killed a deranged college student who'd gravely wounded a classmate, his medical history and revelations of childhood sexual abuse were played out in the national media.

His minor act of heroism—if it could even be called that—has come to define him, and now part of him regrets not bowing out shortly after the shooting, when his retirement package became fully vested.

The painful irony is that for all the attention and honors bestowed upon him for his bravado, he's ended up feeling like a coward for not walking away when he should have. His reticence (or was it ambivalence?) has created problems for him at home. His wife feels that if he wants to continue working, he should retire, take the monthly pension that's due to him, and pick up some consulting work on the side. They can then use the extra money he makes above and beyond his current salary to help support her family in Nicaragua. He agrees, it makes a lot of sense, but he just isn't the type of guy who sees himself hustling for consulting or private-eye gigs, which means he'll be stuck at home having his wife hassle him about getting extra work so they can send more money to her relatives. And he'll feel guilty if he doesn't.

"You're always complaining about the politics, the silly problems," she keeps reminding him. "Why do you stay? For what?"

For this, he thinks, as he exits the neighbors' home and is greeted by a barrage of flashing red, blue, and white lights. With the help of the fire department and the Atherton police, they've closed off the end of the block and set up a wide perimeter. The line extends around the neighboring houses, designated part of the crime scene because the killer could have entered and exited the property from any direction and left trace evidence yards away from the body. From the MPPD, all four on-duty patrol officers, plus three detectives are at the scene, along with half the fire department and two ambulances. And more folks are on the way. While they haven't had a murder in Menlo Park in over a year, one thing Madden can count on: whenever there is a killing, it's all hands on deck; everyone wants a piece of the action.

The victim's house is on a street called Robert S Drive, a cul-de-sac lined with very pricey homes. A block to the north, on the other side of Valparaiso, is the even wealthier enclave of Atherton, where plenty of properties fetch $5 million and higher. But Menlo Park's Robert S rivals Atherton in terms of affluence and exclusivity. For years the same families lived on the block and turnover was rare. But the Great Recession reached even this moneyed patch and Madden had heard that a couple of homes had gone up for sale in the last few years. This must have been one of them.

The McGregor-Hill property, like some of the neighboring homes, has a gate that controls access to the driveway. Madden has ordered that it be kept shut and that no one be allowed through the door to the right of the driveway without his approval. Passing through the little checkpoint at the door, he reminds the officer at the gate, a freckled, red-haired guy named John Frawley, to keep off his radio. The longer they can keep the media away, the better.

The McGregor-Hill home has a bit of French country flair to it, with a stucco exterior, small balconies on the upper-floor windows, and a high-pitched gray slate roof. Even at nighttime, Madden can see the property is heavily landscaped. He hadn't really considered the house's size before, but now he guesses it's probably a good six to seven thousand square feet, and that doesn't include the detached three-car garage (with a second-floor guest room), where they'd found the body.

The garage isn't right next to the house, but a bit behind it and off to the side. Down at the end of the driveway, standing in front of a twelve-foot-wide blue privacy shield that's been erected in front of the entrance to the garage, he sees Greg Lyons looking down at his BlackBerry, tapping out a message with latex gloves on his hands. He's in his late thirties, a fit-looking guy who wears his longish blond hair in a ponytail.

Madden always marvels that if you were to see Lyons sitting at a coffee shop your first thought would be that he's some sort of artist, a guise perpetuated by his smoking habit. You'd never guess he was the San Mateo County chief deputy coroner in charge of the Investigations and Pathology unit.

"Well, if it isn't Mr. Minimum Wage Madden himself," Lyons greets him in his navy blue windbreaker with the Coroner's Office logo on the front. "Looks like you folks caught yourself a big one. The hits, they just keep coming, don't they?"

"Apparently so," Madden says, feeling his face redden.

The new nickname comes courtesy of an article written about him in the *Almanac*, a small local paper, about his decision not to retire. Under the state and city's "3 at 50" pension formula for public safety employees, cops who were hired before 2010 could retire as early as age fifty and receive 3 percent of their highest annual salary for each year they'd worked for the city, up to thirty years. That meant Madden was eligible to retire and collect 90 percent of his current salary for the rest of his life. The article's headline asked, WHY IS THIS MAN WORKING FOR MINIMUM WAGE WHEN HE DOESN'T NEED TO?

It was a good question, one he should never have agreed to answer. He ended up sounding like a Boy Scout, gushing how he was grateful to have been given the opportunity to serve his city in the capacity he had, even though earlier in his career some people thought his handicap might be a liability. "I happen to love my job," he told the reporter, "I worked hard to get here, and I'm not ready to retire, even if many of my peers have left the force. So, call me stupid but I'm happy to work for minimum wage to give back a little to the community that's given me so much."

After Billings saw the article, he told Madden he hoped he was running for office or that someone had slipped him some Prozac, because that was just about the goddamn hokiest thing he'd ever heard. "Christ, man, I know you think this is Mayberry, but Andy Griffith wouldn't have read that if it was in the script."

As a kid, they'd called him Chester after that character on *Gunsmoke* who had a limp. Now he's Minimum Wage. Not exactly an improvement. Looking at Lyons now, Madden wonders whether he's taking a jab at him or just giving him a little good-natured ribbing.

"Well, one thing's clear," he hears a woman's voice say from behind the screen. "Guy had good taste in his vehicles. That this year's model, Mr. Lee?"

"Last," says Vincent Lee, the diminutive crime-scene photographer.

Madden walks past Lyons and looks behind the screen. Lydia Ramirez, one of Lyons's investigators, wearing orange goggles, is examining something on the pavement just outside the garage, he can't tell what exactly, near the front wheel of a metallic blue BMW M6, as Lee snaps pictures of the spot. Ramirez is short and muscular, a workout fiend. She's generally quiet and brooding but has a passion for restoring sports cars from the eighties.

Mark McGregor's body is positioned exactly as it was when Madden saw it earlier. It's lying in the middle of the garage next to a black Porsche Cayenne parked on the right. What's interesting is that both the M6 and the wife's Mercedes SUV are parked outside. Inside, the garage is neatly in order, with tools and gardening items either put away in drawers or hung on the wall. He makes a mental note to ask Hill about whether they usually left the cars parked outside the garage or pulled them in.

McGregor's body is mostly on its stomach, though the right arm is tucked awkwardly underneath so the chest and torso aren't completely flush with the cement floor. However, his head—or rather the right side of his face—is pressed against the floor, resting in a pool of blood that's six or seven feet in diameter and stretches all the way to the wall of the garage. His nose and cheekbone appear to have taken the brunt of one blow and a huge gash is open on the right lower portion of the neck just above the clavicle. Three additional deep gashes—one on each side of his upper back, the third about eight inches down on the right side—are plainly visible.

What a goddamn mess, Madden thinks again. However, the clinical giddiness he felt when he initially encountered the body is gone, replaced by a more uncomfortable feeling he can't quite pinpoint.

McGregor was twenty-nine when Madden first encountered him eight years ago, a programmer turned entrepreneur who later got a big payout when his online-payments company was swallowed up by an enterprise firm. He vividly remembers McGregor sitting there on the grassy embankment by the side of the road, his head in hands, muttering to himself, still in shock after the vehicle he was in ran a red light and T-boned another vehicle, killing a young woman driver and badly injuring her friend and coworker. McGregor was the passenger in the vehicle that caused the accident. However, the following day McGregor's friend, Richie Forman, insisted he wasn't driving, despite all the evidence to the contrary. Thus began the saga of the Bachelor Disaster, which would play out over the following thirteen months and end with a jury siding with McGregor.

Looking at the guy now it's hard to tell how the years between had treated him. Judging from the minivilla on at least an acre, the Rolex on his wrist, and the three high-performance German cars a few feet away, he seems to have been doing just fine—financially anyway. Beyond the mortal wounds, his body shows some signs of more mundane wear and tear; his slicked-back hair is flecked on the sides with gray and has receded an inch or so. He seems heavier, too. Not fat, but his face, the part that isn't smashed in anyway, seems fuller and his body thicker than Madden remembers.

"Bit of a mixed message, don't you think?" Lee says, turning his lens on a wallet that's lying several feet away from the body, splayed open with a couple of credit cards half out of their slots. Not far from the wallet, someone has scrawled a single word on the garage floor using what appeared to be the victim's blood: HACK.

"On the one hand," Lee goes on, "our killer made a halfhearted attempt to make it look like a robbery gone awry. On the other, we have what appears to be the word 'Hack' written on the ground near the victim. That would seem to put the crime in a new context. Of course, 'hack' could mean a few things, couldn't it?"

Madden takes a step forward and goes down to one knee, keeping his back straight as he descends. If he's not careful, sometimes his lower back locks up with spasms. A visit to an orthopedic surgeon and an MRI machine had revealed two bulging discs and some stenosis, which apparently was pretty typical for "someone your age."

"Don't forget the watch," he tells Lee. "Billings says it's a Rolex Daytona. A collector's item. Fifteen grand easy."

"First thing I'd take," Lee agrees.

He's a small guy who wears his hair in a crew cut and has a diamond stud in his left ear. He and Madden went to the same high school, Woodside—or Weedside, as locals sometimes called it, deferring to the 1970s nickname. Lee, in his late thirties, like Billings, graduated twenty-five years after Madden.

"Rolex never did nothin' for me," Ramirez remarks as if Rolex were a perpetually broke ex-boyfriend who had erectile dysfunction.

Earlier there hadn't been much light in the garage, but Lyons's team has set up a couple of portable forensic light source units with multiple blue-and-white LEDs in them so the area is brighter. Depending on what color filter you use, the lights are designed to reveal certain types of trace evidence, everything from hair and fibers to finger- and footprints to bodily fluids.

Madden checks out the watch again. It's got a black face and stainless-steel dial and band. An attractive watch, but Madden has no idea what makes it special.

"His hands looked okay to me," he says, referring to the victim. "I didn't see any defensive wounds."

"I don't think the guy ever knew what hit him," Lyons says. "I think he must have turned around and *wham*, that was it. Could have gotten something out of the Porsche there and then got jumped."

"Weapon?" he asks.

Lyons: "You got about a five-inch gash there. Looks like the killer came almost straight down. So I gotta say hatchet—or something like it. But the wounds to the face were made with a blunt object."

"I was thinking the same thing."

Lyons says that a cursory analysis of the bloodstain pattern—the most noticeable streak at least—suggests the guy was hit mostly from the front, and the killer, if he had to guess now, was probably right-handed because more of the wounds were on the victim's left side. Madden knows that once they complete all their measurements, photos, sketches, and sophisticated computer analysis, they'll have a pretty precise picture of exactly how McGregor bought it. They'll definitively be able to determine if he was struck by a right- or left-handed person and approximately how tall that person is.

Madden turns his attention to McGregor's pants pockets. The one closest to him—the left pocket—doesn't seem to have anything bulging out the side but it's hard to tell if anything is inside.

"You find his cell phone yet?"

"Yeah. Chin's back at the truck working on it. Android model. Password protected. Should have something for you shortly."

Not too long ago, if you found a cell phone at a crime scene, there wasn't much you could do with it. You were supposed to take pictures of where it was found, but after that, you really weren't supposed to mess with it. If the thing was on and not locked, you could take a look at what was on the home screen, but if you started pressing buttons and accidentally ended up deleting something, you could potentially make everything inadmissible in court. Any information from the phone was evidence that had to be handled properly, which meant sending it over to the forensics lab and having them do the extraction and burn all the data to disc. At best, it could take several hours; at worst, several days.

Recently, however, the coroner's office came up with the dough for a mobile field toolkit that included a laptop, some really expensive software, and a whole bunch of connectors that fit just about any cell phone, PDA, or tablet out there.

"Got something else you might find interesting," Lyons says.

Madden stands up, ascending cautiously. He watches as Lyons pulls out a clear plastic evidence bag from his coat pocket. Inside, he sees a small gold-colored rectangular object that he thinks for a moment is a fancy USB thumb drive—but it looks bigger than a thumb drive.

"Ramirez found it on the ground just outside the garage," Lyons said, handing the bag to him. "There's an inscription on it. Lifted a couple of pretty good prints from it. Going to run them shortly."

Nearsighted, Madden raises his glasses, propping them up on top of his head. Then, holding the bag by the top and letting the object dangle there in front of him, he takes a closer look at what he now realizes is an old-school cigarette lighter. On the side facing him, there's a stamp in raised gold cursive letters that reads, "Thanks, Sinatra." The last name appears to be Frank Sinatra's signature.

"Inscription's on the other side," Lyons says.

Madden flips the bag around. The inscription is an actual engraving etched into the lighter in tiny letters. With the reflection of the light and the plastic, he's having trouble making out the words.

"You know where that's from?" Lyons asks.

When Madden doesn't answer right away, Lyons starts humming a few bars, mixing in the lyrics, to give him a clue.

Your love for me has got to be real. For you know just how I feel . . .

"Buddy Holly did it first," he says. "Nineteen fifty-seven. But the Stones did it better. Their first hit in the U.S. The Dead covered it, too. Heard it many a time. 'Not Fade Away.'"

Just then Madden finally realizes what he's looking at, the words coming into focus.

To Richie: Love is love and not fade away, xoxo, Hills

His eyes open wide. "I'll be damned."

Lyons: "That's what I thought. Gotta be him, right? Mr. Bachelor Disaster. Any idea where he is and what he's been up to?"

Madden shakes his head, a little dazed.

"No idea," he says, handing the bag back. "But I'm sure as hell going to find out."

4 / YOU LOOK CLEAN

RICHIE'S FIRST DAY AT THE EXONERATION FOUNDATION, LOURDES Hinojosa started Richie out on the mail. Thanks to being down a person, they were behind a good two weeks and an intimidating stack of letters had piled up inside a large box that was tucked under a desk and doing an awfully good impression of a waste bin.

Hinojosa told him what he already knew: the foundation had strict guidelines for taking on cases and the vast majority of the submissions it received didn't meet the criteria, much less follow the submission guidelines. Defendants or their representatives were supposed to submit a brief, factual summary of the case along with a list of evidence used against the defendant. "No other documents should be submitted for initial review," the foundation's website stated. It also made clear that it only accepted cases on post-conviction appeal in which DNA evidence could prove innocence. No email inquiries, no telephone calls. Other agencies could provide broader legal support. See links below, thank you very much.

"Brief" and "factual" seemed to be the most challenging concepts for prisoners. Richie had read Nathaniel West's *Miss Lonelyhearts* in college, and too many of the letters in the pile were veritable tales of woe that had nothing to do with innocence but instead expressed a more profound form of victimization that was often accompanied by a rant—sometimes a rather eloquent one—against broader societal injustices and inequities. Beyond help, or even sympathy, what they seemed to crave was credit for their pitiable histories. "What can I get for this?" was the con's mentality. "What you gonna gimme?" It had to be worth something. It had to have some trade-in value.

Hinojosa told Richie that sifting through the correspondence pile was like panning for gold in a stream that had been panned out years ago. You got a little dust, some flakes here and there, but the nuggets were few and far between. DNA evidence had been introduced to the legal system in 1989 and now, more then twenty years later, the Exoneration Foundation and other organizations like it had managed to identify many of the legacy cases in California where DNA might be a factor in proving a defendant's innocence. That didn't mean there weren't some still out there—and many they still were working on. But the majority of new cases they took on were typically from the last two to five years.

At around ten he was introduced to a young woman named Ashley Gordon, the second case assistant, who sat down at a desk on the other side of the small room. Petite, with fine, straight dark hair, she was dressed in jeans and a gray Gap hooded sweatshirt and wore nerdy, thick black-rimmed glasses—probably for effect, he guessed. She seemed friendly enough. But she promptly turned her chair away from his, put on a pair of headphones, pulled her hood over her head, and went to work on her computer. As he read and sorted, her back to his, he could hear the faint din of her music leaking out through her earbuds.

Some time had passed, when he heard a crunching noise. He turned around and saw a Ziploc bag with baby carrots sitting on the desk next to Ashley's keyboard, and Ashley pondering her computer screen with a half-eaten carrot in her hand. She took another bite and the mini carrot was gone. The sound of her chewing reverberated through the empty room like a trash compactor. When she went to reload, she noticed he was looking at her.

"Oh, sorry," she said, lowering her hood and tugging the 'buds from her ears. "How impolite. Want one?"

"No. Thanks."

"You sure?"

He nodded, wishing he'd brought his own headphones.

"How's the correspondence?" she asked before he could turn back around.

"Fine. I think it's been breeding in the box."

"Ha, funny. I suppose it's what you expected. I'll tell you something, though. We had an intern here last year who used to read them and get shocked. Most of the letters are pretty earnest, right? But every so often you get one that's really dirty. And this girl—she was still in high school—would open one up and there'd be some guy talking about how he was imagining her reading his letter and masturbating as he was writing it. It got pretty graphic. Of course, he didn't know she'd be reading it, but if you send letters to enough people, you eventually hit on the person you're imagining, right? It's like an odds thing."

He stared at her, slightly dumbfounded. She herself didn't seem much removed from high school.

"What's up with the hoodie?" he asked. "You in training for the World Series of Poker or something?"

He had a feeling the reference might go over her head—and it did. Or at least she let it blow right past her.

"Oh no," she said, "I just didn't want my music to bother you. I know I leak."

She shifted a little in her chair, allowing him to get a glimpse of her screen. He felt his stomach drop, for there was a blog post about Mark McGregor's new company, with a shot of him reclined in a modern, high-backed office chair, smiling with despicable confidence. The site, OneDumbIdea.com, covered start-ups. It was run by Tom Bender, a pompous but audaciously talented asshole Richie had met a couple of times at networking events. That was back in the day when Bender's site was in its fledgling state and nobody thought too much of it. Now the bastard had apparently become the gossip arbiter of all things Valley.

"What are you working on?" he asked testily.

"Background check."

"On who?"

"You."

If it was a joke, he didn't think it was funny.

"Kidding," she said. "Well, sort of anyway. Lourdes wanted me to check on a few things. She likes you."

"What'd she say?"

"She didn't say anything. I can just tell."

"Do you have any say in the hiring process?"

"I should think so. I do good work. They value my opinion."

"I had a bad feeling you were going to say that."

She smiled, looking at him more closely. *Why did she think everything he said was amusing*?

"Okay, I see it more now," she announced after a moment.

"See what?"

"The Frank connection. I see how you can pull it off."

"The hat and suit get me sixty percent of the way there."

"And the rest?"

"Attitude."

"Me, too," she said.

"I see that."

"Well, you've got the eyes. The color anyway."

"She really have you backgrounding me?" He knew they'd be combing through his history, but it seemed oddly insulting to do it right in front of him.

"Don't take it personally. They did it for me, too. They do it for everybody."

"You look clean."

"Pretty much," she said. "When I was sixteen, I had an open-container violation. And a cop once ticketed me for not having my headlights on as I was leaving a lighted shopping-mall parking lot at night. That's the extent of my run-ins with the law. Kinda pathetic, right?"

"Where was sixteen?"

She cocked her head a little, not quite understanding him. "Oh, that's an odd way to put it." Mulling it over, she seemed to approve of the phrasing. "Sixteen was Danville," she said. "Eighteen was UC Irvine. Twenty-four is now. Bad time to find a job. Half my friends are unemployed or teaching English in Costa Rica. I was lucky. I wanted to be an investigative reporter. Had an internship for a couple of summers at a lefty blog where they were focused on old-fashioned muckraking. But they didn't have any paying positions. At least this pays and I've trained under a couple of really great investigators. Same skill set, just no articles. You know, we already have forty applications for this shitty little open position."

"Try making license plates for thirty-eight cents an hour. It won't seem so shitty."

"Sorry," she said, momentarily chastised. "I didn't mean for it to come out like that. I don't mean to be flip or anything. I'm not a flip person."

She fell silent after that. A little while later he went to the bathroom. When he came back and sat down, she asked him whether he'd ever sent in a submission.

He made a slow swivel in his chair to face her.

"Maybe."

"You did, didn't you?"

He shrugged. "I was a poor candidate. White, good legal representation, and my sentence wasn't supposed to be all that long. I was looking at two years with good behavior. By the time they got something going, if they got something going, I'd be out already. That's what you tell half these people, don't you?"

"But sometimes Marty takes on higher-profile cases."

Marty. That made him smile. He liked how Lowenstein was on a first-name basis with everybody. A real man of the people.

"Marty goes low and high, not *higher*," he said. "And when he goes high, he gets in on the ground floor."

She didn't seem to hear his response. Her eyes had settled on something behind him.

"That lighter," she said, nodding at his lighter sitting on the desk next to his cell phone. "It's got Sinatra's signature. Where'd you get it?"

He wasn't sure how she could have seen the signature from where she was sitting. It was pretty small. He guessed she must have looked at it while he was in the bathroom. For someone who seemed awfully introverted at first, she was turning out to be surprisingly inquisitive. He wondered if she'd looked at the inscription on the other side of the lighter. Chances were she hadn't, because he'd have noticed if she'd moved it even a fraction of an inch. If there was one gift prison had given him besides a better physique, it was a keen sense of object memory. Locked up in cramped quarters, you could end up being very anal about your possessions. You were always taking stock of what you had, where it was, who wanted what, and how those things might help you avert conflict and survive better.

"Sinatra used to give them out as thank-you gifts," he said. "You can find them for sale on the Internet."

"How much?"

"Not that much. A few hundred bucks."

"You think it's real?"

"Probably. But it's a bullshit little trinket. He gave away lots of them. To get one he actually used, his own personal lighter, that's a different story."

"How would you know he really used it?"

"I don't know. Maybe we could get Marty on it for some DNA certification. He could start a little side business to help raise money to get all these poor schmucks out of the can."

She let out a little laugh. "You seem a little cynical for someone who's supposed to be idealistic."

"Who said anything about being idealistic?"

"Why are you here then?"

"Same reason that innocent high-school intern was here," he said. "Looks good on the résumé."

"I doubt that."

"Which part?"

"Why do you have a lighter if you don't smoke?"

"How do you know I don't smoke?"

"You have decent skin, no yellow fingernails or teeth, and you don't smell like a chimney. Deduction: you don't smoke."

"It's my comfort object," he said, not totally joking. "I also have a serious fake smoking habit. Part of the act. What's nice is you get all the benefits of smoking without smoking."

"I think I heard that in a Nicorette commercial. You fake drink, too?"

"No, there I inhale."

"Even after what you went through with the accident?"

"I gave up driving instead."

"You don't have a car?"

"Or a license."

"That guy who was in the car with you . . . your friend who you said switched places."

"What about him?"

"You ever talk to him?"

"No. Why would I talk to him?"

"I don't know. What happened to him?"

"Whatever your search engine says happened. I assume you're quite proficient with Google."

She was.

"Well, what does it say?"

"It seems like he made out pretty well."

"Better than well. Like a bandit, wouldn't you say?"

She nodded. At that moment Mark McGregor was very much alive and well, and according to the article, launching a new company. The headline said something about a "private beta," a euphemism for a small group trial.

"There you go," he said. "Google's your friend. Remember that."

The room fell silent. At this rate, he thought, you won't last two days, Richie. Keep it up.

"Look," he said, "it's not something I particularly relish talking about. You know that *Guys and Dolls* song, 'Luck Be a Lady'?"

"Yeah."

"Well, there's a line in it, 'A lady doesn't wander all over the room and blow on some other guy's dice.' You know that line?"

"No, but it sounds kinky."

"Well, every time I sing it I have this picture of this dame, you know this femme fatale sort of dame, who comes over and blows on my dice. When you blow on dice, it's supposed to be for luck, right? Well, my dice got blown on that night and the exact opposite happened. I crapped out. Bad. Simple as that."

"Rick?"

"Yeah."

"Do you mind if I look into your case a bit?"

"Why? What's the point?"

"I don't know. To stop you from reciting cheesy lines from old Sinatra show tunes and talking about some chick blowing on your dice."

"When you say it like that, it does sound kinky."

"Told you," she said.

5/ THE MERCY OF YOUR INVESTORS

WITH THE STREET CORDONED OFF, CAROLYN HAS TO PARK ON VALparaiso and walk back to the entrance of Robert S Drive, where police have set up a barricade. The house is almost at the end of the cul-de-sac on the north side of the street. While it isn't big enough to be an estate, whoever designed it wanted you to think estate, mini one anyway.

"It happened over there," says the young officer with a completely shaved head who escorts her, pointing to a glow of bright lights a little further down the street to the left. She's not particularly tall, just five-four, and dipping her head slightly at an angle, she looks through the bars of the metal driveway gate. Several yards away she glimpses the unmistakable ponytail of the chief deputy coroner, Greg Lyons, who's speaking with a black detective she knows named Jerry Burns. A few other people are milling about, some looking more occupied than others. The rest of the property is only illuminated with ground lights here and there, but it's enough for her to get a sense of the elaborate and meticulous landscaping that surrounds the house.

She feels herself drawn toward the murder scene but when she starts to drift away from the officer and move a few paces closer to the entrance of the driveway, he warns her to stay with the tour and follow him into the house next door.

Going inside, she notes that the foyer has a grand, formal feel to it, with light-colored, polished marble floors. The feel isn't exactly modern—there's a crystal chandelier hanging from the ceiling after all—but somewhere between modern and traditional. One look at the entranceway and a peek into the living room, and she doesn't have to see anything more to know that someone clearly spent a lot of money imbuing every inch of that home with that sensibility.

She can't help but think that if things had gone a little differently she'd be shacked up in a place like this rather than the "cute" three-bedroom cottage she's in now. She'd had her chances, of course, but early on had developed a penchant for dating guys with unique and intriguing qualities, particularly good looks, just not large bank accounts. Perhaps the problem was they always seemed to have dual professions separated by a slash. There was the restaurant manager/nutritionist, a mediator/ski instructor, an architect/political blogger, the landscaper who bred huskies and had Iditarod aspirations. She'd tried to break herself of her habit, rotating in a few techie types, they of lofty titles and nonsensical company names, tier-two Boy Wonders. Invariably she found them dull or unattractive—or both. Meanwhile, the "slashes" kept finding her.

The exception was Ted Cogan, the surgeon. Wealthy, no. Not for around here anyway. But well off, yes, which was just fine with her. The only problem was she'd failed to seal the deal and marry him not once, but twice, and though she doesn't like to admit it, that second defeat triggered the little tailspin that led to her professional grounding.

Fuck him, she thinks, glancing up at an arguably exquisite light fixture that's illuminating the short hallway they're passing through. *Fuck Ted Cogan*. And just then a door suddenly opens in front of her, startling and separating her from her escort. It's a woman coming out of a small bathroom. The two stop just short of colliding.

"My God, you scared me," the woman says, clasping her hand to her chest. Pencil thin, around forty-five, with short sandy-colored hair, she isn't exactly dressed up, but she is well dressed, with khaki slacks and a couple of buttons open on her crisp white blouse to show off a string of white pearls.

"Sorry," Carolyn says. "And you are?"

"Pam Yeagher. I live here. We're the neighbors. This is just ghastly. Absolutely horrible. You must be Carolyn Dupuy. Beth's in the den. She's waiting for you."

Out of view, Carolyn hears the young officer talking to a man with a very familiar-sounding voice, though she only realizes it belongs to Jeff Billings, one of the detectives, when she follows Pam Yeagher into the kitchen and sees him standing there.

"Well, well, if it isn't Ms. Dupuy," he says. "Last I heard, you'd been put on hiatus, Counselor."

"New season, new show," she replies, reflexively winding up to return his jab with a bigger shot of her own. "You guys figure out a way to fuck up the crime scene yet? That why they have you stashed over here?"

Billings face blanches; she's hit a nerve. "Ask Hank," he says. "He's in charge."

Last year, she'd caught Billings in a small fib on the stand in a breaking-and-entering case and made him look bad (he'd testified that a piece of evidence was in "plain sight" when in fact it wasn't). She loves cops but most of them are liars. And they're arrogant. They think they know who's guilty and who isn't, and if they occasionally have to bend their story a bit to make things come out right in the end, well, that's the way it is. As a prosecutor, she was empathetic. She'd overlooked the fudges, even tacitly approved of them so long as she didn't think they'd come back to bite her in the ass. But now it's different. Now it's her job to make them bite back. And leave marks.

"Your perimeter isn't wide enough," she says to antagonize him further. "You've got all kinds of people over there destroying possible evidence."

He forces a smile and sticks his thumbs in the belt loops on either side of his hips.

"Sure they are," he says, smiling, not taking the bait.

Neither the young officer nor the Yeagher woman, who's standing just to her left, knows what to make of the exchange.

"I'm just going to get a glass of water for Beth," Pam says. "My husband's in there with her. He's a doctor. I'll take you in."

A doctor? thinks Carolyn. *Are you kidding me? A fucking doctor's house? That's just goddamn perfect.*

"I'll give you ten minutes," Billings says.

"And I'll see your ten minutes and take as long as I like."

"We need to question her, Carolyn."

"So do I."

With that, she heads into the den. When she enters, Beth Hill doesn't look up. She's sitting on a beautiful chocolate-colored leather couch with her knees pulled up to her chest and her head pressed against her forearms, quietly sobbing. She's wearing black yoga stretch pants and a white T-shirt that's covered by a gray crocheted cardigan. Her feet are bare.

Pam Yeagher's husband, the doctor, also neatly dressed and more well put together than good-looking, has his hand on her back and is doing his best to comfort her, murmuring something inaudible in her ear. His hair is almost completely gray, which makes him seem a few years older than his wife, though they're clearly contemporaries.

"Harry," Pam says quietly to her husband. "This is Carolyn Dupuy. The lawyer she called."

With that Beth looks up at her, then stands up, excited to see her. Carolyn extends her hand but Beth goes right past it, opting for a full embrace.

"Thanks for coming," she says, hugging her tightly.

Under the circumstances she should have expected it. Nevertheless the show of affection feels awkward. She'd always remember the woman's piercing stare in court all those years ago when she was part of the team that prosecuted Beth's fiancé for killing a young woman in a drunk-driving accident. Now they're just acquaintances who see each other in passing in town or at the tennis club where Cogan is a member.

Despite exchanging pleasantries when they crossed paths, Beth always came across as distant, and Carolyn always wondered what she was like under the veneer. Some days she had an urge to come right out and ask her. *You hate my guts, don't you? Go ahead; tell me, it's okay.* But something always stopped her. Once, a friend walked up just as she was about to ask. Another time she was all set to approach when she caught a glimpse of Cogan chatting up some bimbo by the snack bar and became enraged, forgetting about Beth.

Luckily, while the embrace is forceful, it's short, and once Beth relinquishes her grip, she sits back down on the leather sofa. Carolyn notices the doctor mouthing the word "water" to his wife and making a shooing motion with his hand, seemingly encouraging her to complete the mission he'd sent her on, unaware she'd already set the glass on the console to the left, beside a set of family pictures that show off the exploits of the couple's two college-age kids, son and daughter. The gesture indicates that Dr. Harry has had lots of experience dealing with crisis situations and has little tolerance for those who don't. It bothers Carolyn that he's essentially treating his wife like a nurse. *The guy's a controller*, she thinks.

"If you don't mind, Dr. and Mrs. Yeagher, I need to talk to Ms. Hill alone for a few minutes."

She makes the request in her polite voice, but it must still come out sounding abrupt because both husband and wife react as if she's insulted them. When Harry Yeagher reluctantly gets up from the couch, Carolyn realizes he's taller than she thought, over six feet. "I'll get you that sedative," he says to Beth. "In case you need it later."

"Thank you," she says. "Thank you both."

After they're gone, Carolyn sits down in a club chair across from Beth, leans forward, and starts talking in a quiet but firm voice.

"Here's how it's going to go, Beth. The detectives are going to come back in here in a few minutes. They want to take you into the station house. It's purely procedural. They want to interview you in a clean environment. They want to be able to videotape your answers and they have to follow certain rules when they're investigating a case. I just saw my old boss, Dick Crowley, the DA, outside talking to the police. He's making sure that they dot all the i's and cross all the t's."

"I don't want to go to the station house."

"Well, you don't have to go if you don't want to."

"They think I have something to do with this," she says. "Every time I answered a question, I could see it in their eyes."

"Whose eyes?"

"The detective, the older guy. He knew me. He knew Mark."

"Madden?"

"Yeah, Madden. I remember him from the trial."

"But he gave you my number?"

"Yes. I said I wanted to speak to an attorney. Mark has a guy for contracts and stuff. But you were the only criminal attorney I knew. He had your cell number."

She thought of telling Beth that one of the reasons the detectives might have developed a suspicious gaze was that whenever someone close to a victim lawyers up quickly investigators tend to peg that as a sign that something wasn't kosher. Her natural instinct is to concur, but she's also willing to chalk up Beth's paranoid behavior to other factors, most of which involve the shock of discovering her husband violently murdered. But she's also sure that there's more to the story—perhaps a lot more—that Beth isn't willing to share yet.

"Well, I know Hank Madden very well. I was involved in a case with him a few years ago."

"Your boyfriend, the doctor?"

"Well, at the time he was my ex. Now he is again. Anyway, Hank's a solid guy," she says, wanting to change the subject. "Maybe you're reading a little too much into his questions. He just wants to catch whoever did this."

Carolyn explains that she's under no pressure to go to the station now, but she can't stay in her house tonight. The most important thing to do is to give them any information she thinks may help them identify her husband's killer. They'll need the names and phones numbers of all the people who work in their home for them. Housekeepers, gardeners, chefs, personal trainers, anybody who's regularly on the premises or has access to the house. Time is of the essence. But if she doesn't feel up to it—or if there are extenuating circumstances—they should proceed very cautiously.

She's hoping the "extenuating circumstances" comment might elicit a reaction, but Beth just looks at her and without much emotion and says, "No, it's okay, I want to help."

Carolyn decides to be a little more direct.

"Now I don't know the exact situation with your husband. But I'll say this as politely as possible—I heard, well, there was some talk at the club, you know how people talk, about some possible problems. I don't know how serious they were . . ."

She lets her voice trail off, hoping Beth will pick up where she left off. But Beth doesn't respond right away. She stares down at the carpet.

"They were serious," she says after a moment, lifting her head. "Some of the things I didn't know. Mark seemed to be having some problems with his business. Or I should say businesses."

"And that put a strain on your relationship?"

"Sure. He was working late. He was working all the time. A couple years ago he ended up in the hospital with chest pains. Spent the night there."

"But it wasn't a heart attack?"

"No, it turned out to be acid reflux. But he complained of having anxiety attacks. He'd smoke some pot sometimes, but then he got paranoid someone might find out and make him submit to a drug test."

"I thought he owned the company."

"He did. But in many ways you're at the mercy of your investors."

"And how long was this going on?"

"What?"

"The acid reflux, stress, and whatnot."

"I don't know. A couple of years. A while."

"What kind of business was he doing?"

"Well, he had lots of stuff. You know, holdings and investments. But the bigger thing was this start-up. He was pretty secretive about it. Partially on purpose, you know, to create buzz."

"What type of start-up?"

"It's a new platform for geo-location mobile advertising."

"What's that?"

"It's a variation on the whole instant coupon thing where you walk past a store or a restaurant and deals pop up on your phone. A lot of people have been trying to do it for a while. But it's very difficult to do without being intrusive. The messaging part is a challenge."

She grows more focused and energized as she speaks. She clearly enjoys showing her knowledge and appears to have spent some time thinking about the topic. Carolyn wonders whether she's ever done any formal presentations for the company.

"Mark was working on something that made it more of a game," she goes on. "You know, more incentive-based and social. He had something called 'deal docents.' He was essentially bringing multilevel marketing to geo-location advertising. You know what multilevel marketing is, right?"

"Yeah, Amway. Pyramid stuff."

"Right. Well, what a lot of people don't realize is that social networking is built on a multilevel marketing foundation. For a lot of people that's a dirty word. But if you stop and think about it, that's what a lot of this is about—the psychological underpinnings anyway. There's all this talk of building a network, then leveraging the network. Well, what do you think Amway is about? Network marketing folks were talking like that before there was the Internet. The Internet just accelerated the concept."

"And how far along was the company?"

"Well, they were in trials in the Bay Area. They had an app that was in private beta. It was taking longer than they'd hoped to get to the public beta stage but they were planning on extending it to Seattle and LA."

"What was it called?"

"The app was called Francis," Beth explains. "The bigger platform had a code name but no real name yet. That was part of the hype."

"What was the code name?"

"Sinatra."

"Like the singer?"

"Yeah. But they couldn't use that name for commercial purposes."

"Okay. So, whatever he was doing wasn't going well, as far as you could tell?"

"My sense was that it was going well but it wasn't, if that makes any sense. They had an issue with another company offering a similar service. Mark had to buy the company out. But it burned a lot of their capital, so he had to go back to his investors."

"And did they give it to him?"

"They gave him some but naturally it cost him a piece of the company. He used to say that the best time to raise money was when you didn't need to."

"Did you talk about divorce?"

Beth starts to shake her head then changes her mind. "He would bring it up sometimes, but it would always be on me. *You want to divorce me, don't you?* He'd always put it on me. And I'd say, no, I don't want to get divorced. But he wouldn't see a marriage counselor. He didn't like talking to anybody about his problems. He saw it as a weakness."

Her face changes as a wave of emotion overcomes her. Her lips start to quiver a little and she clasps her hands tightly together and puts them up to her mouth, as if to pray.

"Who would do this?" she murmurs, quietly beginning to sob.

Carolyn can't help considering the answer. Mark McGregor, charismatic and wealthy, had always struck her as a very sharp guy who wasn't quite as brilliant as he thought was. He was someone who believed he could charm or bully his way through any predicament. No matter how hairy things got, he thought he'd come through unscathed, maybe even better off. But not today.

"Beth," she says. "I need to know something."

She looks up.

"Beth, have you spoken to Richie Forman? Do you know where Richie is?"

6/ ODDJOB

RICHIE WAS STARING OUT THE WINDOW OF HIS APARTMENT. HE couldn't remember the exact moment the car really registered, but he looked out his blinds that morning, the Saturday before McGregor was killed, and thought he'd seen it before. It was a boxy Ford SUV, the Flex, silver bottom, black top, parked on the south side of Brannan. He might not have thought all that much about it except he saw a guy sitting in it. From his vantage point on the second floor, he couldn't get a clear view into the car, but the window was cracked enough to see a beefy arm and shoulder and an occasional flash of the side of the guy's face.

Before the guy could see him standing at his window, gazing down upon him, Richie retreated a few steps back and sat down on the couch and turned on his TV. The studio apartment was only about five hundred square feet, with a counter separating the kitchen from the living area and a bathroom and large walk-in closet off to the right of the kitchen. His furniture was minimal: a futon couch, coffee table, two bar stools, and a 32-inch LCD TV that sat atop a simple black IKEA media stand with a cable box and PlayStation 3 inside its two shelves. With the shades drawn, he could still catch enough of the street to keep an eye on the car.

About ten minutes went by and he noticed a second guy came back to the car with a couple of coffees in a tray along with some food. It was probably from Crossroads, a café around the corner, a neighborhood mainstay. Richie only caught a glimpse of the second guy, but it was enough to see that he wasn't white or black but something in between. Hispanic or maybe Pacific Islander. Not tall but thick, with a tree trunk for a neck.

They didn't leave once the coffee arrived. Watching the car sitting there got Richie's heart going a little faster. At one point he was sure the guy in the passenger seat was looking up at his window. It was hard to say for sure, because as soon as the guy looked, Richie turned his eyes back to the TV and pretended to watch.

Finally, he got up and went to the kitchen to make a bowl of cereal. He tried to convince himself he was being paranoid; there were plenty of reasons two guys in a Ford Flex would be parked outside his apartment building. He decided to take a shower. If the car was still there after he got dressed, he'd plot his next move.

Fifteen minutes later he found himself on the phone to Howard Kantor, an unemployed programmer who looked just enough like Dean Martin to impersonate him. Kantor's Dino didn't get nearly as many gigs as Richie's Frank. For starters, he wasn't good (he couldn't sing worth shit), but more often than not, to keep costs down, a company preferred to hire one person—Sinatra—not the whole Rat Pack.

Even though he was unemployed, Kantor, who was originally from outside Boston, had cobbled together a living through a combination of odd jobs that included focus groups in which he had no right to participate ("Dude, do you know where I can get my hands on an owner's manual for a BMW? Need to bring one Tuesday night"). He also managed a building in Pacific Heights, in return for which he paid a reduced rent for a ground-floor apartment in the building. A disciple of the radio host Tom Leykis, who was famous for preaching how to get laid as cheaply and effortlessly as possible, he'd been mourning the loss of the *Tom Leykis Show*, which had ended a few years ago. Lately, however, rumors that the show was being resurrected had Kantor's spirits up.

"What's up?" Kantor said when Richie called.

"I need you to do me a favor."

"What?"

"I need you to drive over here and park over on Brannan and keep your engine running."

His plan was pretty simple. Get a picture of the license plate, email the photo to himself, then confront the guys. He wanted Kantor there in case he needed to make a quick getaway—or just be a witness.

"Now?"

"Yeah, now. I'll pay you to drive over."

"I can't."

"Why?"

"I'm with this nice young lady here."

She must have been right next to him because his voice became muffled as he either moved his mouth away from the phone or covered it with his hand. "What's your name?" Richie heard him say. Then a beat later: "I'm kidding. Here, talk to my friend Frank Sinatra."

A woman's voice on the phone: "Hey, Frank."

She sounded drunk but probably wasn't.

"Hey. How 'bout you and the douche bag you're in bed with take a quick ride for me."

"I heard that," Kantor said, grabbing the phone back.

"How many parties have I gotten you into?"

"How many rides have I given you to get to those parties?"

He had a point. Their relationship was somewhat symbiotic, as were most of his relationships these days. His small social circle was comprised of friends, if they could even be defined as such, who tended to serve some sort of purpose.

"Howie, I need a favor."

"Dude, you need to grasp the situation at hand. I'm with a woman. She's seen my place in the light and hasn't left yet. I'm telling you, she's at least an eight." Richie heard a slapping sound with a little thud mixed in. It sounded like the eight had hit him in the chest. "Sorry, I meant nine," Kantor said.

He wasn't budging. So Richie went to plan B. He texted Ashley. He knew she didn't always answer her phone, but she responded quickly to texts. He wrote, "Need some help. You around?"

A minute later he got a response: "What kind of help? You okay?"

"Car parked outside. Maybe being paranoid, maybe not. Need a little backup."

A few seconds later his phone rang. It was Ashley wanting more details. Over the last two weeks of working together they hadn't exactly become friends, but they'd established enough of a rapport to grab something from the gourmet street taco truck downstairs and eat lunch together a few times in a public outdoor space near the Moscone Center.

"Chances are it's nothing," he said, then explained to her what was going on and what he wanted her to do. She promptly replied that she was on her way with her boyfriend, Jason, who had a Canon digital SLR camera that captured both video and still images.

"You think it's someone from prison?" she asked.

"I don't know. But one of them looks a little like Oddjob from *Goldfinger*, except he's not wearing the bowler hat and a tux."

"Who?"

He almost said ask your boyfriend, but then he remembered the one time he'd met Jason he didn't seem like the Bond type. Pale, with longish sideburns and thick-framed black glasses, he thought the guy looked like a slimmer, healthier version of Roy Orbison. Apparently, he worked as a video editor for a production company that specialized in creating viral video campaigns for companies, but he also did freelance projects on the side, including some work for the Exoneration Foundation.

"Never mind. Just call me when you're close."

Thirteen minutes later Ashley called him back. They lived in the Mission, which wasn't too far away. She said they'd cabbed it to within a safe distance and were now on foot.

"They still there?" she asked.

They were. The Ford SUV hadn't moved and judging from the driver's upward glances at his window, Richie was becoming increasingly convinced they were there for him.

His father had a saying, "Go to trouble." As a kid growing up in Bergen County, New Jersey, Richie remembered him always doling out that advice to his clients and later to him. What he meant by that was that if something was bothering you, stressing you out, you had to confront it, not shy away from it. His father, who'd been an estate attorney back in Jersey before his death four years ago from a stroke, had a reputation as a straight shooter. People were drawn to his honesty as well as his easy sense of humor and they went to him for advice much like they would a rabbi. "Go to trouble" was his father's way of saying "Deal with it," only more macho. He made people feel like they had some control over their fate.

But was it, Richie often wondered, the best advice? Didn't people sometimes bring trouble upon themselves—imagine or create trouble —only to end up in a mess that could have been avoided if they'd done nothing? Still, he kept hearing his father's voice urging him on, telling him he didn't need to be looking over his shoulder, worried a couple of bouncer-type assholes were trailing him. Either they were, or they weren't.

"The car's parked in the middle of the block," he told Ashley. "Silver Ford Flex with a black top. I just need you to text me when you think you're at a good vantage point. I need you to get a shot of the plate and then stand by. You don't need to get that close."

He debated whether or not to take a weapon. When he had insomnia and went for a walk late at night, he wore a scuba diver's knife strapped to his ankle under his pants. He'd go out to the Embarcadero and walk the path that ran along the water. In some strange way, part of him missed the tension of prison. When he was in high school, he ran track, the four hundred meters. He'd throw up before almost every race, he was so nervous. Even though he was good, he hated racing, but after he'd stopped for a few years he missed it; he actually missed throwing up.

Now that he was out, he sometimes got the same sort of empty feeling. At one or two in the morning, he'd go over to little Rincon Park, a small grassy area near the water where a giant, somewhat gaudy bow-and-arrow sculpture called Cupid's Span was stuck in the ground at an angle. He'd talk to the homeless people who'd stop in there. Some of them were shockingly regular people and others were total mental cases. So far, no one had bothered him. Maybe because even the wackos sensed you weren't quite right if you were standing around in a parka looking up at the Bay Bridge in the middle of the night.

"Can't jump off that one," he remembered one guy saying to him, in all seriousness. "The one you want is further down the road."

His cell phone dinged. Text from Ashley: "K. We're good."

The scuba knife was on the kitchen counter tucked away in its hard black plastic sheath, looking harmless enough. He picked it up and quickly strapped it to his ankle and headed out, the door automatically swinging shut behind him. It took a little less than a minute to take the elevator down one flight and make his way out of the building. He saw Ashley and her boyfriend as he came out. They were standing on the other side of Brannan (the same side the car was parked on) but back toward the corner.

Without acknowledging them he crossed the street and turned left toward the car. The driver saw him coming through his side-view mirror but Richie didn't go up to the car on the driver's side. Instead, he passed behind the car and onto the sidewalk. As he walked past the car, he heard both doors open almost at the same time. He took a few more steps, then pulled up abruptly and turned around. The two guys stopped in their tracks, a little startled.

"Hey," he said, "you guys heading out anytime soon? My friend's coming in a minute and looking for a space."

"We're not going anywhere, bro," said the driver. He had a longish, straggly soul patch protruding from a spot under his lower lip. He was the smaller of the two, but he made up for his lack of stature with a menacing stare. *Definitely Pacific Islander*, Richie thought. *Probably Tongan.* "Where are you going?"

"Why would you care?"

"We have a message for you," Soul Patch said.

"From whom?"

"From someone who cares about your well-being."

Richie smiled.

"You two don't seem like the caring types."

Soul Patch: "Oh, we are, bro."

"What's the message?"

"Go fuck yourself. No one's paying you shit."

He looked at them incredulously.

"Excuse me."

"Not a dime."

"Who says so?"

"Who do you think says so?"

"I'm not a fucking mind reader."

"You know who," the big one said, making his first contribution to the conversation. His voice wasn't as intimidating as his stature, which was probably why he didn't speak.

"Sure, I do."

"And stay away from the bitch," Soul Patch came back. "We know she's in on this."

"*The bitch?*"

"Yeah, if you go near her again, if you contact her in any way, the next message we deliver won't be so friendly."

Richie started laughing.

The thicker one took a step closer. "What's so funny?" He was a real beast. Not big enough to play pro football but maybe college, D2. Could have played linebacker or fullback. Big as he was, though, he didn't look like gang material. The guy was wearing a black short-sleeve T-shirt and didn't have any visible tattoos on his forearms or neck.

"You assholes," he said. "That's what's funny. Who the hell are you? *Stay away from the bitch*," he said, mocking their menacing tone. "What's up with that?"

The guy took another step forward and was now really in his face. He was literally breathing down on him, coffee breath and all, his nose at forehead level, ripe as hell for a head butt. But the smaller guy, Mr. Soul Patch, pulled his partner away. The guy budged, not much, but enough to put some distance between them.

"Perhaps we should refresh your memory," Soul Patch said, suddenly sounding almost British.

He motioned for his buddy to get something from the car. *Funny how the little ones always seem to order the big oafs around*, Richie thought. The big guy went back to the Flex and returned with a manila envelope and handed it to Richie, who opened it and took out three eight by ten photos. They were shots of a woman with short blond hair walking out of his building. His eyes opened wide. He couldn't quite believe what he was seeing. The "bitch" was Beth. Or rather Beth with short blond hair.

"That was taken two afternoons ago," the smaller guy said.

He stared at the photo, then compared the front of the building in the image to the real one he could see from where he was standing. The photos looked like they were taken from just a few feet closer to the corner, but it was basically the same vantage point. It was hard to argue, they looked authentic, but he still didn't think they were real.

"This is bullshit," he said. "I haven't spoken to Beth Hill in over a year. I haven't seen her in close to four years."

Soul Patch snatched the photos from him.

"No, you're the one who's full of shit, bro."

Both his new friends laughed. He wasn't sure why they thought that was funny, but they did.

"How long have you guys been following me?"

Soul Patch: "Longer than you think."

"Who sent you?"

"An old friend who doesn't take kindly to threats. You had a chance to resolve this amicably before you got out. The offer was quite generous."

"That's why he sent you? Because he says I threatened him?"

"Yeah, you and the bitch have cooked this shit up. And we're here to tell you it's not gonna work, understand? No money, cuz. ATM out of service."

With that, the linebacker decided to add a little extra vigor to the verbal response. You could see it in his eyes: he'd been itching the whole time to rush the passer and tick off a sack on the stat sheet. All that time on the bench, waiting in the car, sipping lattes had gotten to him. He just couldn't contain himself anymore.

He grabbed Richie by the top of the shirt and shoved him into the side of the building, just to the left of the entrance to a wine store. As the top of his back met the wall, Richie felt his breath go out of him. But the guy made the mistake of not pinning him there because as hard as he hit, Richie bounced right back, slammed his forehead into the guy's nose and drove his knee into his groin almost at the same time. The first hit left him blinded, the second buckled his knees, and as he fell to a heap on the ground, Richie looked over and saw a woman pushing a baby stroller about ten yards away, frozen in the middle of the sidewalk, a horrified look on her face.

Richie motioned for her to back off, then turned his attention to Soul Patch, who seemed as shocked by the turn of events as the woman with the stroller. If the guy had a gun, Richie thought, now was the time for him to use it.

"Tell your boss that if I wanted his money, I'd take it."

Soul Patch flashed him an intense look. Searing. "You really shouldn't have done that, bro."

The guy on the ground noticed that his nose was bleeding. "Fucker broke my nose," he said, picking himself up. A little stream of blood was running from the right nostril down the top of his lip and into his mouth.

"I didn't break shit. That was a love tap."

"We could put you back in prison," Soul Patch said. "You understand that, don't you?"

"And I could put you both in the hospital. Or better yet, I got a couple of friends who'll take you on a nice boat ride out on the Bay. You ever been to the Farallons? They've got great whites out there. The size of minivans. They usually put you in a protective cage and don't chum, but in your case, they'd make an exception."

"This is your only warning, Mr. Forman," Soul Patch said.

"And this is yours, too. Now get your piece-of-shit fake gangster vehicle out of here before I call the police."

He started to walk away, continuing to face them as he made his exit. By the time he got to the corner they'd returned to their car. A moment later they pulled out onto Brannan and headed over to the Embarcadero, where they made a right turn. Richie was repeating the license plate ID to himself as Jason and Ashley approached.

"Holy shit," Jason said. "What was that about?"

"I'm not sure," he said. "Something weird's going on. What'd you get?"

Jason handed him his camera and showed him which button to push to scroll through the images on the LCD. Richie's hand shook a little as he flipped through the images. His heart was still racing.

"You okay?" Ashley asked, noticing the tremor.

"Yeah," he said. Jason had nice shots of the license plate and had also managed to snap a dozen or so shots of his new friends handing him the manila envelope. You could see him looking at the photos of Beth, but only one or two shots clearly revealed what was in the photos and it was hard to tell just how good the focus was. He wanted to see them blown up on a bigger screen.

"Who's the woman?" Ashley asked.

"My ex-fiancée."

"Beth?"

"Yeah."

"That looks like it was taken right here. When did you see her?"

"I didn't. Or at least I think I didn't."

"What does that mean?"

He wasn't listening. He was looking at the photo of the photo. There was something incredibly eerie about it. It was as if someone had taken a picture of a scene in one of his dreams and now it had somehow found its way into the real, physical world.

"What did those guys want?" Ashley asked.

He told her he didn't know, even though he did. Or at least he thought he did. Someone appeared to be trying to blackmail Mark. *But who? And how much were they were looking for?* At the same time, he wondered whether it had anything to with what Ashley was up to, poking around on his old case. At his request, he'd told her he didn't want to hear about it, but now he was a lot more interested.

"Ash, who've you been talking to about my stuff?"

"Why?"

"Just who."

"A couple people. Mainly court clerks and I've been trying to track down the woman who was in the vehicle you hit. The friend."

She looked at Jason, who gave her a hard look back. Richie saw her bite her lip nervously, a tell if he'd ever seen one. Poker wasn't her game after all.

He looked at her, waiting.

"Tell him," Jason finally said.

"Okay," Ashley said. "We were down there the other day."

"Down where?"

"Down on the Peninsula. Menlo Park."

"Doing what?"

"As I said, talking to a few folks. Down at the court."

"And we shot a little," Jason said. "We filmed some."

"Some what?" Richie asked.

"Well, just the scene of the accident. There's still a marker there. You know, alongside the road. A cross."

Richie shook his head. He'd seen the cross a long time ago but hadn't realized it was still there.

"I'm sorry," Ashley said. "We should have told you. But you said you didn't want to know what I was doing."

No wonder they were in such a hurry to get over with their camera, he thought. They're making a fucking documentary.

"You okay, Rick?" Ashley asked.

He looked at her, then at Jason.

"I'm going to need a copy of those pictures," he said. "And from now on, I need to know everything that's going on. Everything. Understand?"

7 / THE NUANCES OF HATE

MADDEN HAS ALWAYS FELT BAD FOR BETH HILL. IF THERE WAS A victim aside from the women in that Toyota Corolla, it was Beth. Her wedding was cancelled at the last minute, her life plans dashed, and she wasn't in either car, though there were times when she must have wished she was. Then she might have known exactly what happened that night.

A faded white cross still stands there, a memorial to the accident, planted on the embankment just feet from where he first encountered Mark McGregor. A couple of times a year, someone, probably the family of the victim, comes by and hangs a wreath of flowers on the cross. The only time he really notices the marker is during the few weeks the wreath has color; otherwise it sort of blends in with the dirt on the shoulder.

That open stretch of Sand Hill Road between the 280 off-ramp and Sharon Heights has always attracted its share of mishaps, though the injured are mainly bicyclists, not drivers. Everything west of the freeway is Woodside. East is Menlo Park. And after making the loop off the highway, the road runs downhill and the cars really get going, especially late at night when traffic is light.

Years ago Sand Hill was largely undeveloped. It was all Stanford land; the university owned it. Then one day it became too valuable. Now there is a luxury hotel next to the freeway and all the venture capital firms, most of them anyway, have set up shop along on the north side of the road. There aren't as many businesses on the south side because the mile-long Stanford Linear Accelerator has been there since the sixties. That's where the two women in the crushed vehicle worked.

At approximately 12:52 that night their Toyota Corolla pulled out from the entrance of SLAC to make a left onto Sand Hill (going west toward Woodside) and an old Cadillac convertible ran a red light and slammed into the driver's side of the smaller car, hitting it almost flush, T-boning it. The driver of the Cadillac hit the brakes at the last second but the skid marks weren't longer than ten feet.

An officer showed up within six minutes of the accident. Four patrol cars were out that night, each patrolling within a zone. Typically, most of the action took place on the east side of town, the majority of it closer to the 101 freeway, where the town's pocket of ethnicity, Belle Haven, met East Palo Alto, which, during the crack epidemic of the nineties, had earned the distinction of having the highest per capita murder rate in the country. One car was patrolling quieter West Menlo, but the zone was actually pretty large in terms of square miles, and when the 911 call for the accident came in, the nearest officer was a good three miles away.

He found the driver of the Cadillac groaning and bleeding from the side of his head. Lab tests would later reveal that his blood-alcohol level was just north of 0.12, clearly over the legal limit of 0.08. Meanwhile, the passenger, who was wearing a seat belt, was conscious but dazed. Tests would later reveal his blood alcohol content was within the legal limit.

Tapes from a San Francisco parking garage showed Beth Hill's fiancé, Richie Forman, driving the car out of the garage. The officer at the scene of the accident identified Forman as the driver. Blood on the steering wheel and driver's seat matched Forman's. And yet Forman, saddened as he was for the victims and their families, said he wasn't driving. Yes, he took his car out of the garage, but he just drove it a few blocks to pick up his friend Mark McGregor, who he'd left talking to a woman in a bar. McGregor had asked for the car keys, telling him he was in no shape to drive all the way back down to the Peninsula. Forman didn't know what had happened, but he said he wasn't behind the wheel of the car that killed that woman and injured her friend. His friend must have moved him after the accident, switched places with him.

At his trial months later, after nearly two hours of questioning, after going through every last detail of that night, not twice, but five times, Carolyn Dupuy, the deputy DA cross-examining Forman, got what she was looking for on the stand. It wasn't exactly a confession, but a moment of doubt, a brief hesitation, and an admission that he couldn't be 100 percent sure he wasn't behind that wheel.

Forman's lawyer tried to suppress his answer, but it was too late; it was there, and that moment, when you played it over and over to a jury, started to sound longer and more profound. It started to sound like a confession. And that's how Richie Forman ended up with a felony manslaughter conviction. With gross negligence thrown in, he got three to seven and a ticket to a civil lawsuit. Few bachelor parties had ever cost as much as his.

If the jury didn't believe him, did Beth Hill? During the trial, she'd sat impassively in the gallery with a mostly helpless, drained look on her gaunt face. She had the appearance of someone who hadn't gotten a full night's sleep in weeks, maybe months, and hadn't been eating enough.

"I know Richie better than anyone," she told a reporter. "He's not someone who lies. And he's not someone who backstabs his friends. So, no, he wouldn't accuse a good friend of doing something so nefarious as to pull him into the driver's seat unless it was true. He wouldn't do something like this just so he could stay out of jail."

The only problem was Beth Hill was good-looking. Very good-looking—in a natural way that wasn't manufactured. Even if the people who knew her before the accident said she appeared haggard at the trial, when she took the stand to describe her communications with Forman that evening, the rest of the world—and those jurors—thought she was beautiful. She was fairly tall, with long dark hair, a clear complexion, and elegant, slender hands that her stress-induced weight loss only seemed to accentuate.

Madden remembered overhearing one of the elderly jurors say after the trial that Beth reminded him of Katharine Ross in *The Graduate*. Another said she looked like a model. Whatever the case, when you saw her there, reticent yet forceful, demurely pulling strands of hair away from her eyes between questions, you indeed thought a guy like Richie Forman—any guy really—would say whatever it took not to lose her.

Now, looking at her sitting on the couch next to Carolyn in the Yeaghers' den, Madden still has the same sentiment. Yes, her forehead has a few more lines and her hair is short—dramatically so—and bleached blond. But she's as pretty as ever.

"Before we talk about the past, Ms. Hill," he says. "I need to know where you were tonight. Please."

"I was at a yoga class."

"What time did you leave the class?"

"Right around five thirty. But then I got my nails done. The nail salon is right next to the yoga studio."

"Okay. Let's assume you have someone who can confirm you leaving at that time . . ."

"Ms. Yeagher, her neighbor, has already confirmed it," Carolyn cuts in. "She was there. She left literally five minutes later."

"Okay. Then Ms. Hill, let me ask you, do you have any reason to suspect that someone wanted to kill your husband?"

Beth looks down. When she doesn't say anything, Billings decides he'd better step in.

"Ms. Hill," he says, "what Detective Madden means is, is there anything your husband may have said to you in the last few days that may have indicated any concern on his part? Did he mention anything to you?"

Beth rubs her eyes with her fingers and shakes her head.

"There was no friction in his life?" Billings continues in a quiet voice, his eyes filling with sympathy. "No arguments with business associates?"

"Yes."

"Yes, what?"

"Yes, there was friction," she says.

"What kind?"

"Just day-to-day stuff. I don't know. There were some heated arguments over the direction of the company. But nothing you'd think would cause something like this."

Madden: "If you don't mind my asking. Where were you married? I didn't see an announcement."

She looks up at him, then over at Carolyn. She doesn't seem to know quite what to make of the question. But Carolyn gives an assuring nod, telling her it's okay to answer.

"Out in Napa," she says. "Almost four years ago."

"And you were previously engaged to his friend Richie?"

Another glace at Carolyn, who again gives her the green light. "Yes. But as you know, the accident altered things." She takes a sip of water from a glass that's sitting on the sand-colored marble-topped coffee table, next to where Harry Yeagher had placed two white pills on a napkin. She picks one up, but Madden stops her before she can place the pill in her mouth. He asks if she wouldn't mind refraining from taking any medication until they're through questioning her. He makes the request calmly enough, but his emotion still shows through. He's furious that this doctor, this neighbor, has given her anything. *Goddamn arrogant bastard*, he thinks.

Beth puts the pill back on the napkin and says, "You were hard on him, Mr. Madden."

"If it were your daughter who was killed, you'd probably say I was easy on him."

"You're right," she says. "Well, you were hard on Richie, Mr. Madden. You broke him."

"I was hard on both of them."

Beth smiles. It's an odd, self-knowing smile. "Mark cracked," she says. "But he didn't break. Richie broke."

Now it's Billings's turn to get politely blunt.

"Mr. McGregor was previously married, was he not? At the time of the accident, he was married, wasn't he? I seem to remember that."

"No. He had a girlfriend."

"I find something a little curious," Madden says. "When your call came in, you were listed as B. Hill. Did you keep your maiden name?"

"Yes."

"Any reason?"

She shrugs. "It's just not something I believe in. I was Beth Hill. I will always be Beth Hill. I just couldn't see taking another name. It's also a pain to do. Maybe I'm just lazy."

Somehow Madden doubts that—the lazy part anyway.

"And when did you and Mark get closer, so to speak?"

"I left the Bay Area for a couple of years. After Richie went to prison, I went back East. To New York. That's where I'm from originally. Upstate."

She explains that Mark called her one day. He was in Manhattan for a tech conference and asked her if she'd consider having a drink with him. He told her he'd broken up with his girlfriend. Beth wasn't going to meet him at first, but he said he wanted to tell her something and needed to say it in person. That's how it started, she said.

"What did he tell you?"

She smiles again, seeming to relive the memory fondly in her mind. "He just wanted to apologize for ruining my life."

"He felt responsible?"

"There wasn't supposed to be a bachelor party. I didn't care, but Richie didn't want one. And then Mark and some buddies sprung it on him. It wasn't supposed to be that big a deal. Some sushi and karaoke, like they usually did. Richie had a good voice. He could sing really well. He'd taken lessons when he was younger. He'd been in some school plays. They had this group of guys who met up in the city once a month. Sushioke, they called it."

"And you accepted his apology?"

"Not really. Not then. But he kept calling."

He began by checking in every few weeks. And he sent her some gifts. Nothing serious. A box of apples, for example, because she'd once told him about an orchard she'd visited in Oregon that had the most delicious apples she'd ever tasted. He sent the kind of gifts that were more thoughtful than expensive. Then one day she called him. They hadn't spoken in a couple of weeks, and she wondered why he hadn't called. It was bothering her, which she found kind of surprising. So she picked up the phone and called. And that was really the turning point. She just became more open to the relationship. There wasn't really anyone who understood what she'd been through, she said. She was having a hard time with guys. She was pretty closed off.

"Mark understood where I was," she explains, "and frankly, used it to his advantage. He really wanted to make my life whole again. Well, really our lives, because it was as much about him as it was me."

Madden isn't all that concerned at the moment about how Mark McGregor felt or how he wanted to make ruined lives whole. He's more preoccupied with how Richie Forman felt.

"Beth," he says, using her first name for the first time, "do you know where Richie is now?"

"He's up in the city."

"When did he get out of prison?"

"Well over a year ago. But he was in Sacramento for some months. He told me he was working in a restaurant."

"You spoke with him?"

"Yes. A few times."

The way Carolyn looks at her, this seems to be new information.

"What'd he say?" Billings asks.

"He called to let me know that he'd heard that I'd gotten married to Mark. I hadn't spoken with him in three years."

Madden: "And his tone, was it threatening?"

"No, not exactly."

"What does that mean, *not exactly*?"

"He asked me whether I loved Mark."

"And what did you say?"

"I said I was sorry but I did. I wasn't sure how it had happened but it had."

Madden looks at Carolyn. It's hard to fathom. The Beth Hill he knew from all those years ago had seemed resolutely loyal, even when all the details of the evening had emerged. Of course, five years was a long time to wait for somebody. A lot could happen in five years. But this?

If Carolyn feels the same way, she doesn't let on. She gives him a little shrug with her eyes, then looks back at Beth, who seems lost in her own thoughts.

"And what was his reaction?" Madden asks.

"He said he was profoundly disappointed in me. Understandably."

"That's it?"

"Well no, but that was the gist of the conversation. Frankly, the whole thing was rather awkward. I think we both seemed like strangers to each other. He'd changed in prison. He used to be a very buoyant person, someone who really enjoyed life. And then he became sullen. I guess that's the word. Not exactly bitter. Whenever I visited him, his eyes just had this piercing look to them that wasn't there before. He was always seething."

Madden: "Did you tell your husband you spoke to him?"

"Yes. He was concerned. I mean, we'd heard he was getting out. He served his full sentence and then some because he'd had a tough time the first year or so. He'd been involved in a few altercations. One very serious. He stabbed someone. Or rather, slashed him badly with a razor. The guy lost a lot of blood. He had a stroke."

"Hank," Carolyn says, "I think we can cut to the chase here. Your ten minutes is going to be up pretty quickly. The fact is Ms. Hill isn't aware of any explicit threats that Richie Forman may have made to her or her husband since his release from prison."

"How about before that? I know there was a lot of resentment. Did he ever express a desire to get back at Mark?"

"He was certainly very bitter," Beth says. "But I can't tell you exactly how he felt these last years. I stopped visiting him about eighteen months after he went to prison. As I said, he had a rough time. He changed. He became very remote. We had arguments. He accused me of cheating on him, of being unfaithful."

"And then you were."

"Look, Hank," Carolyn interjects again, "we can go over this in more detail tomorrow. Mr. Forman is obviously a person of interest—"

"Miss Dupuy, don't tell me how to run my investigation."

"I'm not, Sergeant," she says, returning the formality. "I'm just acceding to my client's wish to keep this short. Her husband has been murdered. She found his body. She's distressed. And right now it's closing in on midnight and I need to discuss some matters with her before she tries to get some rest. Tomorrow's going to be a very difficult day. But I assure you she fully intends to cooperate. We have the list of staff that you requested and will be putting together a longer list of people we think you should question."

Madden looks at Beth Hill to get confirmation of those intentions, but she again seems lost in her own thoughts. He wonders if she's trying to sort out for herself whether Forman killed her husband.

"I don't know whether Richie still hated Mark or not," she says. "I assume he did. But he could have hated me just as much. Why wouldn't he have killed me?"

Good question, Madden thinks.

"You were at the trial, Detective," she goes on. "It wasn't as black and white as you're trying to make it out to be. Richie was convinced he wasn't driving that car. Everybody else, including you, thought he was. So he felt betrayed by a lot of people. It's easy to say he hated Mark, but it was more complicated than that. Hate can have its nuances."

Madden looks at her, a little perplexed by her tone.

"And did you believe Richie?"

"I tried to."

"You mean you wanted to?"

They all look at Billings, the poser of the question. Usually he was very good with his timing and phrasing. But this question, delivered just a decibel too loud, a tad too forceful, belly flops. Instead of drawing her out, it shuts her down. Her hands come up over her face. The curtain closes.

"I can't believe this is happening," she says. "I can't believe I'm talking about this. My God. I thought it was over."

Carolyn lays a hand gently on her back.

"Who did this?" Beth mutters. Then, her voice growing louder: "Tell me, who could have done such a thing? He didn't deserve this."

Just then they hear a little knock on the door, and Burns, the lone black detective in their crew, pokes his head into the room. He's been out canvassing the neighbors, hoping to find a witness who saw something. He motions for Madden to step away.

"Nothing from the neighbors," he says in a low voice when he approaches. "But they've got something just outside the garage you might want to check out."

"What?"

"Shoe print. Appears freshly made. Didn't belong to the deceased."

Madden nods.

"They size it?"

"About a ten," he says. "Male."

"Okay, give us a minute. In the meantime, get SFPD on the horn, and let 'em know what's up, and that we may be heading their way shortly."

"Okay if I stay down here, work this end, Hank?" Burns asks.

Madden looks at him, trying to gauge his motivation for the request. Seeing his consternation, Burns adds, "Got a bit of stomach bug. Wouldn't mind staying near a john."

Madden smiles. "You had me worried there for a second. Thought you wanted to keep out of trouble."

"That, too," Burns says.

Madden starts to walk away, but Burns stops him.

"Hank."

"What?"

"We're gonna need some help here."

"I know."

"Everybody's going to want a piece."

"I'm good at sharing."

"Since when?"

"Since you told me to."

With that, Madden turns around and walks back into the den, where he notices Billings scribbling something in his notebook. Beth is quietly weeping, her face still buried in her hands. Madden wishes they could get her down to the station house. Moments like these are what you want to get on video, not only to retain a record of her emotions but also to capture something for experts—and maybe a jury—to look at and analyze down the road.

"Thank you for your help, Ms. Hill," he says. "Again, we know how difficult this is. One last thing: Can you remember what size shoe Richie wore?"

Beth looks up, suddenly more alert—and seeming more alarmed. "I'm not sure. Not huge but not small. Why?"

"Just curious."

8/ A PARADOX

ON THE MONDAY THAT MARKED THE END OF HIS TWO-WEEK VOLunteer period, Lourdes Hinojosa called Richie into her office.

"I said I'd talk to you at the end of two weeks," she said.

Actually, she hadn't—he'd been the one to suggest the two-week time frame in their initial meeting, but nothing had been said about it since he started. But he didn't contradict her. He just nodded, sensing from the tone of her voice and body language that the news wasn't good.

"You've done an excellent job, Rick. You're hard working, courteous, insightful, in short, everything you said you'd be."

She paused, a foreboding, overly sympathetic look coming into her eyes. She took a deep breath, and he noticed the reading glasses hanging from her neck, mingling with a small gold cross, rise a little with her bosom.

"But . . ." he prompted her, trying to make her job a little easier.

"Some issues have arisen concerning your time behind bars."

"You don't say."

"We've hired ex-cons in the past, but they tend to be folks who've been exonerated of their crimes or are recovering drug addicts. So-called nonviolent offenders. And truthfully, I'd like to hire you but my superiors at the national office in New York who have final approval have raised some concerns."

"Let me guess. They're not so worried about what initially landed me in prison, but what happened there, what cost me three years."

She nodded, almost embarrassed. "The violent nature of the incident raised a red flag."

It was the third time she'd said "raised"—or some derivative of it—and he wished she'd find another word. He asked her whether her superiors in New York were aware that there were bad people in prison and that some of them might want to do bad things to you.

"We're quite cognizant of that, Rick. And the truth is we're generally very liberal in our thinking, but legally we need to protect ourselves."

Oh yes, he forgot, they were a law firm.

"Look, I'm working on a compromise," she said.

She explained there was now some question whether they had enough money to fully fund the position. They'd budgeted for it, but sentiments had changed. The foundation relied on donations and grants, and while it had enough funds to meet its current budget, questions had arisen (*again, that word*, he thought) about how generous some backers would be in the coming year.

"A few days ago they froze the position," she said optimistically.

Last he checked his labor vernacular, freeze had a negative connotation. So why'd she seem pumped? Because it turned out her superiors were amenable to opening the kitty for some part-time help. However, even as she outlined her plan to employ him in some capacity, he thought he detected a hint of reticence in her voice.

"What's the catch?" he asked.

"No catch. It's just, well, we've asked the people in the office to sign a waiver declaring they're aware of your background and that they're okay with it—and you."

"Indemnification," he said.

"Something like that. But I just wanted to give you a heads-up and let you know what's going on. I understand you had some trouble over the weekend."

"Who told you that?" he asked, knowing damn well who told her.

"Ashley said you had a little run-in."

"Did she?"

"Did you call the police?"

"To report what?"

"That you'd been attacked."

"I wasn't attacked."

"It sure sounded that way."

"Well, Ashley might have exaggerated the situation."

"You should file a report."

"As you might imagine, I'm not too keen on interacting with the police."

"Take the day off, Rick," she said.

"Look, I hope that nothing Ashley said factored into your decision regarding my potential employment here. She really shouldn't have said anything to you."

"Oh no," she said a little too defensively. "As I said, this has been in the works the last few days. That said, I'd prefer it if you didn't place her in harm's way."

"The woman's at San Quentin every few weeks. I think she can handle herself just fine. It was nothing. Believe me."

"I hope so."

"Look, tell me what the limit is in terms of how much I can work. Whatever it is, I don't have a problem giving you a little extra, you know, pro-bono."

"I haven't told you how much I'm going to pay you."

"Can't be worse than what I'm making now."

"True." She paused briefly, looked at him and then said, "You were in sales before."

"Marketing," he corrected her.

"Close cousins."

"What's that have to do with anything?"

"I don't know. It just shows sometimes. You're convincing."

"I was a framer, Ms. Hinojosa. A packager of concepts and ideas that others took out and sold, sometimes to lucrative effect."

"A framer who got framed. How paradoxical."

He had a flashback to a cartoon a friend had drawn for their high-school newspaper: Two docks sitting side-by-side in a watery expanse of ocean. The caption read, "A paradox." He'd forgotten a lot of other things from high school, but for some reason that image had stayed with him.

"Sorry," she said. "I didn't mean for it to come out like that."

"No, it's okay," he said, smiling at the memory of the cartoon.

"If it's any consolation, I kind of laugh every time I say the name of this place."

"Why?"

"The Exoneration Foundation," he said with the touch of an English accent. "It just sounds so lofty. So highfalutin. And here we are dealing with a lot of folks who don't even know what the word means. Some of these guys can barely write English."

"This isn't about what they understand," she said imposingly. "This is about making other people understand."

"I know."

"It's a powerful word," she said. "It's one thing to be released from prison for a legal technicality. But to be exonerated is another thing altogether. It's on a different plane. We do lofty things here, Rick. We right God's wrongs through science."

"I'm aware of that."

She rolled her eyes. Not a major roll, but definitely detectable. He realized he'd made a mistake. Sure, she tolerated a certain amount a cynicism during the course of a workday—and had even exhibited a dry wit—but the brand was the brand, and no one messed with it. Someone, maybe Marty, had ingrained her with that notion, and she'd stuck to it. That was good. He could understand that. But fuck her, she didn't really understand.

"Look," he said. "People assume that because you experience an injustice you want revenge. But the fact is, the thing you're most preoccupied with is removing the tag you've been stuck with. You don't know what it's like to have a victim's parents look at you like you're the scum of the earth for killing their daughter. For days on end. You don't know. It's like a stink you just can't wash off and no amount of cologne can mask. It doesn't go away."

"It'll diminish. You'll see. You were part of an unfortunate incident but you're not a monster. You keep your head up—and your heart in the right place—you'll smell fine. You're doing okay, Rick. Trust me."

"Maybe. But I watched that video of Joaquin Cruz after he got out of prison. You know, the thing Ashley's boyfriend put together for you guys. He had the big crowd, the press conference—"

"Yeah."

"Well, I gotta admit, watching it, I got a twang of envy. For a second there I wished I was still in prison . . . you know, that I had a more serious charge that might have made my case more worthwhile for folks like you to pursue. I actually asked myself whether I would have traded another six years to walk out like that."

"What was the answer?"

He shook his head. "Nah. Prison blows. Sure, there were some interesting characters, but the thing that people sometimes forget is that the people who are locked up are the ones who got caught. The majority range from not too bright to downright dolts. That's what makes it so tiresome."

"That moment you saw in the video is just a moment," she said. "It's something we work toward every day and it's incredibly gratifying to achieve it. But the crowd goes away pretty quickly. And yeah, Joaquin Cruz sued and got some money for his troubles. But he still has to figure out a way to live the rest of his life and come to terms with what's been taken away from him. And he didn't have the wherewithal to learn to sing Sinatra like you did."

"I still want that moment."

"I know you do. And I know that's part of the reason you're here even though you say it isn't. And that's okay."

He looked at her, wondering how she'd come up with that. He'd never said anything to her about why he was interested in the job beyond what he'd told her in his initial interview.

"I didn't ask Ashley to look into my case if that's what you're talking about. I told her it was pointless."

"I never said you did."

He paused a moment, reflecting on their conversation. He hated that she pretended to be one step ahead of him, knew him better than he knew himself. Couldn't she just take him at face value and leave it at that? Why was everybody trying to fucking psychoanalyze him all the time?

"Lofty things, huh?" he said. "You correct God's wrongs through science?"

She smiled. "We do."

"That seems rather paradoxical. I thought God is never wrong."

"Exactly," she said.

PART 2

9/ CRAPPY CONSTRUCTION

SAN FRANCISCO IS THIRTY MILES NORTH OF MENLO PARK, AND depending on the time of the day and what freeway you choose, the trip can take anywhere from thirty minutes to twice that. This time of night there's no traffic, and going eighty most of the way, they get up to the city in twenty-four minutes.

Most of the officers drive sedans but Madden gets to charge around in a fancy Chevy Yukon SUV, one of the perks of being a sergeant that he doesn't really like. For starters, he isn't a flashy guy, and after so many years of driving a sedan he's still not totally comfortable riding so high in a big car. But when his old boss, Pete Pastorini, was bumped up to commander, Madden was promoted to detective sergeant and they made him take the truck, which is what he and Billings are in as they head up to the city.

Directly in front of them is Brian Carlyle, the sergeant in charge of the patrol officers, a former Marine with the requisite barrel chest and a crew cut. In his matching SUV, Carlyle has another veteran officer with him, Sam Wycoff. Both have spent time in Oakland as part of special drug-related task forces, so they are probably the most battle-tested cops in the department in terms of heavy action.

One of the reasons they get there so quickly is that Richie Forman lives in the southern part of the city, right near the ballpark and the entrance to the Bay Bridge. They pull over on Third and Brannan, where a couple of SFPD cars are waiting for them. Madden knows the officer in the lead vehicle, Felix Hernandez. He's the patrol officer in charge of the precinct, which covers a large portion of the South of Market area.

Felix Hernandez gets out of the car and shakes Madden's hand through the open window. As soon as Madden gets out of the truck, he's glad he has his extra jacket in the back. A brisk breeze is blowing off the bay, and it's a good fifteen degrees colder up here, maybe more.

"Hey, Hank," Hernandez says. "Thought you retired."

"Yeah, the joke is I'm so old I got dementia and forgot to."

A smile. Hernandez is approaching fifty, might be there already. "Know what you mean. So, you've got a person of interest in our neck of the woods. How much interest are we talking?"

Madden gives him the background, tells him about Forman, how he's gotten out of prison eighteen months ago, and how he may be carrying a little grudge. They already have some evidence linking him to the crime scene.

"Forman," Hernandez says. "Name rings a bell."

"He was that Bachelor Disaster guy from eight years ago. I don't know if you remember. Started the night up here. Ended up in a DUI fatality down our way."

"No, I think he paid us a visit the other day." He turns to a black woman officer who's standing nearby: "Something about an assault and a couple of Tongans, right Joyce? He had a license plate and some photos."

"Yeah, the Sinatra dude," Joyce says. "We traced the plate to some woman's car in Burlingame. It had been swapped out and she didn't even know it. The plate, not the car."

"He get beat up?" Madden asks.

"No," Joyce replies. "Just said these guys had hassled him. Didn't know why. He said he didn't want to report the incident but his boss made him. When he's not being Sinatra, he said he volunteers at some nonprofit."

"Interesting," Madden says, half surprised, half perturbed by the news. Assault? Tongans? Stolen license plate? None of that sounds good.

"So you're looking to chat or collar?" Hernandez asks.

"We're hoping he might take a ride with us willingly and answer some questions. Just wanted to let you know we were showing up for a visit."

"Well, we're here for you if you need us."

Hernandez gives him a lay of the land, explaining how the Bayside Village complex is set up. There are basically three possible exit routes. He suggests they have one officer set up in the courtyard and one in the garage in case the guy decides to run. Madden and his partner should come at it from the front of the building and just buzz and see if Forman will let them in.

They finish the briefing and split up. Madden parks a little further down on Brannan and Carlyle parks on a side street adjacent to the Brannan entrance of the building. After a few minutes, a slight, middle-aged Asian man walks out of the front door of the building, his eyes darting around, looking very concerned. Seeing Madden's Menlo Park police vehicle, he comes over and introduces himself. He's the building manager, who's going to let them in the main entrance if Forman doesn't.

"In position, Hank," Carlyle says. He sounds pretty amped up, probably hoping the guy will run. This isn't exactly Iraq, but it's a step up from Menlo Park. "We better get going. Brewster just texted me that word's out. It's all over Twitter. That webhole Bender got wind of it."

"Webholes" are what Carlyle calls dot-commers he considers assholes. Tom Bender is more of a blogger than a dot-commer, but he reports on them and has managed to develop a rather oversized ego in the process, cultivating the perception that he can make or break fledgling companies while building his own one-man media empire.

"I forgot the guy lives like six blocks away," Madden says.

"Actually two," Carlyle corrects him. "He moved last year. His mother's in his old house now."

Despite their better efforts to keep the killing quiet by staying off the radios, Madden knew that it was only a matter of time before it leaked. You just needed one cop to shoot his mouth off to a couple of bystanders and the jig was up. Or perhaps the county coroner's car had been the tip-off. It didn't take much.

"We're at the front," Madden says. "Stay on the line."

Billings goes up to the intercom and buzzes the number for Richie Forman's apartment.

No response. The manager had already pointed out Forman's second-floor apartment from outside. The window is easily visible from the street; his apartment is dark, with the shades drawn.

Madden buzzes again. This time, Billings walks across the street and looks up at the window. He shakes his head. No change. No light comes on. No one looks through the blinds.

Madden asks the manager to open the door.

"Do me a favor," the guy says. "Don't break his door down. I'll let you in if you need to get in."

"Don't worry," Madden says. "We can't go in."

They don't have a warrant. Not yet, but they're working on it.

"You want me to stay here?" the manager asks. "Guard the entrance?"

"Yeah," Billings says. "Hold the fort."

Madden goes to the elevator and presses the up button. In a minute, he and Billings are upstairs, looking down a long hallway that's painted off-white, with gray carpeting that appears to be in good condition, probably replaced in the last few years. It's a clean, generic-looking building. Forman's apartment is in the middle of the hallway on the right.

Madden takes one side of the door and Billings the other. Madden knocks. No answer. He knocks louder.

"Mr. Forman. Are you in there? Menlo Park police. Please open up. We'd like to have a few words with you."

Madden purposely raises his voice, hoping to wake the neighbors. He repeats the request and while they don't get any response from Forman, a door down the hall opens a crack. A young Asian woman looks out.

"He's not here," she says.

Madden walks slowly toward the other apartment. He takes out his police badge and flashes it.

"Hank Madden. Detective from the Menlo Park police," he says. "How do you know he's not here?"

"He's over at the View, that place on top of the downtown Marriott," she says. "He's singing tonight. Wait a sec."

She closes her door, but returns quickly enough. She hands Madden an odd-looking business card from the top of a small stack she has in her hand. It has the logo for the joint and Sinatra @ The View, along with an offer for a free beer or glass of wine. The card has a perforation in the middle. It looks like you're supposed to tear it in two.

"He gave me some of these the other day. Told me to pass them out to friends. He's there on Fridays, I guess. Just started. Have you been? Great view, expensive drinks. I took my parents there when they came to town."

"Do you know him?"

"A little."

"Did you see him tonight?"

She shakes her head. "I went out to dinner. Just got back a little while ago."

Billings takes out a picture of Beth Hill.

"You ever seen him with this woman?"

More curious, she opens the door a little more. She takes the photo and looks at it. After a moment, she shakes her head.

"No, but I've seen him with other women. I've heard him fucking."

Madden and Billings look at each other, surprised at the F-bomb. She seems rather prim and proper in her Hello Kitty T-shirt and pink velvet sweat pants.

"Actually, I shouldn't say I've heard him. But the women. I've heard them. These walls are paper thin. My dad says it's pretty crappy construction."

"He has a girlfriend?"

"I don't think so. I don't ever really see him hanging with anybody. And you know, the voices sound different each time. Why, did he kill someone or something? Is he a serial killer?"

Madden ignores the question.

"You've spoken to him?" he asks.

"A few times. I see him in the building gym. It's not really much of a gym. It's like a hotel gym. A lot of people in the building get a membership to a real gym. But he's in there a lot. The guy's pretty ripped. I mean serious. He offered to train me, said he would do it for half of what the building trainer was asking. He said he was looking for extra money."

"Did you do it?"

"No. But I was thinking about it. I saw him working out with another woman from the building. What'd he do?"

Madden smiles. "We're just looking to ask him some questions about something that happened down on the Peninsula. Mind if we take your name and phone number in case we think of anything else to ask you?"

She nods. Billings takes her number down and Madden gives her his card.

He starts to return the card she's given him, then asks whether they can keep it. She says that's fine, she has more, and gives an extra one to Billings. Flashing a little smile, she says, "He did tell me to hand them out."

After she closes the door, they take one last look down the hallway, then go back to the elevator. As the door opens, Billings says, "Anybody for cocktails?"

Madden looks at the perforated card, then at his watch. If the information on the card is accurate, Richie Forman is about to start his last set.

10/ TEARS TO DRY

MADDEN DOESN'T WANT TO MAKE A SCENE, SO WHEN THEY GET TO the Marriott he tells Carlyle and his partner, who are in uniform, to wait downstairs with the vehicles while he and Billings go upstairs.

Rising swiftly in the elevator, Madden feels his ears pop. Next to him Billings looks ready for a night on the town, not the interrogation of a possible suspect. Madden is wearing a coat and tie; Billings has his top two shirt buttons open, exposing a little chest hair. A couple of women in their early forties are in the elevator with them, dolled up in heels and short skirts underneath long leather coats. One of them flashes Billings a smile.

"How you ladies doing tonight?" he asks, his hands on either side of his belt buckle.

Madden jabs him in the side.

"What?" Billings says.

"We're working," he whispers.

"Intermezzo, man. Intermezzo."

Madden doesn't know what the hell Billings is talking about. When the elevator doors open to the lounge, Billings, channeling his inner Matthew McConaughey, says, "You ladies have a good night. Y'all be safe now."

The Southern drawl kills Madden. Billings is from Southern California, not *the South* South. Lately he's been tossing out his "be safe" sign-off so often that some of the guys have started calling him Officer Condom, which doesn't seem to bother him. When Madden asks about it, he just shrugs. "Envy, man. It's a bitch."

A tall, dark-haired hostess tucked into a formfitting blue dress greets them. The women from the elevator blow past her, seeming to know exactly where they're going.

"Gentlemen," she says. "Welcome."

Madden doesn't hear music or anybody singing, but he does hear someone who sounds a lot like Frank Sinatra speaking over the sound system. He's saying something about smoking.

"Are you meeting folks, or is it just you two?" the hostess asks.

"Just us two," Madden says, and hands her one of the cards they picked up a little earlier.

"Sorry," she says, "those expire at midnight."

"Sorry, I didn't see the fine print."

"There isn't any."

With that, she steps out from behind her station and leads them to a table.

"Not too close," he requests, eyeing Forman on the small stage in the center of the room. The lights of the city shimmer through the large, almost floor-to-ceiling windows behind him. He's wearing a suit with a thin black tie and a dark fedora hat like the one Madden's father used to wear. The hat's tilted just so. Sinatra circa 1960, he thinks. His second prime.

"We're almost at last call," the hostess says as they sit down. "If you want, I'll put your orders in before the bar closes."

Much to Billings's chagrin, Madden asks for two beers. Bud Lites.

"I don't want a beer," Billings says.

"What's the difference? You're not drinking it."

"It's the principle, man." He smiles at the hostess and says, "I'll have a Patron Silver on the rocks."

"Give him a beer," Madden says, waving her away.

As she goes off, Billings gives a little a pout, and murmurs something about how he has an image to uphold.

"I will not waste taxpayer dollars on your personal extravagances."

Billings isn't listening. He's staring at Forman, who's broken into "Come Fly with Me."

"Damn," Billings says. "He's pretty good."

* * *

Richie's in between songs, riffing on how he can't smoke in clubs anymore, when he sees two guys walk in and sit down at a table on the outer perimeter. The place has a decent crowd, but there are a few open tables here and there, and he's happy at first to see a few more folks come in, gay or straight. Then he's not.

Though Madden looks familiar, it's his indelible gait—that prominent limp—that jogs his memory and sets the alarm bells off. The last time he saw the detective, his hair and moustache were a little darker and he had more of it on his head. His hairline had been receding back then, but now, he notes, he has less on top and what's on the sides is trimmed closely. It's stubble really. And while he's still thin, he isn't as slight as he remembers.

His initial reaction is shock. Not so much at seeing them, but that they'd come so quickly. They must have gone to his apartment, poked around, and someone told them where he was. How else could they know?

The cards, he thinks. He'd given them to two people on his floor. The damn things were his booking agent's idea. Per, a Swede who'd lived in the States for twenty-five years and still had a slight Nordic lilt when he spoke, has worked at the periphery of the dot-com scene since the late 90s. He's technically an event promoter, but he dabbles in talent management and assorted other endeavors, including a ninety-second "hyper" speed-dating circuit and this latest venture, a "referral" business card he's invented called the Rip-it.

"Isn't there an app for this?" Richie asked when he first saw the cards.

"Just hand them out, okay?" Per said, not appreciating his decided lack of enthusiasm. "I can get you five bucks for each referral. I told the manager you had a big following. Don't let me down."

He didn't want to let Per down. So he took a stack of cards and distributed a few dozen of them. Now, launching into the breezy "Come Fly With Me," which he can do in his sleep, he thinks the tipster was most likely the young Asian woman, Lynn, who sometimes opens her door to check on who's out in the hallway when he dumps his garbage in the chute at the end of the hall or hauls his clothes to and from the laundry room in the middle of the floor.

* * *

Come fly with me, let's float down to Peru
In llama land there's a one-man band

Friendly yet suspicious, Lynn didn't seem to know exactly what she wanted. She asked once whether he'd work her out, then abruptly cancelled. Then one night she'd knocked on his door and asked if he had any Sweet'N Low. Not sugar, but Sweet'N Low or some other "artificial sweetener." She had wine on her breath and her teeth had a slight pink tinge to them. When he said he didn't, she hovered, peeked around him into his apartment, half inviting herself in. He considered acting on the cue then decided he'd better pass. One or both of her parents stopped by every few weeks and she had the whole "daddy's girl" vibe going strong. He just wasn't confident in her ability to navigate the intricacies of a fling, especially at such close range.

That still doesn't explain why Madden and his partner have come up to the city so fast. He'd expected the detectives tomorrow, maybe the next day, but that they're here now means that they have someone or something that links him to Mark. And it's not just his past. They have to have something more concrete.

After an initial wave of alarm an odd calm comes over him. This time at least he knows what's coming. He finishes the song and picks up his half-full drink glass that's sitting on a nearby bar stool. He takes a sip and smiles at the audience.

"I can't smoke," he says, holding up half an unlit cigarette he's been using as a prop, "but they said it was okay for me to bring my old friend from Tennessee." He takes another swig of the Jack Daniel's and soda, savoring the bite as it goes down.

"I've got a few more," he goes on. "Real nice songs. This first one I'd like to dedicate to an acquaintance who just showed up. We go way back. Can't say it's good to see him."

He takes a fake drag on the cigarette, then holds it out in front of him, down by his side.

"I see he's with his partner," he says, smiling that cheerful, sardonic smile he's worked hard to perfect. "I don't know him but he looks like a handsome fella. A good catch, if you know what I mean."

He goes over to the sound system behind him, where he has his iPod Nano cradled in a little dock. He sets his drink down and scrolls through the list until he finds the song he wants.

All those great musicians Sinatra recruited for his live performances and recordings are now packed into a tiny iPod that's smaller than the gold lighter Ashley had been so curious about. When he hits the play button on the little remote he keeps in his pocket, all the instruments will be there except Frank's voice. You can never replace or measure up to something as big or special as that. No one can. But there's a way to be more right than wrong, to express a profoundness of emotion that moves people enough to overlook the limits of your talent. Sure, sometimes you end up looking and sounding like a street performer. But if you get a good venue with a decent sound system—like this place—you can go beyond glorified karaoke. You can transcend it.

"They sometimes ask me which song I like to sing the most," he says, facing his audience again. "And I say, I don't know, I like to sing them all. But this is one of my favorites."

He hits the button on the remote. A moment passes, then the sound of fingers strumming a guitar, slowly, almost mournfully. One strum, then two . . . on five he starts in:

The torch I carry is handsome.
It's worth its heartache in ransom.

People know the popular songs: "My Way." "New York, New York." "Summer Wind." "Come Fly with Me." The iconic crowd pleasers; he mixes them in, usually finishing with "My Way." But the real money songs, the real swoon-inducers are the songs that most people don't really know. Stuff like "Guess I'll Hang My Tears Out To Dry" and Peter Allen's "You and Me." They are both harder and easier to do. Easier because you don't have to compete with such a strong frame of reference. Harder because a lot of those tunes are dangerously schmaltzy—and he'd seen and heard plenty of less capable acts butcher them to cringe-inducing effect.

Somebody said, "just said forget about her."
So I gave that treatment a try.

As he sings he looks over at Madden from time to time, then shifts his attention to a group of four women and two guys who're sitting at one of the front tables. Two of the women have just shown up. He doesn't know who's with whom, but he figures the numbers are in his favor, and soon enough the new women are gazing up at him with an expression approaching rapture. He moves a little closer, leans down toward them, and sings as if it's the last song he'll ever sing.

Madden's eyes remain glued to Richie when he finishes his set. There's no dressing room or private side room for him to slip away to. He simply takes his bows, unplugs his iPod dock, and walks over to the bar, where he has a drink waiting for him. A few people come over to congratulate him, including a few women, who appear to be groupies in the making.

Madden doesn't think he'll run, but just in case, he has Billings go stand by the elevators. After the initial wave of well-wishers pays their respects, Richie glances over and sees Madden sitting alone at the table. The two lock eyes and Richie gives him what looks like a salute or tip of his hat. And then he comes over, sets his drink on the table and sits down in Billings's chair.

"Hello, Detective," he says, his voice unchanged from the one Madden had heard on the stage.

"Very nice job, Mr. Forman. I didn't realize you had that kind of talent."

"Had some time to practice."

"Well, we were impressed. I played some drums back in the day. Was even in a band for a bit, so I know how difficult it can be to perform."

"Percussionist, huh? I pictured you for something a bit more cerebral. Piano maybe. Or bass. Where's your partner? Guarding the exit? Tell him to come back and have a drink. I'm not going anywhere."

Madden swings around in his chair and motions for Billings to return.

"I heard," Richie says.

Madden: "Heard what?"

Richie pulls a cell phone out of his inside coat pocket, hits a button, and aims the screen toward Madden. Lifting his glasses, Madden leans forward and looks at the text message that's on the screen:

Just got a Google alert. Someone tweeting Mark McGregor is dead. Where are you?

It's time-stamped just before midnight. Whoever sent it did so an hour ago.

"Who's that from?" Madden asks.

"Someone I work with. Is it true?"

Madden nods.

"How? What happened?"

"Why don't you tell us?"

This is Billings. He's just come back to the table and flips around a chair. He sits down, his elbows on top of the backrest.

Richie smiles. "Now why would you go and say something like that, Detective? I feel hurt."

He says the last part with a comical, over-the-top looney tunes Jersey accent. *I feel whoort.*

"Because that's what they pay me to do."

"I didn't get your name."

"Billings. Jeff."

Richie raises his glass to toast him. "Pleasure's mine."

He's still in character, still doing Sinatra, and Madden doesn't like it one bit. He says, "Mr. Forman, would you mind telling us where you were earlier tonight?"

"Would you mind telling me what happened?"

"Your old pal Mark McGregor was murdered earlier this evening," Billings says.

"How?"

Madden: "Bludgeoned to death with a sharp object."

Richie grimaces. "That doesn't sound good."

"Cut the funny talk," Billings says. "Show's over. Where were you?"

"Have a drink, sonny. Be sociable. This is me. This is how I talk. Get used to it."

Billings looks at Madden, who puts up a hand, gesturing for him to hold off on the bad-cop routine.

"We can't drink," Madden says. "We're on the job."

"Well, I hate to drink alone. You want me to call some of the gals over? Until you guyz showed your mugs 'round here things was looking pretty promising. One over there looks like some San Quentin quail. Not sure how they let her in. Maybe you guys should check her ID."

"Look, we just want to ask you a few questions," Madden says. "We don't think you did anything."

Richie lets out a little laugh. "Right," he says half under his breath.

Madden: "We want to rule you out. So just help us out so we can do that."

"Well, I'd like to, fellas, 'cause as much as I disliked Mark, I sure as shit didn't kill him. But that's all I gotta say."

"So you got someone who can vouch for your whereabouts the last several hours?" Madden prods gently. "That's all we need."

Richie doesn't answer. He stares down at his drink, silent. It's hard to tell what's going through his head, but Madden sees him clench his jaw, so he suspects that despite the cool exterior, he's under significant duress. The longer he doesn't answer, the more they'll consider him a suspect. He has to know that. Yet he's also eminently familiar with the criminal justice system to be well aware of the hazards of speaking with the police, particularly if he has anything to do with the crime.

A good ten seconds pass. Then Richie finally says: "What time was he killed?"

Madden looks over at Billings, who already knows what he's thinking. The door has opened. A crack. And in the next moment, depending on their response, it can shut or they can bust it wide open. Billings, as cocky and quirky as he can be, recognizes the moment and knows to defer to Madden, who instinctively does exactly what he's supposed to do in just such a situation: he lies.

"Well, the coroner's investigator showed up at ten," he answers quickly and smoothly. "Says the guy was dead less than two hours. The 911 call came in at around eight twenty-five and the body was still warm when we got there. So that puts us at around eight, give or take twenty minutes."

Richie nods. "I was on a Caltrain at that time. Or, actually just getting into the station here in SF. I took the six forty-five. Got into the city at quarter to eight."

“Where were you coming from?” Billings asks.

“Menlo Park,” he says without emotion.

Madden blinks. “Menlo Park?”

“Yeah. My ticket doesn’t have a time stamp but I’m sure there’s a camera on the platform that can verify I was on that train.”

Madden is stupefied. “The six-forty-five?”

“Yeah.”

Another glance at Billings, who appears to be running the same calculations in his own mind. The 911 call came in around six thirty. The CSU unit showed at just before eight. Rodriguez, the coroner’s investigator, had said they were looking at the guy being dead somewhere between two to three hours. Eight minus two was six. Six-forty-five was well within the window.

Madden didn’t tell him that, however. “What were you doing there?” he asks instead.

Richie reaches into his left coat pocket and produces a small, light blue velvet pouch. It has the Tiffany logo on it. He opens the pouch and turns it upside down, letting the contents roll out onto the table. It’s a ring, a very distinct-looking one, with a big stone and a ring of pavé diamonds around the setting. It seems familiar to Madden. And then he remembers the finger he’d seen it on once upon a time.

“I went to get this,” he says.

They all stare at the ring on the table for a moment. It’s Beth Hill’s engagement ring. Then Richie says something odd.

“The broad said I’m pragmatic. Do you think I’m pragmatic, Detective?”

11/ REAL PHONY

CAROLYN'S CELL PHONE STARTS RINGING AT SEVEN IN THE MORNING. The first call is from Steve Clark, her colleague and partner at the firm. She'd spoken to him briefly the night before, told him there'd been a murder in Menlo Park and that the victim's wife had retained her as an attorney.

"I'm at the scene now," she said. "I'm calling you as a courtesy because you're going to be hearing a lot about it. We'll talk in the morning."

She hung up as he was in the middle of asking her who the victim was. Both Clark and her other partner, Bill Kirshner, called her later in the evening once the news broke on Twitter. She'd ignored them. However, in the morning, Clark's voice mails had a greater urgency; he seemed genuinely panicked. After the police revealed that Carolyn was representing the deceased's wife, the press had started bombarding Clark, Kirshner, and Dupuy with both voice messages and email. It didn't help matters that her office voice-mail greeting directed callers that she was on leave and to contact her partners in her absence.

"Damn it, Carolyn," Clark texted her, "I don't know what the hell to tell anybody."

He's one of those quixotic guys who, if something doesn't go his way, huffs, puffs, shouts, and has a general tizzy, then apologizes almost immediately afterwards. She senses that he's in full combustion mode but is doing everything in his power to restrain himself, fearing she might try to cut them out of a lucrative payday. The thought has crossed her mind, but she knows it's not worth the trouble. Besides, at heart she's a loyal person. That's why she was so hurt in the first place when Clark went all corporate on her.

After his third call in less than ten minutes she calls him back and apologizes for not getting back to him sooner but she's been in the shower.

"What's going on, Carolyn?" he asks. "What am I supposed to be telling people?"

"Give them my email," she says. "I've prepared a statement. I'll respond through email. I took the out-of-office reply off."

"Carolyn, we need to discuss strategy," he pleads.

"The strategy's set. She's my client. I'm in charge. The firm will get its cut as it usually does. I'll let you know when I need your help."

"But—"

"Look, if she's charged, it wouldn't surprise me if she goes with someone higher profile. She can afford it."

"You're an employee of this firm," Clark says.

"I'm on leave."

"You can't be on leave if you're working."

"Sure I can. Watch me."

Next, she gets a call from a reporter, the *Chronicle*'s Gary Newbart, a heavyset guy with a boyish face who'd unfortunately saved her cell phone number after she'd given it to him a few years earlier when she was desperately trying to get some publicity for a client.

He fires off several questions in rapid succession. To each she responds, "You know I can't answer that, Gary."

"Come on, Carolyn, you gotta give me something," he implores. "Even off the record."

"If I had anything to give you, Gary, I'd give it to you. You know how much I like and respect your work."

Hanging up, she thinks how much she misses being able to talk in riddles and doublespeak. It always amazes her how much you can say without saying anything. Of course, depending on how things play out, she may have to change her tune. She may soon be looking at a serious pivot and spin move if they have anything on her client, which is why she threw Newbart the compliment. She didn't want any ill will.

A few minutes after she hangs up with Newbart her cell phone rings again. She thinks of letting the call go to voice mail, but at the last second she decides to pick up because the caller ID shows a local 650 number. Turns out it's a guy named Tom Bender from some tech blog. The way he announces himself, he expects her to know him and his blog and seems incredulous that she doesn't.

"We cover start-ups," he says, impatiently explaining his background. "We've profiled Mark McGregor in the past. Had him on our video podcast, *The Hot Seat*. You sure you don't know us?"

"Maybe," she replies. "How'd you get my number?"

"I know people," he says. "Most of the time, I can make three calls or less and get anybody's number I want. Fact."

"Do you mind telling me who gave you my cell phone number?"

"Yes, I do."

"Wrong answer."

"Look, I can't tell you that. Live with it. I just need you to verify a couple of things."

"You do, huh?"

"My sources are telling me that the crime scene may have been contaminated."

"Who are your sources?"

"I can't divulge that."

"Well, I don't have a comment at this time," she says. "And please don't use anything I say. Nothing I say is for quotation except what I just said. No comment."

"Look, I'd think it would help your client if word got out that the police bungled this thing. It works in your favor. By you saying 'no comment' you're essentially validating my source."

"No. I'm saying 'no comment.'"

"I'm just stating a fact, Ms. Dupuy. That's what people will think when they read my piece."

"Since when do you cover crime?"

"When it happens to one of our own—and in our backyard."

She almost laughs. He sounds like a Marine talking about a fellow Marine.

"I literally live two blocks away from where this happened," he adds. "I was there last night."

"So, what's your angle?"

"I'm going to blow the lid off this thing."

"By saying stuff that isn't true?"

"Don't belittle me. My source said the word 'Hack' was written next to the body. In the victim's blood."

"Is that a fact?"

"The word has a lot of connotations. I don't know if you know that. Look, work with me, I can help you. Don't, I can make things difficult for you."

"Is that a threat?"

"No, it's a friendly suggestion. So let me ask you again: Are you aware of the crime scene being contaminated in any way? My understanding is that this Detective Madden allowed people into the house that shouldn't have been there."

"Look, whatever your name is—"

"Tom. Bender."

"Okay, asshole. Here's the deal. I don't know how you got my number or what you want but we're going to pretend this conversation never happened. Because if anything I say ends up on the Internet, I'll have your ass."

He laughs. "How do you plan on doing that? You going to sue me? People sue me every other week. My key investor's my lawyer. Works cheap. Litigation's just a form of advertising for us, Ms. Dupuy. We bake it into the budget. So, I'll rephrase. How the fuck do you plan on doing that?"

"I'll tell you how. I actually remember why your name rings a bell. You know why I remember?"

"No, why?"

"I have a girlfriend. She's works in PR for a tech firm that shall remain nameless. And I now remember that she had sex with some guy named Tom Bender who runs some sort of tech blog he thinks is influential."

"I don't think it," he says. "Others think it for me."

"Whatever. You know what she said about Tom Bender?"

"What?"

"She said for some guy who's so full of himself he sure has a small penis. And we're not talking small as in average. We're talking comically small. Humiliatingly small."

Bender doesn't respond right away.

"Who's your friend?" he finally asks. "What company does she work for?"

Carloyn gives a brief pause. "She doesn't," she says. "I made her up. But your silence speaks volumes, needledick."

Another silence, this one slightly shorter. She expects him to explode in rage. But he doesn't.

"Well played," he says. "I like you, Ms. Dupuy."

"Go fuck yourself," she says, and hangs up.

She barely has time to take a breath, let alone calm her rage when the doorbell rings. *Shit.* Her first thought is that the press has shown up and she hasn't showered or dressed yet. She isn't ready. But when she peeks out the kitchen window, it's just Dr. Ted Cogan, her ex-boyfriend twice removed. He's standing there in his clogs, wearing green scrub pants and a lightweight navy-blue Patagonia jacket that she bought for him as a birthday present almost two years ago. He must have just gotten off his shift at the hospital.

Bracing for the early-morning chill, she zips up the lavender-colored fleece she's wearing over her pajamas and opens the door. The temperature will hit the low sixties later in the day but it's in the mid-forties now.

"What do you want, Ted?" she says. "What are you doing here? This is really not a good time."

She notices him trying to look past her to see if there's someone else in the house. "No, I'm not with anybody, if that's what you're wondering."

"I heard," he says.

"Really? On the radio? Was it on the morning news?"

"No."

"Well, it was all over Twitter and Facebook," she says, "so I guess everybody's heard by now."

"You're shitting me. You put it on Facebook?"

"No, not me."

She stares at him, a little surprised by his aggressive tone. A thoracic surgeon who also does trauma work, he isn't one to fluster easily. Yet he appears genuinely agitated, even a little disheveled, like a drug addict in search of a fix. His hair's standing up on one side but not the other, and it looks like he's been running his hands through it, even pulling at it a bit. He has a day or two of Brett Favre stubble that's the same salt-and-pepper color of his hair, and his blue eyes, penetrating as ever, seem more bloodshot than usual. Despite all that, she can't get over how good he looks.

"Well, who the fuck did?" he demands.

Squinting, she flashes a quizzical look. It suddenly dawns on her that they're talking about two different things.

"What are you talking about, Ted?"

"I'm talking about you having a baby on your own."

"Oh."

"What are *you* talking about?" he asks.

"You know Mark McGregor? From the club?"

"Yeah."

"Well, someone killed him last night."

Now it's his turn to say, "Oh." After absorbing the news, he says: "Christ. How?"

"He got hacked. Literally."

"Where?"

"At his home. It's in Menlo Park, right off Valparaiso."

"Hacked? Like with a machete?"

"I can't talk about the details, but it was apparently pretty messy." She says that after the police showed up last night, McGregor's wife called her, requesting she come over.

"You know her from the club, too, don't you?" she asks. "Beth Hill?"

"Did she do it?"

"I don't know. But she didn't like the questions Madden was asking. She thinks he thinks she killed him."

"He probably does."

After making the comment, Cogan goes silent, staring at the ground. He's intimately familiar with Detective Hank Madden. A few years ago he'd been accused of raping and causing the death of a former patient, a teenager named Kristen Kroiter, who'd tragically hanged herself at home. Madden had been in charge of the investigation. If the nature of the alleged crime wasn't disturbing enough, complicating matters was the fact that, when Madden was a child, his pediatrician had molested him (the revelation of his ordeal had come out in a newspaper profile years earlier). Needless to say, a few people, including Carolyn, felt the detective harbored some resentment toward doctors, and that he'd let that resentment influence how he approached the case.

She wonders whether Cogan is thinking about all that. Then, for a brief, horrifying moment she has a vision of him on top of Beth Hill, passionately screwing her. She has no reason to believe he's slept with her, yet there she is, suddenly thinking he has, incensed.

"Man, I played tennis with that guy last summer," he mutters. "Rinehart and I had drinks with him and his friend afterwards. Interesting cat. Real talker. I couldn't tell whether he was full of shit or not, which I liked. He tried to get us to invest in his company."

She takes a breath, relieved. His assessment reminds her of a great line from *Breakfast at Tiffany's* that she's always liked. In the party scene in the middle of the movie, the actor Marty Balsam says, "She's a phony, but she's a real phony." The line seems somehow apropos of Mark McGregor. He was charismatic and seemed to make friends easily, but he also made a strong first impression that not everybody bought into.

She says, "Well, Beth Hill married the guy after he testified against her fiancé in court, so he must have something going for him."

"I forgot about that." Cogan smiles, a memory returning. "Rinehart actually asked him how he'd pulled it off."

Maybe because he's used to having frank and open discussions with his patients about their perceived physical flaws, Cogan's plastic-surgeon friend, Rinehart, God bless him, is never one to shy away from asking blunt, personal questions. His nickname's the Rhino because he has short, thick legs and a big gut and he once charged the net to get to an opponent's drop shot and ended up plowing through it, snapping the net off its moorings without injuring himself.

"Really? What'd he say?"

"He said he was a good listener. That was the way to a woman's heart. That and a lot of money and a big dick."

"For real?"

"His very words. I swear."

"Well, he was right about the money and the big dick," she says. "Any schmuck can listen. Doing anything about what you're hearing is the hard part."

"Ouch," he says. "It just got a little colder out here. Can I come in for a minute?"

Discipline, Dupuy, she thinks. She'd promised herself that if he ever showed up or called, she'd keep her cool—and her distance. It would be tempting to fall back into the old routine. When they were dating, he'd come over some mornings, walk into her house (he used to have a key) and get in bed with her. "How many?" she'd always ask. And he'd report the number of trauma victims who'd come into the hospital. More than half of the time, he'd say, "Slow night." But usually he had a story or two to recount, which she loved hearing.

They live just a few miles apart; she in Palo Alto, he in an area of Menlo Park called Stanford Hills, which is just off Sand Hill Road, very close to where Forman killed the SLAC researcher with his car. Cogan's house is a little bigger and sits on a bit more land, but it arguably isn't as charming (she had a three-bedroom cottage, he a four-bedroom ranch).

They'd talked about moving in together and had even had a three-month-long cohabitation trial, with the understanding that if things progressed they'd sell both houses and get a larger one. But things didn't progress. A series of niggling arguments (mainly over his interactions with other women) mushroomed into something more menacing and destructive. She felt like she'd pulled out of the parking lot one day and instead of encountering the usual speed bump, she'd run over a set of severe-tire-damage "Tiger Teeth." It got ugly.

Then she started drinking. Heavily.

"I've got to get showered and dressed," she tells him now. "I've gotta deal with the press and my asshole partners, not to mention my client."

"This is a big deal, right? When was the last time something this big happened around here?"

"You," she says. "That was big."

"No, I mean a murder like this."

"A while."

"Are you really having a kid on your own, Carolyn?"

"I am, Ted. Trying anyway. I'm doing a cycle right now."

She wonders who'd told him, though she didn't really care. She'd informed enough people to ensure he'd hear about it. It had actually taken several days longer for the news to reach him than she'd anticipated. Funny how people could be more discreet when you were open with something and totally indiscreet when you requested they keep it a secret.

"Who's the donor?" he asks.

"I don't know. But he seems good on paper."

"ADI, huh?" Anonymous donor insemination. She'd heard the term, of course, but didn't know he had. "So, you're really going to do this?"

"I told you I was going to."

He shakes his head disapprovingly.

"If you want in, Ted, you've got a week," she warns.

"I've got shitty genes, Carolyn. I told you that."

She laughs. It still strikes her as comical for someone who looks like George Clooney to stand there and tell you he has shitty genetics. But Cogan, who's been married before to a woman who left him for her suddenly rich ex-boyfriend, is a doctor, and Alzheimer's runs in his family. On top of that, his father died relatively young of cancer. So, he does have something to worry about. But the way she sees it he's simply come up with a clinical excuse for birth control.

"The only bad gene you've got is an anti-Dad gene," she says.

"You know, I think about her sometimes."

"Who?"

"Kristen."

Kristen is his former patient, the girl who died. He rarely, if ever, speaks about her. Carolyn had told him to get some counseling after everything that went down, but he'd shrugged off her suggestions. He'd done a rotation in psych, he explained to her, and didn't think much of the discipline, which had become much more about changing people's outlooks and demeanor through drugs rather than through conversation. Like a few other doctors she knew, Cogan was good at dispensing his own medical opinion but not so good at accepting others'.

"What do you think about?" she asks.

"Just what happened, why she would have done that to herself. How irrational it really was and how I could have prevented it. And then I think about all the bad things that can happen to kids. I see it every day in the hospital, Carolyn. Have you ever had to tell a parent their kid has died in a car accident?"

No, she hasn't.

"So is it the genetics or just a dour outlook?" she asks. "Or is it just me? Or all of the above?"

"It's not you," he says.

"Then what is it, Ted? We've been through this over and over. Why are you here? You said you were out."

"I did."

"So?"

"I heard. It bothered me. So I'm here. And now I'm fucking cold."

"I gotta go, Ted."

"How are you doing with the shots?"

"Shitty."

"I thought so. And you're going to continue even with all this going on? Those fertility drugs can make you a little wiggy, you know?"

"Tell me about it," she says. "I just told some asshole tech blogger to go fuck himself. Probably not a good idea. But it could be over tomorrow. They might find the killer. Or if Hill really gets charged, someone's going to tell her to get some big-name attorney. I've done two murder cases as a defense attorney, three as a prosecutor."

"Well, let me know if I can help with anything."

"I will."

"Hang in there, okay? This is good, Carolyn. This is really good for you. I'm happy for you."

She doesn't know whether he means the case or the kid but suspects the former.

"Go home, Ted. You're not making sense anymore."

12 / MONEY ON MONEY

OUTSIDE THE HOLDING CELL ON THE LOWER FLOOR OF THE MENLO Park police station, a sign affixed to the wall reads, "It is a felony to possess or to bring into this jail any narcotic or paraphernalia, alcoholic beverage, firearm, tear gas or explosives. Violators will be imprisoned for up to four years in a state prison. Sections 4573 & 4574 California Penal Code."

Purposely slurring his words, Richie reads the sign aloud as Madden stands behind him, unlocking the handcuffs his partner clamped on Richie's wrists earlier. "You *guyz* is a bunch of party poopers," he says after he finishes reading. "How do you expect to have any fun around here?"

The truth is, it isn't much of a jail. The room they put him in feels more like a small, austere, windowless office, with its cement floor painted gray and cinder-block walls painted white. Integrated into the wall on one side of the room is a sort of bench or shelf made out of a Formica-like material that has child-friendly rounded corners. On top of the bench is a bed mat the color of green hospital scrubs. The mat's only a couple of inches thick and not as comfortable as the futon couch he sleeps on up in the city, but at least it has some padding.

The station is nicer than he remembers from his one other visit years ago. He realizes why: it's new. During his trial, he'd heard people talking about redoing the station and the civic center, and now the project is completed.

"If you need to go to the bathroom, knock on the door," Madden says.

Back at the View, before they'd arrested him, he'd downed another whisky—a double—and made his last substantive comments before he stopped talking. "Someone was putting the heat on Mark," he said. "They wanted some dough. I think he thought it was me. He sent over some muscle to send a message. I reported it to the SFPD. That's all I gotta say. This nonsense, I got nothin' to do with. I didn't kill nobody."

Not long after that Madden took a call and stepped away from the table. He was gone awhile. A good ten minutes. When he came back, the place was getting ready to close. He said:

"Good news, Richie. The judge just issued a warrant to search your apartment. You want to come along?"

He rode back with them to his apartment and waited outside while they snapped some pictures and searched it. About forty-five minutes later, Madden and Billings came out with some of his belongings sealed in plain paper evidence bags, which got his heart racing more than it already had been.

What the hell did they take? The diving knives? My laptop?

"What you got there?" he asked Billings, who was in the process of lifting the hatch to the trunk of Madden's SUV.

"You'll know soon enough. You got a lawyer?"

"He's dead."

"You want us to get you a lawyer? You need some numbers?"

He shook his head, the gravity of what was happening finally sinking in. He'd already texted Ashley three times, asking her for help. "They got a warrant," he wrote. "Searching apartment now."

"Don't say anything," she wrote back. "Keep your mouth shut, whatever you do."

Too late. Now he was fucked. They were going to arrest him. And to make matters worse, they were getting cocky about it. Which could mean one of two things. They either thought they had him nailed or they thought they almost had him nailed but were missing the hammer and were hoping he'd give it to them.

His original lawyer, Max Fischer, actually had died, but he could have called the attorney from the firm, a woman named Gail Stevens who'd represented him at his parole-board hearing. The only problem was he couldn't afford her. And more than getting charged, the thought of how he was going to pay for decent representation was what was really weighing on him. He might as well have been walking gravely injured into an emergency room without insurance. He'd be in debt for years. If his father were alive, he would have called him, because his father wouldn't forgive him if he didn't. But he'd already cost his family so much the first go-around, he couldn't bear the thought of making the call to his mother. She'd be devastated. He just couldn't. He asked Ashley to speak to Lourdes. He'd seen that guy Krisberg in the office. Maybe he'd cut him a deal.

"When do I get a call?" he asked.

"Face the vehicle," Billings said, taking him by the arm and gently turning him. "You'll get your call when you get to the station house. But looks like you've been texting your head off. Who you talking to?"

Richie was sober enough to know that in some ways they actually didn't mind him texting. It would later give them a record of whom he'd contacted and what he'd said. And all too often people made incriminating statements in texts.

"A friend," he murmured as Billings cuffed him.

That was how it went down. In the car ride down, he kept hoping he'd drunk enough to keep them from questioning him right away. Sure enough, when they got to the station house, they allowed him to go to the bathroom and make a call (he spoke to Ashley), then left him in the holding cell.

Richie sat on the bench for a few minutes, waiting for someone to return, but no one did. Madden hadn't said anything but Richie knew they needed him completely sober. Taint the beginning, you taint the end, he thinks now, lying down on the bench, reminded of something a lawyer had once told him. He likes the sound of that. *Tainted beginnings, tainted ends.* And then for some reason he remembers a book he'd read in his high-school advanced-placement English class. *The Painted Bird*, by Jerzy Kosinski. A goddamn holocaust novel. Perfect.

Tainted beginnings, tainted ends, he repeats to himself over and over, finally falling asleep.

They wake him at seven thirty. A younger, clean-cut cop with short blond hair who looks like he lifeguards on the weekends gives him a towel and a cheap travel toiletry kit that reminds him of something you'd get on an airplane when you fly overseas coach class. He tells Richie to get his shoes on. He can brush his teeth and wash his face if he wants.

After he's through in the bathroom, two more uniformed cops lead him into an interrogation room. It looks very similar to the "cell" he'd slept in but is about twice as large and has a rectangular gray institutional-looking table in the middle of it with a single chair on one side of the table and two chairs on the other. There's a window on the wall across from the single chair. He can't see out the window but assumes whoever is on the other side can see into the room.

They make him wait in the room by himself for almost ten minutes. Then Madden enters, trailed by a tall, thin black guy Richie vaguely remembers. Short-cropped afro, pleasant eyes and a strong, angular jaw. Would be better-looking except his face has pockmarks on his cheeks and neck from cystic acne.

"Good morning, Mr. Forman," Madden says. "This is Detective Burns. I believe you've met before."

"Déjà vu," Richie says.

They'd brought breakfast. Madden puts a cup of coffee down in front of him along with a bag that he says contains a bagel and cream cheese, a banana, and a bottle of water.

"If you've got any special requests, we'll see what we can do," Madden says accommodatingly.

Richie rubs his eyes. His contacts are bothering him a little.

"How 'bout some contact-lens solution?" he asks. "My peepers are starting to bark like hell."

"Fair enough."

"And a newspaper wouldn't be bad. I like to read the sports section in the morning, you know."

"We switched to iPads," Madden says without missing a beat. "Since we got the new digs, there's been a push to go green. We're running a little experiment. Going as paperless as possible."

"For real? All you guys got iPads?"

"Not everybody. We got ten. Corporate donation."

"Nice. And I heard Facebook has taken over the old Sun campus over by the 101. That's gotta feel pretty good. Little civic pride."

Madden shrugs. He's hard to read. "City's happy," he says. "Free publicity. And they'll probably get some concessions down the road. Who knows, maybe Belle Haven gets a new community center. But I'm not sure what it really does except make it more expensive to buy a home here after they go public. They're on the other side of 101, basically off on their own. They're building it out. Meals in-house, all that fun stuff."

"Kind of a self-contained little utopia," Burns comments. "I wouldn't leave. Ever. They should have a free senior center and crematorium on campus."

Richie takes the bagel out of the bag and inspects it. It's plain and passably soft. He then pulls the top off the coffee and takes a look.

"Milk and one sugar," Madden says.

"You remembered."

"I've got a good memory."

They let him eat for a bit before they finally get down to business.

"You understand the seriousness of the situation you're in, don't you?"

"Sure."

"We just want to make that clear, Mr. Forman," Burns adds. "And we're going Mirandize you now. I'm going to read you your rights and then have you sign a Miranda waiver. You don't have to say anything. You don't have to answer any questions without a lawyer present. Do you want to make another call?"

Richie takes a sip of the coffee, doing his best to appear nonplussed.

"I'm good for now. Go ahead. I'll be grading on elocution. No pressure."

Burns, who's got more of a sense of humor than Richie first thought, cracks a smile. He then reads him his rights slowly and deliberately, enunciating each word. "How was that?" he asks when he's through.

"A for effort," Richie says.

If Madden's getting impatient with his shenanigans, he doesn't show it. He lets him have another bite of his bagel, then makes him read the top of the form aloud and sign it at the bottom. After he signs, Madden says, "We're going to ask you some questions now."

"Shouldn't we do a sound check first?"

Madden looks at Burns, then back at Richie. Before either of them can respond, Richie says:

"Those pictures of the Tongans, the ones in my laptop case, you find 'em?"

Madden nods. "We did."

"You seen either of those mugs before?"

"We've got them up on the wire," Burns says. "The SFPD said they didn't turn up anything."

Madden: "So, you really think someone was trying to blackmail Mr. McGregor?"

"Looked that way."

"And you had no part in that? You didn't say to one of your old buddies from prison, hey, I've got an easy mark, you just have to put the screws in a little and we can pick up some fast cash."

He laughs. Not a defiant snort, a real chuckle.

"What's so funny?" Madden asks.

"Just the way you said it, like they were guys I'd gone to school with or something. You know, college buds you meet up with at a reunion and knock back a couple of cold ones, talk about the good ol' days raping and ripping people off."

"You were in there awhile," Burns says. "You had friends. Anybody you close to out now? You talk to anyone?"

He shakes his head, a touch of sadness coming into his eyes.

"You sure about that?" Burns says a little more aggressively. "I noticed a little tentativeness there."

"No," he says firmly.

Madden: "You wanna give us some names, so we can check on their status?"

"You remember this guy Dr. Jaron? Dr. Ben Jaron?"

"The anesthesiologist?" Madden says.

"Yeah, him."

"Man, I haven't heard that name in a while. You remember him, Burns?"

Burns remembers.

"Well, he's still locked up," Richie says. "Go talk to him."

Madden: "You guys were tight?"

"Whatever you want to call it. We played board games, philosophized about the state of the world, traded dating stories. His batting average was a lot better than mine. I tried to sleep with broads while they were awake, which can be challenging."

His closest friend in the pen was a rapist, an anesthesiologist who brought women back to his home, knocked them out, took pictures of them naked and had sex with them while they lay there unconscious. It only took about two years and ten victims before he got caught.

"Who else?" Burns asks.

He tells them he had another pal, Alain Dessain, who liked to rent apartments for the week then sublet the same apartment to fifty other people for the year, walking away with their deposits. He was popped doing it in San Francisco, got off with probation, then moved to New York, pulled the same stunt there, went to jail, came back to San Francisco and picked up a five-to-seven bid for defrauding charities and violating his parole. The guy was a three-time loser but he was smart. His biggest flaw was his limited repertoire; he kept committing the same crimes over and over. A light-skinned black guy who moved well among the various prison factions, he talked a good game. Richie thought he'd have made a great political fund-raiser and organizer. Dessain agreed. But now it was too late for that.

Way too fucking late.

The big problem, Dessian liked to point out, was that once you got a record you ended up behind the eight ball. It was hard to get hired, even for crappy jobs, especially when the economy was bad and especially when you were black and had no college diploma. He didn't want to drive a bus. Menial labor wasn't part of his DNA. What was he supposed to do? He liked hanging out with successful people. He felt that's where he belonged, he just didn't want to do what it took to really get there. He knew he was being stupid but people were stupid. They were consumed with their own political correctness and they kept giving him their money because they didn't want to appear racist for not trusting him. Was that such a crime, showing "wine-sniffing Marina bitches" how stupid they were?

Richie smiles at Madden but he's really smiling at the memory of Dessain's perverse logic. There was a lot of that in prison. A lot of perverse logic.

"Mark offered me some money when I got out of prison," he says. "I didn't take it. Why would I then go out of my way to try and squeeze it out of him now?"

Burns: "Circumstances change. Maybe someone was trying to squeeze you. Maybe you owed someone."

"Look, I reported the incident to the police. Yeah, it was a few days later, but I reported it."

"Why'd you wait?" Madden asks.

"I hate to break it to you, but based on previous experience, I don't have much fondness for cops. But a couple of friends convinced me that it was in my best interest to put something on the record."

"In case you got caught?" Burns jumps in.

Richie sighs. "Come on. If I were blackmailing him, why would I report it?"

Madden: "To cover it up."

"That's rich," he says, kicking the Jersey accent up a notch. "You fellas got a fertile imagination. You do an internship at Disney Imagineering? You'd be good. I'd give you the gig."

Madden smiles. "You'd be surprised by the crazy, stupid stuff people do. Even here in Mayberry."

"Yeah, you'd be surprised," Burns agrees. "What about that guy a few months back, the one who got stabbed by his wife?"

"Yeah, that's a good one," Madden says. "Tell him about that."

"Okay, get this. A couple months back a guy calls 911. Says his wife stabbed him. So we go over there and the paramedics are there and there's actually a decent amount of blood. And the guy has a wound on his side. It's not insignificant but it's right above his belt, you know, right where his tire roll is. He'd gotten stabbed in the fatty part. It looked like he needed stitches. And the guy's yelling about how his wife tried to kill him. Well, she tells a different a story. She says she never went near him."

"We brought them in separately," Madden says.

"And we go back and forth," Burns goes on. "And I think to myself, the wife actually sounds pretty convincing. A little hysterical at times but she sticks to her story and never deviates from it. Very consistent."

"The guy, however, starts to introduce some small discrepancies.

How she approached him. From what side. You know, little stuff like that. We brought him back a second time and finally after about an hour of questioning he admits that he stabbed himself. You know why? Because he knows he and his wife are going to get divorced and he doesn't want her taking the kids. So, he thinks, hey, I'll hit her up with something that'll stick her with a police report. And maybe it doesn't mean I'll get custody, but I'll use it as leverage so I don't get screwed. That's how he's thinking. Intelligent guy. A VP at some tech firm."

"Marketing guy," Madden says

"Oh, those marketing guys," Richie says. "They're not so bright."

"Well, you get the idea," Madden says. "You wouldn't believe the twisted crap people do, Mr. Forman. So yes, we have fertile imaginations."

"Well, I'm telling you someone was trying to blackmail the guy."

"We know someone was trying to blackmail him."

"You do?"

"He reported it himself ten days ago to the Sunnyvale police."

"He filed a report?"

"Yeah, someone had sent him a letter saying they wanted two hundred fifty thousand dollars."

"And what was the threat?"

"He got a note. It said, 'I know you were driving that car that night.'"

"Yeah. And?"

"Apparently, whoever sent the note threatened to provide evidence to the authorities that he'd been driving the car."

"I'd like to see that evidence."

"I'm sure you would."

"And how was the exchange supposed to take place?"

"It never got that far."

"Well, did you analyze the note? Send it to the FBI?"

"We just heard about it late last night."

"Why Sunnyvale?" Richie asks.

"That's where his office is. That's where the note was delivered."

"By snail mail?"

"We're not at liberty to discuss that," Burns says.

"Well, what were the next steps?"

Madden: "Next steps?"

"I don't know what you guys call it. What was the action plan? You guys have action plans, don't you?"

"Look, let's talk about your trip down here yesterday," Madden says, realizing his suspect is controlling the conversation too much.

"I'm not at liberty to discuss that without my lawyer present. I've told you I was on the six forty-five train. I came in at around noon. I forget the exact time. I brought my bike 'cause I don't got no license. You can confirm that."

"Where's your lawyer?" Madden asks.

"I don't know. Someone's working on it for me. What I'm willing to discuss right now is what I discussed already with the SFPD. When do I get my hat and ring back?"

"I don't know," Madden says. "What do you need the hat for? What's in the hat?"

"Nothin's in the hat. It's just like, you know, sort of like an appendage."

"You mean part of the act," Burns says.

"What are you worried about?" Madden says. "You got a nice full head of hair. The only reason Sinatra wore that thing was because he was losing his."

"Ah, we have ourselves a fan. You a fan, Detective?"

"My father," Madden replies. "And I know a thing or too about going bald."

Burns isn't happy with the conversation's direction. "About those Tongans . . ."

"Alleged Tongans," Richie counters. "How 'bout we call them Pacific Islanders until we know for sure? I don't want to cast racial aspersions."

"They said they were working for McGregor?"

"They didn't say his name, per se, but they made it seem that way."

"So you have no proof they were working for him," Madden says, "We just have to take your word—"

"What am I being charged with?"

"Well, right now you're looking at murder," Madden says. "But hey, maybe it didn't go down like that. Maybe you've got something to tell us that might help get it knocked down to manslaughter."

"When am I getting arraigned?"

"You're looking at Monday morning. With what we got, the judge will remand you back to prison. You're okay with that, right?"

Richie: "What do you have?"

"We got a couple of nice prints. One off the panel of the buzzer to the house and one right near the body. And I bet when we run the cell-phone data, you're going to be right there in the window."

Fuck, Richie thinks. He'd wiped off the buzzer but he didn't think he'd touched the panel. But what was this bullshit about a print near the body? What the fuck was that about? He had to be bluffing.

When he doesn't respond, Madden goes on. "Here's the deal. You're going to be locked up for a while. This here's a country club compared to the county jail next door in Redwood City. Clean, new building like this. Private room. Nice, right? But if you don't give us something soon, we're going to have to pass you on to the folks over there. So what you got, Richie? What can you tell us that will help us help you? Because the fact is I like you. I think you're a good guy who's had some bad luck. I really do."

"I like you, too, Detective. You know that. But my own personal opinion is that I think you're too old for this shit. I don't know why you don't pack it in. Can't you get ninety percent of your highest salary for the rest of your life? Oh, wait, I get it, you keep pulling all nighters, you'll pick up some nice overtime, bump your salary up a little more this year, then retire at an even higher rate."

"You know what they call me?" Madden asks, leaning forward a little.

"No, what?"

"Minimum Wage Madden. You know why?"

"Because you're only working for that ten percent you could get if you retired."

Madden glances at Burns, who nods, impressed he's figured it out so quickly.

"You got it," Madden says. "And do you know why I keep working?"

"Because you like what you do and don't like the idea of the city losing experienced officers and you want to give something back to the community. Yeah, I read that article. Dug it up on Google one day. Very noble of you, Officer. If I was a taxpayer in this county, I'd be touched. Really tickled. But you know how much it cost to keep me in prison each year? Around forty-five, fifty grand. A real menace to society like me costing taxpayers fifty grand a year when instead I could have been making, I don't know, a quarter million, and giving back eighty or so to the government. What's the tax rate for rich people these days?"

"I didn't put you in prison," Madden says, his anger showing for the first time. "You can thank the DA for that and the jury of your peers that convicted you."

"You were part of it. You testified."

"I questioned you and McGregor, that's it."

"Well you didn't do a very fucking good job of it."

"Well, next time take a fucking cab," Madden fires back, edging toward, him, a tiny fleck of his saliva hitting Richie on the cheek. "Oh, and, here's another thing you might think about. Don't drive around in an ancient car that doesn't have airbags. If you'd been driving around in a car from the era, you'd have both been pinned to your goddamned seats. You thought you were so cool with your classic Caddy, lot of good it did you. What, don't tell me, Sinatra drove that kind of car?"

Burns puts a hand up in front of Madden as if to restrain him.

"Easy Hank," Burns says.

Richie smiles, feeling a weird sense of accomplishment. It's the most emotion he's ever seen Madden display and he's thrilled that it's on tape. But at the same time he knows Madden's right about the airbags. He'd thought about that a lot—that fucking car. He hated that car. Still, he can't help taking one last swing, just one more little potshot.

"You should have retired after shooting that kid," he says. "You're never going to top that."

"I'm not trying to top that," Madden replies more calmly.

"You think you got enough? Really? You got a witness? An actual fucking witness? Let me be absolutely clear, Detective. I did not kill Mark McGregor despite your circumstantial trumped-up bullshit."

Madden's eyes meet his. They really bear down on him.

"Mr. Forman, I have one question for you," he says.

"What's that?"

"Do you still love Beth Hill?"

Richie doesn't flinch. He stares right back at Madden. A good five seconds pass.

"Your question assumes I loved her at some other point in time," he finally says.

Madden seems taken aback by the response.

"You were engaged to be married."

"Yes. We were."

Again, Madden goes with the hard, probing eyes. They're in full-on stare-down mode, when Burns says:

"See the thing is both me and Detective Madden here are kind of romantics. We believe that if you really love someone, you never stop loving them."

"Even if she completely betrays you?"

"Maybe things don't appear exactly as they seem," Burns says.

"What are you implying, Detective?"

"That maybe Ms. Hill had ulterior motives for marrying Mark McGregor."

"Really? That's news to me."

Madden: "We don't think Ms. Hill is telling the truth. She's already made some contradictory statements. And she's hired a lawyer."

"Last night?"

"Asked for one right away."

His jaw tightens. *Not good*, he thinks. *Why the hell did she do that*?

"Where is she?"

"She's here. Or she'll be here shortly. But she was questioned some last night."

Richie shrugs. "Did you ask whether she still loved me?"

Burns looks at Madden, who looks back at him. Then Madden says:

"Look, if you've got anything to tell us, you should tell us now. If you're protecting her in any way, you're an accessory to murder. You're going away for the rest of your life. You tell us what happened now, how she's involved, and we'll see what we can do for you."

Richie sits there impassively, clenching his teeth, getting more and more aggravated. *What the fuck do these assholes know about love?* he thinks. *About what we went through? And what I went through because of their ineptitude? What right do they have asking me if I still love her?*

"What do you say, Richie?"

This is Burns trying to prompt him. He looks at the detective, then slowly and deliberately leans forward, puts his elbows on the table and clasps his hands in front him.

"This is all I got to say to you guys. Stop talking about love. No one ever does anything for love in the Valley. People obsess over deals. Over networking. Over building a company. But not genuine love. A woman once told me this was one of the most asexual places on earth. She said people were more interested in her introducing them to investors than fucking her. And let me tell you, she wasn't bad-looking. So cut the love bullshit. No one killed Mark because someone loved or didn't love someone."

"So why'd he get killed?" Madden asks.

"Well, that's up to you to find out now, isn't it? But my money's on money. And not no piddly-shit one hundred thousand."

"Two hundred fifty thousand," Burns corrects him.

"Whatever," he says.

13 / SCOOP WHORE

"Nice work," Billings says sarcastically when Madden comes out of the interrogation room. "You got a lot out of him."

"Don't start," Madden grumbles.

"Give me fifteen minutes alone," Billings says.

"Not now."

"When?"

"After Burns is through. I gotta deal with the commander. He just texted me."

"And Crowley."

This is news to him. He didn't realize Dick Crowley, the San Mateo County district attorney, is already in the office.

"He's here?"

"Yeah. Just saw his car pull in. What are you going to tell him?"

"What he probably doesn't want to hear."

Madden starts to walk away.

"You sleep?" Billings calls after him.

"A little."

"I got four hours," Billings boasts.

Madden, who rarely ever swears, uncharacteristically holds up his middle finger, extending it over his shoulder, backwards. "One for me," he says without turning around.

Commander Pete Pastorini's door is open. He's sitting at his desk, an iPad in his hand, while Dick Crowley, the DA, sits in a chair on the other side of the desk. Pastorini's a big man, imposing, and though he's lost some weight, he still has the look of an operatic tenor, with dark, wavy hair that he wears slicked back.

Back when he was a sergeant, some of the guys would good-humoredly call him "Luciano" or "Maestro," but since his status was elevated to commander, those nicknames haven't been heard. However, they still occasionally mock him for his caffeine addiction, referring to him as Commander Loca. Pastorini used to drink eight to ten Diet Cokes a day. Now he's moved on to Java Monster Loca Moca energy drinks. He prides himself on cutting down his fluid intake, going from that eight to ten to two to three cans. The only problem is the stuff he's drinking probably has three to four times the amount of caffeine as coffee, so he's as amped as ever.

When Madden walks in, Crowley swivels ninety degrees toward him, so that his back is now facing the window.

"Morning, Hank," Crowley says.

"Morning, Dick."

Tall and lanky, near six-nine, Crowley has big features and sandy brown hair flecked with gray. He played basketball in college for Cal in the late 1970s and comes across as easygoing and genial, a guy who shakes your hand with both of his while looking you in the eye. There's something good-natured, even almost bumbling about his demeanor. But underneath that exterior layer lies a more manipulative, calculating side that has a tendency to sneak up on people just as they've let their guard down. Madden learned to stop underestimating him long ago.

Pastorini motions for Madden to sit in the open seat next to Crowley. Feeling pretty beat, he gladly takes a seat. He's even tempted to ask Pastorini for one of his Loca Mocas.

"How's it going in there?" Crowley asks. "We got our guy or not?"

"Maybe."

"He talking?"

"Sure. He's saying the same thing over and over. Singing a little, too. He's been making a living as a Sinatra impersonator."

"Pete told me," Crowley says. "Richie Forman doing Sinatra. He any good?"

Madden: "Actually, yeah. Takes it very seriously. In fact, he's been in character pretty much the whole time we've questioned him."

"You think he's going to try for some insanity thing?"

"He could."

"Does he think he's Sinatra?"

"I don't know exactly what he's thinking. He's straddling this line. I'm not sure how he thinks it's going to help him. He's got a lot of cards stacked against him and he's playing it like he's got a full house."

"Strange," Crowley says. "You got the prints on the lighter and the buzzer panel. That's pretty good. Anything else?"

"Nothing concrete so far. But the fact that this guy lives up in the city and is down here during the window says a lot. And, of course, he's got motive. In spades."

Crowley nods. "Still no weapon?"

He tells Crowley they'd picked up two diver's knives at Forman's apartment. However, from what he can tell, he thinks they're too small to inflict the kind of damage he saw on the body.

Pastorini: "And why would the guy keep the murder weapon in his apartment?"

Crowley agrees. "You'd think he'd be bright enough to ditch it."

"The weapon may have been there already. In the garage, I mean."

He explains that there was an empty, open slot on the wall for a missing tool. The wife seemed to remember some sort of hatchet being there. They were going to go through credit-card records to see what they could come up with.

"But he admits to being down here yesterday?" Crowley asks.

"Says he took the six forty-five home. Told us to check the video."

"And what time did he come in?"

"Around noon."

"Where'd he go?"

"Won't say. He's waiting for legal counsel to talk about certain details. But he may have met with Ms. Hill. He picked up his engagement ring, he says. Someone returned it to him."

"And between noon and seven, how did Mr. Forman get around town?" Crowley asks.

"On a bike."

"A bike?"

"He doesn't have a driver's license. He brought a bike on the train. We got that out of him."

"Anybody see him? I mean, we've got motive. We've got the prints. And we've got a guy who admits to being in the general vicinity at the time of the crime. But someone must have seen him."

"We're working on it," Madden says. "As you know, a lot of those folks on Robert S have security cameras. Unfortunately, McGregor didn't. He's got a home security system but no cameras. But some of the neighbors say they have cameras that are pointed at the street. We're also going to get his cell-phone data, though that'll take a few days. If he had his phone on, we should be able to pinpoint exactly where he was at what times. The satellite may be our best witness."

"You should be able to pinpoint where his phone was," Crowley corrects him. "Not him for certain."

Crowley is old-fashioned. He likes his witnesses to be real people if he can get them. But so much more detective work these days is being done through cell-phone tracking, with investigators combing through call logs and location-based data that carriers keep stored on their servers. In many crimes, the smoking gun often turns out to be a cell phone in a pocket, not a weapon in a hand.

Crowley stares past Madden, mulling things over. After a moment, he says:

"I think we've got to consider that maybe this wasn't premeditated. You know, the guy comes into town, and against his better judgment, decides to pay his old friend a visit. And, you know, they get into it."

"Forman doesn't have a mark on him," Madden counters. "Go see for yourself. And there are no defensive wounds on the victim."

"I'm going to have a word with him later. And with Ms. Hill. When's Carolyn bringing her in?"

Madden: "We said eleven but I'm not banking on it."

Crowley shakes his head. "I bet Sinatra boy sings."

Pastorini: "I'm going with the wife cracking first."

"You, Hank?" Crowley asks, as if he's somehow the tie-breaking vote.

"I don't know. I'm working on one hour of sleep." He rubs his eye. "Been a while since I did that."

Madden regrets making the statement as soon as he says it. Pastorini looks at Crowley, their eyes locking for a second. It's one of those knowing looks that speaks volumes. Madden gets the distinct feeling they were discussing him—and perhaps his ability to handle the case—before he walked in.

Pastorini picks up the iPad and turns it around toward Madden. "You see this?" he asks.

Madden leans forward, squinting. When Pastorini hands the iPad over to him, he lifts his glasses, propping them up on the top of his head. It's an article from Tom Bender's site, OneDumbIdea.com—or ODi, as the site's prominent red logo reads. The piece is written by Bender himself, with a typically inflammatory headline: EXCLUSIVE: SILICON VALLEY ENTREPRENEUR HACKED TO DEATH, BUMBLING DETECTIVES MAY HAVE CONTAMINATED CRIME SCENE.

Madden skims through the article, which is a first-person account of how Bender stumbled upon the crime while walking his dog and, with a little investigative fortitude, gained access to important details that he claimed were anonymously leaked to him by reliable sources. As he reads, Madden feels the heat rise in his face, his heart pounding in his chest. The guy's taking potshots at him left and right.

"What do you think?" Pastorini says.

Madden shrugs, doing his best to feign indifference. "I think the guy's looking for traffic. That's what he does."

"Yeah. But where's he getting his info? You think it's someone from our side or is our little lady counselor making a play here? Dick says she said something to him last night about how the crime scene was being handled."

"Look, half of it is innuendo. There were people in the house before I got there. It took us a little while to get the wife out of there and over to the neighbors' house. We secured the crime scene, which was out in the garage. That's it, end of story."

"This guy Bender," Crowley says, "I hear he may have a little ax to grind. Maybe we can provide a little context to the media if we get any questions."

Bender used to have some pretty big parties, which his neighbors frequently called the police to complain about. The MPPD had paid at least ten visits to his previous home, and Bender, who was fond of the expression "What you do in your own home is your own business," hadn't exactly been accommodating. He'd ended up paying several fines and had to make a court appearance or two.

"I told Dick about the citations," Pastorini says. "Between him and his mother—"

Crowley: "Who's his mother?"

"A life coach," Madden says, glad to shift the conversation. "Or at least that's what she calls herself. Does nude group sessions in her backyard. Cleansings."

Crowley lifts an eyebrow. "I think I heard about this."

"Neighbors complained about her, too," Madden goes on. "Didn't like that she was running a business out of her home."

"And that she couldn't get more attractive clients," Pastorini deadpans.

"Look, I'll take care of him," Madden says after a moment.

"How?" Crowley asks.

"Give him what he wants."

"What's that?"

"An exclusive. He likes to be first. For him, it's all about being first. He's a scoop whore."

"An exclusive on what?" Pastorini asks, obviously concerned about what information he's going to release.

"Let me think about it. But I think he can be useful."

They both look at him like he's off his rocker.

"Is that a real term, 'scoop whore'?" Crowley asks. "Or did you just make it up?"

"I don't know. I might have."

With that, Madden says he has to go.

"I'll be back in an hour," he says. "I gotta check on something with Lyons. He might have something."

"What?"

"He said he found a couple of needle marks, one on each arm."

"So the guy was a user?"

"I don't know. That's what I gotta find out."

14 / BLINDSIDES

At a little after nine in the morning Carolyn heads out to pick up Beth. She'd put her in the Rosewood Sand Hill Hotel under the name of the neighbor, Pam Yeagher, who'd trailed behind them in her car and spent the night in the room with Beth in the second bed.

Carolyn had picked the hotel because she knew it well. Pretentiously casual, it was a favored meeting spot of wealthy venture capitalists, entrepreneurs, and other business leaders, and she had a friend who sometimes came down from the city and stayed there for a night or two to take in a few spa treatments and, hopefully, land a "lifelong investor," which she'd shortened to the more text-friendly LLI.

Carolyn likes how the hotel's a little bit out of the way, right next to the 280 freeway off Sand Hill, rather than closer to downtown, and feels more like a hotel you'd find in the southwest; picturesque, with views of the Santa Cruz mountains—"Napa light" as her friend fondly calls it.

That the hotel is just up the road from the entrance to the Stanford Linear Accelerator, where the accident had occurred all those years ago, hadn't factored into her decision, but that was because she hadn't considered it until she pulled her car onto Sand Hill the night before. Her hands had tensed little on the wheel as they passed through the intersection, but Beth, sitting next to her in the passenger seat, didn't react or show any emotion. She just kept staring straight ahead.

At nine thirty in the morning, Beth and Pam are waiting for her in the hotel's restaurant, plates of half-eaten food strewn about their table. In their black leggings, fleece pullovers, and running shoes, they both look ready to work out. The large restaurant, with its high, arched ceiling, has just a smattering of patrons, several of whom are eating alone, reading newspapers, or checking email on their phones.

Carolyn asks Beth how she's doing.

"Okay," Beth says. "And not."

"She actually slept really well," Pam remarks as if she'd been by her bedside, monitoring her all night. "Did you eat already? Do you want some coffee?"

Carolyn has already decided she really doesn't like Pam, though she can't quite put her finger on why. The woman seems boxed in, harried, and insecure all at once, yet she has this irritatingly perky disposition. Carolyn feels she's compensating for something—or perhaps coping is the kinder way to put it. She senses her relationship with her husband is far from copacetic. And while she sympathizes with her plight on a certain level she doesn't have the time or patience to deal with it now.

"If you don't mind, Pam, I've got to talk to Beth alone. We need to head to the police station in a little while."

"You want me to leave?"

As quickly as possible. "Yes. And I mean that in the politest way."

"Oh." She seems a little shocked. "Okay."

After some hugs and naive, clichéd parting words ("Everything is going to be okay, I promise") she's on her way, her purse tucked under one arm, a to-go cup of coffee in her other hand.

"She means well," Beth says when she's gone. "She just tries too hard sometimes."

"Sometimes?"

"Okay, all the time. But we've had some good talks. She needs a friend."

"Her husband fools around, doesn't he?"

"It's a little more complicated than that."

"How so?"

"He wants her to fool around with him."

"Oh." Carolyn considers that a moment. "You mean swing?"

Beth nods. "She tried it a few times but she's having trouble with it."

"I can see that."

Not much surprises Carolyn anymore. Still, she had Harry Yeagher pegged as more of a bang-a-nurse-on-the-sly kind of guy, not a wife swapper. This scenario is better, but only if everyone is on board with the program. *Poor woman*, she thinks.

The check comes. After Beth settles up, Carolyn asks whether she has any preference where they talk. Does she want to find a more private lounge area?

Beth looks away, absently staring out the window at a terrace that has a row of tables lined up along it.

"I'm going to be cooped up in a little room for a while, aren't I?" she says. "Why don't we go outside? The hotel has a nice garden. I saw it on the way to breakfast."

The weather is still on the cool side, but they find a bench in the sun, where it's considerably warmer. The garden—or the Cypress Garden, as it's officially named—is in a courtyard between two of the complex's several two-story buildings. As its name implies, it's sprinkled with slim, perfectly straight Cypress trees. Manicured gravel paths run among native grasses, plants, and flowers.

Carolyn starts the conversation by saying what she says to just about every client: "I'm your attorney, Beth. And you should know that anything you say to me is guarded by the attorney-client privilege."

Then she gets specific about what she wants:

"I need you to speak frankly with me about your relationship with your husband and Richie Forman so I can help you. And then I need you to go through your day yesterday, hour by hour. You cannot lie to me. That's Rule Number One. I don't want to get blindsided and I don't want you to get blindsided."

Beth smiles. "So you don't believe me either?"

"I'm going to believe whatever you tell me, Beth. And based on what you say and the facts we have before us, I'm going to do everything within my power to attain the best outcome possible."

"Are you still dating that doctor? Cogan his name was, right? I saw you two together at the club a few times."

Carolyn's a little taken aback by the question. "No," she says. "We broke it off about six months ago."

"May I ask why?"

"Why?" Carolyn smiles. "I guess that would depend who you ask."

"I'm asking you."

She hesitates to answer, reluctant to dive into the private details of her love life with a client. But then she thinks that maybe if she's more open, Beth will relax.

"Simple," she says. "I wanted to have a kid and he didn't."

"You wanted to get married?"

"No, I didn't care so much about the married part. I'm just at the point where if I'm going to have a kid, I need to have it already."

"I've heard that one before. I'm sorry it didn't work out."

"I am, too."

Carolyn is hoping the inquiry will end there, but Beth isn't through. "So what's his story? Why would he say you split up?"

"Him? He'd probably give the same reason. At least that would be his official response. But get a few drinks into him and I bet he'd say I was psycho, exceedingly jealous, and prone to irrational outbursts."

"But you don't seem that way at all. You seem very even-keeled."

"Mostly. Which is why you probably wouldn't believe Ted. But objectively speaking, he's right."

Beth's eyes turn to a group of small birds that have landed nearby and are pecking about, searching for food while glancing over at them, hoping for a handout. "So, two truths," she remarks. "Or should I say perspectives? Sometimes it's hard to know who to believe."

"With Richie, I was just doing my job. You understand that?"

Beth looks up at her. "That's a bit of a non sequitur, isn't it?"

"Yes. But I wanted to say it. I've wanted to say it to you for a long time."

"I wasn't asking for an apology."

"And I wasn't giving it." She lets her client chew on that for a second. Then she says, "Look, I don't mind discussing my personal life. But right now I need you to tell me what happened."

"Where do you want me to start?"

"Let's start with your relationship with Mark. Where were you guys at?"

Beth gives a little shrug. "Things, you know, just didn't turn out exactly as I thought they would. As I said, the Mark I married was a different guy from the guy I ended up with. It wasn't a whirlwind romance. He got under my skin, gradually. My feelings evolved. He made me feel good about living again. There I was, dealing with Richie, who was angry all the time, talking about how he'd been screwed over. I could understand it. But it just got oppressive, you know? And then after the incident—he wouldn't talk about it, but I assume he was raped—he just became very sullen."

She pauses, takes a breath, and exhales hard, a sadness coming into her eyes.

"I didn't think he'd ever be the same again, which I could live with, but the problem was, he didn't think he could ever be the same again. He was a different person and part of him despised the person he'd become. He'd lost this sort of wonderful innocence he had; he'd been uncorrupted. There was something really pure about him. Sure, a lot of the marketing stuff has a snake-oil side to it, but he was such an optimistic guy. And he was good at taking people's cluttered ideas and turning them into a focused, sellable message. And there was something pure about that, even noble. There's a lot of great technology and great ideas out there that never make it because someone couldn't figure out how to frame it the right way. So much of the stuff is pretty incomprehensible to begin with and then you throw in some poor naming and it's no wonder it goes nowhere."

"And then he got those extra years tacked on to his sentence," Carolyn says. "For what he did to that guy."

"Yeah, he waited. I don't know, it was maybe three, four weeks after he got attacked. He was patient, which is like Richie. The next time the main instigator—I guess that's what you'd call him—the next time the guy came after him, he hit him in the neck with a homemade blade of some sort. He was pretty messed up. I think he almost died. Thank God he didn't."

"Did Richie regret doing it afterwards?"

"I don't think so. He made it seem like he didn't have a choice. He wasn't totally stupid about it. He tried to make it look like a fight. Said it was self-defense. I think he'd gotten to the point where he just wanted to lash out at someone. And there was some satisfaction in it."

"Even if it meant losing you."

"I think he already felt he'd lost me. He could see that part of me had just had enough. You gotta remember, I'd already lived with all this for over two years."

"So then you end up with Mark. And he ends up changing on you, too?"

"Well, in his case, I don't know if he really changed."

"You said he was a different guy from the one you married."

"Yeah, I guess I did say that."

"Well, this is important, Beth. You have to be very precise in your statements. And you have to stick to what you say. So let's try to clarify this before you get in there. Did he change or not?"

"I think it just turned out that he was more in love with the idea of me than actually loving me. I think he thought having me as his wife would impress everyone, from his cronies here in the Valley to his father."

"Who's his father?"

"Some wealthy guy from St. Louis who ran a medical supply business. Made products for hospitals and doctors. He sold it before I met Mark."

"He's still alive?"

"Yeah, but I've never met him."

"Not even at the wedding?"

"We had a really small wedding. At a friend's house in Napa. We basically eloped. Mark grew up more with his mother, who died back in 2003. His father had kids with three different wives. Mark grew up in Cleveland with number two. He mostly lived with his mother, but he spent a lot of vacations with his father. He'd see him four or five times a year for a week or two at a time. He was always frustrated that his father didn't understand what he did. He didn't get all this web stuff. He was a manufacturing guy. Real, physical products. He didn't get bits and bytes."

"Mark didn't want kids?"

"He said he did. But it wasn't like he was in any hurry and when we got married, neither was I. I was thirty-two. I felt I had a couple of years to make that decision."

"And then what happened?"

"He didn't behave very well. That's what happened."

"How so?"

"Well, I'd say there were some substance-abuse issues."

"Like what?"

"Pot, alcohol, some prescription drugs, a line or two of coke. He dabbled. Didn't seem to play favorites."

"And he'd do this in front of you?"

"We did it together sometimes. And let's be clear, there was something casual about it. Every once in a while, he'd go pretty hard, but he wasn't a heavy-duty partier or anything. He was too worried about his reputation."

"So what'd you do?"

"I didn't do anything. Which probably made things worse. I just got very passive aggressive. He was out a lot at these networking things, trying to create buzz for his new business. The Silicon Valley Circle Jerk Association, I like to call it. The CJA. A lot of nights I curled up in bed with my own glass of wine. And then he kind of had a mini nervous breakdown."

"What do you mean?"

"At work one day he started to get dizzy, got some tingling in his arm, shortness of breath, and chest pains. He thought he was having a heart attack. Don Gattner, his right-hand guy, drove him over to the Parkview Hospital emergency room. Turned out it was just a bad case of acid reflux."

Okay, Carolyn thinks, *she's repeating what she said last night, which is good.* She watches Beth as she speaks. She's one of those women who just don't have a bad side to their face, which looks a little longer and thinner with her hair short. Her nose is finely shaped, not too big or small, and she has greenish blue eyes and a clear complexion. She's barely wearing any makeup, just some eyeliner. The only thing that strikes Carolyn as odd is why Beth changed her hair. She looks a little edgier, more artsy with the cropped blond hair, sort of like a younger version of Sharon Stone.

"Did you dye your hair because he wanted a blonde?" she asks.

"Actually, no. He didn't want me to change my hair or appearance at all. He loved how natural I looked and how people thought I was such a natural beauty and all that."

"So why'd you do it?"

"I just felt like it. I knew it would piss him off."

"And did it?"

"Like I said, he would go around saying, you want a divorce, don't you? And I would say no."

"But you did?"

"Well, I made a mistake. One day I keyed 'adultery divorce California' into Google. He must have looked through my search history because he asked why I'd Googled it. But he thought it was because I'd cheated on him and wanted to know the fiduciary consequences in case I got caught. You know, if he accused me of adultery, what could that mean? So he assumed I was cheating. But I actually thought he was cheating."

"California's a no-fault state so it doesn't really mean anything," Carolyn says. "You can allege adultery but it usually doesn't do that much for you except ring up a big legal fee."

"I know. But he could never get over that. Three words typed into Google and the guy never trusts me again."

"No marriage is destroyed just by that."

"Well, it felt that way."

"What made you think he was cheating? Did you stop having sex?"

"Normal sex."

"What does that mean?"

"It means that he only seemed to want to have sex when I didn't, which quickly became most of the time. In a weird way it turned him on that I didn't want to. He could just sense it. And he'd start kissing me and I'd say, not now, I don't feel like it. And he'd say, 'Why, because you're fucking around? Is that why?' And I'd say no. And then, you know, he'd assert himself on me."

"You mean he'd *force* himself on you."

"Well, yeah, in a way. But it was more complicated than that. Because some of the time I was into it. There was like this flip point where it became a turn-on."

Carolyn doesn't mean to frown, doesn't mean to judge, but her anger must be showing through her eyes, for Beth suddenly turns away, ashamed.

"I know what you're thinking," she says. "I'm sick. But you wanted the truth and that's the truth. I know it wasn't healthy. Some relationships are based on trust. Ours happened to be based on distrust."

"But it didn't start out that way."

"No. No, it didn't. Or maybe it did and I just didn't realize it."

"Why didn't you leave him? Why didn't *you* find another guy?"

"Well, part of me was fearful of what he'd do if I did leave. He'd put spyware on my phone and he had someone following me."

"He had someone following you?"

"Sometimes. And the rest he did through technology."

"Did you report it to the police?"

"No. I didn't really have any proof he'd done anything. He wouldn't hit me or anything. We didn't have big shouting matches and domestic disputes. I mean, a lot of the time, he pretended everything was fine."

"So, what was your plan? To let this go on indefinitely?"

"No, I'd given myself a deadline to figure things out."

"What date was that?"

"June third. My birthday."

"Was there a prenup?"

"No."

"He didn't try to get you to sign one?"

"I refused."

"So he asked?"

"Yes."

"Did he have his lawyer draw up papers?"

"No, it didn't get that far. I just said I wasn't signing anything. It was his idea to get married, not mine. I mean, here I was marrying this guy who'd been my fiancé's close friend, plus all the circumstances of the accident and he wants a prenup for me to get on board. I don't think so. Fuck that."

"Well, I could see how he might not trust you completely."

"Sure."

"Sure, what?"

"Sure, he might be concerned. But I was committed. Really, I was. But that meant that he needed to be, too."

"Okay. I'm not sure what exactly that means, but it's good. Say it just like that. Because right about now Madden is going to ask you something like, 'Well, Ms. Hill, how much was Mark worth when you married him?'" She pauses, waiting for an answer, but when it doesn't come, she says, "Did he tell you how much he was worth?"

"Not exactly."

"How much do you think he was worth when you got married?"

"I don't know. Not that much. Somewhere north of twenty million."

Carolyn lets out a little laugh. "Not that much?"

"For around here, no."

"And if you were to get divorced, how much did you expect to walk away with?"

"I don't know. I didn't really think about it."

Was he worth more to her dead or alive? Carolyn thinks. That's something she's sure the detectives and Crowley's office would be looking at. It depends on the will, of course—and any life insurance policy. But if she can show that it was in her best interest to keep him alive and just divorce him, that will help eliminate her motive—or at least reduce it considerably.

"You're wondering about his will, aren't you?" Beth reads her mind, which feels a little eerie.

"Yes. Did he have one?"

"We both did."

"And do you know where you stand?"

"He said I would be 'taken care of.' That's all he said. We didn't discuss it much."

"And what about a life insurance policy?"

"I don't know. He never mentioned it. I just said that if he didn't want me to work that I needed my own bank account and I needed two hundred thousand dollars put into it at the beginning of each year. That was my main concern."

"An allowance?"

"You could call it that. But I really saw it as my salary. He wanted me to work for him."

"At the office?"

"At being Mrs. McGregor. I was expected to support him. You know, I used to have a fairly prominent role at a nonprofit called Jumpstart. They organize volunteers from nearby colleges and schools—students—to go in and read to little kids who come from homes where their parents never read to them. It really makes a big difference in their lives. I was the West Coast regional director."

"I thought you were in wine sales."

"I was. When I met Richie. But frankly, it's not the best job to have when you're depressed. At the end, I was doing some consulting for the Idaho Wine Commission to help try to popularize Idaho wines, and let's just say I was educating myself to the product a little too much."

"Idaho has wine?"

"Yeah, it's called Sawtooth. Quite good in fact. They were more known for their whites but have been doing some nice reds lately. Anyway, Mark finally said, enough, you can help organize fund-raisers and we'll give money, but it's ridiculous for you to be working full-time for seventy thousand a year. He was right. It didn't make much sense. Except I need to work, for my own good. But he didn't really understand what it meant to me. I ended up resenting the fact that he didn't want me to work."

"Okay, so if I'm to understand this correctly, you basically didn't like your husband much anymore."

"It was a bit more complicated than that."

"You keep saying that."

"Well, imagine it like this. You're hooked on a drug. And that drug is incredibly intense and wonderful for about twenty minutes. It's awesome. But the side effect, the hangover, whatever you want to call it, is just brutal. It lasts days. You know the ratio is off. And part of you hates yourself for knowing it and still doing it. But then the other part, that part that can't forget the twenty minutes, keeps you coming back. Does that make any sense?"

Carolyn nods, wincing a little as she does. There may be something to work with there but it would take serious sculpting. The word "unconventional" popped into her head. *Ms. Hill and and Mr. McGregor had an unconventional relationship.* Where do you go from there? How much do you say? *Christ.*

"Okay," she says. "We're going to have to get all this down to shorter responses. But let's move on to Richie for a minute. Why don't you tell me about your more recent interactions with him. You said you'd spoken to him a few times after he got out of prison."

"Yes, twice altogether on the phone. And then I saw him yesterday."

Carolyn blinks. At first, she doesn't think she's heard right. *Did she say yesterday*?

"Excuse me. Yesterday? Is that what you said?"

"Yes. I saw him yesterday. I gave him his engagement ring back. I figured he could use the money."

Carolyn is stunned. "Is there some reason you didn't tell me this last night? Is there some reason you didn't mention that to the police?"

"I wasn't thinking incredibly clearly last night. And they never asked me specifically when the last time I'd seen him in person was."

Carolyn puts her hand across her face. Feeling a headache coming on, she briefly kneads her right temple with her thumb. *You've got to be fucking kidding me*, she thinks, remembering something Cogan had once told her about how certain patients wouldn't always tell him exactly what was wrong when he first started examining them. After going through a whole battery of questions and getting poked and prodded, the patient would casually mention that he or she had some pain or symptom that made it obvious what their real problem was. Cogan called it the oh-I-forgot-to-tell-you moment. This is clearly one of those moments.

"I'm sorry," Beth says. "I just couldn't handle it. Imagine you wish something and it actually comes true. But it's a bad thing—a really bad thing. I felt horrible."

Carolyn lets her hand drop from her face. "Look, you should know something. I was going to tell you this after we spoke but I'll tell you now. I just got a call this morning from Detective Madden. He says they arrested Richie last night on suspicion of murder. They have some evidence he was in your garage last night."

Beth doesn't react. She doesn't seem surprised. She just lowers her head, then closes her eyes for a moment, as if she's taking a moment to make a silent prayer.

"You don't seem surprised by that," Carolyn says.

"He didn't do it," Beth says. "He wouldn't have."

"How do you know that?"

"Because when I saw him yesterday I didn't just see him. I didn't just give him his ring back."

"What did you do?"

"I slept with him."

If Beth's first admission has left her stunned, the latest one leaves aghast. Her mouth hangs open.

"You had sex with him?"

"Yes."

"Where? At your home?"

"No. We went to a place."

"What place?"

"Watercourse Way."

Watercourse Way. She's heard of it. It rings a bell. *A motel? No. Not a motel, a . . .*

"You mean that spa place in Palo Alto? On Channing?"

"Yeah. You can rent a room out. You know, with a hot tub."

"Christ."

"I know," Beth says.

Carolyn stares straight ahead, lost in thought. She's trying to figure out how she can spin that one. She looks at her watch. They're supposed to be at the police station in ninety minutes. There's no way she can prep her in time. Not with all this. And now she wonders whether Beth should be saying anything at all. For the first time, she feels like she may need some help. She thinks of calling Clark.

"Do you know if Richie told them anything?" Beth asks.

She looks at her. She hadn't considered that. What had Richie said?

"No, I don't."

Beth's expression changes. Suddenly, she seems helpless and terrified all over again. Her lip trembles a little as she speaks. "I'm sorry. I should have said something earlier. They're going to think I'm lying now, aren't they? They're going to think I had something to do with it."

Carolyn puts her arm around her shoulders. For a second she feels as if she's her friend. But if she were her friend, she'd probably toss off some throwaway line like Pam had earlier. *Everything is going to okay. We'll get through this.*

But instead she says:

"Well, I can see why you called me now."

15 / SEDITION

LOCATED IN THE FOOTHILLS OF SOUTHERN SAN MATEO A FEW MILES from where the 92 freeway intersects the 280 freeway, the San Mateo County Sheriff's Forensic Laboratory and Coroner's Office is a 30,000-square-foot modern one-story warehouse-like structure that, back when it opened in 2003, was heralded as the greenest building the county had ever built. Whenever Madden sees it now, he thinks it's something out of the shelter magazines that his wife, who's developed an alarming interest in interior design, keeps bringing home. It has solar panels splayed out across nearly its entire sloped roof, eco-friendly bamboo flooring, energy-efficient lab equipment, and large windows that have been designed to flood the open workspaces inside with natural light.

Since it's a Saturday morning, just a handful of people are in a building that normally houses close to forty full-time employees, and the parking lot is practically empty. Lyons is waiting for him on the steps leading up to the main entrance, wearing a white lab coat and smoking a cigarette. Madden manages a smile as he gets out of his car.

"You got here quick," Lyons says.

Typically, it takes a good twenty to twenty-five minutes to get here from the Menlo Park police station in light traffic, but Madden has made it in around fifteen.

"Saturday morning," he says. "No one's on the roads."

"Don't remind me."

"When did you get in?"

"Around seven."

Lyons takes a long drag on the cigarette, turns his head upward, and exhales hard through pursed lips, watching the tight stream of smoke blow away with the wind. The strong breeze plays with the ropes on the flagpole at the entrance of the building, pounding against the metal rod with a discordant, percussive *clang*. An enormous American flag flies overhead, fluttering noisily.

Madden pops his trunk and removes the evidence bags, which are stacked neatly on top of one another.

"What you got for me?" he asks.

"Shoes, laptop, couple of diver's knives, some other personal effects," Madden says.

"How'd the apartment look?"

"Neat."

Lyons takes another drag, then taps the tip of his cigarette on the pavement, killing it gently. After inspecting the tip, he sticks the stunted cigarette into his white lab-coat pocket, stands up, and takes the top two evidence bags from Madden, leaving him with the bag containing the laptop.

"Come on," he says. "I have something to show you."

He takes Madden inside. A Hispanic-looking woman security guard waves them past the front desk. They walk down a hallway, pass through a cubicle area, then proceed through another hallway, where they pass a door marked Chemicals Lab, followed by the ballistics testing area, and finally they reach the forensics lab. Because this is where they process DNA evidence for severe crimes and perform autopsies, security is tight. Lyons swipes his ID card through the scanner and the door buzzes open.

"You haven't been here for a while, have you?" he asks Madden as he places the plain brown evidence bags down on a counter. Each bag is sealed with tape and has an evidence description and "chain of custody" label affixed to the side, which Madden has filled out with the required information.

"Not since the Hughes case," Madden says.

The lab room looks a lot like a high school or science lab. The black tables are high so you can stand at them, and tall swivel chairs are parked at the half dozen or so work stations, most of them with white coats hanging over the backrests. There are microscopes and other testing equipment on some of the tables and various bottles of chemicals perched on shelves around the room. Each work area has a special overhead light attached to an adjustable arm and track, but there is plenty of natural light streaming into the room.

"They never prosecuted anybody on that one, did they?" Lyons says, starting to enter the numbers on the bags into the computer.

"No. Crowley didn't like the percentages. And no one seemed to care too much."

Early last year a drug dealer and general scumbag named Louis Ramos had been shot outside his home in the Belle Haven section of Menlo Park. No witness came forward and the subsequent month-long investigation yielded almost no information. Then they had a little break. Burns learned that Hughes had gotten into an altercation with a former girlfriend's current boyfriend a few days before the slaying. Harsh words were exchanged along with a blow or two. Burns's source said that three days later, the boyfriend walked up to Hughes while he was sitting on his porch, drew a gun, and shot him. Simple as that. But they never came up with the weapon, didn't have a witness, and the probable killer had concocted an alibi they'd failed to puncture. Crowley wouldn't touch it, so the case was still open a year later.

"That was your last murder, wasn't it?" Lyons says.

"Yeah. Been busy—but more with weird stuff. Had an audio sexting case the other week."

"Audio sexting? What the hell's that?"

"Guy records him and his girlfriend having sex. Then, after they break up, he starts texting her saying he's got the recording and is going to put it up on the Internet if she doesn't continue having sex with him."

"Bluffing?"

"Oh no, he had it. Very clear. High quality, too. You could definitely tell it was her. And the kicker is the guy was slightly autistic, which made things even worse. It was a goddamn mess."

"Minors?"

"She was. He wasn't."

Lyons is a silent a moment, then says: "You ever think about quitting? A lot of people asking that, you know. If it were me, I wouldn't risk it."

"Risk what?"

"Them changing the rules on me. I'd be out of here in a heartbeat if I'd done my time like you."

"They're not taking anything away. It's all grandfathered in. And we were excluded from Measure L."

"I don't know if you noticed, but the state's fucking bankrupt. And the pension fund is down a third of what it was."

"Menlo Park's okay," Madden says. "If anything, they're just going to freeze our wages and hit us with a higher healthcare contribution. That's what they're talking about."

A couple years ago, the city council agreed to raise officers' pay close to twenty-five percent over a period of three years to help offset a wave of departures to other, higher-paying police departments and government agencies. Between retirements and defections, the Menlo Park Police Department had lost thirty of its fifty officers between 2005 and 2008. Now, though, in the "new economic reality," the city council's tune had changed. They were looking to shave where they could and control costs for the future. Measure L's passage had raised the retirement age for new non-safety city employees to 60 from 55 and allowed them to collect only 60 percent of their salary for 30 years of service instead of 81 percent. However, the police were excluded from the measure and had retained their retirement equations.

Lyons laughs. "You're crazy, man. You could retire, get a little consulting gig, maybe do some PI work, really rake it in."

"I know. That's what the wife wants me to do. Wants to send some extra money to her family in Nicaragua, maybe even help her sister who's here. I already send a thousand a month now."

"Just say no. You got kids. You need to look out for them first. Doesn't she want what's best for you guys?"

"She wants what's best for her family. That includes me and Henry Jr. and Bella, but it also includes a bunch of other folks. Guys like you and Billings got these side gigs. He wanted me to go in with him on a couple of places in EPA, but I just couldn't do it in the end. Probably stupid on my part."

One of the advantages of being a cop is that you have block-by-block, even house-by-house, insight into transitional neighborhoods. Many were thinking that it was only a matter of time before once-troubled places like East Palo Alto and Belle Haven, which border fairly affluent neighborhoods, became gentrified. And they gradually are. But you really have to know the spots that have the most potential and will give you the lightest headache as a landlord because you aren't looking at a quick flip. You're looking at a five- to ten-year hold, maybe longer.

Lyons smiles. "Bills has got that whole long-term view going, God bless him. I wish I had that kind of patience. He doesn't have an ex-wife sending his kid to private school just to spite his ass."

"Well, you did cheat on her."

"People make mistakes."

Once is a mistake, Madden thinks. Multiple times is a girlfriend on the side. But he doesn't say that to Lyons. Instead he asks, "How's Sam?"

"He's doing good," Lyons says. "He'd do just fine in public school, too, just like your kids. I don't know how a gimp like you produces an all-star pitcher and I have a kid that's a klutz, but such is the way of the world. Gotta tell you, though, your wife never struck me as a ball-breaker. When you first got married, I remember some of the guys talking about how you imported your wife, she didn't speak English, she was your housekeeper. But the few times I met her I thought she was good people—and good-looking."

Though he knows Lyons is paying him a compliment, it always makes him feel uncomfortable, talking about how he'd met his wife. People are always getting it wrong. She was a housekeeper, but when they first met, she was working for Pete Pastorini. She never worked for him. They barely understood each other at first—and were an unlikely match. But their marriage had gotten better as she became more fluent in English and he in Spanish. Now, however, the extended family situation has developed into something he hadn't quite bargained for.

"The thing is," Lyons goes on, "you hit with an iPhone app now, you can make in two weeks what Bills would make in ten years on his little real-estate transactions. Two fucking weeks. I'm telling you."

"If it was that easy," Madden says, "everybody would be doing it."

"Everybody *is* doing it. That's the problem."

When he's through logging the evidence, Lyons walks Madden over to the autopsy room. Before opening the door, Lyons stretches a pair of surgical gloves over his hands.

Madden has only been in this room a few times, and he isn't too keen on going in there again. In spite of the state-of-the-art ventilation, the smell, which he once described to someone as a mix of formaldehyde and raw sewage, is decidedly unpleasant when you first encounter it, though it fades as you acclimate to it.

The body is in a refrigeration unit, lying on a stainless-steel gurney and covered with a sheet. Lyons rolls the gurney out and pulls the sheet down to waist level, exposing McGregor's arms. On the inside of each arm, at the elbow, are a few small, asymmetrical red dots. They look a little like mosquito bites that have been scratched, the telltale sign of track marks.

"Any idea what he's been shooting?" Madden asks.

Lyons shakes his head. "We'll know soon enough. Used to be heroin but now we're getting people shooting all kinds of shit. Oxycontin's been popular lately. Had a kid in here who OD'd last month," Lyons says. "Was shooting it between his toes so his parents wouldn't find out."

Madden, keeping his eyes focused on the dots, replies, "We popped a guy about three months ago who was selling it out of the Marsh Road Chevron. Guy was a full-service pharmacy."

Lyons has opinions about the efficacy of the delivery method. Shooting it doesn't enhance the experience; it just makes it more dangerous, opens you up to infection.

"Truth is, you're better off snorting oxy," he says. "But people do crazy shit. One guy tells another you can get a euphoric high shooting it and he believes him. It's an opioid, so it's easy to convince someone there's a benefit to shooting it. But it's got all kinds of impurities in it. The goddamn coating on the pill is nasty, so you gotta dissolve it at just the right temperature and skim the shit off the top before you inject it."

"Could that have killed him?"

"Nah. For starters, these weren't fresh injections. However, I did find a couple pills in his stomach. Only partially dissolved. Probably took them fifteen, twenty minutes before he was killed. So they didn't kill him either. I think taking out his jugular and emptying his blood onto the floor probably didn't do him much good."

Madden lets his eyes drift up the body. Now that they've been cleaned up, the wounds look even more gaping, though not as grotesque as they had back in the garage. The way McGregor's cheekbone and nose have been smashed, leaving his face partially caved in and both eyes black and blue, was tougher to absorb. He puts his hand up to his mouth and lets out a little cough.

Lyons cracks a smile, slightly amused. "You okay?"

Madden turns to his left, looking away from the body. "You think a diver's knife could have made those wounds?"

Lyons shakes his head.

"Looks more like a hatchet to me. Or even one of those tomahawks. You ever seen those? Amazon sells them."

Madden has seen them. They're modern variations on the Indian tomahawk. Lighter than an axe, with a thinner, sharper blade.

"But what do you think hit him in the face?"

"Blunt object of some sort. Not a big diameter."

"How 'bout the back of an axe? Or a tomahawk?"

"Possible. Some of those have sharp backs but some have hammerlike backs."

"Well, let's see if we can narrow it down."

Madden starts to walk toward the door, but Lyons calls him back.

"I got one other thing to show you. That tattoo you were telling me about."

"Oh yeah."

When they'd asked Beth Hill whether her husband had any distinguishing marks on him, she said he had a small snake tattooed horizontally to his right hip, just below his belt line. Though she'd identified the body, it was standard protocol in any suspicious death to look at any distinguishing characteristics such as tattoos, moles, or scars, as well run a fingerprint analysis (Lyons got a thumbprint match from the DMV), call in dental records, and create a DNA profile.

Lyons lifts the top corner of the sheet, exposing McGregor's right side. "Well, like you said, he has this little snake here. But what's kind of interesting is that I looked at it with a magnifying glass and there's actually a word in the snake and some numbers. You gotta look closely."

He takes out a lighted magnifying glass and shows him what he means.

Madden reads aloud the characters, carefully enunciating each letter and number. "S . . . E . . . D . . . I . . ." When he's finished, he puts them together. "Sedition 1918," he says quizzically, lifting an eyebrow. It rings a bell but he doesn't know from where.

"Sound familiar?" Lyons asks.

"Yeah."

"I looked it up. There was something called the Sedition Act of 1918. During the First World War. Woodrow Wilson was president."

"What the hell is that about?"

"Did the wife say anything about the word?"

"No, just the snake," Madden says.

"I mean, it's possible she didn't even see it. You really have to look."

"Sedition 1918," he repeats again.

With that, Lyons slides the gurney back into its refrigeration unit. After they leave the autopsy room, Madden asks how long it will take to process and analyze the items from Forman's apartment along with other crime-scene evidence.

"I've got a few folks coming in any minute to help out. I can't promise anything, but I know you want this stuff expedited as quickly as possible." Contrary to what the TV dramas show, crime labs work at a slow, deliberate pace. DNA evidence takes weeks to process. "We should have some preliminary toxicology results late today and we'll just bang on all this stuff hard. I'm going to go home in a little bit, take a shower, and head back down to the crime scene for another look-see in the light."

Lyons locks the evidence bags in a locker, then walks Madden out.

"What is it, Hank?" Lyons asks when they get outside. He takes the remaining half of his cigarette out of his coat pocket and lights it. "You've got that worried look on your face, like something isn't right."

"I don't know." He stands there, reflecting on the previous night. He pictures Richie Forman in the club singing, the words to the one song still running in his head.

Somebody said "just forget about her." So I gave that treatment a try . . .

"The guy can sing," he says.

"Who?"

"Richie Forman. He's a Sinatra impersonator."

"No shit?"

"He was good. Seems like he was doing okay for himself. Aside from the obvious, I just don't know why he'd go ahead and do something like this. And it just seems too neat and too messy at the same time. Does that make any sense?"

Lyons takes a drag on his cigarette. "Sure," he says, exhaling. "But anyway I look at it, this wasn't a random killing. Someone was making a statement. Someone had something against this guy. You got the method of the slaying and then the whole 'hack' angle. It was personal."

"But I don't know if that's just a red herring, you know? I mean, whoever did it left the wallet to make it look like a robbery. Why not dash off 'Hack' while you're at it?"

"Well, there's a couple meanings to the word. Hack, as in you're mediocre. Hack as in to write code, you know, program, which is what Zuckerberg meant when he put the word up on the wall at the Facebook offices. A hack in a malicious sense. Identity theft. Malware. Virus creator. Hack as in hacker, bad guy."

"That's three, not two," Madden points out.

"Yeah, I guess you're right. Anyway, I'm not sure where McGregor fit in on the scale. I've heard him talk before. If anything, you could argue he was mediocre. I mean, he talked a good game, but like a lot of these guys, he had a bullshit quotient. Guy probably did a mean PowerPoint. You saw him at the trial. He was slick, right?"

"Yeah," Madden answers, though his thoughts are elsewhere. He needs a witness. And he needs to know who the Tongans are and if they were really working for McGregor and why.

Just then a car pulls into the lot. A petite, dark-haried woman gets out and nods a curt greeting to Lyons.

"One of yours?" Madden asks.

"That's Sue Romero, one of my technicians. Not the cheeriest of personalities. But at least the reinforcements are starting to roll in."

"Look, I don't need to say this, Greg, but you know the scrutiny level we're looking at on this thing. You've got to be buttoned down all the way on this. Batten down the hatches. You understand?"

"We always do."

"Well, we know Colletti has had his issues. You guys didn't look so hot for a while."

The coroner is an elected position and Drew Colletti is going on his fourth term. But he faced vigorous challenges in the last election after his office was hit with a sexual harassment suit and several workers were accused of looking at pornography on their work computers.

"Come on, man," Lyons says. "Ancient history. Just bullshit politics."

"Well, you got that 'chief' in your title because of bullshit politics."

That's true. Colletti needed a fall guy, and the previous chief deputy had been that guy.

"Look, Hank, I'm well aware what a big deal this is. I wouldn't have been here at the crack of fucking dawn if I didn't. You get any security-camera footage from the neighbors yet? There's gotta be one camera on that block that caught something."

"We're working on it. Billings is going through some footage this morning."

"You think Forman will submit to a polygraph?"

"I don't know. He didn't suggest it yet. The first thing we gotta do is get him to turn off the Sinatra act."

"What do you mean?"

"He's still doing his goddamn impersonation routine."

"Under questioning?"

"Yeah. I mean, it fades in and out, but it's getting a little ridiculous."

"You think it's a tactic?"

"I don't know."

Just then Madden's phone rings. Caller ID shows the main number for the Menlo Park police station.

"Madden," he answers.

"Billings," Billings answers back.

"What's up?"

"Where are you?"

"Still up at the coroner's, talking to Lyons."

"Forman's attorney showed up."

"When?" Madden asks.

"Five minutes ago," Billings says.

"He or a she?"

"He. And you're not going to believe who it is."

"Who?"

"Marty Lowenstein."

Madden falls silent. He doesn't know any local attorneys named Marty Lowenstein. The only Marty Lowenstein he knows is the famous Marty Lowenstein.

"Yeah, that guy," Billings says.

"The DNA Dude?"

He looks over at Lyons, who's in the process of pulling the cigarette toward his mouth for a final drag but suddenly freezes with his hand is a few inches away from his lips.

Billings: "Yeah. Just flew in from LA."

"How did he get him?"

"How the hell should I know?"

"Okay, I'm on my way back. Gotta make one stop. But I'll be there by eleven. He talking to Forman now?"

"He just went in," Billings says. "There's also some kids here with cameras. Came with him."

"What do you mean?"

"Couple of kids, one male, one female, showed up with Lowenstein. Say they're working on a documentary."

"You're kidding me. I hope you kept them out."

"Sure I did. They're upstairs. With the guys from Channels Five and Two."

"Shit," Madden says. "I'm on my way. Call me with any updates."

He hangs up and looks over at Lyons, who doesn't seem so relaxed and nonchalant anymore.

"Did I hear you say what I think I heard you say? The DNA Dude? Marty Lowenstein?"

Madden nods.

"How the fuck did he get him?"

"I just asked Billings the same question."

A smile creeps across Lyons's face. "Well, shiver me timbers," he says. "Marty fucking Lowenstein. I always wanted to meet him."

"Well, you may just get your chance."

"This is awesome," Lyons says.

Madden doesn't think it's awesome. In fact, he thinks it's the farthest thing from awesome.

"Greg?"

"What?"

"You got your A game on, right?"

"Yeah."

"Well, that's not going to be good enough. Add another gear."

Lyons doesn't take kindly to the comment.

"You find another gear, Hank. I got plenty of gears. This thing's on you. It's your fucking case. I'm just the support team. Chill, man."

"I don't do chill, Greg."

"I know you don't, Hank. But don't stress on me. I got enough stress. I'm trying to quit smoking."

"That seems like it's going really well."

"It was," he lamented. "Until last night."

16 / TALK TO THE MITT

"FORMAN, WAKE UP."

He's been lying on the thin green mat, his cuffed hands resting on his stomach, staring up at the ceiling in the small room where he'd spent the night, when the door opens. Billings, the detective, pokes his head in and tells him that his attorney is here.

Still lying there, he turns his head to see a face he knows looks familiar but can't place at first. He sits up on the bench. Once vertical, he realizes who it is.

"Goddamn if it isn't Marty Lowenstein, the DNA Dude."

"Marty," Marty Lowenstein says, extending a hand. "Call me Marty."

He's shorter than Richie had imagined. Heck, he's practically eye to eye with the man before he even stands up from the bench. The guy has to be like five-three, five-four, with a head, nose, and ears that seem disproportionately big for his body. He has a mostly full head of tight, curly gray hair and is wearing a navy blue suit and a crisp white shirt, but he doesn't have a tie on, which gives him a hipper, more casual look, which is only accentuated by the fact that he appears to have a baseball mitt under his arm.

"Lourdes gave me a call last night and said you were in some trouble. I happened to be in L.A. Got here as soon as I could. Ashley picked me up at the airport."

Richie can't stop smiling.

"Marty fucking Lowenstein," he says.

"Marty," Marty says.

"Sorry. She here—Ashley?"

"Upstairs. With her boyfriend. He tells me he's doing some sort of documentary about you."

With the intonation of his voice, he might as well have said, *What the fuck is up with that?*

"That isn't official."

"Well, we'll talk about that later. You make any statements?"

He answers with a little shrug. "Nothing bad," he says quietly.

"Nothing bad? If I had a nickel every time a client said, 'nothing bad' or 'I just told them the truth' I'd have a pile so big I could ski down it. You know the part that goes, 'Anything you say can and will be used against you in a court of law?' Well, strike the 'can.' It *will* be used against you."

Now Richie really feels stupid. If someone had told him last night he'd have Marty Lowenstein standing there next to him now, he'd have clammed up and not said a word. But no one had told him Marty Lowenstein was coming.

"You give them an alibi?" Marty asks. "Is that what you tried to do?"

He nods. "I'd just finished performing. I was a little drunk, to be honest. I don't think any of it's admissible."

Marty doesn't respond. Instead, he looks up at the ceiling and Richie thinks he's going to roll his eyes in disgust. But no, he's actually looking at the ceiling—or rather the corner of the ceiling. He does a little pirouette, his eyes examining the walls as he does.

"What are you doing?"

"They said there were no cameras or mics in here but I never believe them," Marty explains.

When he's done with his inspection, he sits down next to Richie and hands him the baseball mitt, a tan Rawlings that looks ancient and is folded so flat it might as well have been ironed. It must be at least thirty years old.

"What's this for?" he asks.

"Just put it on. As a precaution. I know it's a little tough with the cuffs. I want you to speak into it. Pretend I'm the catcher and you're the pitcher and we're having a mound conference except we're doing it in the dugout."

"Where's your mitt?"

"I don't need one. I work barehanded." He waits for Richie to put the glove on, then leans forward, put his elbows on his thighs, and clasps his hands in front in a modified prayer position, and says: "So what other statements did you make?"

He tells him everything he'd said. Or at least everything he can remember saying. They go back and forth, Lowenstein quietly and methodically firing off question after question. At first, it feels silly to have to keep covering his mouth with the mitt whenever he speaks. But after a few minutes, he gets used to it. Is Lowenstein really concerned the cops are recording the conversation? Maybe. But he also gets the feeling the mitt is just a prop that's designed to help break down his inhibitions.

It's working. But the more he talks, the worse he feels. It's like the time he thought he'd nailed a job interview then realized he'd totally botched it once he went over the conversation with a buddy who already worked at the firm. He kept saying, "You said what?" Marty doesn't do that, but the way he keeps grimacing, he may as well have done.

After he's through, he gets the damage assessment. "Well, you hit the fast-forward button, that's what you did," Marty says. "As soon as you admitted you were down there, that convinced the judge to grant the warrant. They've obviously got something else. Some piece of evidence to link you to the crime. They need that to establish probable cause. But you allowed them to move faster than they probably should have. The good and bad news is they won't arraign until Monday morning, which means you're stuck here until then. I need to know exactly where you were, who you might have talked with and who might have seen you. We're going to need to find these people right away and try to get statements from them to corroborate what you've said. I'm going to get Ashley on it. She's as good an investigator as you're going to get for what you can afford."

Richie rocks back and forth a little, staring at the floor. The mitt's still covering half his face. He can feel Marty's eyes on him. There's still a lot he hasn't told him. He wants to disappear into that mitt now.

"Rick," he says. "Is it okay if I call you Rick?"

Richie nods.

"Look, you know everything you say to me is protected by attorney-client privilege. You know that, right?"

Another nod. Sure, he knows.

"I've been up since four thirty," he explains, not making an effort to cover his mouth. "Lucky for you I'm on New York time. But normally I don't like to be woken up at four thirty unless it's for a goddamn good reason. Are you a goddamn good reason?"

Before Richie can formulate an answer, he goes on: "Lourdes Hinojosa seems to think so. She told me we've got to find a way to help you. Those were her words, 'We've got to help him, Marty.' And you know, it's not like I don't like to help people, but at four thirty in the morning I'm not always in the most helpful mood. Then she reminds me you're the ex-con who's been volunteering for us, the Sinatra impersonator who had some bad luck with that car accident. And I think to myself, Okay, I've got to meet this guy. You know why? Because way back when, when Sinatra was alive, I had a dream I represented him. It was a very vivid dream. I remember it to this day."

"What'd he do?"

"He killed Ava Gardner. Well, that's how it was at first. But you know how dreams go. First, he killed Ava Gardner but then it became someone else. In the end, it wasn't really clear who he killed. In fact, in the end, I determined he was making it all up. He thought something had happened but it was really just a movie script he was working on. He'd come to embody one of the characters, was into the whole method-acting thing, and was drunk half the time, which didn't help—and doesn't seem to be helping you either."

"Did he pay well?"

Marty laughs.

"Funny you should ask. No. But he played my kid's Bar Mitzvah."

"For real?"

"No, in the dream."

"That's what I meant."

"Actually, I think that's what precipitated the dream. I was trying to figure out who I could get to play at my kid's Bar Mitzvah. And there I was representing Old Blue Eyes and he said he couldn't afford to pay me but he could come to my backyard and sing."

"You got any other Bar Mitzvahs coming up?"

"Kids all graduated college. But I'm sure we can work something out. You do weddings?"

"Sure."

"Okay. I've got a niece getting married next September. So talk to me. What really happened yesterday? You see your ex over there at this Café Barrone near the train station and she gives you back your ring. You're missing about five hours after that. You wanna clue me in as to what happened in those five hours?"

Richie takes a deep breath. He waits a moment, then puts the mitt up to his mouth.

"I'm going with the curve," he says.

"Bring it," Marty says.

"I slept with her."

Marty leans in a little closer. "With who? Your ex?"

"Yeah."

"Where, at her house?"

"No, a place called Watercourse Way in Palo Alto. It's kind of like a spa. You can rent a room with a hot tub in it."

"Okay. Very Cali. On the East Coast, we don't have hot tubs. We have Jacuzzis."

"I know. I'm from Jersey."

Marty smiles. "Just like our pal Frank."

"Yeah, only I'm from Teaneck."

"Teaneck, huh? So, tough-luck Richie from Teaneck, did you tell our police friends you fucked your ex in some watery zen chamber with flutes playing in the background a few hours before her husband was killed?"

"No."

Marty Lowenstein nods, then falls silent a moment, seeming to mull over the revelation.

"I take it there's more to the story."

"Lot more," he says into the glove.

17 / UNINTIMIDATABLE

MADDEN REMEMBERS THE DAYS WHEN DEALING WITH THE PRESS WAS a lot easier. When he started as a cop, you had the *Chronicle*, *Examiner*, *San Jose Mercury*, and smaller papers like the *Peninsula Times Tribune*, since folded, which had different local sections geared to various towns along the Peninsula. The papers planned stories to run in the morning edition or, in the case of the *Examiner*, the afternoon. It was all pretty straightforward. You granted an interview or did a press conference and the story would appear in the paper the next day. If you wanted to draw some attention to a case, the department's PR person would call reporters and try to get them to bite on a feature. Sure, you got the occasional wrinkle or misquote and every now and then things went south, but for the most part, the encounter was pretty predictable—and manageable.

Is he being too nostalgic? Probably. But that doesn't stop him from lamenting the fact that the entity formerly known as the press has become an ambiguous, slippery blob. It reminds him of a toy he'd bought for his daughter last Christmas, a concoction called GobbledlyGoop that comes in a small bucket. You mix it with water, add a few drops of color, and soon you have a batch of what the company accurately describes as the most "ooey, gooey slime imaginable." Depending on how much water you mix in, you could change its consistency, make it thicker or thinner. The kids love it. He finds it repulsive, but it does entertain and even educate, kind of like guys like Tom Bender.

It's around ten when he gets to Bender's house. The Great One opens his front door wearing a white T-shirt and jeans, and holding a piece of toast in one hand and a squirming and excited pug puppy in the other. His short hair is gelled and spiked, he looks freshly showered and crisp yet tired and weary at the same time, with dark bags under his eyes, and his white, pasty face has small clusters of spider veins high on both cheeks. He looks thinner than the last time Madden saw him; he's lost weight.

"Do you know who I am?" Madden asks.

Bender looks at Madden for a second—then looks past him, as if he's expecting a larger contingent that has yet to materialize.

"Yeah," Bender comes back disinterestedly. Then to his dog, "Say hello to Detective Madden, Beezo." Next, he takes a bite of his toast and keeps talking. "I was just writing about you," he mumbles. "A sidebar really. How's the case going? I hear you may have got the guy."

"Sorry for the unannounced visit," Madden says.

"If you're looking for me to reveal any sources, I'm not going to do that. And don't bother with any of that police intimidation crap. I'm unintimidatable."

Madden isn't sure that's a real word.

"This is an off-the-record visit," he says. "I just want to ask a couple of questions, if you don't mind."

"Okay, sure, come on in. Last time I think I saw you in person you were raiding one of my parties."

Madden follows him inside. "Ancient history," he says. "Different house."

The new house actually reminds Madden of Bender's old one—probably from the same era, designed during the 1960s with a simple Frank Lloyd Wright flair, with large bay windows in the living room. It feels open and airy. But the big difference is Bender is no longer a renter. He owns this place and has clearly put considerable thought and effort into making this a showcase home, with expensive modern furniture, artwork, and sleek appliances. And while his new yard seems a bit smaller, not a twig seems out of place.

Bender ushers him into the kitchen, which is connected to a deck. Madden peeks out to see a teak dining table, lounge chairs, umbrellas, and planters with flowering plants. How mature. Madden marvels how he's gone from geek frat boy to nester. He's come a long way in just a few years.

"I sold out," Bender says, opening the sliding door to the porch. "And I don't mind saying it. I'm a sellout. In case you were wondering, this is what selling out buys you."

He sets Beezo down outside and slides the door closed as the little dog tears off into the yard.

"You see this coffee machine here?" Bender points to a contraption that looks like it belongs in an upscale restaurant. "This cost more than the car I used to drive. I have my assistant fill it up at the beginning of the week and then I just push a button and bam, I get whatever fucking style coffee I want. That's what selling out buys you. Latte?"

Madden shrugs. "Sure."

Bender retrieves a glass mug from a cabinet, sets it the machine, and presses a button. The machine goes to work, grinding beans.

"I take it you saw what I wrote last night?"

"The time stamp said four in the morning."

"Morning, night, who gives a shit what time it is anymore?"

"Yeah, I saw it."

"What'd you think? Pretty good, huh? Beat the *Merc*, the *Chron*. I had it first and now it's everywhere. I take it you dispute its central hypothesis?"

"I took a journalism class or two, and back then, at least, one anonymous source didn't make something true."

"Whoever said anything about true? I simply present the information that's available to me at the time. If I don't do it, someone else will. That's a fact, Detective. Do I think you contaminated the crime scene? I don't know. Maybe. My source is pretty good. Or at least I think it is. So now it's up to you to prove me wrong."

"I can't."

"Exactly."

"That's irresponsible."

"Maybe. But the fact is I get things right more often than I get them wrong. In the old days you had to bat a thousand—or very close to it. Nowdays you hit seven fifty, eight hundred, it's good enough. 'Beyond a reasonable doubt' has become 'more likely than not,' a preponderance of evidence. It's—"

"Look," Madden says, "I'm not here to have a philosophical discussion about how you do your job."

Bender hands him his coffee.

"Sugar?"

"No, thanks."

"Try it," Bender encourages him.

Madden obediently takes a sip.

"Good, right? Fucking better than that Starbucks crap. That's what selling out buys you, Detective. Kona. Premium. Organic. Twenty-five dollars a pound. Or something like that. Who cares?"

"Mr. Bender—"

"Tom."

"Okay, Tom. Here's the deal. I'm here to make a deal."

"Really?"

Now Bender seems intrigued.

"What are you looking for?"

"I'm looking to take advantage of your considerable knowledge."

Bender nods. He seemed to be willing to concede that point—that he has considerable knowledge to offer.

"Honestly, you probably know a lot more about Mark McGregor than we do right now. I need to learn as quickly as possible about this latest business he was tying to get off the ground, who I might talk to about it, and what your sources might know about his business dealings."

"I thought you had the guy. I'm hearing it was a straight revenge thing. His old pal Richie Forman, Mr. Bachelor Disaster. You arrested him last night, didn't you?"

Madden is impressed that he knows as much as he does. Whoever the source is, he or she is good.

"We did. But that doesn't mean we shut down the investigation."

"You didn't get a confession then, I take it?"

"I can't discuss that."

Bender laughs. "You wouldn't be here if you did. That's a fact. So, in exchange for tapping my great knowledge base—and it is great—what are you offering in return?"

"Exclusives."

Bender leans a little closer.

"I like the sound of that, Detective. How 'bout a badge? You know, in the movies, the sheriff gives the guy the gold star, you know, deputizes him."

"You want a badge? I'll give you any badge you want."

"I'm just kidding. Truth is—and perhaps you guessed this—I never wanted to be on the side of the prosecution. I always wanted to be a defense attorney. Criminal. But then my grades in law school weren't quite as good as they should have been. I know that's hard to believe. But I had a little too much fun for my own good. My only regret really. Anyway, bouncing around the bottom of the legal profession is sort of like being dragged behind a car. So I fell into all this tech stuff. Turned out there wasn't much competition. Ambitious, talented writers generally don't gravitate toward tech. You can rise to the top quicker than you think. The first Comdex I went to—you don't know what that is, but it used to be a huge computer trade show in Las Vegas. But anyway, the first Comdex I went to I weaseled my way into the hot party, the Spencer the Cat party. And there I was, dancing next to Bill Gates and Michael Dell and some other billionaires I didn't know. I'd been on the job two months and there I am, boogeying with the big guys. It told me something. Height was easily attainable."

Madden doesn't really care what it told him. He wants information that's pertinent to the here and now. "I know about Comdex," he says. "I used to build my own computers. What do you know about Mark McGregor?"

Bender takes another bite of toast, finishing what's left of the remaining piece. But this time he chews and swallows before he speaks.

"Pretty good track record," he says. "Had two start-ups with decent exits. Nothing anybody could really retire on, but his investors were happy and he made out well himself."

"What kind of money are we talking?"

"I believe he sold the first company for something like sixteen million. Nothing sexy. B to B stuff. The technology behind the technology. He sold the second company for more, but he had more investors. But he knew the drill. You do that a few times, raise money, you start to get the hang of it. You learn how to waste less time, know who the players are, and who to go to and who not to."

"What was his latest venture?"

"Sinatra?"

"Yeah, whatever it was called."

"Ah, but what it is called is key."

"That was the code name, though, right?"

"Sure. Code names are important, too. The company's name was actually Crune. It was pretty interesting. His first real consumer play. Had some buzz going. Basically was the gamification of geo-advertising. What I thought was interesting was the human element. You took something that had traditionally been automated and you brought in what were essentially these guides—or docents I think they were calling them. You'd essentially follow certain people who were experts in one particular zip code. The idea was you have this warehouse of deals and these docents would comb through them and then select ones they liked to broadcast out to their followers. Kind of like Twitter but on a more micro level. Anyway, he'd managed to combine a few hot concepts, got a few of the right people on board, and he'd peddled it right. Was fairly low-key about it."

"How much did he raise?"

"Something like fifteen. He put the seed money in himself, then did a first round of twelve, thirteen million that was followed by some more, recently. Foreign guy. Cahill. An Aussie, I think."

"Isn't that a lot?"

"For a first round, yeah. That's actually a shitload. People used to do a couple million. But you get somebody with a track record and a seemingly hot concept and the numbers can get silly."

"The wife said the company seemed to be in a little bit of trouble."

"Most start-ups are," Bender says. "They're one catastrophe away from being a start goner."

"Even well-capitalized ones?"

"Well, in the case of Crune the problem was someone had a similar idea and they had to go buy those guys out."

"What was the name of that other company?"

"I forget. Wasn't a great name. Which is why I forget."

"You said McGregor had brought in the right people. What was right about them?"

"Well, you get one or two Google or Facebook engineers in the mix—or preferably both—you can raise a good chunk of change right from a PowerPoint deck. McGregor had a couple of names. Not big names—but big enough. And then his partner, this guy Don Gattner, is a take-no-prisoners kind of guy. In it to win it, if you know what I mean."

Madden doesn't know what he means.

"The guy started out as a recruiter," Bender explains. "As you've probably heard, programmers and engineers are in high demand. They're the lifeblood. The biggies pick off the all-stars, throw all kinds of packages at them. Well, Gattner started out as one of the guys who supplied a lot of the second- and third-tier companies with talent. He was at a headhunting firm. And you know, he worked on commission, and pretty quickly worked his way up the ladder. You know what his secret was?"

Madden shakes his head.

"The wife, the girlfriend. A lot of these guys—and most of them were guys—are moving from somewhere else. And they may like where they are or they may have a girlfriend or wife who likes where she is. Well, these nerdy dudes aren't in the habit of making rash decisions without some serious input from their significant other. So you gotta work on the woman. In the end, she makes the call a lot of the time. And Gattner was particularly ruthless about getting the gals on board. He'd lie, he'd offer them things he knew might not pan out, stuff like that."

"And that didn't come back to haunt him?"

"Nah. He got where he wanted to get, then bolted for a start-up. He became an operational guy. And look, sometimes things turned out okay for some of these people. And if they didn't, well, they could always go somewhere else if they were any good."

"People still got hurt, though."

"People got fucked. But people are always getting fucked. For there to be winners, you gotta have losers. Fact. But if you're looking to talk to someone inside his company, I'd go to Gattner first. He'd have the dirt. He was really running the thing from an operational standpoint."

"Okay. Thanks for the tip."

"Now what do you have for me? Where's my exclusive?"

Madden pauses for a moment, pretends to think about it, then takes out a folded up piece of paper from his coat pocket. He hands it to Bender.

Bender unfolds it and looks at what's on the paper. It's a shot of the two Pacific Islanders who Forman said had harassed him. Madden had photocopied the photo.

"Who are these guys?" Bender asks.

"They may be involved in the murder," Madden says. "But we don't know who they are."

Bender lifts an eyebrow.

"You think these guys killed McGregor?"

"We've had strong indications they were involved somehow."

"Who told you that?"

"I can't say. But I need someone to get their faces out there. I've got a digital file on a thumb drive. You can't say where you got it. If you don't want it, I'll send it over to the *Chronicle*."

"And what do you want me to say?"

"Whatever you want. You always do."

Bender smiles. He knows Madden is playing him. He's not a fool.

"Who are these guys, really?"

"We'll just have to find out now, won't we?" Madden says.

Just then Bender sees his dog outside eating something he shouldn't. He bolts outside and reprimands the dog, telling him to release whatever's in his mouth. "Drop it, Beezo. Drop it now."

After the dog relinquishes the item, Bender picks it up and throws it as far as he can in the direction of his neighbor's yard.

Afterwards he comes back inside and goes to the sink and washes his hands. "Dog likes to eat the shit of other animals," he says. "I named him after Jeff Bezos 'cause he kind of looks like him."

Madden tries to remember what Jeff Bezos looks like. He's not sure he sees the same resemblance.

"Bezos doesn't take shit from anyone," Bender goes on, "and my dog eats the shit of other animals even after the gourmet grub I feed him. You know how much it costs a day to feed that animal? Eighteen bucks. Goddamn dog costs me eighteen bucks a day just to feed. But that's what selling out buys you, the stupidity to feed your dog gourmet canine delicacies while he prefers to eat shit."

Madden looks at him, not quite sure how to respond. But before he can say anything, Bender says, "I'll take that thumb drive now if you don't mind."

18 / CONTROLLING THE NARRATIVE

Carolyn looks at her watch. It's just after eleven o'clock and she's still at the hotel when she's supposed to be at the police station with Beth. She tells Beth to go to the lobby, where she can keep an eye on her and still be out of earshot while she makes a call.

"Hey, Hank," she says cheerfully when Madden answers the phone.

"I know that tone," Madden says. "It's the sound of someone who's about to disappoint me."

"We're running a little late."

"Late as in a few minutes late or late as in not coming?"

"I'm not sure," she says. "Those sedatives my client took last night have left her pretty sluggish this morning. I'm trying to get more coffee into her."

"I thought you were going to cooperate."

"We have every intention of doing so. We heard you arrested Richie Forman last night. You have a confession yet?"

Silence on the line.

"You should get her in here, Carolyn," he says after a moment. "Apparently the two of them saw each other yesterday. I wouldn't like to see Forman controlling the narrative. He's doing a pretty good job of it."

"What's he saying?"

"You'll get a full report soon enough, Counselor. You still haven't thanked me yet for sending this one your way."

"She asked for me, you didn't send her."

"Oh, but I gave you my full endorsement. And your cell number."

Just then Carolyn gets a text from her partner, Steve Clark. "Where are you?" Then a few seconds later he sends another one with a link to a website: "Did you see this?"

"Well, I'd give you a referral fee," she says to Madden while reading the messages, "but I know you can't accept it. That would be unethical."

He lets out a little laugh. "Meant to ask, how's Ted?"

"Ted's not happening."

"You two couldn't work things out?"

"Sadly, negotiations broke down," she says.

"Well, I'm sorry about that. Really, I am."

She now has the website up on her phone. It's an article by Tom Bender, the guy she'd spoken to that morning. The headline reads, SILICON NOIR: COPS HUNTING ADDITIONAL SUSPECTS IN MCGREGOR KILLING (Exclusive photo).

"I am, too," she murmurs absently, spreading her fingers to zoom in on the image. The picture is of two male Latino or Pacific Islanders, one a big, squat guy, the other smaller with one of those silly hipster soul patches dangling from his lower lip.

"You should know something, Carolyn," he says.

"What?"

"Marty Lowenstein's here."

The name rings a bell, but it takes a second for it to sink in.

"Marty Lowenstein, the lawyer? The DNA guy?"

"Yeah, him."

"What's he doing there?"

She realizes it's a stupid question as soon as she asks it. What she really means is, what's he doing representing Richie Forman?

"Forman got him somehow. No one seems to know how."

"Marty Lowenstein," she repeats, glancing over in the direction of Beth, who's sitting in a chair in the lobby.

"I really think you need to get down here," Madden says.

"Is there press?"

"Some," he says.

"Can you get rid of them?"

"I don't know about that."

She glances at Beth again and this time notices her talking to someone. The guy looks familiar, though it takes her a couple of seconds to realize why. She looks down at her cell phone again, then back in the direction of Beth. *Is it possible? Mr. Soul Patch? Here?*

"Carolyn, you still there?" Madden asks.

"Yeah." She takes a few steps in the direction of Beth to get a better look, careful not to draw attention to herself. Beth glances back her way once or twice, but overall doesn't seem fearful or intimidated.

Carolyn isn't sure what to do. If this really is one of the guys the cops are looking for and Beth is somehow associated with him, it could be potentially damning. But at the same time, she knows that if this guy really is a suspect then she has to report him. She's torn for a moment, then says to Madden:

"Word is you guys are looking for a couple of ethnic-looking dudes."

"Where'd you hear that?"

"It's up on the Internet," she says, lowering her voice, trying to remain out of Beth's view. "This guy Bender's got a picture up."

"Really?"

"Cut the bullshit, Hank, I know you leaked it. Just get a car here now—to the Rosewood Sand Hill."

"Why?"

"Because I think my client is talking to one of the guys in the picture right now."

19 / GOING LOW

SINCE THE HOTEL AND THE STATION HOUSE ARE ON OPPOSITE SIDES of town, Madden's first impulse is simply to send the nearest patrol car. But just as he's getting off the phone with Carolyn, he sees Carlyle pulling his Yukon into the parking lot. He rushes out to intercept him before he can come inside.

"Come on," he says, grabbing him by the arm and turning him around. "We're going for a ride."

Carlyle couldn't be happier. He jumps back in the driver's seat and peels out of the lot. Soon they're barreling across the El Camino, heading west on Santa Cruz Avenue, lights flashing, dipping in and out of the opposing lane to pass cars.

Carlyle slows for a tricky intersection and red light where Santa Cruz crosses Alameda de las Pulgas, then accelerates when Madden tells him he's clear and to "go, go, go." Carlyle, who doesn't need any encouragement, slams down the gas pedal and shoots up the remaining bit of Santa Cruz, then makes a sharp right onto Sand Hill.

Just then the radio crackles and David Consuelo, the patrol officer who'd gone ahead of them to the hotel, says he's at the location and that the suspect has reportedly left the premises. That's when Madden spots a Ford Flex as it passes them on the other side of Sand Hill and something clicks in his mind. *They were driving a two-tone Ford Flex*. Forman had said it last night. At the time, Madden hadn't given the descriptor a second thought, but the car that just went by had a black top and a silver body. *Two-tone*.

"Turn around," he tells Carlyle. "I think that's him."

Carlyle's just gone through the intersection with the turnoff to Sharon Heights and won't hit the next turnaround point for another few hundred yards. But instead of waiting for it, he says, "Hold on," hits the brakes, and makes a hard left over the raised divider, hitting the curb hard. The SUV lurches forward, then bounces up when the back tires climb the curb. Madden pops up in the air, his chest slamming up against his seat belt, which has locked and gone taut.

"Jesus," he says as Carlyle guns the car and they drive away in the opposite direction.

Up ahead is a major four-way intersection where Sand Hill meets Santa Cruz and Junipero Serra. The light has already turned green and Madden, because they're at the top of a slight crest in the road, catches a glimpse of the Flex heading down the hill on the other side of the intersection. Just off to the right behind a high chain-link fence is the Stanford golf course.

"Straight, straight," he tells Carlyle, who floors it through the intersection. Madden feels his stomach drop as they almost catch air hitting the down slope on the other side.

Carlyle passes one car, then another, once again weaving into the opposing lane, forcing a couple of cars to swerve out of their way. The traffic is relatively light—it is a Sunday morning after all—but it's heavier than the traffic they encountered on Santa Cruz Avenue, thanks to shoppers on their way to Stanford Shopping Center.

Carlyle makes one more pass and suddenly they're behind the Flex. He grabs his radio handset and announces their location. "We have the possible suspect in sight. Send backup. Alert the Palo Alto police that they've crossed onto their turf."

"Right behind you guys." It's Consuelo's voice over the radio. "On my way."

Carlyle gives the siren a short blast, signaling to the occupants of the Flex to pull over.

"You sure it's them?" he asks Madden.

He isn't. The vehicle matches the description but it's hard to tell who's inside because the back window is tinted. The car in front of the Flex drifts to the shoulder and slows, but instead of pulling over behind it, the Flex cruises past it, slowing slightly but mostly maintaining its speed.

Madden grabs the mic and hits a button to activate the car's integrated bullhorn. "You in the Ford Flex, pull your vehicle to the side of the road," he says. "Pull over now."

A moment later, the car starts to drift to the shoulder, gradually slowing.

"Just got a peek in the side mirror," Carlyle says. "Ain't no white boy, I can tell you that. Tongan, you said? We're in the right color spectrum anyway."

The Flex stops on the shoulder just after the turnoff to Stanford Hospital.

"The good news is that if anybody gets hurt, we're within yards of world-class medical care," Madden says.

"You got your vest on?" Carlyle asks, reading the number off the plate and punching it into his onboard computer. The small computer is perched up on a flexible gooseneck.

Madden shakes his head. He didn't put it on before he'd left the station house. "Doesn't matter," he says, and realizes he means it.

"Fuck that," Carlyle replies, then lets out a low whistle. He swings the screen over in Madden's direction. "Take a look at this."

Madden's eyes open wide. The vehicle is registered to Mark McGregor. *Had the plates been changed?*

"I'll take point on this," Carlyle says. "But get out of the car and back me up. I'm not getting a good vibe here. You ready?"

Carlyle exits the Yukon, draws his gun and takes the safety off. He waits for Madden to get out, then, keeping his weapon down by his hip, cautiously approaches the Flex on the driver's side. He doesn't come right up to the driver's window but stops slightly behind it and says loudly and authoritatively:

"License and registration."

He waits for the window to come down but it never does. The car suddenly lurches forward, the wheels spinning, dust and gravel kicking up in the air. For a second, Madden considers taking a shot at a wheel, but just as he starts to take aim, he finds himself with his hand in front of his face, shielding his eyes from the flying bits of gravel he feels pelting his glasses.

He and Carlyle hop back in the Yukon, slamming their doors shut at the same exact instant.

"Motherfucker," Carlyle says, shifting into drive and slamming down the gas pedal almost simultaneously. If he was amped up before, now he's really jacked. "Where's this asshole think he's going?"

Wherever he's going he's now opened up a good hundred- to hundred-fifty-yard gap between them. Carlyle gets back on the radio to report what's happened and which direction the suspect is headed. Within seconds they see flashing lights behind them. It's Consuelo; he's caught up.

Up ahead, they can see the Flex approaching the intersection at the northwest entrance of the Stanford mall where Aboretum Road cuts into Sand Hill. Take the right there and you head toward the Stanford campus. Keep going straight and Sand Hill traces the periphery of the mall and ends up hitting the El Camino Real, one of the main north-south arteries on the Peninsula.

The suspects continue straight through the intersection without turning onto Aboretum but having to slow down to avoid traffic. Carlyle is gaining. He fully expects the Flex to continue to the El Camino but then it suddenly makes a sharp right into the mall's parking lot.

"What's this dumbfuck doing?" Carlyle says, trying to keep the Flex in sight as they work their way around the periphery of the lot. In an hour or two the place will be filled with cars, but now plenty of spaces are open, especially ones toward the outside of the lot. He follows the route of the Flex.

As they make the turn, Madden says, "There! He pulled into a handicapped spot. See, over by Williams-Sonoma."

Carlyle leans on the gas pedal a little harder.

"Two of them," Madden says. "They're making a run for it. You go after them, I'll take the car around to the other side."

Madden guesses that since the car isn't registered to these idiots, they'll just ditch it and somehow disappear into the mall before anybody gets a good look at them. It's actually not a bad plan, except for the fact that both Madden and Carlyle have a pretty good idea what they look like.

Carlyle cuts through the lot, makes a hard left into the lane that runs just adjacent to the mall, the back of the truck fishtailing to a stop. He jolts the car into park, leaving the engine running. "Time to get some exercise," he says, and dashes off.

Madden jumps out and sees Consuelo pull up behind him a few seconds later.

"Secure the vehicle," Madden shouts, coming around the Yukon to get into the driver's seat. He points at the Flex. "The Ford SUV right there. Don't touch anything. Just make sure no one goes near it." Then he gets in the car and drives off.

As he reaches the front of the mall on the El Camino side he hears sirens coming up the El Camino from the south. Two squad cars in the distance. Palo Alto PD. Not theirs. He looks to his right toward the mall but doesn't see either of the Tongans or Carlyle, so he circles the mall until he's on the opposite side from where he left Carlyle.

"I'm on the other side by the Gap," he tells Carlyle over the radio. "You see them?"

"They split up," Carlyle says, breathing hard. "I went after the bigger one. More my speed."

"Where are you?"

"Right in the middle. Just went by Gymboree."

Madden stops the Yukon in front of Häagen-Dazs and gets out. It's hard to tell exactly where he is in relation to Carlyle, but he decides to head right and then cut left into the mall just before Bloomingdale's, breaking into a brisk walk that makes him more aware of his limp. He turns to make his way to the center of the mall and suddenly hears a woman's scream. Then a man yells, "Hey, watch out." Then it's Carlyle shouting at everybody to get out of the way and a moment later the quarry appears, wide and wild-eyed, charging toward Madden.

The guy's a fucking bull, but instead of reaching for his gun, Madden freezes, startled that he's coming directly at him. His first thought is *How do I stop this guy?* and then he thinks, *He doesn't know I'm a cop, he expects me to get out of the way.*

So he doesn't. In a moment of inspired stupidity, he does what any punter with limited tackling skills would do when faced with a speedy return man streaking through a hole into the open field: he decides to go low.

He dives in front of the guy, aiming for his ankles, and feels a sharp pain as the beast clips his right shoulder and is sent tumbling to the ground, landing hard on his side. Stunned, he looks back at Madden, who's also laid out on his side, grimacing in pain. The guy gets up and just as he does, Carlyle comes flying in, doing his best imitation of a blindside cornerback blitz, hitting the guy full force with his shoulder and wrapping his arms around him at the same time.

The blow knocks him back to the ground, but it doesn't have quite the incapacitating effect that Carlyle had hoped for. He tries to keep him pinned, but the guy's got a good eighty pounds on him. He manages to shed Carlyle, then literally lifts him up and chucks him toward the Bloomingdale's entrance. Madden, who's watched too many professional wrestling matches with his son, thinks the guy's next move will be a pile driver, but he's not that crazy. Instead, he scrambles to his feet and turns to resume his run only to find himself staring at the barrel of Madden's Glock.

"Freeze, asshole, or I'll blow your fucking brains into Bloomingdale's."

The guy looks him in the eyes, gauging his sincerity. Madden adjusts the grip on his gun, adding his left hand to show he's not fucking around. Out of the corner of his eye he sees a woman cowering behind a cement garbage can.

"Hands behind your head and on your knees."

The guy complies—halfway anyway. He does a modified lunge and drops down on one knee. "I didn't do anything," he says, clasping his hands behind his head.

Madden notes that his English is perfect. No trace of an accent. He's a kid really. Probably twenty, twenty-one, Madden thinks.

"Then why are you running?"

"There's a big sale today," he says. "Just trying to get my Christmas shopping done early."

"A goddamn comedian, eh?" Madden says to Carlyle, who's back on his feet, cuffs out. "We've got Sinatra, now Don Rickles. Who's next?"

"Why don't you tell us the one about the guy who got caught driving around in a dead man's car?" Carlyle says, binding his wrists behind him with a plastic cable, a wrist tie. "We'll see how that goes over."

Just then two Palo Alto cops appear from the same direction Madden came from. One has his gun out, the other a Taser. Out of the corner of his eye, Madden can't really tell exactly who they've got their weapons pointed at, but everybody seems to know who everybody is, which is what he's mainly concerned about. Both officers are fairly young, in their early thirties. Madden has met them before but he doesn't remember their names.

He lowers his weapon, waving them on. "Keep going," he says. "There's one more. On foot. Also APA but smaller and has a prominent soul patch below his lower lip. Don't know if he's armed but he's probably as stupid as this idiot."

"I'm not stupid," their captive protests.

"Just wait," Madden says. "It'll sink in soon enough."

20 / FORBIDDEN FRUIT

"FORMAN, YOU GOT COMPANY."

One look at Madden's wry smile and something tells him that this may not be such a welcome visitor. At first he thinks it's someone from the DA's office, but then he looks past Madden and sees the cop from last night, Carlyle, escorting a familiar character, the Oddjob look-alike, which makes his eyes light up.

"We found one of your Tongan friends," Madden says.

"Bravo, Detective. I didn't think you had it in you. Where's his buddy?"

"Still looking for him."

"You holding anybody else?"

"No."

"Wouldn't he be more comfortable in his own cage?"

"Sure."

Madden opens the door and steps out of the way, leaving Richie face to face with his old acquaintance, Oddjob, who doesn't seem terribly happy to see him again. The guy gives him a hard stare, followed by an almost comical guttural noise, a cross between a growl and grunt.

"Marty's not going to be pleased about this," Richie says.

"Probably not," Madden says. "But I'll let him know this is how we roll here in Mayberry."

Smiling at the comment, Carlyle removes the Tongan's wrist restraint, then gives him a nice nudge into the room and shuts the door.

Richie braces for confrontation but once inside the guy just brushes past him and sits down on the bench, rubbing his wrists. He decides to give him space—the little he can give. He takes the few steps to the other side of the small room and leans his back into the wall and looks up at the ceiling, searching one more time for the microphone or camera that Lowenstein had suspected was there. He'd promised to keep his trap shut, but he's curious as hell to know why they arrested the guy.

"What'd they get you for?"

He waits for a response but none comes. So he rephrases:

"What'd they charge you with? They told you what they charged you with, didn't they?"

His new roommate turns his head a little to the right—away from him—and mumbles something out of the side of his mouth that he can't decipher.

"What, bro?"

"I ain't your bro."

"Fair enough. But what'd they charge you with?"

"Failure to stop and assaulting an officer."

Richie lets out a low whistle. "Assault, huh? A cop? That could get you some jail time. You got a record?"

He shakes his head. The guy still refuses to look at him when he speaks. Dressed respectably enough in gray cargo pants and a black collared untucked short-sleeve shirt, he seems like a relatively normal kid. He's just big, with a wide, round face, a buzz cut, and dark, dull eyes. Shark's eyes. A little puffy. Tears? Maybe. Despite the earlier growl, Richie detects a touch of fear.

"What's your name?" he asks.

"Why?"

"I don't know. You seems to know who I am, so it only seems fair I should know who you is. Unless you prefer I make up a name. I'll try to keep your weight out of it but I can't promise anything."

"Tevita," he says quietly after a moment. "But people call me T-Truck."

"As in tow truck?"

"No. As in I will run your shit over, bro."

"Charming. You Tongan?"

"Why you talking like that?"

"Like what?"

"With that accent?"

"I didn't know I had an accent."

"Well, you do."

Silence.

Richie: "So how'd you get wrapped up in this little mess?"

"Fuck if I know."

"I know how you feel. But how'd you end up working for Mark McGregor?"

"Who said I worked for Mark McGregor?"

"Oh no? Who then?"

"His wife."

Richie pushes himself forward off the wall. "His wife?"

"Yeah. Ms. Hill."

"Why were you working for her?"

"She offered us double what her husband was paying us."

"Really? And did you keep collecting from McGregor?"

He smiles. "Yeah."

"Sounds like a pretty awesome arrangement. So he's paying you to follow her around and she's paying you to do what exactly?"

"She had us working on a couple projects."

"Like what?"

"You."

"Me?"

"Yeah, we were supposed to hang out in front of your building, keep tabs on you for a couple of days."

Richie takes a step closer.

"Why?"

"You don't know?"

"No."

"To get your attention. Reverse psychology, bro." He taps his temple a few times, a smile breaking across his face. He seems rather pleased with himself. "You tell someone to stay away and they can't."

"The old forbidden fruit trick."

"Yeah. Forbidden fruit."

Regrettably, he's right. After the run-in with the Togans, he'd only been able to hold out for a day before the urge to contact Beth had grown too powerful. He hadn't called her from his cell. Instead, as a precaution, he'd called her from a public phone, which hadn't been easy to find; he had to go to the Caltrain station, a ten-minute walk from his apartment. She'd answered on his third try, her voice tentative. As soon as she figured out who was calling she got nervous. "I can't talk," she said. "Just wait. I gotta go." And then she was gone.

He did wait. About a minute later the pay phone rang. He thought it was Beth calling back so he picked up. But he got a man's voice.

"Who's this?" the caller asked.

Richie's first reaction was to hang up, but then he reconsidered.

"I don't know," he replied. "Who this?"

"Ms. Hill's assistant." The accent was English, poorly done. "Are you trying to reach her?"

"I think you have the wrong number."

"You called, bro."

"No, *you* called," he said, and hung up.

His heart was pounding. What the hell? Was that who he thought it was? And his heart was still pounding a minute later when the phone rang a second time. *Let it go*, he thought. But then he heard his father again telling him to go to trouble. And he thought, *Fuck it*, and picked up. This time he didn't say anything.

"Richie? Richie, are you there?"

It was Beth's voice.

She'd called him back from a friend's phone. She said Mark had installed some sort of spyware on her phone. He could hear who she was talking to, see who she was texting and emailing. She'd heard a weird echo and had taken her phone into the Verizon store. A repair guy there told her she had spyware on her phone and that there was no way to get rid of it. He told her to trash the phone but she hadn't because then Mark would know she'd replaced it.

"It's bad, Richie," she said.

He thought of mentioning the call he'd just received from her fake assistant, but she already sounded stressed enough. "How so?" he asked.

"Mark's gotten really weird. He's paranoid. He thinks I'm having an affair. He thinks people want to kill him."

"Maybe he's right."

"He started a new company."

"I heard. Riding high. The next big thing."

"It's not like that," she said. "There's a lot of anxiety. He had to go back to investors. I don't know how much longer I can live like this."

"Did you come to my apartment building, Beth?"

Silence.

"The other day, you were there, Beth, weren't you?"

If she denied it, he was ready to say he'd seen the photo, but he didn't have to.

"I was up in the city. I stopped there. I rang your buzzer, but you weren't in. Then someone let me into the building. I waited a bit, then left."

"How do you know where I live?"

"Mark knows. He told me at some point. A few months ago he said you were living in the same building that Christopher Markus used to live in years ago. Bayside Village."

"Why'd you come, Beth?"

A moment of hesitation, then a soft voice. He could barely make out what she was saying. She was going to give him something. He thought he heard her say "rug." But that didn't make any sense.

"My what?" he asked, and just as he did, he realized what she'd really said.

"Your ring."

She enunciated the word this time, said it very clearly, and it hit him harder than he expected. Maybe it was how she said it. The way it came out made it sound as if it had never belonged to her. She was harboring stolen goods. Or rather, she'd borrowed it and now really wanted to return it. She didn't want it on her conscience anymore.

How he got all that from two short words she'd uttered he wasn't sure, but he suddenly felt sick.

"I thought, you know, you should have it back," she said. "That you might be able to get good money for it. I know what it's worth."

So did he. He'd bought it for $24,000. He'd gotten a deal on it through his father's friend in New York. A real rock.

"I told you I didn't want it back," he said.

"I know. But I thought your sentiments might have changed."

"I gave it to you, so it's yours. It always will be."

"It's a beautiful ring, Richie. You should have it."

The whole thing was killing him. The goddamn ring not only reminded him of sweeter times, but of his father, who'd helped pick it out and had died while he was in prison. A wave of anger swept over him and he released it in a way he was all too familiar with toward the end of their relationship. He let her have it.

"So let me get this straight, you've got a paranoid husband who put spyware on your phone and you're coming to my place? Did it occur to you that someone might be following you? If he's got shit on your phone, he's also probably got something on your car."

"I made sure no one was following. I was careful."

Not careful enough, he thought.

"Did Mark say anything about me demanding money from him? Did he say I was trying to blackmail him? Anything about notes or calls or emails or anything like that?"

"No. Why?"

"I don't know. I think someone may be trying to get money out of him using me as leverage."

"Who?"

"I don't know. Just stay away, Beth. And tell that psycho husband of yours to stay away. I don't need this shit. I'm doing okay here."

"Richie?"

"What?"

"I don't know what I'm going to do."

"Go to the police, Beth. Go right now, do you understand? File a report."

"What am I going to report?"

He heard an echo of himself in that response.

"Show them your phone," he said. "Show them the spyware."

"And what?"

"And I don't know. It's not my problem."

"I don't want the ring, Richie."

"I don't want it either. So we're even."

"You think about it."

"I don't want to think about it."

"You will," she said. "I know you will. You're stubborn but you're also practical. I know you've changed, but some things never change."

No, they don't, he now thinks. *You knew, didn't you? You knew saying that would remind me of that stupid song. You knew exactly what you were doing, didn't you?*

"The bitch done you good, bro."

Richie looks over and realizes T-Truck's been talking but he hasn't been listening. For a moment, he'd forgotten he was there.

"That your buddy who was monitoring her calls?" he asks him. "Mr. Soul Patch? It sounded like him."

T-Truck looks at him quizzically. "What are you talking about?"

"She had spyware on her phone. You guys were monitoring her calls."

That gets a chuckle.

"That what she told you?"

"Yeah."

He laughs again. "She played you good, bro. Spyware. That's a good one. I certainly hope you aren't—"

He coughs in the middle of the sentence, garbling the end of it.

"What?" Richie asks.

T-Truck takes a moment to clear his throat. "I said I certainly I hope you aren't protecting her. 'Cause she set you up, bro. Just like she set us up."

"How'd she set you up?"

"She gave the cops a picture of us. Made it seem like we got something to do with this. We're all over the fucking Internet. That's why the cops was after us."

"What do you mean? I told the cops about you stupid fucks. I was the one who—"

A sound at the door. The jangle of keys. They both look that way. In the little window, they see Carlyle, who yanks the door open. He's standing there with Madden and another officer behind him.

He motions for T-Truck to come out.

"Your lawyer's here, shithead."

"Lawyer?"

"Yeah, your mama sent over a lawyer. It's your lucky day."

"Am I getting out now?"

"Not that lucky."

21/ INTERCOURSE WAY

"YOU THINK YOU GOT HIM OUT IN TIME?"

Madden's back in the commander's office, sitting in the same chair he was sitting in earlier that morning, but this time there's no Crowley. It's just Pastorini seated at his desk and Carlyle standing behind Madden, leaning up against the wall, brooding a little, holding an icepack to his elbow. Pastorini keeps encouraging him to get over to the clinic and have it checked out, but Carlyle keeps insisting he's okay.

"I don't know," Madden says. "We'll see."

"Mr. T was doing well until he started whining about being a victim himself," Carlyle remarks.

Madden thinks: *How many times had they told the kid to let Forman do the talking? How many?* But he should have expected it. There's only so much coaching you can do in twenty minutes.

Pastorini had agreed the chicanery was worth a shot. If they could get Forman thinking Beth had sold him out, maybe he'd give her up. But Pastorini was concerned about the case falling apart on some technicality. "You can try it, Hank," he said, "but I want him in and out of there. If it's going nowhere, you pull him, tell him his lawyer's here. Understand?"

So after one last quick rehearsal, they'd tossed Tevita in with Forman and retired to a small room just down the hall. Not much bigger than a walk-in closet, the room was filled with high-tech equipment and looked like a mini recording studio. They each put on a pair of headphones.

It was going a whole lot better than Madden thought it would, especially considering an hour ago the guy was sitting in the back of the Yukon, a blubbering mess, with Carlyle showing him his heavily bruised elbow and telling him they were going to "lock his ass up," that he'd ruined his life and his mama was going to be disappointed.

Carlyle played the mama card early and often after they learned the kid's mother was a nurse. "I bet your mama puts in long hours at the hospital so you can go to college," he said. "Doesn't she?"

His name was Tevita Taupa and he said he was enrolled at Foothill, the junior college that some kids mockingly referred to as Harvard on the Hill. He claimed he had a year's worth of credits and was hoping to get a football scholarship somewhere.

"This is the kind of shit you get yourself into?" Carlyle went on, keeping up the pressure. "And with your luck, you're gonna pick yourself up a murder charge. You know you were driving a dead man's car? You worked for him? As an intern? Really? I'm not buying that—Hank, you buying it? A fucking intern. I ain't never seen no intern who looked like you. At a tech company? Come on. All they got there is fucking geeks and little hotties to give the geeks some reason to work at the company. McGregor may have had you on the payroll as an intern but you weren't no intern."

"I didn't do anything," Tevita said, tears running down his big, round face. "I swear. We were just supposed to follow the guy's wife around."

"Did you have an encounter with Richie Forman a couple of weeks ago in front of his apartment in the city?" Madden asked.

"Yeah. Fucker broke my nose."

"That doesn't sound like you were just following the guy's wife around."

No response. He just lowered his head.

"Yes or no, asshole?" Carlyle said. "What's the answer? We want some fucking answers."

"Mr. McGregor said this guy Richie was trying to get money out of him and might have something going on with his wife. He was the ex-boyfriend, I guess. Mr. McGregor wanted to send a message. Let him know he was being watched."

"Why'd you go see Ms. Hill at the Rosewood Hotel this morning?"

"I told him not to. I told him we shouldn't."

"You told who?"

No answer.

"Who, Tevita?" Madden cut in. "You partner? You got a name for us?"

"I can't do that."

"Well, it isn't going to make a difference because once we catch him we're going to tell him you coughed him right up. And I bet if I go through your phone, he's going to show up pretty quick. So you might as well tell us."

He shook his head, which made Madden think that his buddy must have a real hold over him.

Carlyle: "Why'd you go to the hotel to see Ms. Hill?"

"Because Edwin thought the bitch set us up."

"Edwin? That's his name?"

Realizing his mistake, Tevita winced.

"Why would he think that?" Madden asked.

"Someone texted him that our pictures were up on the Internet. And as soon as we saw that, we were like fuck, she fucked us. That shot was from the day we were up in the city with Forman. It makes it look like we were talking to him, you know, like having a meeting. She purposely went up there, knowing we were following her. And when we went back later, she followed us and she took those pictures. That or someone who was working for her."

They both knew there was a different explanation, but it did make Madden wonder whether Beth knew she was being followed. A guy like Tevita didn't exactly blend in. He'd be an easy spot, especially after you saw him a couple of times.

"So let me get this straight," Madden said. "You were following her and then she started following you? That's what you're saying?"

"Something like that."

Carlyle: "How'd you know she was at the hotel?"

Good point. Madden hadn't thought of that.

"We could track her by her phone," Tevita explained.

"By her phone?"

"Yeah, as long as she kept it on we knew where she was. There was a program on the phone. It kept the GPS on even if she tried to turn it off. Mr. McGregor installed it."

Carlyle looked at Madden. That seemed to confirm what Forman had told them. He'd said something about McGregor putting spyware on her phone.

Madden: "So you go talk to her at the hotel and—"

"I stayed in the car."

"Okay, so your buddy Edwin goes in and talks to her . . ."

"Yeah. He thought he was going to have to go looking for her but she was sitting right there in the lobby."

"What'd she say?"

"She denied it. She said she had nothing to do with the photo."

"And then what?"

"She asked him if we saw anything, if we knew anything about her husband getting killed."

"What'd he say?"

"He said fuck that."

"Those were his exact words? *Fuck that*?"

"I don't know exactly what he said. She just asked whether he knew anything about her husband getting killed. She wanted to know if he'd seen anything. He got the sense she was kind of worried he had seen something."

"Had he?"

"Fuck no."

"That's it?"

"Then she told him he'd better turn himself in to the police."

"Good advice," Madden said. "Why didn't he listen?"

"I don't know. He kind of panicked, I guess."

Carlyle: "He got a record, your friend? We found some pills in the car. He do a little dealing on the side?"

He nodded, the tears welling up again. "That's how he met Mr. McGregor. He met him at the gas station." He stared down at his feet, sniffling loudly. "I don't want to go to jail," he said. "I didn't do nothin'. Honest. Mr. McGregor wanted a big guy. But I did some intern stuff. I worked in the office some days. You can ask. What if—"

His voice trailed off.

"What if what?" Madden said.

"If I help you. Will I have to go to jail?"

"That depends."

"On what?"

"How helpful you are."

Never mind that if he was who he said he was and got himself a half decent lawyer, he probably wouldn't do any jail time. They leaned, he swayed, that's how the game was played. Like Carlyle said, the kid was doing fine until he went off-script. But Madden heard it coming. Holed up in the recording room, he thought they were toast as soon as Tevita said, "Just like she set us up." Carlyle's eyes lit up at the same time as his and they both tore off their headphones and bolted out of the room.

When they replayed the tape it seemed clear that Forman had a strong inkling something was amiss. But hopefully they'd intervened before he could start connecting too many dots. At least that's what they're telling Pastorini, who's called them into his office and now takes a sip from his tall can of Java Monster Loca Moca "energy" drink and says:

"I want you boys to listen to something. While you were busy playing around with our main suspect, we had multiple tips come in from people who claim to have seen Forman and Hill around town."

He turns to his computer screen, which is facing away from Madden, and maneuvers his mouse onto something, and clicks on it. A moment passes, and they hear a male 911 dispatcher's voice speaking to them through Pastorini's crappy little PC speakers, asking the caller to "state your emergency."

A woman's giddy voice: "This isn't really an emergency. But you know the guy who got arrested for killing that Mark McGregor guy? Well, I saw him yesterday and I'm pretty sure he was with the guy's wife. In fact, I'm certain."

Dispatcher: "Okay. Thank you for calling. Can you please give me your name and the best number to reach you at?"

The woman, who sounds young, states her name and gives a phone number.

"So where did you see them?" the dispatcher asks.

"At Watercourse Way. I'm a receptionist there."

"Watercourse Way? I've heard of that. The spa? In Palo Alto?"

"Yes, we're sorta like a spa. I mean, we *are* a spa, we have spa services, but we're also, you know, a bathhouse with hot tubs."

"And what time did they come in?"

"Right before two. The woman made a two-o'clock reservation. She didn't use her real name."

"A reservation for what?"

"A tub."

"Okay, and you say she was with this man you say was arrested."

"Yes. I just thought, you know, that someone should know. That it might be pertinent."

"Yes, thank you. I just want to let you know that we're recording this call and I'm going to pass on your info to the detectives here. Is there anything else you can remember that they should know?"

A pause. "No. Well, she paid in cash. I don't know if that's important or not."

"Okay, that's good to know. Someone will get back to you soon."

"I'm working today. I'm here."

"Okay, someone will definitely be in contact."

The call ends. Pastorini closes out the audio player on his computer, then swivels his chair toward Madden and says:

"Watercourse Way. You ever been there, Hank?"

"Can't say I have."

"Me neither. But last I checked, people went there to relax or fuck. In this case, I'd bet on fucking."

"They don't call it Intercourse Way for nothin'," Carlyle murmurs, coaxing a smile out of Pastorini.

"No, they don't," he says. Then, looking at Madden: "You don't seem surprised, Hank."

"I didn't think she was being completely honest with us."

"The question is why," Pastorini says. "She had to know it would eventually come out."

Madden: "People have a bad habit of developing selective memory under duress."

Pastorini shakes his head. He seems dismayed. "All I can say is that if Forman did it, he sure didn't plan it out too well."

"Maybe that was his plan," Madden says.

"To make it look like he's a fucking idiot? That was his plan?"

"Maybe. He's a smart guy. Maybe that's his defense. I'm a smart guy so why would I not plan this thing out better."

"I still think he didn't plan it out. That was his problem. I bet McGregor found out about this little excursion to Watercourse Way. He confronts Forman and they get into it. He takes a whack at him and Forman goes berzerko. Years of pent-up aggression."

"Why would Forman be at the house?" Madden asks.

Pastorini considers that.

"I don't know," he says after a moment, stumped. "If she set him up and brought him there hoping he and her husband would have it out, why not just come out and say that's what happened? The other thing I don't get is if she's involved, what does she really have to gain? She divorces McGregor, she does all right. Why risk so much for an extra five or ten million when you've already got a nice chunk of change coming to you?"

Madden: "What if it's more?"

"How much more?"

"Say twenty."

"Twenty? You know that?"

"No, but I'm just saying. Hypothetically speaking."

"Well, no more guessing," Pastorini says. "I want to know exactly where these people were and when. I want cell-phone data. I want witnesses on the ground. I want a murder weapon." He holds up his iPad and practically thrusts it in Madden's face. On the screen is a Google Maps satellite image of McGregor's street. "I want some goddamn virtual pushpins in my goddamn virtual map."

"Pete?" Madden says.

"What?"

"How many of those drinks have you had today?"

"I don't know. Two. Three. Why?"

"I'm getting a contact high just sitting across from you. And I think your iPad's charging in your hand."

Carlyle lets out a little laugh that elicits a surprisingly sharp, reproachful look from Pastorini. Normally, he takes ribbings about his caffeinated soda habit in stride.

"Pushpins, Hank," he repeats. "Start with this receptionist at Watercourse Way. When you get it all confirmed, I want you to ask Carolyn what her client was doing there with Forman at two in the afternoon. And if she keeps stonewalling, I want her arrested."

"On what charge?"

"I don't know. You'll think of something. You always do."

22 / HAPPY HUNTING

Carolyn calls Madden's cell phone once at eleven thirty, then again at noon. He isn't picking up, so she leaves two short, matter-of-fact messages, each stating the time of her call and telling him to get back to her when he gets a chance.

Finally, just before twelve thirty, she sees his caller ID info come up on her phone.

"Did you get the guy?" she asks.

"We got his partner."

"Partner?"

"Yeah, the big one. Ask your client about him."

"You get anything out of him?"

"Maybe."

"What's that mean?"

"We've still got some work to do. Where are you?"

She smiles, looking around. She's standing outside her car in a small park down the road from the hotel on Sand Hill. The setting is particularly significant for Madden—as well as her. It's where the shooting took place. She witnessed it from a surveillance van not more than fifty yards away from this very spot.

"I'm in that little Stanford Hills Park you made famous."

"What are you doing there?"

"Don't ask," she says. "You in your car?"

"Yeah."

"Where are you going?"

"Don't ask."

"Fair enough. When are you going to be back in the office?"

"An hour or so. Gotta make a couple of stops. Why, you coming in?"

"Looking that way."

"I don't want to warn you again, Carolyn, but I will. I'm not trying to play you. Her story's taking on water. She's sinking fast."

She's been waiting for this. The moment when he really shows his cards. Not all of them. But enough to make it clear he's not bluffing. The only thing to do is call his bet.

"I guess you know about Watercourse Way then."

Silence.

"Hank, you there?"

"Yeah, I'm still here."

"Is that where you're off to?"

"Maybe."

"Well, I'll save you some time. She was there with Forman yesterday."

"What was she doing there?"

"What do people do there?" she asks.

"Pastorini says either make love or relax."

She laughs. "I somehow don't imagine him saying it like that."

"He didn't."

"You're such a prude, Hank. Maybe they fucked, then relaxed. Did you ever think of that? You can do both, you know?"

"Well, as you might imagine, I'm more interested in the fucking part."

"I'm sure you are."

"Did they go back to the house afterwards?"

She takes a breath, hesitates a moment, then says: "As far as I know, she did not take him into the house."

"Now you're getting all Bill Clinton on me. What does that mean?"

As she weighs her next response, she sees a car turn off Sand Hill and head down the street toward her. Midsized sedan, generic-looking, has all the earmarks of a rental. *Got to be him*, she thinks, though she notices there are two people inside the vehicle.

"It means what it means," she says, giving a little wave to the car's occupants. "Look, I gotta go. My lunch date is here."

"I'll give you till the end of day."

"Then what?"

"Then I'm bringing her in myself—in cuffs. The media should enjoy that."

"On what charge?"

"I figured I'd start with obstruction of justice and work my way up."

"Good luck with that, Hank. Happy hunting."

As she hangs up, the sedan pulls over and comes to a stop behind her. A petite young woman emerges from the passenger side and gets out. Then Marty Lowenstein and his trademark shock of frizzy gray hair emerge from the driver's side. He flashes a warm, welcoming smile.

"Hello, Ms. Dupuy," he says. "Thank you for meeting us on such short notice."

"Pleasure's all mine, Mr. Lowenstein."

"Marty," he says, extending a hand. "Call me Marty."

23 / CROSSED-UP

LEAVING THE CARS PARKED WHERE THEY ARE, THEY SET OFF ON FOOT back to Sand Hill, heading up the pedestrian path a couple hundred yards to the entrance of the Stanford Linear Accelerator.

The young woman's name is Ashley and she reminds Carolyn a little of Tina Fey. She's no dead ringer, but change up the glasses and Carolyn thinks she'd get a few double takes. Turns out she's been working up in the city with Forman, who's been volunteering the past few weeks at the Exoneration Foundation. At least that solves one mystery: the Lowenstein connection.

When Lowenstein called just before noon, she'd figured he was fishing for information on what Beth was saying. But after dispensing with the introductions, he quickly asked whether she didn't mind meeting him at her earliest convenience—preferably later today or early tomorrow—at the scene of "the accident." He said he was hoping she could answer a few questions for "background purposes."

It was an odd conversation. Despite being abundantly polite and complimentary, in his own peculiar way he seemed to be challenging her. To what end, she wasn't quite sure, but it bothered her, and instead of saying she'd get back to him in a little while, as she'd initially been inclined to do, she ended up pushing to meet earlier. After all, she was nearby, and it behooved her to try to get a sense of where things stood with Forman. Oh yeah, and she was just a little curious to see him in the flesh.

He turns out to be a little taller than she'd expected. He's always struck her as someone who's cultivated his vaunted status pragmatically and prudently. He probably could have gotten even more exposure, but her impression is that he's deliberately avoided becoming a media slut, knowing that doing so would diminish him. TV builds you up but it can also water you down. Lowenstein seems to have found a happy medium.

"We saw this driving down," he says, stopping in front of the faded white cross planted beside the pedestrian path: "I'm always fascinated by roadside memorials. There's an immediacy to them even years later."

He stoops to take a closer look at the memorial. It's pretty understated—no ribbons, laminated pictures, or wreaths of any sort. The initials of the accident victim are written on the vertical part of cross and RIP is notched neatly into the wood horizontally. Lower down, on the front of the cross and on the sides, people have carved short messages in small letters. Most appear to be from friends or relatives, though could have been written by strangers.

"How did the parents feel about the outcome?" he asks, standing again and talking more loudly so his voice carries over the sound of passing cars. The traffic along Sand Hill alternates between sporadic and steady; when the light at the intersection is green, which is most of the time, the cars zip by pretty quickly, probably pushing sixty.

"Outcome of what?" she asks.

"The trial. Richie's conviction."

"They were religious people. They'd put their faith in God. So, in that sense, I think they were willing to accept whatever resolution the court gave them."

"The victim had a brother and sister?"

"Yes. They were more vocal in their desire for a conviction. They were incredibly angry. They would have been heartbroken if he'd walked."

"I think that's one of the more brilliant things you did, Ms. Dupuy."

"What?"

"The subtle way you got it into the heads of the jurors that if they didn't convict Richie Forman, no one would be convicted. You managed to raise the stakes."

Damn, she thinks. *The great Marty thinks you're brilliant*. She feels her face redden, a smile involuntarily creeping onto her lips. But then she catches herself: *He's trying to soften you up. Don't go mushy.*

"Like you, I pride myself on my rapport with juries," she says. "You know what I tell people who say they don't want to serve? I tell them, 'Hey, you're going to want to see me in action. You don't want to miss this.' People want theater. They want to be entertained. That said, the evidence in the Forman case was very solid. The one big unknown was how he'd play on the stand. Therefore my main focus was to undermine his credibility, even just slightly, because the evidence was so strong. He actually gave me a little more than I was hoping for."

"Ashley took a look at that evidence," Lowenstein says. "It was solid but not overwhelming. There were holes that the defense failed to exploit fully—or at all."

"Such as?"

"Mr. McGregor was never examined. His injuries were never documented. The detectives made a few notes about his condition, but he was never examined by a doctor. And the way the crime scene was processed was lackadaisical. Everybody was under the assumption that Forman was the driver, so the investigation was tarnished by that assumption."

Ashley: "It's also unclear that the injuries sustained by Forman were consistent with someone who was seated in the driver's seat."

Carolyn feels her nostrils flare. This Ashley looks like she's fresh out of college. "And that's some sort of great revelation? I've been through all this before. We called our experts. They called theirs. If you want to play Monday-morning quarterback and tell me you would have got Forman off, go right ahead, but I don't really have time for that now."

Lowenstein dismisses her indignation, motions for Ashley to hand over a yellow folder she's carrying. He takes it and opens it, leafing through the various pieces of paper until he gets to a set of photos printed out on photographic paper. Most are eight by tens but a few are five by sevens and four by sixes. He removes them from the folder and hands the folder back to Ashley.

"I take it you've seen these." Pictures of the accident. He holds one up and glances over it. "This one seems like it was taken just a few feet from where we're standing."

"Where'd you get those?"

"Ashley's very good. She's been making some inquiries in her spare time."

"At whose behest?"

"We were doing a background check on Rick for the foundation and I got curious," Ashley explains.

"Rick?"

"Yes, Richie goes by Rick now," she says. "I told him I was looking into his case a bit and he seemed somewhat ambivalent about it but didn't object too strenuously. He didn't think there was much point in it."

Carolyn has a flashback to handling a similar assortment of photos years ago. "A lot of those are official police photos," she says. "How'd you get them?"

Ashley: "I contacted the accident victim's family and, well, they didn't want to have anything to do with me. But I had more luck with the friend, the woman who was in the car and injured in the accident. She lives up in the city."

"Dawn?"Carolyn says, suddenly remembering her name.

"Yes, Dawn Chu. She's had a rather rough go of it. I don't suppose you've kept track of her."

"No. I actually have my own problems, which I'm sure you're aware of given your apparent crack investigative skills."

"She works at Centerfolds, over on Broadway."

Centerfolds. Sounds familiar, but she can't remember why. Then it hits her. "The strip club?"

"Yeah."

"Really?" She pauses briefly to consider how a woman with an advanced physics degree ended up a stripper. "Well, I guess the only upside is she must be fully recovered physically. I took a pole-dancing class once. That shit is hard."

"She's still nearly blind in the one eye," Ashley says. "And she still has memory issues."

"And she had the photos?"

"Yes, she'd asked the police for anything they had on the accident. As disturbing as some of the pictures were, she wanted them. She told me that she had a premonition that someday someone would come asking about the accident."

"And there you were."

"There I was."

"That's not all," Lowenstein says. "Apparently, she's had some contact with Forman."

"Contact? What kind of contact?"

Lowenstein glances over at Ashley, queuing her to answer. "Well, as part of the settlement, he had to pay restitution," she says. "There was a larger settlement of hundreds of thousands but then he was supposed to send a check for one dollar on the anniversary of the accident for each year of her life."

"Yeah, I remember that. To the parents."

"And Dawn. Anyway, she says that along with the check each year, he'd also been sending a note, which wasn't required. She showed them to me. He'd always say that on this day, the anniversary, he was thinking about her and her friend and how sorry he was for what happened. And then he'd write about himself and how he was doing. Some of it was quite personal. You know, he was sexually assaulted in prison."

"I'd heard that," Carolyn says. "And that he'd taken a sharp object to the jugular of one of his attackers. Nearly killed him. If I were still a prosecutor, I'd—"

Ashley's eyes narrow, bearing down on her. "How'd you feel about that?"

"About what?"

"That he was assaulted."

You entitled little bitch. "What I felt is irrelevant. But to fulfill your curiosity, I felt bad. Mr. Forman's sentence was heavy enough as it was. More importantly, did she write back?"

"No. She said a friend advised her not to write back. He said Forman was just trying to suck her in, manipulate her. That's what people in prison do."

"But she saw him after he got out?"

Ashley nods. She explains that Dawn found out Forman was doing these Sinatra gigs, and she went to see him at one. Afterwards, she saw him up at the bar and introduced herself. But she gave him her stage name, Toni. She had some work done after the accident, so he didn't recognize her.

"She has these big fake boobs now," Ashley goes on. "Wears her hair short and spiky and talks with a Texas accent."

She told Forman she'd been a Dallas Mavericks cheerleader for a while and that she worked at the club and he should come by sometime and say hello. A few days later, he dropped a hundred bucks on a lap dance and then she hooked up with him a week or two later "back at his apartment, free of charge."

"You've got to be kidding me," Carolyn says, stunned. "And she doesn't say anything the whole time, doesn't reveal who she is?"

"Nope. But she gets him to talk about how he went to prison and how his friend switched seats on him and all that. She seems to take some weird, perverse pleasure in him not knowing it's her. Says it was the best sex she ever had."

"Jesus Christ."

Carolyn glances over at the cross, then turns and looks out onto the intersection where the accident took place. She can't believe what she's hearing and where she's hearing it.

She looks over at Lowenstein, who seems to be enjoying her agita. "Why are you telling me all this, Marty?" she asks.

"Did Ms. Hill tell you anything about somebody blackmailing her husband?"

Carolyn almost falls into Lownstein's trap, but then backs away at the last second.

"So that's why we're here, eh? I'm not sure we had to meet by the side of the road if you were interested in discussing my client's statements."

Lowenstein smiles, unruffled. "You're an insider here, Ms. Dupuy."

"Carolyn."

"Yes, sorry. Look, you're an insider here and I just showed up four hours ago and I'm trying to get my head around a lot of stuff. I'm looking for a little help. My client is the one locked up at the police station, not yours. But I do get a strong sense that Ms. Hill is not telling the entire truth about what happened and where she was yesterday."

"What makes you think that?"

"I'm a fast learner. And by that I mean that I learn things quickly from people. One of the good things about being a celebrity attorney is that folks are more apt to meet with and talk to you, even by the side of the road. Because they've seen you on TV before, they think they know you, and more importantly, they have a tendency to be accommodating."

"Everybody's a starfucker."

"In a manner of speaking."

"So you think Dawn was somehow involved in blackmailing McGregor?"

"So you are aware that someone sent a note to McGregor saying they had evidence he was driving the car and wanted two hundred fifty thousand dollars to keep quiet?"

"Yes, I'm aware of that. I was not aware that she was suspected."

"She isn't. Not by the police anyway. But a copy of a photograph apparently was attached to the note."

"What did the photo show?"

"We're not sure. The Sunnyvale police aren't saying. But McGregor seems to have claimed it was altered. Photoshopped."

"I only knew about him reporting something to the police. I wasn't aware of the photo, if that's what you're asking."

"And you saw all the photos from the crime scene? Did any bystanders take additional pictures? Or police officers or firefighters? I know the technology wasn't what it is today, but most cell phones had cameras back then."

"If you're asking whether any photos were suppressed, the answer's a definitive no. We may be inept by your standards, but we're not corrupt."

"I didn't say anything about ineptitude." He turns around and points up to the traffic light. "So these lights didn't have any cameras in them at the time of accident?"

"They still don't. Well, not the kind that would have helped document what happened. They have something in there that measures the speed of passing cars. That's it."

"And the Linear Accelerator had no video?"

She looks over at the guard station, a good fifty yards away up an inclined driveway. While they're standing next to the turnoff to the Accelerator, the guard station—and real entrance—is up the hill a bit, away from the road. The cluster of office buildings is even further up the hill, well beyond the guard station.

"They had video of the guard station—and the cars going in and out—but the camera back then didn't go all the way down to the road. I believe it does now. Someone's probably watching us, wondering what the hell we're doing here."

Lowenstein glances over at Ashley, who's just finishing getting everything back in order in her folder.

Lowenstein nods, seemingly satisfied. He says, "Well, thanks. I appreciate you coming out and meeting on such short notice. I don't want to keep you any longer."

He extends his hand to say good-bye.

"Come on, Marty," she says, not accepting it. "Cut the shit. You give me something, I'll give you something. Let's go. Is Forman going to sell Hill out?"

She actually seems to catch him off guard. For a brief moment, he's taken aback. His mouth moves to say something, but nothing comes out. A beat, then: "You always this aggressive?"

"Yeah. But being jacked up on fertility drugs probably doesn't help. So let's go. You turn a card, I turn one."

Lowenstein seems to consider his cards and which one he's going to turn. After a moment, he says:

"Has your client told you about this hot-tub place they went to?"

"Yes."

"And what's she told the police about that?"

"Nothing. But they know. They got tipped off."

"And what did you plan on doing about it?"

"Honestly, I'm not sure. She spoke to the police initially. I wasn't there for the first round. Now we're in a little hole."

"How's the truth look?"

He squints a little, peering at her more closely. He doesn't hide the fact that he wants to see her reaction to this one and glean something from it.

She smiles. "The truth? I was actually thinking about it before I came over here. It reminds me a little of an iTunes card with the scratch-off code on the back. I got one of those the other day and started scratching the film off with a coin and I somehow screwed up and it turned into a mess. I couldn't figure out what a couple of numbers were. Or maybe they were letters. How 'bout you? How's it look on your end?"

"I can read the code but I may have some trouble redeeming it if someone's already redeemed it herself."

"What do you want?"

"Well, I'd take anything she's got that helps Rick. Short of that, I'd take anything that won't hurt him."

"No votes for insanity? I hear he's been in character the whole time. Thinks he's Sinatra. Or playing like he does."

"Just a defense mechanism. Helped him get by in prison. No one fucks with 'Frank.' Right?"

"They want her to come in, Marty. They're pressing pretty hard to get her in there."

"You can go in but it doesn't mean she has to say anything."

"True. While I'm her attorney, my obligation is to her, though."

"You say that as if you're not confident you'll remain her attorney."

"Well, until nine o'clock last night I was mothballed, contemplating a career change with a pit stop at motherhood. So I'm not exactly certain about anything."

She half expects him to ask whether this is her first time trying to get pregnant and whether she's married. But he just says: "You seem in fine form."

"I feel rusty."

"Well, you know where to reach me if you want to talk. Ashley will text you her number, so you have that, too."

She looks at Ashley, who's been quietly listening the last few minutes, then turns her attention back to Lowenstein, who seems as calm as ever. Or does he? Is that a touch of self-doubt that she sees in his eyes? *What's bothering you?* she thinks. *Me or something else?*

"How much do they have on Forman, Marty? What's got you so worried?"

If someone had asked her the same question, she'd have let him or her have it. Sent the bulldozer in. But Lowenstein just cracks a smile. He seems to like her bluster.

"I'm the DNA Dude, right?" he says. "That's what I'm known as."

She looks at him quizzically, wondering whether it's a rhetorical question or whether she's supposed to answer it. Before she can, he goes on:

"We come in and we analyze how labs and the police handle evidence usually months or even years after a crime has taken place. DNA's great, but it's slow, and today's cases are starting to be increasingly decided by digital, not biological DNA. It's your digital trail—emails, texts, location-based tracking from your cell phone—that's telling the story. And that information is being obtained increasingly quickly by the police."

"That can be good, though," she says. "That can be exculpatory."

"Absolutely. But it also doesn't look good when the evidence shows the defendant may have paid a visit to the victim's home, then turned his cell phone off during the time the crime he's alleged to have committed took place."

"Oh," she says. "Where does he say he was?"

Lowenstein turns to his right and looks up the road. He points in the direction of the freeway and Woodside.

"Up there somewhere. On his bike."

As if on queue, a group of five or six cyclists coasts down Sand Hill toward them, returning from their morning ride, which could have taken them all the way to the ocean and back. They go by in a blur of colors, shaved legs, and high-tech gear. After they pass, Lowenstein says:

"If you needed someone to identify a lone rider coming down this road at dusk, you might be a little concerned, too."

"Maybe he wasn't on this road," she says.

"That, too. But let's not go there yet. One way or another, I'm getting him out on Monday."

"Is that a threat?"

"No. Just the power of positive thinking."

24 / THE ISSUE OF CUSTODY

"WHEN THEY READ THE CHARGES, YOU DON'T SMILE, YOU DON'T look sad, you don't let any emotion cross your face. You just give a little shake of your head. Not the whole time. Just for a couple of seconds. And that's it. Nothing else, understand?"

Those are Lowenstein's instructions. Standing in the courtroom on Monday morning for his arraignment Richie does his best to follow them to a T, even if every bone in his body is aching to show defiance. Sinatra would have sneered at the judge, mugged for the cameras, and maybe given a little wink to the cute Hispanic stenographer transcribing the proceedings. But stoic with a dash of disdain is what Lowenstein wants, so stoic with a dash of disdain is what he gets.

The charge is murder in the second degree. After he enters a plea of not guilty, Judge Marta Jones, a heavyset light-skinned black woman with an attractive face and tightly cropped afro, turns to Crowley, the DA, and says, "On the issue of custody?"

Lowenstein warned him that the odds were stacked against his making bail. Judges, he said, even so-called liberal ones, are inherently conservative and averse to risk. Given the choice between keeping an accused killer locked up or allowing him to roam free and possibly committing another crime, it was in their best interest—and the public's—to go with the safer option. So it didn't matter whether he was a flight risk or not. What mattered was how she felt about the prosecution's case.

Crowley's argument comes as no surprise: "The defendant should be remanded back to prison due to the seriousness of the offense and the fact that he presents a flight risk."

Lowenstein respectfully disagrees. "Your Honor, this case is very circumstantial at best. Notice the prosecution makes a very general bail application because they know their evidence is flimsy. Based on my understanding of these facts, there's no way they're proving this case against my client."

Every time he moves a little or raises a hand to gesticulate, the sound of camera shutters firing in rapid succession permeates the courtroom. Only two photographers have been allowed into the room, but it sounds like red carpet at the Golden Globes. *Fucking locusts*, Richie thinks. He's always hated that sound.

"Well, Mr. Crowley," the judge says, "what shows that this case is provable?"

"Your Honor, we have a lighter that was found just ten feet from the victim's body. A fingerprint on it matches this defendant, who's a prior felon."

Lighter? Richie thinks. *Did he say lighter? But I—*

"We also have a second fingerprint on the outside buzzer panel showing that the defendant was at the residence," Crowley goes on. "In addition, there was a past relationship between the defendant and the victim and the defendant blamed the victim for his being convicted of a crime. And I would further submit to the court that it was no coincidence the victim ended up marrying the defendant's former fiancé. The defendant was clearly angered by that because in the past he spoke of killing the victim."

Just as Lowenstein's about to respond, Richie leans over and whispers in his ear: "I gave the lighter to Beth. She had the lighter, not me."

Lowenstein gives a little nod and Richie expects him to pass his comment on to the judge but he doesn't. Instead he says, "Your Honor, the felony the prosecutor mentioned was a nonviolent offense and the fact that they found a lighter proves nothing. And so does a fingerprint on a door buzzer. They have nothing. They have no blood, they have no weapon. And what they do have doesn't prove anything. There's nothing that directly ties the defendant to this crime. The prosecution's assertion of a possible motive is speculative at best.

Once again, he's not pointing to any direct proof but is rather casting a general aspersion. Your Honor, under these circumstances, bail is appropriate."

The judge doesn't say anything to Lowenstein. Instead, she turns to Crowley and asks, "Counsel, is there anything else you want to add?"

Crowley stands there impassively, staring at her. "That's what we have to share at this time, Your Honor."

Again, Judge Jones doesn't respond right away. But her deliberation is short. "I tend to agree with the defense," she says after a moment. "Based upon your representation to the court, it appears you may have an uphill battle proving this case. If you're able to indict this defendant, you'll have a second opportunity to address the issue of custody at that time. Therefore I find that bail is appropriate and I am setting bail in the sum of two million dollars bond or one million dollars cash."

Crowley knows he's beat, but he fights back anyway in an attempt to eke out a victory, even a token one.

"Your Honor, in light of the fact the court has not remanded the defendant I would ask that the court require the defendant to wear an ankle bracelet to monitor his whereabouts."

"So ordered," she says without hesitation. And suddenly, that's it. Lowenstein isn't given an opportunity to respond. They're done and the next thing Richie knows he's being taken into custody. He doesn't have a chance to say anything to Lowenstein at the table, but the two are able to catch up for a moment in the courthouse cell.

"Why didn't you say anything to them about the lighter?" Richie whispers to him. "I told you I returned it to Beth that day. She must have dropped it."

"Or planted it," Lowenstein says.

"Either way, I didn't drop it. Why didn't you say anything?"

"That would have been a rookie mistake," Lowenstein explains. "You want to save information like that. You never draw early if you don't have to. You tuck something like that away, it's your ace in the hole. I wasn't there to argue the case. I was there to argue for your bail. Be happy. You got lucky."

He doesn't feel that lucky.

"Two hundred K for the bond, Marty. Tell me you've got that kind of coin lying around. I'm good for it."

"I don't," he whispers back. "But I'm working on it."

The officers are on either side of Richie now. One takes him by his left arm, the other by his right. His wrists are cuffed to his waist in front of him.

"If I had someone for you to call, I'd tell you," he says.

"I know," Lowenstein says. "Hang in there a little longer."

Richie smiles. "Get me out and I'll buy you another mitt."

"I like my mitt."

"Yeah, but I wanna play catch for real. With a ball."

"You will," he says. "Just hang in there."

PART 3

25/ THE GOLDEN ARCHES

RIGHT AROUND ONE IN THE AFTERNOON, HE HEARS KEYS AT THE DOOR, and a moment later it opens. Madden is standing there with a white paper bag in his hand, which looks a lot like the same bag Richie's breakfast came in.

"Congrats, Forman, you made bail."

"No shit," he says getting up from the bench.

"You seem surprised."

"I was expecting lunch. This is better."

Madden sets the bag down on the bench. "We got it for you. You might as well take it to go."

Madden uncuffs him, then leads him down the hall, where a small group of officers and detectives is mingling around a common area, waiting for him while trying not to look like they're waiting for him. The commander, Pastorini, who he spoke to briefly yesterday, is among the officers.

"Getting the royal send-off, am I?" Richie says, addressing the group. "You'll be happy to know I filled out the feedback form in the cell. Personable staff. Firm mattress. Clean sheets. You need to work on your interrogation techniques, but other than that, five stars all around."

Pastorini smiles. "You think this is all a joke, Mr. Forman?"

"It'd be awfully depressing if it wasn't, wouldn't it, Commander?"

Richie peeks into the slit of the window of a nearby cell, checking to see if it's occupied.

"Where's the big fella?" he asks.

"We let him go," Pastorini says.

"How 'bout his friend? You pick him up yet?"

"Found his phone. Not him. But we will."

Carlyle hands him a large brown paper bag with a sticker on it that has his name and some numbers on it. "Check that everything's there," he says. "We've got some papers for you to sign and then we'll just fit you up with your ankle bracelet and you'll be good to go."

Richie opens the bag. His jacket is there along with a separate Ziploc plastic bag that contains his watch, wallet, and the rest of what was in his pockets, including the ring case, his iPod, and a pack of gum. He flips open the ring case and sees that the ring is inside, still ensconced in its slot. *You little fucker*, he thinks, and snaps the case shut.

"All here," he says.

Once he's done signing the release forms, he sits down in a chair, lifts his pant leg, and watches as Carlyle clamps the bracelet on. He looks around, expecting Lowenstein to appear. But he's not anywhere to be seen.

"You need to test this thing?" he asks, standing up.

"We did," Carlyle says.

"Where's my attorney?"

He nods in the direction of Madden, who's standing on the other side of the room with his cell phone to his head. "He's talking to him," he says.

Shortly, Madden comes over and hands the phone to Richie. Lowenstein tells him that the media's still crawling all over the station. As a favor, he's asked the detectives to slip him out to a nearby meeting point, which they've agreed to. Apparently, there's a little good will going around now that they're about to lose custody of him. Lowenstein says he thinks they're also a little embarrassed he was granted bail and would prefer that he slip out quietly.

Moments later he finds himself exiting the back of the building and diving into the back of Madden's SUV, which is parked practically next to the door. Someone shuts the door behind him and he lies down on the seat, face up, keeping low, his lunch bag on his stomach.

"You boys aren't thinking of dumping me off the Dumbarton or anything like that, are you?" he says to Madden, who's driving. Burns is in the passenger seat. "That stuff I said about you being washed up, I wasn't serious about that. You know that, don't you?"

"You're a piece of work, Forman," Madden says. "Shut up or I'll consider it."

The ride lasts a little more than a minute. Madden makes a few turns, then a sharp right into what feels like a driveway. From his horizontal position Richie catches a glimpse of a familiar site: the golden arches. He realizes then that they're in the McDonald's parking lot on the corner of El Camino and Santa Cruz Avenue.

Madden pulls the car to a stop, and looking into the rearview mirror, he says, "You're free to go. You know where to reach us if you have anything you want to talk about."

"Will do," Richie says, and gets out on Madden's side.

When the car pulls away, he looks over to see Lowenstein and Ashley standing in an open parking space between two cars. He goes over and shakes Lowenstein's hand and gets a full hug from Ashley, who's brought him a small duffel bag that's filled with clean clothes, his toiletry kit, and a pair of running shoes from his apartment. Lots of smiles all around, and for a brief instant, Richie gets a whiff of what it must feel like for one of Lowenstein's clients to be exonerated. Then he remembers he's not off the hook and there's potentially a big debt to settle.

"Who put up the money?" he asks. "The foundation?"

Lowenstein shakes his head, his smile disappearing. He glances over at Ashley, who doesn't give him any help. She looks down, averting her eyes.

"Who, Marty?" he asks again.

"I had to make a little deal," he explains.

"What kind of deal?"

"I had to sell you."

"Sell me?"

"Just for a little while. It'll be all right. I worked out the terms. Might actually help us."

"What are you talking about? Who the hell did you sell me to?"

Lowenstein nods at someone or something over Richie's shoulder. Then he says: "To that guy."

Richie turns around. Emerging from the McDonald's is a small man in a T-shirt and jeans carrying a cardboard tray that has a bag in the middle of it and a couple of drinks stuck in its corner cup holders. The guy plucks a couple of french fries out of the bag and stuffs them in his mouth as he walks toward them. As he gets closer, he starts to look more familiar but Richie can't quite place him. Then it hits him.

"Hey, killer," Tom Bender says. "Got you a shake. Nothing tastes like freedom more than a Mickey D's vanilla shake. Am I right?"

26 / YOU SAY GRAIL, I SAY FAIL

LOWENSTEIN WASN'T KIDDING WHEN HE SAID HE'D SOLD HIM. IN exchange for putting up $200,000 for a bail bond, plus his house as collateral, Bender bought himself two days of Richie Forman. He said he wanted five, but in the end he got two, and Richie's now his for the next forty-eight hours, with a few hefty strings attached.

Bender has his exclusive all right, but he also has to adhere to strict guidelines over what he can post and when; everything has to be approved by Lowenstein before it goes up online. Lowenstein has worked the contract so that Richie will benefit mightily—and monetarily—should Bender fail to live up to his end of the bargain. But despite Lowenstein's assurances that there's more upside than down to the unusual arrangement—and their best option given the circumstances—Richie still thinks that once again he's drawn the short end of the stick.

Their first stop is Bender's gym, the Equinox just off the El Camino in Palo Alto on Portage Road, where his newfound benefactor says he can get "cleaned up and recharged."

After being locked in an austere, windowless room for more than two days, it's something of a culture shock to be suddenly among the Lululemon set in an old warehouse that's been transformed into a hip, modern gym and tagged with the "industrial chic" label. Wearing sweatpants, a T-shirt, and baseball cap plucked from Bender's swag-filled car trunk, Richie walks around in a bit of a daze, doing a set here and there on various weight machines until settling in on a treadmill for twenty minutes. He then heads upstairs to the roof, where there's a small lap pool.

It's bright and sunny outside, though a little cool, in the midsixties. Only a couple of swimmers are in the pool, and when he retires to one of the chaise longue chairs surrounding it, he notices someone's left a copy of that day's *San Francisco Chronicle* under it. There, on the bottom of the front page, is a story about the murder, with a picture of McGregor and him from the old days, when they were friends.

The *Chronicle* had run the same picture years ago during his trial and the story is really just a rehash of the trial and the accident, though after the jump, he comes across a jarringly large picture of him doing his Sinatra routine. It seems oddly out of place, if only because it would seem more at home in the Sunday Datebook section.

There's something surreal about sitting there by the pool, reading the article. While he knows it's about him, at times he feels like he's reading about someone else, a total stranger. He knows the story through and through, but he has nothing to do with it, which is probably why he's less concerned now than when he first walked into the joint that someone will recognize him or notice the tracer bracelet.

Yeah, I'm Richie Forman, he thinks. *But so fucking what? Who fucking cares?*

Before dumping the paper he peruses the sports section, then heads back down to the locker room, stopping along the way to catch a bit of Bender's manic workout, which involves jumping from a stationary bike to a treadmill to an elliptical machine and engaging in a furious two-minute sprint on each machine before taking a gasping forty-five-second break, then repeating the process.

Later, as they make their way down to the underground garage where his Audi covertible is parked, Bender explains what Richie's witnessed: it's his new All-in, All-out Circuit Method, copyright pending.

"As I like to say, either you're all in or you're all out. Or, in my case, both."

Richie asks whether a defibrillator is included. "I was kind of hoping you'd drop dead of a heart attack," he says, getting back in the car. "It seemed well within the realm of possibility."

Bender ignores the remark. On the way out he'd picked up an açaí berry–wheatgrass "cleansing" smoothie at the club's juice bar. He drops the cup into a well built into an armrest between the seats. Then he checks his email on his phone and taps out a quick message before plugging the phone into a car charger.

"Look, the idea here is not to be pissed at me," he says, backing out of the space. "I am the savior here. I am the Good Samaritan. Your ass would be on its way back to prison if I hadn't come along. Do you know how many companies would pay money to get twenty minutes of my time? Do you?"

He does. The souvenirs of Bender's meetings are littered across the floor of the trunk behind them—T-shirts, hats, coffee mugs, and assorted other tchotchkes emblazoned with a cornucopia of nonsensical company names and logos, all by-products of the golden rule of start-up naming: keep it short, seven letters or less.

"Here you are," Bender goes on. "You have my undivided attention for the next forty-eight hours. And you're still worried about the bad call you got back in the fourth and you don't realize you've just yanked one yard and cleared the bases. Enjoy the trip. Take a curtain call. Soak it in."

Tires screeching, he peels out from the underground garage, accelerating toward the intersection ahead. The light's green but seems in danger of turning yellow thanks to Bender's urgency.

"Where are we going?" Richie asks, a little alarmed that they've veered left onto El Camino instead of turning right and heading north toward Menlo Park, where Bender lives.

"To catch the killer."

"Excuse me?"

"Well, if you didn't do it, someone else did, right?"

"That's not part of the contract," Richie says.

"There's no contract on innocence."

"What the fuck does that mean?"

"I don't know. I just made it up. As you're probably aware by now, I tend to make shit up as I go along but it's all perfectly planned out. That's the beauty of me."

"Charming."

Bender reaches over and picks up his smoothie from the cup holder, takes a long drag on the straw.

"You know why I ponied up the cash for you?" he mumbles after a moment, his mouth still half full with the supercharged concoction.

"It's not what you think. It's not about making money off your story. That's a given. No, the real reason, quite frankly, is that I was bored. I needed intellectual stimulation. I needed a mixing of the disciplines."

"Where are we going?" Richie asks again. "Specifically?"

"Sunnyvale."

"What's there?"

"McGregor's office."

"Why are we going there?"

"To talk to Don Gattner, McGregor's right-hand guy. I know him."

Richie knows him, too. He tells Bender they crossed paths back in the day. He'd been part of their karaoke group at one point. Richie asks whether Gattner knows that he's coming.

"Sure," Bender says. "I've got an appointment."

"No, I mean me."

"What fun would it be if he knew you were coming?"

"You do understand that the police are probably following us?"

Bender glances up at the rearview mirror and takes a look at what—or rather who—is behind them.

"Oh, yeah? With the way I drive, you think they can keep up?"

They don't have to, you arrogant bastard, Richie thinks. Bender seems to have forgotten he's wearing a tracer bracelet.

"I'll stay in the car," he says.

"Fuck that. I didn't spend two hundred grand for you to sit in the car. That's like telling a hooker you just want to talk. There's no story in that. The story is in you walking into McGregor's office and getting some answers. This is about the money, friend. Screenshot this moment." He takes his hands off the wheel for a second, shapes his figures in to the bottom of a frame, and makes a little sound with his mouth that comes off as a cross between a camera shutter and gun going off. "This guy went down for money. Mark my words."

It's the first sane thing he's said.

"If I'm going in, I've got some questions I want to ask."

"I'm asking the questions," Bender says. "You'll be distracting him."

"From what?"

"His computer."

"Why?"

"Don't worry about it. Just when I give the signal, occupy him."

"What's the signal?"

"You'll know."

"I'll know?"

"Believe me, you'll know."

McGregor's office is in a business-park complex that's made up of several small two- and three-story structures surrounded by a parking lot. The complex is in a decent location, and while it's a bit nondescript, the architecture is attractive enough and the building seems fairly new, which means McGregor had probably been spending a decent chunk of change on rent, unless he'd gotten a deal subletting from a friend or investor.

Not surprisingly, the receptionist is a knockout: early twenties, with short dark hair, full lips, a perfect complexion, and bright, intelligent eyes. Knowing McGregor, she's getting paid well to sit around, look good, act friendly, and set a wow-these-guys-aren't-fucking-around tone, though today she looks pretty somber.

Bender takes her appearance in stride. "Well, you're fucking hot," he says. "We're here to see Don. But you know that. Because not only are you beautiful but you're clairvoyant."

That gets a little smile out of her. "I'll tell him you're here." As she picks up the phone to call Gattner he appears behind her. Richie guesses his office is close enough to the front desk that he's heard the whole conversation.

He comes out and shakes Bender's hand. "Hey, Tom."

The guy looks glum and weary, like he hasn't slept much in the last couple of days. Aside from the dark bags under his eyes, he doesn't look too different from when Richie last saw him. He's one of those guys who went bald at a young age and keeps his dark hair shorn very short. And his uniform of choice hasn't changed: jeans, running shoes, and a crisp white dress shirt with the top two buttons open, exposing a white T-shirt underneath.

"Sorry for your loss," Bender says perfunctorily, then steps to his right to give Gattner a better look at Richie, who's hung back a little. "You know, Rick, I think."

"Hey," Gattner says, extending a hand while looking up at Richie's baseball cap. "You affiliated with those guys?" he asks, referring to the scripted logo on the front of the hat.

Maybe it's because he's wearing the hat—or that he hasn't seen him in so long—but Gattner doesn't recognize him.

"No," Richie says. Out of the corner of his eye, he sees Bender studying Gattner's face, waiting for a reaction. Finally, he gets one.

"Shit," he says, taking a step back, his eyes opening wide. "Is that you, Richie?"

"Yeah, it's me, Don. How are things?"

Gattner looks at Bender, his expression now one of deep alarm. "What the fuck, Tom? What's he doing here?"

"I've got an exclusive. We're making the rounds. You're our first stop."

"What the fuck?" Gattner says again. Behind him, Richie catches a glimpse of the receptionist, who's trying to figure out what's going on. "I didn't know he'd even gotten out. I thought they'd sent him back to prison."

"I bailed him out a couple of hours ago," Bender says.

"Why'd you do that?"

"'Cause I'm kind and generous."

"The fuck you are. Are you fucking crazy bringing him here? Are you out of your mind? Get the fuck out or I'm going to call the police."

"Go ahead," Bender says. "You'll be out of business by tomorrow."

"What are you talking about?"

"I'll write that you're insolvent."

"That's bullshit. Look," he says, pointing to the room behind him, where a half dozen or so heads are visible through the cubicle windows. "Everybody showed up for work. Paychecks are going out tomorrow as usual. We've got cash in the bank. We're not insolvent. Far from it."

"After I write it, you will be."

"But it's not true."

"You don't own the future. It belongs to everyone."

Gattner, his head about to explode, now turns to Richie.

"Look, I'm sorry, man," he says, unexpectedly opting for a more conciliatory tone. "You know, I always liked you. You were a good guy. But this is wrong. This asshole calls me saying he's doing a tribute to Mark on his site and wants a few quotes and remembrances and would I mind meeting with him for a few minutes. Now there's clearly another agenda here. This is fucked up."

Richie smiles. Bender has some nerve. The guy's truly a dick. But Gattner's an idiot for agreeing to see him. He obviously couldn't resist the opportunity for some free publicity.

Richie: "A tribute, huh?"

"That was the plan," Bender says. "Plans change."

Gattner: "You're fucking demented, you know that? Threatening to write that we're insolvent if I don't talk to you. You'd go ahead and flat-out lie, that's what you're saying?"

"The road to the truth is often paved with lies. I forget who said that but I think it was someone famous. Oh, wait, it was me."

"Fuck you. I'll sue your fucking ass."

"Please do. I would thoroughly enjoy that. Lawsuits are my after-shave. I like to splash them on in the morning."

Bender then reaches for his wallet in his back pocket, and extracting a card from it, walks over to the receptionist and hands it to her.

"Email me," he says. "When you guys shut down, I'll get you a job. I also want to invite you to a benefit concert I'm planning. We're raising money for this guy's defense." This is news to Richie. *Concert? What concert?* "I want you to tell all your friends. And not just the hot ones. The clairvoyant ones, too."

He then turns to leave, motioning for Richie to follow him. From the defiant look on Gattner's face, Richie doesn't expect him to stop them, but just as they're about to hit the exit, he folds.

"Wait," he says.

Bender swivels slowly around.

"Yes?"

"You know you're a fucking bully," Gattner says. "We're all pretty traumatized here."

"I'm here to help you, Don." Bender's voice is surprisingly sincere. "I mean that."

"What do you want?"

"I want numbers. I want to know where you're at, where you've been, and where you're going. And who the players are."

"I can only tell you what's public already."

"You need to do a little better than that. Even if it's off the record."

Gattner lets out a little laugh. He knows Bender well enough to know he has a way of accidentally confusing "off" with "on."

"Have a little fucking respect," he says. "Just a smidgen. Would you?"

"Play a little ball and I will. I'm not going to fuck you, Don."

"I'm going to tape the conversation. If you make anything up, I'm going to post the recording."

"I don't make shit up unless it's true. That's the truth."

Gattner shakes his head, clearly questioning his judgment. He weighs his options one more time, then tries to set the terms.

"Okay, you can come back," he says. "But he stays here."

"You sure you want to do that, Don?" Richie counters, inspired. "Leave an accused killer out here with your lovely traumatized receptionist? You may end up with a lawsuit yourself."

Gattner looks at the receptionist, who now truly does seem traumatized. "Fine," he says. "Let's go."

The office is just an open room or "pen" with cubicles in the middle and some small offices around the perimeter that have glass fronts with shades you can draw for privacy. The place doesn't look much different from the outfits where Richie worked a decade ago. The décor, the minimal amount of it anyway, is right out of the Grind School of office design, exuding a creative, merry-band-of-misfits vibe that doesn't quite ring true. A small electric car is parked toward the front along with an electric scooter propped up against the side of a cubicle. On the floor, he notices a Nerf football, a Frisbee, and a cardboard box with a remote-control helicopter sitting on top of it in the middle of a homemade bull's-eye that marks its landing pad. It's fucking FAO Schwarz, the Lite version.

He suspects there's a small break room somewhere with Ping-Pong and foosball tables and perhaps a large flat-panel TV with a game console connected to it. Knowing McGregor, they probably also have access to some sort of outdoor space for "unwinding." The guy could be a slave driver but he'd also been a big believer in throwing impromptu celebrations for irrelevant successes. Richie remembered him walking out into the middle of the office on more than a few occasions and gustily proclaiming, "Are we having fun yet?" Plenty of people loved him but just as many came to the conclusion that he was a raging asshole.

Gattner is an equally polarizing character, but for different reasons. Where McGregor's charm was in his alpha-male bluster and directness, Gattner's good-intentioned straightforwardness is tinged with a touch too much weasel, like a diet soda with a questionable aftertaste.

Needless to say the guy is cagey. He says he met with detectives on Sunday and that they seized McGregor's work computer and some other items in the office. They questioned him for over an hour, asked the things you'd expect them to ask: Had McGregor expressed any concern that someone might want to do harm to him? Did he have any trouble with any particular individuals? When did he leave the office? And finally, did he mention having had any contact with Richie Forman?

At least from what he's telling them now, Gattner didn't seem to offer up any terribly revealing leads. He says that McGregor told him that someone claimed to have evidence that he was driving the car the night of the accident all those years ago and was now trying to blackmail him. While McGregor suspected Richie might have something to do with it, he wasn't sure.

"He told me that he was going to get to the bottom of it even if the police didn't," he tells Bender. "He was determined to figure out who was behind it. That's what I told the police."

Richie's sitting next to Bender, across the desk from Gattner, but he feels ignored, excluded. Gattner addresses only Bender, making it a point to pretend that Richie isn't in the room. Which is why he's surprised when all of sudden Gattner turns to him and says, "I'm going to take a SWAG and assume the cops asked you about blackmailing him."

Richie: "SWAG?"

"Scientific wild-ass guess."

"When did he hire the Tongans?"

Gattner's eyes blink, not once, but twice, then a third time. The question's clearly caught him off guard, but he decides to feign ignorance anyway.

"Who?"

"Come on, man. You fucking know damn well who."

"I'm not going to talk about them. There is an ongoing police investigation."

Richie leans forward in his seat and in a low, conspiratorial voice, says: "I heard they worked for the company. They were on the payroll."

Gattner's eyes shift to Bender, then back to him, then back to Bender.

"Where'd you get that photo of them you posted on your site, Tom?" Gattner asks. "Did Beth give that to you?"

"McGregor's wife?" Bender replies. "Why would she give it to me?"

"I don't know."

"Well, something made you think she'd give it to me, what was it?"

Gattner suddenly takes on the look of someone who's cornered. He realizes he's dug himself a little hole and it's not going to be easy to get out.

He shrugs, offering up a second "I don't know."

"Try again, Don," Bender says. "I know when someone's full of shit because I'm so full of shit."

Gattner falls silent. After a moment, he says, "They were interns. They did a little office work. Errands and stuff mostly. But McGregor was also using them for security. I didn't ask what they were doing but I know Mark was paranoid, clearly for good reason. And I know he was concerned with what Beth was up to. He didn't trust her. I can't say it any more simply than that. After hours, I think he paid them out of his own pocket. My impression was he was paying them extra because I can tell you they weren't making much here. I cut the checks."

"But why would you think Beth gave me the photo?" Bender asks.

"Because she knew they were following her. After that photo ran on your site, one of the guys—one of the Tongans—called me and said he was sure Beth had given it to you. He said he always knew she was a conniving little bitch. She was setting them up."

Richie: "That you calling her a conniving little bitch or them, Don? 'Cause the way you said it methinks it was more you than them."

"No, it wasn't me. Those were his words."

"Beth didn't think too highly of you, you know that, don't you?"

"News to me. We got along fine."

"She said you were unhappy with how much stock Mark had given you," Richie goes on. "She said you'd didn't think it was fair given how much work you were doing and how instrumental you were to the company."

"Did she? When did she tell you that?"

"Recently."

"Just before you killed Mark?"

Richie gives him a hard look that Gattner returns with his own don't-fuck-with-me stare. They lock eyes for a moment, then Gattner says, "We might as well get specific here while you're insulting me. I know where you were that day. I know you were with her. How did she convince you to do it? Tell you she still loved you?" He starts laughing. "Is that what she did, you dumbfuck?"

Richie sees himself stand up and grab Gattner by the collar and violently yank him over the desk and slam him to the floor. But before he can actually do it, Bender says:

"How much of the company do you have, Don?"

Gattner looks over at him, a little surprised by Bender's flat, unemotional tone.

"What?"

"You heard me. What's your piece of the pie?"

"Around five percent or so."

"So, what are we talking about, a thirty, thirty-five million dollar valuation. I think that's what I heard."

"Something like that."

"And you haven't made a dime."

"Course not. But we've got plenty of strategic partnerships lined up. We've been signing up vendors for the last three months. We've got over a thousand on board so far. We'll have over twice that at launch."

He then gives them a brief history of their financing. Gattner says McGregor put up the better part of a million in seed money and had then gone out and raised close to twelve million. They hadn't expected to raise that much. They were looking for more like half that. But the mobile market was so hot and this Australian investor, Grant Cahill, came along and didn't blink twice at the valuation they insisted on.

"We talked to a few of the big VCs and the truth is we could have gotten them to invest based on Mark's track record. But they were going to drive a much harder bargain and Mark didn't want them up his ass all the time. You know how it is."

Richie knows that one of the big benefits to having a Sequoia, KPCB, or Andreessen Horowitz on board is that it's easier to hire engineers and programmers. They figure that, with one of the heavies behind you, the odds are greater for an exit event, which is ultimately what all these guys are after. But the heavies also keep very careful watch over their investments. They dole out payments in smaller chunks and do rigorous due diligence every step of the way.

"Truthfully, Mark's strategy was to get a foreign investor all along. He dabbled with the Russians and Chinese, but was happy as hell this Aussie Cahill came along. The guy was like eight thousand miles away and he spoke fluent English. He'd made a fortune in minerals but wanted to broaden himself into high tech. Mark knew he'd be much easier to deal with."

Gattner says everything was going well until they discovered that another start-up was basically on their way to doing the exact same thing they were doing—except their way seemed better and they seemed about six months ahead.

"Mark kind of panicked," Gattner says. "These guys—it was only two of them—were in stealth mode and somehow Cahill got wind of it. Mark tried to convince him that it would be okay, but then we just ended up buying the company. It was the easiest thing to do."

"How much did you pay?"

"We didn't disclose that," Gattner says.

"Ballpark?"

"Let's just say it ate up a nice chunk of the initial investment."

"So how much do you have left?"

"Enough. Mr. Cahill put up some additional money recently and he has no intention of letting this thing go down the drain, especially with us so close to launch. He called to tell me that yesterday in fact. If you want to speak with him, I'll give you his number. He's got deep pockets."

Bender isn't impressed. He says they all say they have deep pockets until they have to reach inside them.

"Shit, they could have pockets to their goddamn ankles, but what good is that when they suddenly develop stubby thalidomide arms."

"I sent you a code for our private beta," Gattner says. "We've got twenty-five thousand people using the service. I don't suppose you checked it out."

"It was on my plate and then it slipped off."

"Well, maybe you should check it out before you dismiss it."

"Frankly, I didn't see the there there. It seemed derivative, another Groupon/Living Social clone."

"It's far more sophisticated than that. These are real-time deals in real space. This is the grail."

"You say grail, I say fail."

"Well, if that's your fucking attitude, I don't think we have anything else to talk about."

"Come on, don't take it personally. What the fuck do I know? I'm only batting nine twenty and was the Tech Blogger of the Year five of the last seven years. But who's counting?"

Gattner shakes his head. "You know what your problem is? You're so morally and emotionally bankrupt that your sole goal in life is to bring everybody down to your level."

"I can't totally disagree with you, so I won't. But here's my question. The company McGregor picked up, who were the guys? Who were the coders? I assume that's why he paid what he did for the company."

"For competitive reasons, I can't disclose that."

"I'm going to find out."

"Go ahead."

"Are they still at the company?"

"I'm not going to disclose that. I'm honestly not sure what I should and shouldn't be saying, so I really have to talk to someone before I overstep myself."

"Tell me this then: how hands-on was McGregor? You can answer that, right? He doesn't do any coding himself anymore, does he?"

"Nah. Not that it's beneath him or anything. I mean, I'd see him talking to some of the guys about certain bugs—we had a couple of marathon bug-bash sessions recently. But at this point, we were mainly tweaking the interface and talking about features we wanted to add in the next version. He'd draw up wireframes and give it to the programmers and tell them what he wanted. The engine was done. We were just refining it. We were planning a one point five version for next year that was more robust."

Bender: "Who's is in charge now?"

Gattner flashes a smile. "For the moment, me. But it depends on what the will says, right? Mark had the controlling interest."

"Did he leave it to his wife?"

"I'm not in a position to comment on that. I think we should know soon enough, though." He pauses for a moment and when Bender doesn't say anything right away, he says: "Is that it? Are we done here? Because I think I've been pretty damn accommodating if you ask me. We've got nothing to hide. As hard as it will be, the company can survive this."

Bender nods, then gets up and extends a hand, suddenly and remarkably kicking into affable Tom mode. "I owe you one," he says, and promises to cover the app when it officially launches, please give him an early heads-up.

Gattner sees them back to the reception area and begins to say his farewells when Bender mumbles something about his protein smoothie running through him and that he needs to take a leak. Is there a bathroom he can use?

Gattner points him back toward the offices. "All the way down to the left," he says. "There's a little hallway. First door."

Richie realizes that this is the you'll-know-when moment Bender was referring to back in the car.

"I've seen it," he says to Gattner.

"Seen what?"

"The app. Beth showed it to me."

"What'd you think?"

"I actually thought it looked pretty good."

He then begins to critique it, making sure to keep Gattner looking in the direction of the exit rather than behind him toward the pen. The more kind words he has, the more Gattner is drawn in. He talks about the interface, points out what he likes about it and mentions a couple of things he thinks could be improved. As he gives his two cents, he catches a glimpse of Bender walking back toward them. He then disappears, presumably checking into Gattner's office, which is out of Richie's line of view.

Come on, asshole, he thinks, listening to Gattner rationalize one of the design choices they've made. *Hurry up*. He wonders how long he can hold his attention. Every time Gattner turns to look in the direction of his office, he quickly reels him back with a compliment.

As Gattner starts to swivel around again (he's obviously started to wonder where Bender is), Richie reaches into the barrel one more time, scraping bottom.

"To me, it's just a scalability issue," he says. "Like all this stuff, it's live or die on that. You need to ramp up the users at warp speed or it just isn't going to work. I know you have a big social element, but I'm just not sure how viral this thing can be without better incentives. It doesn't seem to lend itself to building organically through search engines, so I think you're going to have to market the hell out of it in pretty traditional ways, and you know, then it comes down to money and good ideas."

Gattner seems to have forgotten whom he's talking to. It's not Richie, accused killer. It's like the old days, the two of them talking shop—or shit—as the case often was.

"You know, here's the fucked-up thing," he says. "I told Mark to bring you back. You know he was so fucking paranoid about you and what you were going to do to him, I said Mark, you know the old saying, 'Keep your enemies close.' Well, I said bring Richie back. We could use him. No one else is going to give him a shot with a decent title and all that. Ask him. I bet he goes for it. And he kind of looked at me like I was crazy at first but then I could see it hit home. He said, 'You know, that's not bad idea. I'm going to think about it.' And I said call Richie, feel him out, because frankly I didn't know if you'd be interested. I'd heard the Sinatra stuff was going pretty well. But at least he could get a sense of where things stood. I just said, fuck, confront this shit directly. I know he tried to contact you when you first got out and to offer to help you out with some cash and you blew him off. But who knows, maybe things had changed."

Richie looks down, absorbing Gattner's little speech, no longer concerned about Bender.

"Well, I wouldn't have done it, Don. I didn't want to have anything to do with Mark."

Just then, over Gattner's shoulder, behind the receptionist, he sees Bender reappear, smilling as he flashes a quick V for victory signal with his fingers.

"Maybe he would have made you an offer you couldn't refuse," Gattner says.

"He wouldn't have."

"Why not?"

"Because it would've killed him to do it."

27 / ASS OR ARM

CAROLYN IS PEERING INTO HER REFRIGERATOR, COMTEMPLATING cracking open a bottle of white wine, when she hears the familiar *ding* of a text message from her phone in the other room. Her text communications have been in the unpleasant camp, so the sound makes her apprehensive. But this time when she goes to look at her phone, she's happy to discover the message is from Cogan, who's simply written: "Shot up yet?"

"Nope," she responds. She's just just come back from having dinner with Beth Hill and is still wearing her work clothes, a blue pants suit and white blouse. "Long day," she adds. "Against doctor's orders staring longingly at unopened sauvignon blanc."

She watches the phone's screen, waiting. It has been a long day. In the morning, she and Beth met with McGregor's estate attorney about the will and spent the better part of the day going over finances, which she'd used as an excuse to keep stiff-arming Madden. Meanwhile, Richie Forman had posted bail and Lowenstein was busy filing discovery motions. She'd been trying to keep abreast of all of that and more.

Ding.

"Want some help? With shot, not bottle. But can help there 2."

Shit yes, she thinks. Then, mustering every reserve of willpower, she writes:

"I'm ok. Thx for offering."

His reply takes a little longer this time, but not much.

"Saw you on TV today. Looked and sounded good."

She's gotten similar messages from a dozen or so other people.

She's about to type another "Thx" when he tacks on another sentence:

"Have some info for you."

"About what?"

"Ok if I stop by?"

"When?"

The next text that comes through is actually a picture. It's thumbnail sized and while she can see that it's a picture of him, she taps on it to enlarge. The background looks familiar despite the poor lighting.

She goes to the door and opens it, and there he is, standing there with his phone in his hand.

"Oh, hello," he says.

Expressionless, she stares at him a moment, then looks down at her phone and types: "Not amused."

After the message arrives, he types back, "Don't be a hardass. I know you're happy I'm here. I saw you smiling through the window when you were reading my texts."

"Really not amused now," she types. "Spying on me?"

"Yes," he writes back. "But not in a creepy way."

She struggles to suppress a smile. To stifle it, she looks up and says: "What's the info?"

"Let me shoot you up and I'll talk to you about it."

"You drive a hard bargain, Cogan," she says, then turns and walks back inside, leaving the door open behind her.

"Ass or arm?" he asks, following her into the living room.

"What?"

"Where do you want it?"

She ignores the question, giving his appearance a more thorough inspection. On second glance, his clothes seem neater than usual. His hair is combed, too, which leads her to believe he's on his way out rather than returning home.

"You work today?" she asks.

"Was off. But I went in. For you."

"You didn't have to."

"You were curious about McGregor's health so I poked around a bit. For the record, let's just say I overheard a couple of nurses gossiping in the courtyard over coffee."

"Cheeky. What'd you hear?"

"Like you said, the guy had some tightness in his chest, so he went to the emergency room. Told the attending that he had some pain in his arm, some light-headedness and shortness of breath. You know, classic heart-attack symptoms. So they do an EKG and some blood work and he seems okay. It's most likely a GI issue because GI issues end up presenting a lot like cardio issues, which can cut both ways. You get people thinking they have heartburn when, in fact, it's a much more serious issue. Anyway, you've got to run the blood test a few times over a twenty-four-hour period to get an accurate reading. There's this enzyme called CKMB—it's a form of creatine kinase—whose levels rise if you have any damage to your heart muscles. Usually if the levels aren't elevated on the first test you haven't had a heart attack, but that isn't always the case. To be safe, the attending decided to keep him overnight for observation and to run the follow-up CKMB the next day, along with a stress test."

Usually, she likes hearing all the medical terms, which is why he went into the detail he did. But tonight she's tired and impatient.

"Okay," she says. "That's it?"

She's kind of hoping it is because that would mean he'd used this pathetic little report as an excuse to get to see her.

"Come on," he says. "You know I'm better than that."

"What'd you get?"

"How 'bout we do the shot first?"

"Don't worry about the shot. I can do it. When you're genetically involved, you can do the shot."

He looks at her, his eyes boring into her, their sudden intensity startling her.

"Just let me do the goddamn shot for you, Carolyn," he says testily and suddenly it dawns on her that something's a little different. Something's changed.

"Okay, okay. Geez."

"Ass or arm?" he asks, his voice calm again.

"I've been doing it in the stomach," she says, leading him to the bathroom, her heart beating harder. "I'm supposed to pinch the skin, get a little hunk to jab into. But I'm such a baby."

The capped, preloaded syringes are in a box on a shelf in a small linen closet next to a syringe disposal container that has a biohazard warning symbol on its label. She fishes a syringe out of the box and hands it to him along with a couple of alcohol swabs.

"Drop your pants, Counselor," he says nonchalantly, tearing open one of the alcohol swabs.

She knows full well she can just expose the top of her rump and that'll be enough. But with a little glint in her eye, she decides to take him literally. She unbuttons her pants, pulls the zipper down, then tucks her thumbs under the elastic band of her panties and slowly slides both layers to her knees, leaving her blouse dangling there, providing a bit of coverage. Turning away and bending forward slightly, she rests her left hand on the counter and then lifts the back of her blouse from the bottom with her right hand.

"Don't miss," she says, looking back over her shoulder.

She watches his eyes drift downward and his Adam's apple rise, then fall, as he goes to work with the alcohol swab on a spot just below her hip on the right side. He pulls the syringe's cap off with his teeth, and jabs her with the needle, causing her to wince. It's over in a second. He sets the syringe aside, applies some pressure to the pricked area with the second swab, then guides her blouse back down her ass, conveniently managing to brush the back of his hand against her skin.

She turns to face him and they stand there for a moment staring at each other. But before he gets too many ideas she reaches down and slowly and deliberately wiggles her pants and underwear up her legs. When everything's back in place, she goes to the closet and gets the container for the used syringes and hands it to him.

"So what'd you hear? Or were you just bullshitting me so you could stick me?"

"Come on."

She heads back to the kitchen and decides to open the bottle of wine after all. She needs something to do with her hands, afraid what they might do if they're not occupied. But just as she's about to give the screw cap a twist he says, "Hold up," and takes the bottle from her.

"Here's the deal," he says. "The guy was in the hospital almost two years ago. I pulled his chart. Nothing too exciting. They prescribed antacids, referred him to a GI, told him he might consider getting an endoscopy for piece of mind. Who knows, it could be severe heartburn, an ulcer, maybe even an anxiety attack. Whatever. They discharged him the next afternoon. I figure I'm going to leave it at that but then I decide what the hell, I know one of the nurses, Janie, who did the blood work on him the next day, maybe she remembers something.

"I find out she's on duty so I swing over to have a chat with her," he continues. "And I say, 'Hey, I don't know if you noticed but this guy McGregor who got killed the other night and who's been in all the papers spent the night in the cardio wing about two years ago. And I figure she'd draw a blank but instead, you know, her eyes open wide and she asks me whether the police have talked to me. I shake my head, and playing it dumb I say, 'Uh, no. Why, have they talked to you?'

"She kind of mumbles something and I can't quite tell what she's saying, so I ask her to say it again. And then she tells me she put in a call. They had some sort of tip line and she put in a call. And, you know, I'm a little surprised. I say, 'Why would you do that?'"

Now Carolyn's the one with the wide eyes.

"She spoke to the police?" she asks. "Why?"

"I'm getting to that."

He says Janie didn't want to talk about it in the hospital so he met her a little while later for a cup of coffee outside in the courtyard. That's when she told him why she remembered the guy: He'd said some things in the hospital that had concerned her at the time. She didn't know if he was joking or exaggerating but he said a few things that were a little disturbing.

"To her? What, did he try to pick her up or something?"

"Actually, no. He wasn't talking to her. She just overheard him talking in the room."

"To whom?"

Cogan explains that McGregor had apparently asked for a private room but they didn't have one so they stuck him in the bed they had available, which was in a room with this guy in his thirties who'd tried to commit suicide. He'd gone to a motel and taken a bunch of sleeping pills and if a maid hadn't seen him through the drapes lying there on the bed, he probably would have succeeded.

A nurse was sitting in a chair in the room near the door when McGregor got there. He noticed the woman sitting there and asked Janie about it when she came in to give him some dinner. She quietly explained that his roommate had tried to harm himself so they had to keep a nurse on watch to make sure he didn't try it again. It was the manifestation of the term "suicide watch."

McGregor seemed impressed. It suddenly occurred to him that he was in a real hospital with real people who were really sick and that he wasn't in some convalescent home or something like that. And he was joking around about the seriousness of the place when he said, "What if someone is trying to do harm to you, would you get a nurse like that?"

What did he mean, someone? Janie asked.

"Like another person," he said.

And she said no, you'd probably get an actual police officer. And he said something like, "Oh come on, you look tough, you'd protect me, wouldn't you?"

"So he was hitting on her," Carolyn interrupted. "What's this Janie look like?"

"She's fine. She's married and has two kids."

"Never stopped you."

"Please."

"Sorry. That wasn't nice. Go on."

"Well, the guy wakes up the next day, and they bring in a psychiatrist to speak with him. That's standard procedure."

Because there was only a curtain divider in the room, McGregor could hear the whole conversation. Janie came back later that morning and heard the two of them talking. McGregor was asking the guy about what it was like to wake up and find out he wasn't dead. And then he said something to the effect of "Well, at least you don't have your wife wanting you dead." And Janie realized from the way he said it he might not be joking. Innocently enough, she asked:

"Where is your wife, Mr. McGregor? Has she been here to visit you?"

"I didn't even tell her I was here," he said. "I didn't want to give her the satisfaction. She's probably hoping I drove off a cliff."

She vividly remembered him saying that, which really got to her. *I didn't want to give her the satisfaction.*

"But she didn't say anything to anybody at the time?" Carolyn asks. "There's no formal record of this? No police report or anything?"

"I don't think so. I think she just called this tip line now because she saw the number in the paper."

She'd heard from Madden that they'd received several hundred tips about people who'd either seen Richie Forman with Beth Hill the day of the murder or claimed to have information related to the murder. She somehow doubted a conversation in a hospital room nearly two years ago would have made it high on their call-back priority list. But chances were good one of the detectives would eventually speak with Janie to check whether there really was anything to the tip.

She's asking herself that question now. So what, the guy spouts off about his wife two years ago in his hospital room. If it had happened a week or two ago, even last month, it would have carried more weight. But a couple of years? Big deal. People were always spouting off about their spouses. She had a friend who said she could never have a gun in the house because she was afraid she'd shoot her husband. She was completely serious, though that hadn't stopped her from being married to the guy for twenty-one years. They were mostly good years but he sometimes pissed her off so much that she didn't know what she was capable of.

"If McGregor thinks his wife wants to kill him, he doesn't leave her most of his estate," she says to Cogan, thinking aloud. "That just doesn't make sense."

"I don't know," he says. "Maybe it was a rough patch. I'm just telling you what I overheard and how it relates to your new client. But you figure that if he's saying this stuff to a nurse in the hospital, he's probably told other people the same thing. That's the way it usually works."

He has a point, she thinks, her mind drifting to what Beth told her back at the hotel. *That drug is incredibly intense and wonderful for about twenty minutes. It's awesome. But the side effect, the hangover, whatever you want to call it, is just brutal.*

"Look, I gotta go," he says. "But a card is going to accidentally fall out of my pocket on my way out, which means I didn't give it to you. It's got a name on the back of it. If the guy hasn't managed to off himself yet, at least you'd have a second witness to go to if something like this becomes a factor."

He slides the card onto the kitchen counter, then kisses her on the cheek and turns to leave.

She looks at the card, which has the Parkview Medical Center logo on the front but isn't personalized in any way; there's just an address and phone number. Suddenly, she realizes he's taken her bottle.

"Hey, my wine," she calls after him.

"Requisitioning it," he says, his back to her, holding it up above his shoulder as if to toast her. "I've got a birthday to go to. Jim Toumey's turning fifty. And I'm late. Thanks."

"No fair."

"You'll get it back. Soon. I promise."

Then he's gone. *Fucker*, she thinks, wondering if he slipped her the card as a misdirection play. She half expects to turn it over and see nothing on the back. But indeed there's a name and number on the other side and she does what most people would do after reading it: she goes to her computer in the other room and types the name into the Google search bar.

"Okay, Mr. Paul Anderson," she says to herself as she types. "Let's see if you still exist."

28 / A RADICAL FORM OF CAPITALISM

"GO HOME, HANK," SAYS CARLYLE, STANDING BEHIND HIM IN FULL uniform, radio clipped on. He's just started his regular shift. "Go see your wife and kids. I'll keep an eye on him on tonight."

"I'm going," Madden says. "In a minute."

He's sitting at the desk in his small office, watching the little blip on his computer screen that's Richie Forman, who appears to be making his way back to Tom Bender's house. The pace of the blip on the map had thrown him at first. It had seemed to be moving too slowly for Forman to be in a car but too quickly for him to be on foot. Madden guessed bike, and sure enough, when he diverted a squad car to do a drive-by, the officer confirmed that Forman was cruising along on a mountain bike.

It seemed like an odd thing to do, riding around after dark, but it had been a day filled with oddities. They'd tracked Forman to the Equinox gym, then the offices of Crune, McGregor's old company, a second office building in Mountain View, then on to a series of more mundane stops at Long's Drugs in the Town and Country Shopping Center and some shops along University Avenue in Palo Alto.

He was momentarily stunned when he found out Forman was palling around with Bender. It seemed beneath Lowenstein to swing such a deal. But then again, if he was in his shoes, he probably wouldn't have wanted to scrape together $2 million in cash or collateral for a pro-bono client—or drop two hundred grand on the 10 percent nonrefundable fee for the bail bond. Which didn't leave him much choice. But Bender? Christ.

Carlyle's radio crackles behind him. The dispatcher mentions something about a house alarm going off. Although last year they did have a string of burglaries over a period of three months (two guys from way out in Merced were behind them), Madden thinks the owner probably tripped it. Armed it when he thought he was disarming it. The usual bullshit.

"He still over at Stanford?" Carlyle asks.

Madden shakes his head. "On his way back to Bender's."

Forman hadn't gone far on the bike. Using mainly side streets, he'd ridden about two and a half miles from Bender's house in Menlo Park to Angell Field, Stanford's track-and field site, where he'd run around the track for around thirty minutes.

Now he's almost back. Madden takes note of the blip's location, then switches to another window he previously had open and brings it front and center on the screen. It's a close-up of the snake tattoo on McGregor's hip. *Sedition 1918*. It's been vexing him. There seems to be no question that the wording on the tattoo refers to the Sedition Act of 1918, which he's spent a little too much time researching. According to various websites, on May 16, 1918, Congress, in an affront to First Amendment rights, amended and extended the Espionage Act of 1917 to make it against the law to say anything "disloyal, profane, scurrilous," about the U.S. government. This included the flag and military institutions.

What's so troubling is that he still has no clue what "sedition" has to do with McGregor. As far as he can tell, the term refers to subversion or a subversive act, and though it occurs to him that some Silicon Valley entrepreneurs view themselves and their products as disrupting markets, McGregor, from what he's learned about him, wasn't exactly the subversive type.

He imagines some sort of secret society whose members run around with snake tattoos on their hips symbolizing their radical form of capitalism. Or a secret order of hackers. That seems more plausible in light of the word "Hack" written in blood near McGregor's body. The only problem with this theory is that if Forman committed the murder, he'd have likely written the word as a diversionary tactic. Should he be discounting its presence as much as he has? Probably not. Nevertheless he fixates on different clues.

But the more he contemplates the tattoo's potential symbolism, the more absurd each guess seems, or as Billings put it: "Hank, man, you've been reading too many Dan Brown novels."

Alas, he's never read a Dan Brown book in his life. Or seen the movies.

"Anything come up?" Carlyle asks now.

Madden shakes his head. "There's one political cartoon with a snake in it."

He's calls up the image on his computer for Carlyle.

The cartoon bears the caption "As gag-rulers would have it" and has a drawing of a large snake with the words "Sedition Bills" written on its tail. The snake's tongue is wagging menacingly at three Little Rascals–looking kids holding small sticks in their hands. The kids represent "honest opinion," "free speech," and "free press." As for the snake, it looks a little like the one in the tattoo, but it's far from being a match.

Carlyle looks at it for moment, shrugs, and says, "For all we know the guy got drunk one night and ended up pointing to something in a book."

Madden doubts that. "I had Billings email this picture to every tattoo parlor around here and a few up in the city. Nothing so far."

"Do you know if he got it in the Bay Area?"

No, he doesn't. That's the problem. He tells him that Beth wasn't exactly sure when or where her husband got it, though she was pretty certain it was after they got married. When she told him about it, she just said he had "a little snake tattoo on his hip." She didn't mention any words.

"You're wasting your time, Hank," Carlyle concludes. "Send it to the feds. Who's your buddy there? Santorum?"

"Santoro," Madden corrects him. Carlyle, a staunch Republican, has been watching one too many Republican presidential debates.

"They've got a serious fucking database. If it's some sort of cult or secret society, they're going to have something. Do it tomorrow. Go home now. Google will only take you so far."

Carlyle's right. He is wasting his time. He closes out the window and calls up the tracking map again. The blip has stopped. Forman's back at Bender's. He minimizes the window, revealing the Google Docs spreadsheet underneath it that Billings has put together for the tips that have come in. Madden's gone through all the tips, one by one, and placed a *1*, *2*, or 3 in the column marked "priority." Billings, Burns, and a couple of other officers have been working through them, inputting their comments on the spreadsheet and flagging promising leads that may be worth an in-person interview. Most of the tips marked with a *1* have remarks in the comments box and probably a quarter of the tips designated *2* have also been investigated.

Once more he skims past the name Janie Cowen in row 241. The tip associated with her name, "Woman overheard McGregor saying wife wanted to kill him approx. two years ago," continues to fail to make much of an impression (he'd graded it a 3). Later, he'll realize he dismissed it mainly because whoever had taken down the tip had been too vague in his or her description. If it had read, "Nurse in hospital overhears . . ." he would have rated it higher.

As it is, only a handful of the tips have proven helpful. They've had more luck with some surveillance footage from one of McGregor's neighbors' security cameras that caught his car driving past followed by a bicyclist twenty minutes later. Because the video was low resolution it didn't have much detail, but the biker appeared to be Forman. After arriving at 4:28, he left the area eight minutes and forty-two seconds later.

Crowley thinks the ID will stand up in court, and they've also lifted a pair of partial prints from the buzzer box outside McGregor's home that matched the prints on Forman's middle and index fingers on his right hand. He appeared to have pressed the button with his thumb while briefly laying his other fingers on the metal part of the box.

He closes the Google Docs window, takes a look at his email inbox, then closes that out, too.

Carlyle continues to hover over him. "You're leaving, right?"

Madden calls up the map one more time. The blip remains motionless, parked at Bender's address.

"If he heads out, I'll call you," Carlyle says. "I'll tail him myself if he leaves."

Madden nods, reluctantly shutting down his computer. He puts on his coat, picks up his keys from the desk, and drops them in the right front pocket of his coat. Carlyle walks him out through the empty office. It's after seven, everybody else has punched out. Most have been gone at least an hour.

"There's one thing that's been bothering me," Madden says, walking out to his car.

"Just one thing?" Carlyle replies.

"Well, a lot of things. But one thing I was thinking about was what does the guy do with the weapon? He's got a bag, right? So, what, he wipes the hatchet down, sticks it in his bag, rides off on the bike, and what, dumps it in the woods up there in Woodside?"

"Sure. He could have wrapped it in a shirt. Or a newspaper or something. Presumably, he has something in the bag or else he wouldn't be carrying the bag."

"I realize that. But we've got the bag and it's clean."

Carlyle considers that. "Look, the thing isn't huge," he says. "It's not a full-on ax. In a lot of ways it's perfect. It's easily concealable. It's easier to use than a hunting knife, does a heck of a lot of damage."

"He could have just left it there. It was McGregor's after all."

"He could have."

"I wanna send someone up there."

"Where?"

"Along his bike route."

Carlyle's radio crackles again. The dispatcher reports they've gotten a 911 call from someone saying he's captured a "wanted man." She gives an address and he and Carlyle look at each other. It sounds awfully familiar.

Carlyle engages the microphone that's clipped onto his uniform near his clavicle and turns his head to speak into it. "Carlyle here. Can you repeat that address, please?"

She calls it out again. It's Bender's all right.

"Did the caller give a name?" Carlyle asks. "Please confirm."

"Yes, Bender. Tom Bender. And he asked for an ambulance for his dog."

Carlyle looks at Madden, then turns his head to speak into the microphone again.

"Did you say dog?"

"Roger that. D-O-G dog."

29 / PROTECTING YOUR SOURCES

RICHIE DOESN'T TELL BENDER WHERE HE'S GOING, HE JUST SAYS HE wants to get out for a bit and clear his head and would he mind lending him the mountain bike he saw in his garage for a quick ride?

Bender isn't keen on the idea. Immersed in dashing off a quick two-thousand-word rant on his site, he tells him to hang tight, he's almost done. The contract, he notes, only stipulates for eight hours of sleep and one hour of "independent recreation," and the trip to Equinox qualified as independent recreation in his book; after all, he'd been permitted to roam the gym freely, had he not?

Everything with Bender is a goddamn negotiation, and in the end, he only relents after Richie offers to amend the contract by hand and extend his stay by an hour.

"You don't come back, there will be serious repercussions," Bender warns.

By the time he gets to the track it's fully dark outside and the lights are on. The facility isn't loaded with people but there's a half dozen or so runners, some going about their business more seriously than others. He knows she probably won't be there yet—he's fifteen minutes early—but he does a quick search before walking the bike over to the infield and setting it down in a spot near the middle where he can keep an eye on it while he runs.

He hasn't been to Angell Field in more than eight years. Earlier in the day, as he and Bender drove past the Stanford campus, he had a flashback of running there with Beth. They'd gone there occasionally at night and he always remembered the place fondly, maybe because she always looked so good in her running tights and Nike running hat.

When he called her in her room at the hotel (Ashley, with a little finessing of a hotel employee and perhaps even a small bribe, had discovered she was staying there under her neighbor's name), he hadn't expected her to pick up. When she did—and then agreed to meet him—he quickly had to come up with a rendezvous point. Angell Field it was.

He stretches his calves, then heads out onto the track, gradually ratcheting up his pace. He's on lap six, the 1.5-mile mark, when he spots her. She's standing by the oval near the entrance wearing a loose-fitting dark gray sweat suit, her head covered by the top's hood. As he goes past, he slows but doesn't stop.

"Come on," he says. "Run with me."

He keeps up the slow pace until she's beside him, then picks it up a little.

"Not too fast," she says. "I haven't been running."

"Anybody follow you?"

"I don't think so. You?"

"I've got a tracer bracelet on my ankle," he says. "They know where I am all the time. Every once in a while I get buzzed by a squad car but I don't think I've got an official tail."

A short pause, then: "I'm sorry about the Marriott," she says.

He'd told her on the phone that not surprisingly he'd lost the gig at the Marriott. The manager said that "regrettably" he was going to have to "hold off" using him for now. Now that he was dealing with an accused killer, the bastard had gone from being Mr. Gruff to Mr. Polite.

"I told him that with my newfound notoriety I could really pack them in and that he was a fool for not booking me, someone else would."

"Someone will," she says.

"This guy Bender wants to do a concert around here somewhere to raise money for my legal defense. But he's fucking crazy."

They run in silence for about a hundred yards and then he says: "You know what I came here to ask you."

"I didn't set you up, Richie."

She'd always had the eerie ability to know what he was going to say before he said it, and he'd never minded it, even found it endearing. But this time her quick response grates.

"You sure about that? Last I checked, you were the one who said you wanted him dead, didn't you?"

She pulls up suddenly and puts her hands on her hips, her jaw clenched. He stops, too, and when he does, she lunges toward him and grabs him, pulling him toward her with her left hand. He then feels her other hand slip underneath his sweatshirt and she begins to grope him. But that's not really what she's doing. She's fucking patting him down.

"Are you wearing a wire?" she says in a low voice, a little wild-eyed. "Are you wearing a fucking wire? Is that what you're doing?"

He tears away from her and pulls off his sweatshirt, then his T-shirt, until he's standing there bare-chested on the edge of the infield grass, giving her his best Marky Mark.

"You want the pants off, too," he says. "Oh wait, you already did a dick-check the other day at Watercourse Way."

He doesn't get the feisty reaction he expects. Instead, she just stares at him the same way she did back in the private hot-tub room when he'd stripped down. Part of her still can't get over his chiseled new body. He was in decent shape before he went away, but now he truly does look like he could be on a billboard in an underwear ad.

When she realizes she's staring, she looks down, embarrassed. "Put your shirt back on," she says. "It's cold." And then she jogs away.

It doesn't take long to catch up to her.

"So you're saying Watercourse Way was a spontaneous act? It wasn't planned?"

"I didn't say I wanted him dead. I didn't."

She's still stuck on that.

"Well, what? What was the exact quote, 'I sometimes wish he was dead. I wish he'd just go away.' *Want*, *wish*, what's the difference? It's fucking semantics."

"I wish I could run a little faster. Do I want to? Not really. There's a difference. And you took what I said out of context anyway."

He laughs. "Context? You'd just fucked my brains out and you're lying there naked on a towel, all fucking splayed out, casually sharing your inner thoughts like you're talking to your shrink or something. Context?"

The image is indelible. More than the sex, more than the sensation of tasting her mouth again, that image of her lying there had remained with him. He couldn't get it out of his head, the way she kept pulling her wet hair back as she spoke, her eyes staring up at the ceiling. She looked completely relaxed and yet possessed at the same time.

"Just leave," he'd said. "File for divorce."

She let out a laugh. "He'll kill me before that happens," she said. "His precious money. His precious fucking company. He can't stand the idea of giving any of it up."

"I told you, go to the police. You have to."

"He's smarter than that. You don't know how smart he is. You always underestimated him."

She was right about that.

"I didn't come here to fight, Richie," she says now. "I shouldn't have let Watercourse Way happen. I shouldn't have brought you into my shit."

"But you did, Beth. And it wasn't an accident. So don't get all hindsight on me."

She falls silent. Several strides later she says, "You know what the funny thing was? Things were okay when you were in prison. Out of sight, out of mind, right? But it all started to deteriorate a few months before you got out. It weighed on him, you getting out. I could see it. And then I wanted to know again. Sometimes I said to myself it was for you but it was really for me."

Now he's the one who pulls up. "Know what?"

She stops, too, and stands there, hands on hips, trying to catch her breath. "I told you not to go so fast," she says.

"Know what, Beth?"

"Whether he really switched places on you. I believed you, Richie, I really did. But part of me wanted to hear it from him. It became sort of an obsession."

She says that was what some of the drinking and drugs were about. She figured she'd loosen him up and get him to talk about it. She'd ask in different ways, approach it from different angles, and every time he'd say he wasn't behind the wheel. He told the same story every time.

Then one morning when things were at one of their low points, they were sitting in the kitchen, each having their coffee, reading the newspaper, when he turned to her and said, "I love you, Beth, and if it makes you feel any better, I was driving."

For a second, she thought she'd imagined it. She was pretty hungover and her head was a little foggy. *Did he just say what I think he said*? Here, she'd tried to ply him with all these substances, she'd even looked into how she might administer one of the so-called truth serums, sodium pentothal or some other barbiturate, and now, totally sober, he'd offhandedly confessed, wedging it between a couple of layers of conflicted emotions. As far as sandwiches go, it didn't taste good, and her first response, ironically, was not to believe him.

"Yeah, I did it," he said. "But not for the reasons you think I did."

And then he got up from the table and left.

"He wouldn't talk about it after that," she tells Richie now. "It was as if he hadn't said it. But he basically replaced one uncertainty with another. It was sick. It was as if he knew I was giving up, that I was losing my curiosity and would ditch him if it disappeared."

The revelation leaves Richie not so much stunned as steamed—and in the cool night air, now that he's stopped running, there's literally steam rising from his body. He should have known that the vindication he's sought all these years would arrive with such a resounding and dissatisfying whimper. *Fucking great,* he thinks. *Just fan-fucking-tastic.*

"Why didn't you tell me this the other day?" he asks.

"You were already so disappointed with me. It was hard to have someone who used to love me so much have so much disdain for me."

"Is that why you had sex with me?"

The question seems to provoke her—and refocus her. "You want the truth?"

"Yeah. Give me your best Jack. I can handle it."

"I just wanted to," she says.

"That's it. *I just wanted to*."

"Hold on, I'm not finished. I wanted to and I didn't give a shit if Mark found out."

"So, you did set me up."

"No. Not in the way you're thinking. I was just being reckless."

Her lip starts to tremble. "I'm so sorry," she says. The tears come after that; she's full-on crying. He moves closer to her, gently pulling her toward him. She rests her head on his shoulder and sobs quietly. He looks around, checking to see who's watching. A runner looks at them as he passes by and Richie raises a hand behind Beth's back, flashing a hi-everything's-all-right-nothing-to-see-here signal.

"My lawyer says they could arrest me," she says after a moment, separating from him and wiping her eyes.

He shakes his head. "I can't believe you hired her. Of all the fucking people. Did you have to? Carolyn Dupuy?"

"I like her. She's tough. She got under your skin, not mine."

He looks at her incredulously, wants to call foul, low blow.

"Well, she's right," he says spitefully. "They probably will arrest you. They just need to get a few more ducks lined up."

"Why do you say that?"

He readies the big gun, the one he's been holding back.

"They check phone records, Beth," he says. "They know you texted me right before Mark was killed. They're probably just trying to get a little more evidence."

"I didn't text you."

He looks at her, his eyes narrowing, trying to read hers.

"Really? You sure about that?"

"I replied to yours, yeah. You asked me if everything was okay, and I wrote, 'y.' One letter. That's it. That was my big text. I sent it when I got out of yoga. I thought your message was sweet but a little dangerous."

"You didn't write anything about Mark knowing about us and that he was coming home and that you were worried?"

"No."

"You didn't give me your address?"

"My address? Why would I do that?"

Shit, he thinks, suddenly nauseated.

"Richie?"

"What?"

"You were there, weren't you?"

He studies her eyes again, hoping they show some glimmer of deceit.

"You didn't send it," he says, but this time it's not a question but an admission.

"What happened, Richie?"

He runs a hand nervously through his hair, his mind racing. If it's true, if she really didn't send the message, it means someone else did. And it means someone else set him up. But who? And wouldn't she see the messages he'd sent back? Someone would physically have to get on her phone, tap out the messages, and delete the thread. The other possibility was that it was done remotely via the spyware she claimed was on the phone. He just didn't know what to believe at this point.

"Tell me what me happened, Richie," he hears her say. He looks up at her. It sounds a little too much like a prompt, so now it's his turn to get paranoid. Moving closer to her, he slips his hand under her sweatshirt. "Do you mind?" he asks.

"I'm not taking off my shirt so you better go under that, too," she says.

"Thanks."

He slides his hand up her shirt and she flinches a little when he strafes her stomach. "Cold hands," she says. He apologizes with a shrug.

"Yeah," he says after moment, "I was there."

He tells her that after they split up after Watercourse Way, he biked over to University Avenue and locked his bike up and walked around. He hadn't been there in a while and wanted to see how much it had changed, chill for a bit, and fill his water bottle and pump his tires up before doing a much curtailed version of a ride he used to do over the hill to San Gregorio Beach through La Honda. He was in the Palo Alto Bicycles shop a little after four when he got her first message.

It said: "Mark knows. On his way home. Scared. Can you come?"

He wrote back: "Where are you?"

A few minutes later she gave him the address, followed by, "Please come now."

He shot her back another text, trying to get more details, but she never wrote back. He didn't go at first. In fact, he contemplated calling the police and dumping it on them. But he couldn't find a pay phone and didn't want to call from his own phone, figuring it might get him into trouble. And he didn't know exactly what to say. So he rode over. It was a detour on his planned ride but not that far out of the way.

It didn't take him long to get there. Maybe ten, twelve minutes. And when he got there it didn't seem like anybody was home. There were no cars in the driveway and he couldn't see the garage from the gate. He gave the buzzer a quick push and no one answered. He wasn't sure what the hell to do. The place was silent. Everything seemed very peaceful. He started to get a bad vibe about the whole thing, so he wiped down the buzzer where he'd touched it, and got on his bike and rode out of there. He turned off his phone, too. He didn't want to get any more messages from her.

He only turned it back on when he got to the train station. That's when he texted her, asking if she was all right. When he got the "y" from her he felt a little relieved, but part of him didn't think everything was fine. That's why he wasn't all that surprised when Ashley, his friend from work, texted him later on that evening, saying she'd seen something on Twitter about Mark being killed. He'd had a feeling of doom all night.

"The spyware," he says.

"What about it?"

"Do you know how it worked? Did Mark control it? Or these guys he had following you?"

"I think they were monitoring it for him. But I'm sure he had access to it. I mean, he was the one who set it up. At least I assume he did."

"And no one had access to your phone at around four o'clock? You had it in your possession the whole time?"

"Yeah." But after she says it, he sees some doubt creep into her eyes. "Well, come to think of it, I did let Pam make a call. She said her battery died."

"Pam? Your neighbor?"

"Yeah. But it was just for like a minute. And I don't think it was exactly at four."

"Was it before or after?"

"After. Closer to four fifteen, I think."

"Did you see her the whole time she was making the call?"

"Sort of. She may have turned her back a little. But why would she text you? Why would she do that? How could she be involved?"

"Did she or her husband have anything against Mark?"

"Against him? I mean, he'd hit on me, but I don't think killing Mark was going to increase the odds of sleeping with me."

"Did you tell the wife about it?"

"Pam? No. But I didn't have to. He wasn't exactly discreet about it."

"Well, wouldn't Mark have noticed?"

"He behaved around Mark."

"But did you say anything to Mark about it?"

"Come on, Richie. Mark assumed every guy wanted to fuck me—whether they did or not. That doesn't explain why she'd text you."

He nods. He'd told Lowenstein about the alleged spyware. Such programs existed, Lowenstein said, and were more common than people thought. But he said that it was a mistake for Richie to think that just because she said she had spyware on her phone that she actually had it. As part of the discovery process, they'd dig through all that. He'd get an independent lab to examine her phone and they'd comb through the phone records just like the detectives were doing. At this point, his job was to figure out what evidence they had against him and to work on ways to refute each piece. He would then build a story to support their case. But the evidence came first. It was the foundation. You had to weaken the foundation until the weight of the prosecution's case collapsed onto itself. It was as simple as that.

Evidence first, Richie thinks. What's he missing? And then it hits him: the lighter! What about the goddamn lighter?

"The one thing I don't get is my lighter," he says. "How did it end up at the crime scene?"

"Your lighter?"

"Yeah, the Sinatra lighter I gave back to you. They found it somewhere near the body. And it had my prints on it. How did it get there?"

She seems stumped. Either she's a great actress or she really is going over in her mind what she did with it and what might have happened to it.

"I dropped it," she says.

"The lighter?"

"No, my purse. When I went to pull out my cell phone, I dropped the bag on the ground. The lighter was in the bag. It must have come out. It was in the side pocket."

He thinks back to when he gave it to her at lunch. After refusing several times to accept it, she'd finally relented and slipped it into her purse. But the bag had been by her feet, so he hadn't seen exactly where she'd put it.

"You didn't notice it was missing afterwards?"

"Honestly, I didn't think about it, Richie. I didn't want it back. I told you that."

He shakes his head, frustrated. Whether she's lying or not, he needs her to tell the police that he gave her back the lighter, and that it was in her possession, not his. He doesn't give a shit what Marty Lowenstein said.

"You need to tell the police that, Beth. You need to tell them I gave you back the lighter and that you dropped it when you got out of the car."

"Okay," she says.

"Tomorrow. Call Madden tomorrow and tell him."

"I will. I'll talk to Carolyn."

"Oh, so you're on a first-name basis now."

"She's okay, Richie."

"First thing tomorrow," he says. "Tell him."

"I will. I promise. But I've gotta go now. I've got to meet with Mark's half-sister Linda. She just came in."

"When's the funeral?"

"We were going to try for Wednesday but the coroner's office asked us to hold off until the end of the week, they need more time to complete their inquest or whatever it's called. So probably Saturday, but she came in. I don't think they were close. Mark wasn't close to Barb or their brother, Scott. But he liked Linda's kids. He left them a little money in his will. Hundred thousand each. But when I told her they might not get it, she came rushing out on the first plane."

"What do you mean, not get it?"

"Mark apparently wasn't as flush as people thought. His personal lawyer, who he named the executor, seems to think he'd been living beyond his means for several years. He lost more in the 2008 crash than he told people. They're still sorting through everything, but it doesn't look like I'm going to be left with much. Basically the house and a company that has no sales and a burn rate of at least a hundred grand a month, maybe more. And even the house is mortgaged to the hilt." She laughs. It's the laugh of someone who realizes the joke's on her but doesn't care. "The good news is, it helps with reducing any motive I might have had for killing him."

"How 'bout an insurance policy?"

"Oh yeah, he did have one of those. A million bucks. Big deal. I'm going to kill him for that kind of money? I don't think so. I could marry that in five seconds. Easy. That's what people seem to be forgetting here."

"But you thought there was more. You thought there was a lot more. That's what's important. That's what they're going to look at, Beth."

"Maybe," she says. "But I can always say I thought he was in trouble, which I did think."

She then reaches out and gives his arm an affectionate squeeze. "I gotta go, Richie. You hang in there, okay?"

With that, she turns to leave, walking toward the entrance. As she's approaching the finish line, he realizes that he forgot to ask her something. He sprints to catch up to her.

"I meant to ask you something," he says, now a little breathless himself. "Did Mark ever say anything about a guy named John Hsieh or Paul Anderson?"

She ruminates a moment, but the names don't ring a bell. So he throws out another one. But this time it's the name of a company, not a person.

"Isn't that the company he bought?" she asks.

"Yes."

"Why are you asking?"

"I don't know. Bender's been poking around. Wants to track these guys down. They don't seem to be with the company anymore. Mark's company, I mean. I have Lowenstein's investigator working on it, too."

She looks at him, seemingly more interested in his face than in what he's saying. She then leans forward and kisses him on the lips, barely touching them, and says softly, "I'm not lying, Richie. I believed you. Now you have to believe me."

Her words hover there, lingering, even after he watches her get in her car and drive away. Trying to shake them, he heads back to the track and does another couple of laps. But they keep following him, riding all the way back with him to Bender's house. Only when he pulls into Bender's driveway and puts the bike back in the garage do they abruptly vanish, for inside the house, he hears shouting.

"You're seriously pissing me off!" a male voice, vaguely familiar, screams. "Who gave it to you? Just tell me who gave it to you and nothing's going to happen."

"I will not reveal my sources," he hears Bender say. "I can't. It's the one thing I won't do."

"Well, you're going to fucking die then, motherfucker."

30 / CHUMPS LIKE YOU

HE SLIPPED INTO THE HOUSE THROUGH THE ENTRANCE IN THE GARAGE, quietly passed through the laundry room, and headed down the hallway toward the living room. Edging closer, his back against the wall, he peeked around the corner and saw Bender sitting there, cowering on the couch, his hands over his head in a sort of modified fetal position.

Tongan Number Two, Soul Patch, is towering over him, a mini baseball bat in his hand that Richie recognizes as one of Bender's tchotchkes. Except it's not a freebie from some start-up, it's his own creation. Richie had seen it earlier, lying around somewhere. On one side, the bat has "OneDumbIdea.com" written on it in bold black letters and on the other, "Speak loudly and carry a small stick, you will go far," a play on the famous Teddy Roosevelt slogan. Bender thought it was very clever. Now the Tongan is threatening to ram it up his ass.

"You've got five seconds to tell me whose photo that was," the intruder demands.

"Mine, asshole."

The answer comes from Richie, now standing right behind the guy, who turns and faces him, his eyes lighting up. He's not only shocked that there's another person in the room but also that it's Richie.

"*You*," is all he has time to say before Richie slams him as hard as he can in the stomach. If there's one thing he's learned over the years, it's that a shot to the body can be just as effective, if not more so, than a strike to the face. And it doesn't hurt your hand.

The Tongan doubles over gasping, the air gone from him. He

starts to crumple, like he's been kicked in the nuts, but Richie doesn't let him topple over. He picks him up and, aiming him toward one of Bender's modernist paintings, chucks him at it, lifting him off the floor.

Man hits painting. Man and painting go crashing to floor.

"Hey, hey," Bender says. "Watch out."

But Richie isn't finished. He takes a look around the room and ponders what he wants to destroy next. The flat-panel TV mounted to the wall looks like a pretty good target and he nails it dead center, cracking the screen right in the middle.

"Get the dog leash," he tells Bender.

He then gives the Tongan one more toss, taking out some vases on an accent tablet. By the time Bender returns with the leash, Richie's on top of the guy and has him pinned to the floor. Bender sees it as an opportunity to get a few licks in with his foot.

"What are you doing?" Richie says.

"Fucker kicked my dog. I'm kicking him."

He yanks the leash out of his hand—it's one of those fancy retractable ones with lots of line—and tells him to make himself useful. After a brief struggle, they manage to hog-tie the guy.

"What are you doing here?" the Tongan keeps saying. "What the fuck?"

"You're the fuck," Bender says. "I invite you into my home. I give you twenty-five-a-pound Kona fucking coffee and this is how you treat me."

That's when Richie notices that Bender has a big wet spot in his pants in his crotch area. He can't resist asking what it is.

"I fucking pissed myself and I'm man enough to admit it," Bender says. "This fucker made me piss myself."

He then winds up with his foot to take another shot, but Richie grabs it midswing, almost causing him to fall over.

"Cut it out," he tells Bender. "What's he doing in your house?"

Bender tells him that he went outside because his dog was barking. And this guy was standing there. At first things were pretty civil. He asked whether he was Tom Bender, and he said, yeah, he was, what'd he want? He said he was one of the guys in the picture that he'd posted on his website and he wanted to know who took it and who gave it to him. Bender told him that was privileged information. But if he wanted to come in, they could talk about it, maybe Bender could shed some light on the case. Maybe he could help him.

"You're an idiot, man," Richie says. "This guy's a fucking criminal."

"You're one to talk, bro," Soul Patch retorts.

"What's your name?"

"What's it to you?"

"If you don't start talking in five seconds, we're calling the police and they'll take your ass away. No one will care what you did to this asshole," Richie says, referring to Bender, "but that dog's another story," pointing to Beezo, who's lying on the ground on his side, whimpering. "They'll fucking lock you up for five years for cruelty to animals. Vick-ify you."

"I barely touched him. He's fine."

He doesn't look so fine. If Richie had to guess, Beezo had himself a couple of cracked ribs and maybe some internal injuries. Bender is now on his knees next to him, trying to comfort him with something that sounds disturbingly like baby talk.

"Dial 911," Richie tells him.

"Gladly," he says, and gets up and starts to head toward the kitchen, where there's a cordless phone hitched to a cradle on the wall.

"Hold on," their captive says. "You'll let me go if I tell you my name?"

Richie: "We're going to need a lot more than your name, bro. But that's a start. And I'll tell you what, you answer a few questions and I'll tell you where he got that picture."

"Okay."

The guy says his name is Edwin Martinez. He's half Tongan, half Mexican. He has a record, but nothing involving "serious" violence, just possessing prescription drugs not prescribed to him. He peddled them, and McGregor was a customer. That's how they'd met—at some gas station awhile back. Then McGregor decided to take things in-house. He offered Edwin a job and asked him whether he had any big friends, bouncer types. They started out doing gofer and "bodyguard-type" work. McGregor had them start checking up on his wife.

"Did he say why he wanted you checking up on her?" Richie asks.

"I don't know, man. One time he called her a vampire. He was worried she was going to kill him or have him killed. He asked me to get a gun for him at one point."

"Did you?"

"Nah, bro. I didn't want to get into any of that shit. I gave him a name. That's it."

Sometimes when he mentions McGregor, he refers to him by a nickname Richie hasn't heard in a while, McGregs. Only he puts "Mister" in front of it.

"I gotta get him to the emergency room," Bender says from the other side of the room, now trying to give Beezo some water. "He needs medical attention, stat. Look how he's breathing."

Richie looks. Beezo doesn't seem any worse than before. "He'll be okay," he says. "Just got the wind knocked out of him. That dog's a fucking horse."

Then he turns back to Edwin and says:

"You put spyware on her phone?"

"I didn't. Mr. McGregs did."

"The day he was murdered, what happened?"

"What do you mean, what happened?"

"Did you follow her like you normally did?"

"It didn't work like that. We didn't always follow her. We kept track of her on the map. We had her on GPS. We could track her calls, her emails, everything. I was the one who called you back that day you called her. I knew it was you," he says proudly. "Freaked you out, didn't it? Got inside your head, bitch."

"You do a shitty English accent," Richie says.

"I know." He winces in pain. "Man, could you loosen this up? It's cutting into my skin. I'm losing circulation."

"In a minute. Just tell us what happened the day he was murdered."

"Okay, okay."

He tells Richie what he already knows. When Beth went to meet him for lunch, she borrowed her neighbor's car and left her phone at home. But it took them a couple of hours to figure that out; they thought she was still at the house. McGregor was pissed when he found out she'd given them the slip. "You realize she's probably with him right now," he said. "And I bet I know where they are."

"That's it, bro," Edwin tells Richie. "She must have come home around three thirty, because the phone started moving again right before four."

"Where'd she go?"

"She went and did yoga like she usually does on Fridays. And then she got her nails done at a place down the street from the yoga studio."

"Do you know for a fact she was there? Or are you just saying that's what the GPS told you?"

"We went to check on her around five or so. I saw her car. And later I saw her go into the nail salon. She was talking to a woman, her neighbor, I think, and that woman left, and she went in the nail place. She waved to me. I mean, the whole thing was a fucking joke. That's what people don't understand. It wasn't like we was being menacing or anything. Everything was kind of out in the open."

"Then what happened?"

"I called Mr. McGregs to tell him. But he didn't pick up so I left a message, saying, you know, where she was and that we were going to go home unless he needed anything else. He usually let us go around six on Fridays unless there was something special going on."

"Did he usually pick up?"

"Most of the time, yeah."

"But you didn't think anything about it at the time? That it was unusual?"

"The next day, yeah. I thought shit, the dude must have been dead, that's why he didn't answer. But at the time, no, bro."

"You send me text messages from her phone?"

The question confuses him.

"On Ms. Hill's phone? Why would I do that?"

"Could you?"

"What?"

"Send a message with the spyware?"

"I don't know. I don't know all that shit. I'm not technology savvy, bro. Look, that's it. That's all I'm saying. I gave you plenty, now you gotta gimme something. And loosen this fucking thing up," he says, holding out his hands.

"He's licking my hand," he hears Bender say. "He seems a little better."

Richie: "One last thing."

"Fuck your one last thing."

"Paul Anderson," he says. "Name ring a bell?"

"Yeah. The queer dude, Paul. Mr. McGregs bought his company. He and this Chinese dude. Didn't talk much English."

"You ever meet them?"

"Yeah. Couple times. The Paul dude was around more."

"You said he was queer—as in gay?"

"Seemed like a homo to me. Sometimes, you know, we wondered about Mr. McGregs."

"Wondered as in what?"

"I don't know. Maybe he liked dick. He had the nice suits and Lacoste shirts and looked all well groomed and shit." He lets out a little snicker. "Sometimes, you know, these guys with the hot wives got all these problems and you think maybe the dude's got some issues. I tell you, bro, that's one sweet piece of ass. I know you had it, so I know you know. I got respect for that, bro."

Respect? Richie has an urge to smack the guy but allows Edwin's poor excuse for a compliment to pass.

"You ever follow Paul around?"

"Fuck no. Look, I'm done here. Call the fucking police I don't give a shit. I can't feel my fucking hands."

"Why you so concerned about the photo?"

"You saw a picture of you linked to a murderer you'd be concerned too, bro. I can't get that shit off the web. I shoulda sued this cocksucker for defamation."

"Please do," Bender says from across the room. "I would enjoy that."

"But why'd you want to know who gave it to him so bad?"

"'Cause she played us, bro. By that I mean you, too. I just got a bad vibe. The way she took her friend's car and all that. She was real calculated, and it got me thinking she'd been cookin' this thing up for a while. As soon as I saw that photo, that's what I thought. So I had to know if she was the one who gave it to him. If she did, I'd know for sure."

"Well, like I said, it was my photo."

"No, it wasn't," Bender says.

The fucking guy just can't contain himself.

"Yes, it was," Richie says firmly, then explains how he had Ashley and her boyfriend come over and take pictures after he saw Edwin and T-Truck sitting outside his apartment.

Bender can't quite believe it. Neither can Edwin. "For real, bro?"

"The cops took the photo from me. I assume Madden or one of the other detectives gave it to him," he says, nodding in Bender's direction. "It's called an intentional leak. Designed to stir things up, flush you out. All they wanted was to question you. They didn't have anything on you. But now they're going to think you had something to do with it."

"I didn't have nothin' to do with it. I'm telling you, bro."

"Don't tell me. Tell the fucking police. Go ahead, dial 911," he says to Bender.

"But you said you'd let me go," Edwin protests.

"You're a fucking idiot. I had to deal with character defects like you every day in prison. People who got fixated on stupid shit and wound up fucked. The good news is with the new overcrowding laws, they're weeding out chumps like you. But I didn't have that luxury."

"Fuck you," Edwin says.

Bender looks on, impressed, though he isn't sure whether or not Richie's bluffing.

"Dial," Richie repeats. "And then you might want to think about changing your pants."

31/ THE PRICE OF ECONOMIC NECESSITY

By the time Madden and Carlyle get to Bender's house, two squad cars are already parked in front with their lights flashing, bringing out a few onlookers.

"I gotta hand it to you guys," Forman greets them when they enter the living room. "You're fucking fast. Two goddamn minutes. These fine officers showed up in two minutes."

Forman's sitting in an armchair on one side of the room while Bender's propped up on an elbow, lying on his side on the carpet next to his dog, who's also lying on his side, strangely mirroring him.

The place is a mess. Cracked TV on the wall, shattered glass on the floor, painting toppled over along with something that appears to be a mangled dog leash. One of the uniformed officers is standing behind their suspect, who's now got his hands cuffed behind his back. His brow is furrowed. He's brooding.

"What happened?" Madden asks.

"We got your boy is what happened," Forman says. "Doing your job for you as usual, Detective."

It doesn't take a genius to figure out that there's been some sort of altercation, but how did the Tongan end up at the house? It doesn't make sense.

"How'd he get here?"

"You could sort of call it an interview op turned ugly."

"Fucker kicked my dog," Bender says. "I want pictures taken of everything. This is real, man. This is some real shit that went down. I want it fully documented."

Bender is so used to fabricating his facts that now that he's experienced something with some semblance of gravitas, he can't quite believe it.

"I didn't do anything," Edwin says. "I was assaulted. This guy's an animal. He tried to kill me."

"Why are you here, Edwin?" Madden asks.

"I'm not saying shit. I want a lawyer. I want proper representation."

"The idiot wanted to know how his picture ended up on the web," Forman says. "And Bender here decided he was going to get himself an exclusive Q and A. The only problem was Edwin was the one who wanted the A's. I walked in after getting a little exercise and the Big Bambino Edwino is threatening to sodomize our host with a miniature baseball bat."

"That true, Edwin?"

"Hell yes, it's true," Bender pipes in. Carlyle, himself the owner of two dogs, is next to Beezo, down on one knee, examining the little pup, stroking his head, muttering, "you're going to be all right, boy." *Christ*, Madden thinks, *the two of them*.

Edwin: "I told you. I want a lawyer. I know how this shit works."

"Why'd you run on us?"

"I got nothing to do with the McGregor thing."

"I tell you why he ran," Forman says. "'Cause he's guilty of something. I'm not sure what it is—I mean, it's probably multiple things—but I'm sure if you offer him a deal, he'll tell you."

"I don't want a deal," Edwin says.

Forman: "Detective, tell him you got the picture from me. He doesn't believe me. Tell him you were the one who gave it to Bender. You leaked it."

Madden, on the spot, doesn't know quite what to say. While part of him wants to curry a little favor from Forman, get him to keep talking, another part doesn't want to give him anything.

"Did you?" Edwin asks.

"Yeah, I did," Madden replies.

"Fuck me."

Just then they hear a knock on the door, and a moment later a woman in jeans and a gray UC Davis sweatshirt walks into the living room. She's short and stocky, with dark hair pulled back in a ponytail.

"I'm the vet," she introduces herself. "I got a call about an injured animal."

Her presence puts everybody in check and things simmer down

quickly. She attends to the dog as one of the uniforms leads Edwin out to the squad car.

While Carlyle takes a statement from Bender—they're suddenly best friends—Madden shuttles in and out of the house, conversing with other officers. Billings has shown up, too; Madden thinks he seems relieved to have Carlyle in charge of processing the arrest, probably because he can't be bothered with all the paperwork.

Madden goes inside one last time to find Forman asleep in the armchair. He gives him a little slap to the side of his knee.

"We're going," he says.

"How's the pooch?" Forman asks.

"Vet says it's not life threatening. They're taking him for X-rays, though."

"That's good news for Edwin. Nothing worse than being labeled a dog killer."

Forman sits up a little in the chair, crossing one leg over the other, pushing the sweatpants up and exposing the tracer ankle bracelet. Madden notices some redness on his shin.

"That bothering you?" Madden says.

"I'm getting used to it."

"You know, I don't know what you're doing here."

"That makes two of us."

"I heard Lowenstein put this together."

"The price of economic necessity."

"What's Bender get out of the deal?"

"An exclusive, of course. Some pictures and video. And now he's got this little incident to crow about. Pure gold. He'll have plenty of material to send his traffic through the roof for a couple weeks."

"Should make for a nice exploitation package."

"Don't worry, I won't go too hard on you, Detective," Forman says. "I'll leave out the part where I tell you now that your days as a police officer are numbered."

"You keep telling me that and I keep ignoring you."

"Yeah, but it's going to be embarrassing, Hank. No, strike that. Humiliating. It's okay if I call you, Hank, right?"

"Not really."

"You're a step behind. We're on to some shit that you haven't even begun to touch."

"Who's we?"

"Everybody but you."

Madden laughs. "I guess we're even then."

"How's that?"

"We've got some stuff on you that's pretty damaging."

"Like what?"

"Like Marty will get it soon enough in discovery. What's mine is yours."

"I was set up. You know that."

"Sure, Columbo."

"You're dating yourself."

"Call me old-fashioned," Madden says. "I say throwback. How much longer you staying here?"

"Another night."

"Well, try to stay out of trouble."

"How much more trouble could I be in?"

"There's always getting your bail revoked. Shouldn't be too hard given what went on here tonight."

"Is that how you treat people who do your job for you?"

"Good night, Mr. Forman. I'm sorry I woke you."

"I bet you are."

Madden walks away to join Carlyle, who's waiting for him at the door. Looks like he won't be going home so fast after all.

"That guy can't shut up, can he?" Carlyle says outside.

"Who? Bender?"

"Well, both of them. Forman, too."

"You hear him talking?"

"Some of it."

"You notice anything different?"

Carlyle shrugs. "Not really."

"The Frank act," Madden says. "He's toned it way down. The accent's almost gone."

Carlyle goes around to the driver's side of his car and gets in. Madden slides into the passenger seat next to him.

"That's a good thing, right?" Carlyle says, firing up the engine.

"No," Madden says. Then, after a beat: "No, it isn't."

32 / HITMWHERETHESUNDONTSHINE

THE NEXT DAY ASHLEY VISITS BENDER'S SPEAK LOUDLY PRODUCTIONS Palo Alto office around noon to give him an update. Lowenstein had had to go back to New York, but she'd held on to his rental car and had been racking up the miles the last couple of days, using a friend from college's place in nearby Redwood City as home base.

Richie doesn't love the fact that Lowenstein split, but he understands. The man is busy after all, and the Exoneration Foundation depends on his appearances to raise funds and awareness for its clients. Promotional considerations also play a role in Richie's relationship with Bender. One of the clauses in their contract states that as part of any article featuring Richie, Lowenstein's pet projects must be highlighted, and during the video interview Richie did that morning in the office, he went out of his way to mention some cases he'd been working on during his few weeks as a volunteer at the foundation.

In fact, most of that morning's interview had nothing to do with the murder. Except for a few prepared statements, Lowenstein had instructed Richie to refrain from speaking about the investigation, which would make it less likely that he'd have to veto anything before it went up. He had said it was okay to be more open about his past (though he should still watch what he said). So, much of that morning's interview was devoted to more mundane background stuff, like his days growing up in New Jersey, how he'd ended up in the Valley, and impressions of working here.

Later, in the afternoon session, they're slated to discuss the accident, his experiences in prison, and the Sinatra connection, all of which Bender seems eager to delve into. If Bender ever asks him whether he killed McGregor, Richie's been coached to say, "No way. Why would I? I was putting my life back together. I was moving in the right direction. Why would I kill that? And why would I kill him?"

The office is on the second floor of a building off of California Avenue in Palo Alto and when Ashley arrives, Richie's sitting at a desk, reading SFGate.com on a borrowed computer. Bender used to have his handful of staffers work out of his old home—or their own homes—but a few years ago he decided to get an office "for appearance's sake," which he claims immediately doubled the value of his company.

Now that he's sold out, his parent company expects his eight full-time employees to come into the office on a daily basis, but he flagrantly doesn't enforce the rule, encouraging them to come and go as they please. "As long as the work gets done."

The office layout is open, just one large room with a few desks strewn about the space rather haphazardly. There's one side office that serves as a conference room, and another smaller room is the video and podcast studio. Clearly, someone has sunk some money into the thoughtfully designed furniture and lighting.

"There's press outside," is the first thing Ashley says.

Richie is well aware of this fact. Bender has even taken a break from interviewing him to be interviewed himself. He posted a short piece on the Edwin incident that morning, taking the opportunity to upgrade it to a "home invasion." His PR agency has been fielding calls ever since.

The article, just a few paragraphs long, is really just a vague and sensational caption for a set of thirty or so photos, several of which feature dramatic images of his wounded pug. Despite suffering "grave internal injuries," one caption reads, "Beezo looks like he's going to make it." The piece ends with a patently Bender cliffhanger: "I can't say as much as I'd like to about this right now. More later. Stay tuned."

It's quintessential Bender times ten, and he's relishing the attention. A couple hundred thousand people have already gone into the main story and, as Bender tells anyone who will listen, "The page-turns on the slideshow have been astronomical." The feedback, barring a few comments lamenting Beezo's survival ("You make me sick" Bender had replied to one), is overwhelmingly positive. "This is the kind of in-the-trenches, tell-it-like-it-is journalism that's sadly missing from today's mainstream press," writes one poster with the handle hitmwherethesundontshine. "Go get 'em, Tom!"

What a goddamn farce, Richie thinks.

"Apparently, there's a secret fire escape," he tells Ashley, who for some reason is wearing a touch of makeup. She looks a little older. "I'm probably going to have to use it."

"Well, I can tell you one thing for sure, this guy Hsieh is gone."

"Gone?"

"Yeah, I've got—"

Before she says anything more, he stops her, realizing that Bender is talking on the phone in the conference room nearby. He may not approve, especially since Richie never told him that he's got Ashley looking into these guys. It's a safe bet that Bender would have a hissy fit, claiming that he owned the rights to anything lifted from Gattner's computer.

Richie gets up and motions for her to follow him, then leads her to the hall outside the office, where they can get a little privacy.

"Okay, go ahead," he says once they're out of the office.

"I've got one person that says he went back to Shanghai and another who says he's in Hong Kong," she says in a low voice. "He didn't leave any contact information. I'm hitting a wall trying to get any. Hsieh is a pretty common Chinese name and there are multiple Johns out there."

"No Facebook or Twitter account?"

"Not that I can find. And Anderson isn't on there either. He used to have a Facebook account but it's no longer active."

"Who doesn't have a Facebook account now?"

"The few, the proud, the abstainers. I got something on him, though."

"Who, Anderson?"

"Yeah," she says. "The guy didn't have too many friends. Hadn't been out here that long. Was from Kansas City, came out here and worked at a couple of dot-coms. Made it as high as director of something but then got demoted, and had his shares stripped down. Six months later the company went public. But he'd already left. So he missed the big exit in more ways than one."

"Why'd he get demoted?"

"I'm not sure. 'Personal issues' was all I could get, which is sometimes code for alcohol or drugs. Or some form of sexual misconduct or harassment. But apparently he was devastated by it. Didn't work for a while and then ended up selling suits at the Macy's Men's Store in the Stanford Shopping Center. That's where I found a guy who knew him."

"Gay guy?"

"Yeah, but he says he's in a committed relationship."

The Macy's guy's name is Vincent. Vincent Purdy. He said he'd run into Anderson in the store about three months ago when Anderson came in to do some shopping. He bought several items, expensive stuff. Even bought Purdy a gift. Anderson told him he'd started a company and had just sold it to another start-up that had the same idea. He was rich, moved to a new place in San Carlos. He gave Purdy his address and told him to stop by if he was ever in the neighborhood.

Purdy said Anderson never mentioned Mark McGregor's name. And he never got in touch with Anderson, though he did keep his information in his phone because "you never know."

"I was tempted to call," he explained. "He's a decent-looking guy. But I heard he's into some kinky stuff, and frankly, I get intimidated by that."

When Ashley's through giving Richie the details of the encounter, she gives him the address she got from Purdy. He keys that into Google Maps on his phone and zooms into the block using the satellite view. It's a small house, nothing special, with a decent-sized backyard.

"I've gotta go back up to the city in a little bit," she says. "I figured I'd stop by on the way up, take a peek inside."

"You don't want to email first?"

"I wanna have a look. Maybe talk to a neighbor or two. If no one's around, I'll try email."

A little smile creeps onto her face, and then she shakes her head, letting out a little laugh.

"What's so funny?" he asks.

"I just remembered what you said about Bender's instructions for searching for sensitive email."

He smiles, too. When Richie asked Bender how he'd come up with Hsieh and Anderson's names on Gattner's computer, Bender didn't hesitate to offer his secret. "First rule when searching for sensitive email is to key 'Do not forward' into the search bar. Always a good place to start."

"You speak to Marty?" Richie asks.

"Late last night. I emailed him and he called me back. You'll be shocked to know he was awake past midnight."

"You tell him about my conversation with Beth and what Madden said?"

"Yeah."

"What'd he think?"

"He found it very interesting. Said he would call you tomorrow, meaning today."

"I mean, shouldn't we be more proactive?"

"I've been working my ass off for the last three days. I think we've been plenty proactive."

"I know, I just mean—"

"Why isn't he here doing something?"

"Yeah."

"He is, Rick. He may not be physically here, but he's here—and he'll be back."

That doesn't sound too comforting or persuasive.

"Look, I'm sorry. You've always been really good to me. I'm not sure why, but I know you have. And I know you're doing your best to help me now."

She gives him a little aw-shucks punch in the shoulder. "I like you, Rick. Don't you know that?"

"But why?"

She shrugs. "Sometimes I think it's because you remind me of this guy I liked from high school. This black guy, Jeff Johnson. Ran track like you did, only faster. He also played wide receiver."

"Did you say black?"

"Yeah, this girl accused him of raping her," she goes on without missing a beat. "Well, forcing himself on her anyway. It became this huge deal at school. There was no proof or anything, but he got suspended for a semester and when he came back he was kind of ostracized. Kids were like, 'There's the rapist.'"

"I didn't think that was fair," she continues. "And I went up and started talking to him as a kind of dare. He was two years older. And then we became friends, we even fooled around a little. And I'll never forget what he said. He said, 'I'm smarter than that. Don't they understand? I'd never do something like that because I'm smarter than that.'"

"Sometimes smart people do dumb things."

"Yeah, well, that's true, too. But it's just something about how you think everything's sort of an affront, that you can't understand how people could actually believe something about you that's so obviously not true. That's the part that reminded me of him. And, you know, I wanted people to see him for who he was."

"Did they?"

"No, not really. Not in high school. And then he was killed in a car accident two years later, when he was in college."

"Oh." A beat, then: "Well, that's an uplifting story."

"You asked."

He shakes his head. For a chipper kid, she sure can be dark.

"Let me know what you find out. Email me later on."

"I'll send you a picture."

"I like pictures," he says.

33 / JAILBREAK

THE DAY STARTS BADLY FOR MADDEN AND THEN GETS PROGRESSIVELY worse. First, he's awakened by a call from Carlyle, asking if he's seen it yet. The "it" he's referring to is Bender's article, which doesn't say much but nonetheless manages to taint the police department with a faint odor of incompetence.

Soon after that, Pastorini picks up the scent and puts him on the spot at their morning all-hands briefing. So he's already on edge when around ten he gets a call from the officer upstairs at the front desk announcing there's a woman there to see him, something about the McGregor case. He tells her to hold on, he'll be up in a minute, because he's dealing with getting Edwin transferred and arraigned.

He feels like he's being pelted from all sides, and then *bam*, he takes one right in the kisser, for there, sitting in the lobby of the building, is Beth Hill's friend and neighbor.

"Hi, Ms. Yeagher, can I help you?" he asks.

"Yes," she says without getting up. "Yes, you can."

Then silence. She looks down at the floor and he watches her bite her lip, obviously nervous about something.

"Ms. Yeagher?"

"I'm sorry," she says in a low voice. "I don't know how to say this so I'm just going to say it. I think I'm partially responsible for Mark McGregor's death."

He blinks. "Excuse me?"

"I may have inadvertently done something that contributed to his death."

"Inadvertently?"

"Well, I meant to do it. But I didn't think it would have the consequences it did."

He raises an eyebrow, afraid to hear what comes next. He moves a step closer, leaning down toward her.

"What did you do exactly?"

"I texted Richie Forman from Beth's phone. I was the one who sent the text, not her."

Madden is stunned. He isn't even quite sure what she's talking about but it doesn't sound good. Not good at all.

"Why would you do that?"

"Mark asked me to."

"He what?"

"He asked me to send a message from her phone saying that he knew about her and Richie getting together and that he was coming home and wanted Richie to meet him there."

Madden puts his hand up to his temple, thinking about what she just said, trying to process it without having a stroke. And then it begins to make sense. She's talking about the text they discovered that Beth had sent to Richie not long before McGregor was killed. Or, rather, it was texts, plural. The whole thread had been deleted a minute after the second message was sent.

He sits down next to her on the long polished wood bench attached to the wall. There's nobody in the lobby but them and Garcia, the female officer sitting at a computer behind the front desk. He clasps his hands between his legs, lets out a long sigh and says:

"You spoke to Mark the day he was killed?"

"Yes. He called to ask me whether Beth was at home. And I kind of hesitated a second and he knew she wasn't there even when I said I thought she was. I'm not a good liar."

Madden rolls his eyes a little.

"I then told him she'd taken my car," she continues. "And he asked if she'd gone to meet Richie. And you know, I tried to lie again, but he knew. And he got angry. He said, 'Why didn't you tell me?' Well, I didn't think I had to tell him, I said. From what Beth had told me he had other people spying on her. That wasn't my job."

Oh Jesus, Madden thinks.

"Did you have a relationship with him?"

"What do you mean?"

"Were you having an affair with him?"

"No. God no. I mean, we were friendly. We'd talk. We had them over for dinner a few times."

From the sudden flush of red on her face and the way she's touching her earring, she doesn't sound totally convincing. Looks a lot like she had a little crush on the guy. Maybe a big one.

"Ms. Yeagher, you're not doing this to protect your friend, are you? Ms. Hill didn't put you up to this, did she?"

"No."

"What precipitated you coming here this morning then?"

"Precipitated?"

"Why did you suddenly decide to tell me this today?"

"I spoke to Beth last night. She mentioned the texts. She didn't know about some of the evidence you had against Richie. Like the lighter. She said she was the one who dropped it, not him. Richie had given it back to her at lunch that day."

Now Madden really does feel light-headed.

"She said that? That she dropped it?"

"Yes. She was speaking to her lawyer about it. She wanted to come in and talk to you."

Madden looks at her, trying to gauge her sincerity.

"She didn't put you up to this?"

"No."

"Are you sure?"

"Yes."

Madden still doesn't believe her.

"How did she find out about these things?"

"I think she read about it online. Or from her lawyer."

"Ms. Dupuy wouldn't be privy to much of the evidence we've gathered as part of our investigation. Her client has not been charged yet. We're still investigating."

Yeagher doesn't seem to know quite how to respond. She stares up at him as if he's speaking in a foreign language she can't understand.

"I'm just telling you what she told me. She seemed upset. We were discussing the lighter and all of sudden she asked me whether I texted anybody with her phone when I borrowed it before yoga class. She said, 'You texted, Richie, didn't you? You were the one.' And I said no, no I wasn't. But I could tell she didn't believe me. And I woke up this morning and just felt absolutely horrible. I knew I had to go to the police before she did and try to make things right. I felt awful."

He puts his hand to his temple again, feeling a headache coming on.

"Ms. Yeagher, I'm going to have to bring you downstairs to make a statement. I'm going to need to record our conversation. Are you okay with that?"

"Yes. Yes, I'm okay with that."

"Before we go down, I've got to ask you one thing. Why did you send the message?"

"I told you, because Mark asked me to."

"Why did he ask you to?"

"Well, obviously he wanted to try to get Richie to come to the house. He said that if he could get him on his property it'd be helpful. I knew what he was trying to do, of course. He was trying to get him in trouble because, you know, if someone comes onto your property, you can claim self-defense and all that. I told him I wouldn't do it."

"But what changed your mind?"

She hesitates a moment, then says, "He said he'd destroy my husband. He'd destroy his career as a doctor. And that it would be incredibly embarrassing for me."

"How was he going to do that?"

"He said he'd put spyware on his phone, too."

"And you believed him?"

"It was hard not to. My husband would go to Mark sometimes and ask him about some computer problem. And Mark would fix it. And then he wanted to use his phone for Wi-Fi with his computer when he was traveling. Mark said he could hack his iPhone. I forget what it's called when you do that."

"Jailbreak," Madden says.

"Yes, he said he could jailbreak it so he could do the tethering thing without paying extra. And Mark said that when he did that he put spyware on my husband's phone. He said he did it just for fun, but guess what, it turned out my husband was a real pervert and that he had all his passwords and it wouldn't be hard for him to hit the self-destruct button on him without ever being linked."

"And you believed him? You didn't think he was bluffing?"

"Let's just say my husband isn't an angel. And neither am I. He had some pictures on his computer. I'd like to leave it at that for now."

"We're going to have to speak to him," Madden says. "He's going to have to come down here. Did you tell him about any of this? After Mark called, did you let him know that Mark had put spyware on his phone? Did you say anything to him?"

"No," she says, then hesitates a moment, thinking.

"Ms. Yeagher, are you lying now?"

"No, no. I didn't say anything that day."

"Are you sure? This is important."

"Later on, a few days later, we were talking about how Beth maybe had spyware on her phone and I might have said something about how we all should check for it, because, you know, you never know."

He shakes his head, still not sure whether to believe her or not.

"You realize how serious this is, don't you? You realize what you've done here?"

"I should have called the police," she says, tearing up. "I know I should have. But I didn't think someone would end up dead."

"What did you think would end up happening?"

"I don't know. Not this. Never something like this."

34/ THE TIMING OF EVERYTHING

RICHIE'S PHONE RINGS ABOUT FORTY-FIVE MINUTES AFTER ASHLEY leaves Bender's office. The caller ID shows a 914 number, which he recognizes as Westchester County, New York.

"Rick?"

"Marty."

"Where are you?"

"At Bender's office, fulfilling the terms of the deal you put together."

"How's it going?" he asks cheerfully.

"Not a big fan of talking about myself on camera."

"Well, someday you may thank me for putting you two together. You got a piece of paper to write a number down?"

He says he does even though he doesn't. He figures he'll just write it down in the Google search bar he's looking at on the computer, then copy it down afterwards.

"I want you to call Carolyn Dupuy," Lowenstein says.

Richie, concentrating on taking good dictation, starts to tap out her name, then stops after the *a*.

"Did you say Carolyn Dupuy?"

"Yes."

"I really don't want to do that, Marty."

"I know you don't, but I need you to compare notes on this guy Paul Anderson you dug up. I can't reach Ashley and Carolyn has some info you might find interesting. Here's her cell number." He reads off the number. "Got it?"

In the background, Richie hears what sounds like the roar of a plane's jet engine.

"Where are you Marty?"

"At the airport."

"Which one?"

"SFO. Took a flight out this morning. Picking up the rental car now."

"You come out for me or something else?"

"All you, bud. It's hole-poking time," he says. "Time to fire the torpedoes."

"You serious?"

"Rawlings or Wilson?"

"What?"

"What brand of mitt do you like?" he asks. "My youngest only does Mizuno. I tell him it's a sign he'll be another Jewish guy marrying Asian. Got a hundred bucks on it."

"Always been a Wilson guy myself. A3000."

"Well, don't pick one up just yet. We've still got a little work to do. Call Dupuy. She's waiting for your call. I'll call you back in a little while."

Richie hangs up and stares at the number he's typed on the computer screen. *He wouldn't ask you to do it if there wasn't a damn good reason*, he thinks, then punches the number into his phone, gets up from the desk, and heads out to the hall outside the office again.

She answers on the fourth ring.

"Dupuy."

"Forman."

Silence.

"Hello?" he says.

"Hello. I just wasn't expecting . . ."

Her voice trails off.

"Marty said I should call you. He didn't tell you I was going to call?"

"No, he didn't. He said his investigator, the young woman, was going to call. But that's okay. How are you?"

"I'm okay." He's about to ask her how she is, but then thinks that's weird, making small talk with Carloyn Dupuy. So he cuts right to the chase. "What's this about Paul Anderson?" he asks. "Marty told me you have some information."

"Beth told me that you mentioned his name last night when you saw her. You really shouldn't do that, by the way."

"Do what?"

"Meet with her like that. You could be charged with witness intimidation."

"Who the fuck cares at this point?"

"You should."

"Thanks for the advice. Now what's this about Anderson?"

A brief pause, then: "My boyfriend . . . well, really my ex-boyfriend. He works over at Parkview Hospital."

"The doctor? The one who had a thing for San Quentin quail?"

"Yeah, that and a lot of other tail," she says, taking his jab in stride impressively.

"I read about the two of you."

"Well, let's just say he overheard some nurses in the courtyard gossiping about the McGregor murder. I don't know if you know this but a couple of years ago, he spent the night in Parkview. McGregor, I mean. He thought he was having a heart attack."

"Shame it wasn't real."

As he paces in the hallway, she goes into some detail about the episode, talking about an enzyme test and acid reflux before getting to the real nugget.

"McGregor didn't have a private room during his stay at the hospital," she says. "He had a roommate the night he spent there. And one of the nurses remembered McGregor because of some of the things he was saying to the roommate."

She explains that the guy, the roommate, had attempted suicide and the nurse overheard McGregor saying something to the guy about at least his wife didn't want him dead.

"Interesting, but what does that have to do with Paul Anderson?"

"The roommate was Paul Anderson."

A little chill runs up his spine.

"You know that for a fact?"

"Yes. One hundred percent."

"And when did you say this was?"

"Two years ago."

He leans up against the wall, a little dazed. "Two years ago?"

"I couldn't find much on Anderson on the Internet. It also didn't help that he doesn't have a more unique name. But when Beth mentioned—"

"Gattner said they started looking at that company like a year ago," he says, talking to himself more than to her. "He said someone had tipped off their investor that there was another company out there like them. That they'd been in stealth mode."

"Yes, that's what I wanted to ask you about. The timing of everything. When I spoke to Marty, he said you had some information about that and that his investigator was trying to track down Anderson and his partner. An Asian guy."

When she says investigator, he remembers Ashley, and thinks, *Oh shit.*

"Did you ever speak to Ashley?" he asks. "Does she know about this?"

"No, I left a message for Marty early this morning but I guess he was on a plane coming here. He called me back just like ten minutes ago. Said he would have her call me."

"Shit," he says.

"What's wrong?"

"I've gotta call you back. She needs to know this. I'm going to try her now."

He hangs up and speed dials Ashley's number. When she doesn't pick up, he leaves a message telling her to call back, then texts her. Waiting for the reply, he taps his foot nervously on the carpeted floor. She doesn't always pick up her phone but she almost always replies to texts within a minute or two. Nothing. He calls her back again, leaving another message. He looks at his watch. She's been gone a little over an hour. It should have taken her only twenty minutes or so to get to San Carlos.

He waits another minute, hoping for a reply. Then Darrin, Bender's video and podcast producer, a tall gawky kid who's all of twenty-three, comes out, a pair of headphones around his neck.

"Hey, Tom's looking for you," he says. "He's off his call. We're going to shoot for another twenty minutes or so, then grab some lunch."

"Okay. Tell him I'll be right in."

He looks at his phone, checks the signal. Still nothing. So he calls Carolyn Dupuy back.

"Have you got a car?" he asks.

"Of course," she says. "Why?"

"I think Ashley may be in trouble. I need you to drive me somewhere. And I need you to do it right now."

35/ SIMPLE AS THAT

MADDEN COMES OUT OF THE INTERROGATION ROOM, LEAVING PAM Yeagher with Burns, and is expectedly greeted by Pastorini, who asks, "How bad is it, Hank?"

"That's depends on how you define bad."

Her revelation had seemed deeply damaging at first, but the more he thinks it through, the more he convinces himself they're looking at a glancing blow rather than anything fatal. Yeah, Billings's theory that Beth had killed her husband, then texted Richie, encouraging him to come over and become implicated in the crime, is shot. But their core case against Forman is still intact.

He explains to Pastorini that in many ways Yeagher's admission helps simplify things. It goes like this: McGregor figures out his wife and Forman have hooked up, he asks Yeagher to text Forman in hopes of luring him over to the house, where he plans to get into it with Forman, maybe he even wants to kill him. But things go horribly awry. He hasn't seen Forman in years and underestimates him physically and the next thing he knows, Forman grabs the tomahawk off the wall in the garage and hacks him to death. Simple as that.

"What about the word 'Hack' written in the guy's blood?" Pastorini points out.

"He does it to throw us off."

"Thinks it up right there on the spot?"

"Sure. Why not?"

"And then he makes sure everything's nice and tidy except he drops his lighter, which Ms. Yeagher is now saying he didn't really drop because Beth Hill really dropped it. Did you miss that part? Because I didn't. Come on, Hank. You're in denial here."

He grimaces, realizes Pastorini is right.

"Are you sure she isn't making this up to protect Hill? Are they really friends?"

He considers this, but his thoughts begin to stray. He can't keep anything straight anymore. *I'm not going to make it,* he thinks. *I'm fucking losing it.*

"I'm not really sure of anything at this point, Pete," he says. "Maybe you better take me off this thing."

"I'm not taking you off shit. You've got to get it together, man. Did Richie Forman do this or not? If he didn't, then who did? What about this doctor?"

"Which doctor?"

"Yeagher. The husband. He's got a motive now. Guy put spyware on his phone. So was he home or not?"

"She says he was in and out. Mostly out. But he works a half day on Friday. He's a dermatologist. Got his own practice."

"Fucking doctors, must be nice," Pastorini says. "What's on the surveillance footage?"

"We should have a record of all the cars that went in and out. I just gotta check it and the times. We weren't focused on him."

He pauses a moment, takes a deep breath, trying to collect himself, but suddenly lashes out at the wall, banging his fist against it.

"Goddammit. We spent so much time looking at the wife. Fucking Billings. That bastard leaked stuff to Bender that first night, too. I know he was the one."

"He didn't leak shit, Hank. I investigated it myself. No one did. Yeah, a couple guys may have made a couple innocent remarks. But Bender blew them up and twisted them. That's what he does. Don't blame anybody for this."

"I'm not. I'm blaming myself."

"Well, don't do that either. What are you going to do with her?"

"Who?"

"The woman in there. Yeagher. Or did you already forget about her?"

"You want me to charge her with obstruction of justice? Providing false information? What?"

"Let's get her husband in here."

Just then Madden feels his cell phone vibrating on his belt. He unclips it, looks at the number. It's Greg Lyons from the coroner's office.

"What fucking now?" he says. Then, putting the phone to his head: "Madden."

"Hank, it's Greg."

"What's up?"

"We have a little problem."

Madden doesn't like the sound of that, especially the "we" part.

"What kind of little problem?"

"I've got Marty Lowenstein standing here. He wants to see the body."

"Well, he can't see the fucking body. Tell him he can't see it."

"I think you need to get up here, Hank. He says he's talked to the FBI."

"About what?"

"The tattoo."

36 / LOST IN THE LIGHTS

RICHIE'S SITTING ON A BENCH IN FRONT OF THE COUNTRY SUN NATURAL Foods store, wolfing down a sandwich, when a maroon BMW convertible makes a sharp left from the opposite side of the street and pulls into a just-vacated parking spot in front of the store, screeching to a halt inches from the curb. In front of him is Carolyn Dupuy, tanned and wearing sunglasses, her dark hair pulled back in a ponytail, looking more glamorous than he remembers. Though he's staring straight at her, she gives him two unnecessary short blasts with her car's horn.

He tosses the remaining bit of sandwich in the garbage but keeps the brown bag with a drink and cookie in it and gets in the car.

"Where are we going?" she asks.

He tells her to head to the freeway, 101. She shifts the car into reverse, steals a quick look behind her left and right, and accelerates hard, going back the way she came—but in reverse. She then hits the brakes, shifts, and guns the car forward all in one motion that's at once smooth and jolting. She and Bender appear to have gone to the same driving school.

"You going to tell me what's going on?" she asks.

He explains that Ashley had stopped by to see him over an hour ago and said she'd come up with an address for Anderson. She was going to stop there on her way back up to the city. She was supposed to call him after she checked it out and maybe even send a picture. She hadn't. And he'd tried to reach her several times on her phone to no avail. It wasn't like her not to answer.

"Thanks for coming to get me," he says.

"Where'd you tell Bender you were going?"

He didn't. He just texted him and said he'd be back in an hour. "I didn't want him involved," he explains. "He can be rather draining."

"Funny. That's what people say about me."

She glances over at her side mirror, changes lanes, then picks up her iPhone and calls Marty Lowenstein's mobile number. She has the phone hooked up to her car's speakers via Bluetooth. After several rings, they get Lowenstein's voice mail.

"Marty," she says, "It's Carolyn Dupuy. Call me back. It's urgent."

Little does she know that at that exact moment Lowenstein is standing at the front desk of the San Mateo County Sheriff's Forensic Laboratory and Coroner's Office, asking to speak with Greg Lyons, and that his cell phone is sitting in a cup holder in his rental car attached to a cigarette-lighter cell-phone charger.

A few minutes later Richie sends Lowenstein a text from his phone—and another to Ashley. Now they're racing up the freeway, going north toward the city, the cooler air outside the car rhythmically pounding his head while a steady stream of hot air from the car's heater blasts his body just long enough to keep him warm.

He tells Carolyn about the deal Lowenstein made with Bender and about Lowenstein himself. She reveals that she met him the other day at the scene of the accident—his accident.

"If there's anybody who's going to get you off, it's him," she says, talking over the wind. She's dressed more warmly than he is, in jeans and one of those thin North Face jackets in avocado green that looks like it's made of down but it's really some synthetic material that's supposed to be warmer than down. "I think he was sorry he couldn't have been there for you back then."

Richie finds this statement weirdly off-putting. It's as if she's lamenting she didn't have a more competent opponent.

"Yeah, well, it was my fault," he says. "I let you beat me."

"No, you didn't. I beat you fair and square."

"I wish you had. I beat myself. You hit one in the gap but it should have been caught. I lost it in the lights."

She smiles, says, "Well, you shouldn't hate me then."

"I don't."

"I know you do. I'm not going to tell you how I know that but you can probably guess. She wants to help you, Richie. She really does."

He doesn't respond right away. He looks down at his phone, which he has sitting in his hand in his lap. Nothing. Still.

"I may hate you," he says, "but I respect your abilities."

"How 'bout respecting me in general?"

"That's pushing it."

Another smile. Then, after a beat: "Bet you didn't ever think you'd be riding in a car with me."

"In a convertible no less."

"You're not too cold?"

"No, I'm all right."

37 / THE TEXAS SHARPSHOOTER FALLACY

PULLING INTO A SPACE NEAR THE FRONT OF THE FORENSIC LAB, Madden sees Lowenstein standing near the entrance, his hands in his pockets, a folder under his arm, talking to Lyons, who's smoking a cigarette.

"Wow, that was fast," Lyons greets him. "That's gotta be a record."

He looks like he's been having a grand old time shooting the shit with Lowenstein.

"You shouldn't be here, Marty," Madden says. "You should have called me first, gone through proper channels."

"Sometimes I'm courteous, sometimes I'm not. This is one of those times I'm not."

"Why are you here?"

"I thought I'd check in personally with Greg and let him know what he was up against. It's a quick shot from the airport."

Great, Madden thinks, *they're on a fucking first-name basis. How long have they been talking?*

"Greg's well aware what he's up against," he says. "He doesn't need you to remind him. I'm pretty good at it."

"Do you know what I do, Detective?"

"Yeah, I know. I think everybody knows. You're the DNA Dude."

"That's great for marketing purposes. Succinct. Resonates with the media. But just a bit narrow in scope, don't you think? So, I ask again, do you know what I really do?"

Madden shrugs. He doesn't know if it's a trick question or not.

"My bailiwick is the use of expert evidence in the courtroom. That includes forensic science in general and particularly forensic DNA tests. And while I'm known more for my work on a few highly publicized cases and the Exoneration Foundation, I've also worked to help convict people with DNA evidence. I work both sides of the DNA fence, so to speak. And I also evaluate statistical testimony because what a lot of people don't understand is how integral statistics are to DNA profiling and evaluating the significance of scientific data. I'm sure you've looked at few electropherograms in your time? Compared the peaks and valleys of alleles at different loci?"

Madden doesn't like the tone of Lowenstein's voice. In his brief encounters with him, he hasn't seemed like a guy who talks down to people, but if Madden's not mistaken, that's what Lowenstein's doing right now.

"I've had several cases where DNA evidence played a key role," he tells Lowenstein. "Not to date myself or anything, but I worked one of the first DNA cases in the country. However, I leave it to guys like Greg here to do the science part. I'm just the evidence collector."

"Well, speaking of that," Lowenstein says, "have you ever heard of the Texas sharpshooter fallacy?"

"The what?"

"Why don't you tell him what it is, Greg?"

Madden looks over at Lyons, who shifts uneasily from one leg to another, and flicks some ashes to the ground.

"What is it?" Madden asks.

"It's a term epidemiologists use—"

"Who?"

"People who study health events. You know, outbreaks and stuff."

"Okay."

"Well, it's a term they use to talk about the way people give too much significance to random data because they're looking at it after the fact from a narrow or biased context. Goes back to this parable of a Texas marksman who fired a bunch of random shots at the side of a barn and afterwards painted targets around the shots. When the paint dried, he brought people over to impress them with what a fantastic shot he was. When they saw he'd nailed each target dead center, they couldn't help but think just that."

"It's a pretty simple concept for jurors to understand," Lowenstein says, taking the baton back. "I use a whiteboard and a Nerf gun with suction-cup bullets. I first draw some targets on the board and then I then ask for one of the detectives who worked on the case, let's say you, to take a couple of cracks at the targets on the white board. For a little extra dramatic flair, I'll throw in a snide comment about how I've heard you're a pretty good shot, judging from your past accolades. Of course, by now your friend Mr. Crowley, the DA, is objecting up the ying yang. He's not having his detective—or anybody else—firing Nerf bullets at a white board. 'What's this got to do with anything, judge?' he asks. 'It's goddamn theater.' Oh, but it does, I say. It has everything to do with everything. Watch. And I hold up the Nerf gun by my shoulder and march off a few paces like I'm participating in a duel. I march right up to the jurors' box and then I turn around and start firing at the white board. As you can imagine, I'm not all that accurate. But then I erase the board, fire some more shots, draw my targets around them, and present my little dissertation on the Texas marksman fallacy. Length of performance: eight minutes. Damage done: priceless."

Madden doesn't know quite what to say but is embarrassed to realize his mouth is hanging open slightly.

"Look," Lowenstein goes on in a flatter, more professorial tone, "everything is fine and dandy when you have a simple DNA case where the alleles are identical at each loci and you get a clear match. But the thing about DNA, and the thing about a lot of cases, is you often don't get a conclusive match. You've got DNA that's degraded or mixed with other DNA. Take, for instance, Ms. Hill, who discovered her husband's body. We now know she'd just spent time with the accused. That means that there's a good chance that some of his DNA transferred over to her. So yeah, while it's possible his DNA may show up at the crime scene, she could have brought it there. That's the way DNA works. It travels. And just because it's there doesn't mean what you might hope it means. You could say the same thing about Mr. Forman's lighter. You presumed because it had his fingerprint and presumably his DNA on it that he brought it there. But I learned recently that he gave it to Ms. Hill and that's how it hitched a ride there."

Madden stares at Lowenstein, growing more irritated. "I've just become aware of the situation with the lighter," he says joylessly. "We're in the process of investigating that further."

"Well, that's not the only thing you're going to have to investigate further. My next stop is the DA's office. I got on a plane this morning to tell you and Crowley that I want the charges dropped on my client by end of day or I go nuclear, news-at-eleven style. I'm giving you an opportunity to redeem yourselves before it's too late. You guys painted the target around the arrow after it was shot and it's going to look really bad when people find out. No one likes a cheater, Detective."

"We did no such thing," Madden objects.

"You don't think you did, but you did. But let's get to the real reason I came by to see Greg."

"I thought you already told us that."

"That was just the opening salvo. Actually, the real reason is this." He takes the folder out from under his arm. He opens it to reveal an image Madden is very familiar with: the picture of the snake tattoo. Even though Lyons had previewed him about it on the phone, his stomach drops a little when he sees it.

"Greg, do you want to tell him what the problem is or should I?"

"You go ahead," Lyons says.

"As we're all aware, this is a tattoo that has been photographed on Mr. McGregor's left hip. Like you, when I saw it, I had some curiosity as to what it was and what it meant, so I sent it over to a friend at the FBI and had him run it through their database. Nothing. *Bupkis*. Okay. But then he says something interesting. He asks whether I knew when the guy got the tattoo and I say, well, according to the wife, it was fairly recently, within the last year or so. And he says, oh, well, that's strange because I gave the picture to an analyst here who thinks it's at least five years old and probably closer to ten."

Madden looks at Lyons, who doesn't have much of a reaction other than to look away sheepishly and take a drag on his cigarette. *Five to ten years?* he thinks. *Why would she lie about that?* He takes the folder from Lowenstein and examines the photo he's already examined too many times. He feels his phone vibrating on his hip but he ignores the call, continuing to stare at the photo.

"It's in good shape because of where it is," Lowenstein says. "It hasn't gotten much sun. But there are still signs of weight gain and loss. And—"

Madden: "He was sure on that? Five to ten?"

"Yeah, but I want to have a look myself. I want to see it up close."

"You can't see the body, Marty. You know you can't see it, so cut the bravado. Answer me this, why would Ms. Hill lie about when her husband got a tattoo?"

"I don't know."

Ha, Madden thinks, *got you there*. However, his small triumph is short-lived.

"Like you, I did my homework on the Sedition Act," Lowenstein goes on. "I thought there might be a clue there. But then on the way over here, I considered the alternative."

"Which is what?"

"That she isn't lying."

Madden takes a moment to mull that one over. "So, she just didn't notice it until a year ago? I'll check my notes, but I'm pretty sure she actually spoke to her husband about it."

"Maybe he was a never-nude," Lyons jokes. "Had a roommate like that in college. No one ever saw him naked. Guy never even took his shirt off."

"Maybe it isn't him," Lowenstein says.

Madden: "What do you mean?"

"Exactly what I said. That guy you have in there on ice, maybe he isn't Mark McGregor."

"Impossible," Lyons says.

"Why?"

"We got a match on his DMV thumbprint and dental."

"What about DNA?"

"Later today or tomorrow," Lyons says. "It's been expedited. I mean, seriously, dude, come on. Who do you take me for? That's fucking insulting. And to think, I had a lot of respect for you."

"Sorry to disappoint you."

"Fuck you, man."

Lowenstein smiles. "You know him at all?"

"Who?"

"McGregor."

Silence.

"What do you mean?"

"You ever meet him?"

"Meet him?"

"Yeah, you ever spend any time in the same room with him?"

Lyons looks to Madden for help, but Madden's not inclined to give him any. He's curious to hear what Lyons has to say.

"Answer the man, Greg."

"Yeah, I met him. How'd you know that?"

"You've got some pictures of him up on your Facebook page. He and a couple of other entrepreneurs from some panel you attended. Some networking event."

"That's not a public photo."

"You know that attractive, innocent-looking brunette whose friendship request you accepted the other day? Well, maybe you should be more careful about who you friend. Not everyone's who they seem."

"You gotta be fucking kidding me."

"So I'm going to ask you again, how well did you know McGregor? From what I gather, you were trying to start a little business of your own. Apps, I believe. Just one dumb idea, right? That's all it takes. Did you ask McGregor for an investment? What'd he ask for in return?"

"I'm not going to dignify that with a response."

"I thought so."

"You've got some fucking nerve."

Lyons takes a step toward Lowenstein. For a moment Madden thinks he may have to step between them, until he feels his phone vibrating on his hip again and decides that now would be a good time to answer it.

"Madden," he says, putting the phone to his ear.

"It's Carlyle. Where are you? I've been trying to call."

"Up at the coroner's office. Why?"

"Richie Forman just broke off his ankle leash."

Madden's stunned.

"Why would he do that?"

"I don't know why. But the alarm went off."

"Where is he?"

"Not far from you. San Carlos."

San Carlos. What the hell's he doing in San Carlos?

"I've got the sheriff's guys on it," Carlyle says.

Since the city of San Carlos has had so many fiscal problems, a few years ago it outsourced its police department to the San Mateo County Sheriff's Office.

"What's going on?" Lowenstein says, moving closer, trying to listen in.

Ignoring him, Madden gets an address, repeats it back, and tells Carlyle he's on his way, breaking for his car even before he hangs up. Lowenstein follows him.

"What's going on, Detective?"

"Apparently, your client removed his GPS bracelet," Madden says. "The alarm went off."

Lowenstein seems equally stunned. "Are you sure? He could have gotten it wet. They go off sometimes when they get wet."

"I don't think so, Marty. This one's waterproof. Now get out of the way before I accidentally hit you with my truck, news-at-eleven style."

38/ TIMID BY S & M STANDARDS

CAROLYN SLOWS THE CAR TO A CRAWL AS THEY NEAR THEIR DESTINAtion and they both start looking in earnest at house numbers while keeping an eye out for Ashley's rental car.

"That's it," Richie says, pointing. Carolyn pauses in front of the house, which is at the end of a cul-de-sac. A two-story home with an attached garage and pitched shingled roof, it's relatively modest in size, painted a yellowish white. Probably a three- or four-bedroom, it looks well maintained, particularly compared with the home across the street, a foreclosure. There's no car parked in the driveway and nothing's going on inside as far as he can tell.

While it's nice enough, Richie's first thought is that it doesn't seem like the home of a guy who recently collected several million dollars from the sale of his company. Of course, he could have bought another home and was waiting on the sale to close. Or maybe he was still house hunting.

"Turn around," he tells Carolyn. "Swing around the block. Maybe she parked on one of the side streets."

They're in cookie-cutter suburbia, a modest neighborhood that's got some larger lots but nothing extravagant. They pass a few other cars and a couple of Hispanic guys who are working on a yard down the block.

They make a couple of loops, taking different streets each time, but don't spot Ashley's car. They turn back into the cul-de-sac and Carolyn, on Richie's instruction, pulls the car over in front of a neighbor's house a couple doors down from the target address.

"I'm going to go check it out," he says. "Watch me. If anything happens, call the police."

He doesn't really have a plan but figures he'll keep things simple and just go up to the door and ring the bell. And that's what he does. He rings the bell and stands there, waiting and listening, but doesn't hear anything. He rings again and waits. Nothing. He gives it another minute, then decides to try to get a better look inside.

The front yard has a small, manicured lawn and a set of high, dense shrubs that come up to a level just above the windowsills and make it harder to see inside the house. Keeping low, he wedges his way between the shrubs and then pops his head up and looks into a large picture window.

The place appears to be empty but lived in at the same time, like a hotel room that's awaiting the next guest. There's a bowl of fruit on a dining-room table, which has six chairs around it. The furniture looks like generic Pottery Barn or Crate and Barrel. He listens for a moment, blocking out the din of a lawn mower down the street. He gives it one last look, then goes around to the side of the house, where there's a wooden gate. Trying it, he realizes it's not locked; it's just a latch. But instead of opening it all the way, he shuts the door and goes back to the car.

"No one's answering," he tells Carolyn.

"You sure it's the right address?"

"I think so. The gate on the side is open. I didn't see any stickers for a security system. I'm going to take a quick peek in the back and then we'll get out of here."

"I don't think that's a good idea," she says. "You're in enough trouble already. Let me do it."

"It's okay," he says. "Just vouch for me if I set an alarm off. And call the police if I'm not back in oh, six minutes."

"You sure her phone's battery didn't die? Happens all the time to me."

"Maybe," he says. But he doubts it. It wasn't like Ashley to say she would call, then not find a way to do so. In the few weeks he'd known and worked with her, she'd proven to be pretty darn reliable and resourceful. "But we're here, we might as well make sure. What time does your phone say?"

She tells him, which of course matches what's on his phone since both clocks are set by the network. They agree on an end time, the hour mark, which is slightly more than six minutes.

"Okay go!" she says.

He heads back to the house. After looking down the street to check that no one's watching, he walks purposefully toward the side gate. This time he opens it all the way and goes through, closing it gently behind him. He finds himself in a sort of alleyway that runs alongside the house and is bordered on one side by the neighbor's high, mesh-textured wooden fence. A strip of dirt, maybe four feet wide, runs next to a cement walkway and contains what appears to be an incomplete gardening project: a few plants in the ground, a few others in plastic containers looking wilted and on the verge of death.

He cautiously makes his way to the back of the house and comes upon a wooden deck with a table that has a green umbrella rising from its center and chairs around it. There's no pool but he spots the cover for the hot tub Ashley mentioned from her conversation with Anderson's former Macy's coworker. The backyard lawn is small, with rosebushes and dwarf fruit trees.

He pauses on the deck, listening again for stirrings from within the house. Then he turns his attention to a set of sliding glass doors that lead into a kind of den or media room. It's hard to see inside because of the angle of the sun, so he presses his face up against the glass, cupping his hands around his head. He notes a leather couch and large flat-panel display in a cabinet but almost nothing on the bookshelves next to it.

Damn, this guy's neat, he thinks, and just then he notices the light shift behind him and a shadow appear on the carpet in front of him inside the room. It takes a moment for it to all register, but in one brief and fleeting instant he realizes someone's standing behind him and that he's in trouble. Deep trouble. Out of the corner of his eye, he sees the flash of a dark object, and a sharp pain streaks through his head. Then nothing.

Come on, Richie. Carolyn says to herself, looking at her phone. *Get back out here. Come on. I don't want to have to call the goddamn police. Christ, what have I gotten myself into?*

Five minutes have ticked away and there's no sign of Richie. Then, just as she's on the verge of panic, the front door to the home opens, and a guy staggers out, clutching his side. He looks around and waves to her, continuing to stagger forward. He's wearing a San Francisco Giants hat and appears to be cut on his face.

What the fuck?

"Help," he calls out to her. "Someone's robbing my house. A guy's robbing my house."

Oh no, she thinks. *Oh Christ.*

"No, no," she says, getting out of the car and going toward him. "He's not robbing it."

As she gets closer, she sees the guy really isn't in good shape. He's got a major scratch running down his cheek, starting from just below his left eye.

"Call 911," he says.

He says something else she can't hear and suddenly it dawns on her that he's not shouting at her. He's just talking in a normal tone voice. And then she recognizes the voice; it somehow sounds familiar, though she's not sure why.

"Sir—" she says, coming up to him, but stops midsentence when she realizes that the face is familiar, too. She peers at him, squinting, and he looks back, his eyes filling with apprehension. He seems to recognize her. *The eyes*. The face is rounder, more moon-shaped, a little bloated even. But those eyes. She remembers them from somewhere. And then, suddenly, it hits her.

"Holy shit," she says, freezing in her tracks, her hand going up to her mouth. She should scream but nothing comes out. And then he has his hand over her mouth and she feels something metal jab her side and stay there.

"That's a gun," he whispers in her ear, the scent of alcohol on his breath. "Don't make me use it."

She tries to pull away, but he jams the gun harder into her rib cage and this time an excruciating pain shoots up her side.

As he drags her into the house, she tries to get away, but he's a big guy, over six feet and at least twice her weight. He pulls her down a short hallway, then opens a door. She catches a glimpse of a set of stairs leading down to a dark space, a basement maybe. That's the last place she wants to go, and with every ounce of energy, she manages to turn her head and bite his thumb as hard as she can. He lets out an angry cry, swears, and whips her wildly through the door, sending her flying into a wall and tumbling down the stairs. Somewhere between the second and third roll, she hears a horrible sound as her leg catches awkwardly underneath her and snaps at the shin, both bones breaking clean through.

The pain hits a second later but what freaks her out more is the feeling of her leg just dangling there and then seeing it lying there on the floor pointed in a gruesome direction. Lying in a heap at the bottom of the stairs, she's screaming now. "Oh my God, it's broken. I broke my leg. I broke my fucking leg!"

Mark McGregor comes down the stairs and stands over her, holding his hand. "Christ," he says, staring at her leg, seemingly shaken by the sight.

"You *fucker*!" she's screaming. "You fucking asshole. You set this whole thing up!"

"Shut up," he says. "What the fuck are you doing here? How'd you find me?"

"Where's Richie? What did you do to him?"

"He's dead."

"What?"

"Shut up," he says again, and drags her by the arm further into the room, which is only lit by a small lamp that's shaped like a gargoyle. She looks over and realizes she's actually in a sparsely furnished bedroom, its walls painted red. There's a white shag carpet on the floor and a king-sized bed in the middle of it with a canopy over it, held up by a metal frame. She sees a big white plastic chair that looks like a cast-off from the set of *A Clockwork Orange* and a dark, oppressively rustic chest of drawers. She feels like she's entered some cheesey bordello but what makes it all the more unnerving is the horrible mix of goth and modern.

McGregor drags her over to the chest, pulls out a set of handcuffs from the middle drawer and cuffs her to the bed frame. In the fog of her agony, she sees Ashley sitting on the floor on the other side of the bed, handcuffed to the opposite bedpost, a strip of silver duct tape over her mouth, her eyes wide with fear.

The pain now is unbearable. Carolyn shuts her eyes, fearing she's about to pass out, and takes a series of short breaths. *Fuck childbirth*, she thinks. *This is worse.* And it's only then that she starts crying. Not because she's terrified but because she realizes all those shots were for nothing. Getting pregnant on a broken leg would be too crazy even for her. And Cogan. She was so close. It all hits her at once.

"*Fuck!*" she screams, and wham, McGregor grabs her by the head and slaps a piece of tape over her mouth.

"Shut up," he says. "I gotta think. I gotta fucking think."

When Richie wakes up, he isn't sure where he is. He hears someone screaming, but the cry is muffled and he isn't sure where it's coming from. He's got a splitting headache and his head feels heavy. His first thought is not to move, he doesn't want to get up, but then he thinks he has to, someone's in trouble. He's in trouble. He struggles to lift his head from the floor, and realizes he's bleeding; there's blood on the tiles in the shape of a ragged half moon where his head has landed.

It takes a moment but he soon realizes he's in a laundry room and his hands are handcuffed together around one of the metal legs of a sink. The sink is large but cheap-looking—plastic, possibly fiberglass.

With a bit of maneuvering he manages to get himself into a seated position, but when he tries to stand, he has to take a knee after becoming dizzy. After a moment, he tries again and this time makes it onto his feet. But because he's limited by the height of the leg on the sink, he's left hunched over, like he's trying to lift a bucket that's too heavy for him.

He pulls up on the sink as hard as he can and gets the legs to lift off the ground an inch or so but no more. The problem is part of the sink is bolted to the wall—or at least seems to be. He sees what he has to do: lift the sink up, then wedge something under the opposite leg and prop up the sink just enough for him to slide his hands down the leg and slip the cuffs out through the gap between the leg and the floor. But when he looks around to find an object that will do the trick, all possible candidates are out of reach.

He tries again to pull up on the sink, the cuffs digging painfully into his skin, but stops when he hears a door open and shut and footsteps nearby. He thinks Anderson's coming back, and still can't understand why he isn't hearing police sirens. *Why didn't Dupuy call? Why has he got me locked up like this?* And then he has a chilling thought: maybe the screams, which have now stopped, were hers.

His heart pounds as the footsteps become louder. He braces himself for the door to the laundry room to open but just when he thinks it's going to happen, it doesn't: the footsteps grow fainter; Anderson's moved on to another part of the house. A momentary sigh of relief, then distress again as he thinks he detects an odor that smells like gasoline.

Think, Richie. Think.

And then it hits him. He's got the object he needs around his ankle. He lifts his leg awkwardly, bringing his foot up to his left hand, and lowers the sock that's covering the tracking bracelet. Once he's got it exposed at the top, he lifts up the sink with all his might and gets the leg up a full two inches this time, maybe more. Holding up the sink, he moves his foot next to the leg and jams its tip into the small space between the bracelet and his skin. He then carefully lowers the sink down a half an inch or so. When he's sure the tip of the leg is wedged in, he grits his teeth and lets go.

He feels a sharp pain as the leg reaches the floor and just catches the side of his foot inside his shoe, pinching it badly. But it's worth it: he looks down and is amazed to see that the bracelet has snapped off. *Fuck yeah,* he thinks, lifting the sink just enough to free his shoe. *Come get me, boys.* Now all he has to do is lift the sink again and, using his foot, slide the bracelet under the opposite leg. That should give him enough clearance to get the handcuffs' chain out from around it.

He hears the footsteps again and on the first try, his nerves get the best of him: he fails to properly align the bracelet with the bottom of the leg and the sink doesn't stay up. The footsteps grow louder, they're coming toward the door. He tries it again, and this time the wedge holds, and he quickly slides the chain down the leg and pulls it out through the open gap.

Just as he gets free of the sink, the door opens and bashes into him, toppling him over. He rolls onto his side and when he looks up he sees a figure standing over him, pointing a gun at him. But he's not a cop. He's a guy in a T-shirt and jeans and a Giants baseball hat. Richie doesn't know why, but he looks somehow familiar. Had he met Anderson before somewhere and didn't know it?

"You were always a determined little fuck, weren't you, Richie?" he says.

When he says his name, it dawns on him that this isn't Anderson. The guy stands there, his mouth breaking into that unmistakable smile and Richie can't quite believe what he's seeing. It doesn't compute, yet it does. The face looks fuller, puffed out. But it's him, isn't it? It's fucking him.

"You—" is all that comes out of his mouth.

"Not who you were expecting?"

"What have you done with Ashley? Where's Dupuy?"

He's so concerned with other more pressing matters, McGregor's resurrection seems almost inconsequential. He can't even begin to process it.

McGregor smiles. "They're getting a very personal tour of Paul Anderson's fetish chamber. It's really pretty timid by S and M standards. But I must say some of his bondage toys have come in handy."

His smile suddenly disappears. He's seen the ankle bracelet wedged under the pedestal.

"What the fuck is that?" he asks.

"What the fuck do you think it is? It's an electronic leash. And it's all over, man. The cops are on their way."

"Get up," he says, waving the gun at him. "Get the fuck up. I don't how you found me. This house isn't even rented in Anderson's name."

"Easy, man," Richie says, standing up slowly, his foot now throbbing along with his head. "Easy. Let the women go, okay? It's me you want anyway."

"No, I don't. But I do want to know how you found me. That Ashley girl says she works for Marty Lowenstein, but she wouldn't say how she found me."

He pulls him out of the little room and nudges him forward down a short hallway, poking him in the back with the gun, telling him not to try anything. As soon as they get out into the hall, the unmistakable odor of gasoline becomes stronger. *He's going to burn the place down*, he thinks, stepping in a wet patch on the floor. There's gas everywhere.

"Let's talk about this, man," he says, resorting to clichés. "You don't have to do this. Let the women go. We'll talk this out. You and me."

"We sure will," he says.

He marches him into the kitchen, where he sees a gas can sitting on the floor next to a door that turns out to be the entrance to the garage. There are two cars in the garage. McGregor presses a button on the wall to open the garage door, then leads him over to the driver's side of the closer vehicle and tells him to get in. Richie opens the door hesitantly, a little discombobulated. *He can't expect me to drive*, he thinks. But it turns out that's exactly what McGregor has in mind.

"Get in," he repeats, giving Richie a nudge with the gun. "You're driving."

He then circles the front of the car, keeping the gun trained on Richie the whole time.

"I can't drive," Richie says after McGregor slides into the passenger seat next to him. "Uncuff me."

"Yes, you can. That's why power steering was invented. Press that button right there," he says pointing to a spot to the right of the wheel.

Richie looks for a key for the ignition but doesn't see one. *Where are the cops?* he wonders, fumbling around by the side of the wheel, stalling. *Come on, boys. Come on.*

"Where's the key?" he asks.

McGregor leans over and presses a button below the dashboard.

"It doesn't use a key. It's a hybrid. I've got the fob in my pocket. It's wireless."

He realizes then that the engine is on, but it's so quiet he can barely hear it. He's never driven a hybrid. What's he do next?

McGregor points the gun at him and says, "Roll down your window."

"Why?"

"It's hot in here. You're sweating."

"Why don't you turn on the air conditioner?" he asks, trying to kill more time.

"Just roll it down." After some more fumbling, this time with the window button on his door handle, he complies with the request.

"There," he says, and just as he says it, McGregor fires the gun. The bullet whizzes past Richie's face and into the house, hitting the gas can near the door, a ball of flames exploding out of it.

"Drive," McGregor says, pointing the gun at his head again. He can barely hear him, his ears are ringing so badly. McGregor jerks the gearshift into reverse for him, then moves the gun closer. "Fucking drive."

39 / NEVER LOST

CAROLYN HAS A HARD TIME CONCENTRATING ON ANYTHING BUT HER pain; then the sound of a bang and small explosion upstairs jolts her to attention. McGregor's turned off all the lights and left the room, but there's some light leaking in from cracks here and there, and she can make out enough of Ashley's face to see that she looks as panicked as she is.

The place is on fire, she thinks. *He's burning the place down. We've got to get out of here.*

And just as she thinks it, she feels her phone vibrating in her back pocket and almost simultaneously hears the muffled sound of the ringer going off. She'd forgotten she slipped the phone in her jeans as she got out of the car and now someone, probably Lowenstein, is calling. But with the way her hands are cuffed to the bed frame, she can't reach the phone, and maddeningly, the call goes to voice mail. Not long afterwards, the phone vibrates again, signaling she has a new voice mail. Then, thirty seconds later, a short but sustained vibration: someone's sent a text message.

She looks over at Ashley again, this time trying to calculate the distance between them. If she can get up on the bed and stretch out width-wise, Ashley might be able to get to the phone by stretching forward as far she can. It's worth a shot. And Ashley, seeming to read her mind, motions with her hands to come toward her.

The only problem is actually getting up off the floor. Her foot on her broken leg is dangling there, a fact that only becomes more apparent as she tries to stand on her good leg. On the first two attempts she can't lift herself up, but then she leans back, letting the cuffs dig into her skin, and uses the bed post as leverage to power up on one leg.

Breathing hard through her nose and sweating, she breaks for a few seconds, knowing the next part is really going to hurt. She rolls over onto the bed, and using her knees and good leg, maneuvers herself toward Ashley.

Another explosion, this one louder. Then she smells it: smoke. Not a strong smell, but it's definitely there. *It's burning*, she thinks. *It's on fire. How the fuck are we going to get out of here?*

By the time Madden gets to the location, the house is already on fire. He sees two San Mateo Sherriff's officers' cars parked across the street from the residence and he pulls in behind them, just in front of a burgandy BMW convertible that seems oddly familiar. He sees flames jutting off the left side of the house and smoke wafting out from the open garage door. He can see a single vehicle inside, partially obscured by all the smoke. The fire trucks arrive as he's literally getting out of his car and a few seconds later Carlyle calls to tell him there's a report of a fire at the location.

"I know," Madden says. "I'm looking at it."

Two cops are just standing in front of the house, one talking on his radio, the other hunched over, his hands on his legs, coughing. Madden comes up and flashes his badge, introducing himself.

"Anybody inside?" he asks.

"Not that I saw," the hunched-over cop says. "But I wasn't in there long. Did find this, though," he says, handing him a Ziploc bag with Richie Forman's ankle bracelet inside. "Your guy wasn't attached to it. But there was some blood on the floor next to it."

"Where in the house?"

"Laundry room. It was weird. Found it wedged underneath the leg of a sink."

For a moment Madden isn't quite sure what to do. The firefighters are busy getting their hoses hooked up and gear on and he just stands there, looking at the house. *Think, Madden, think*. And then it occurs to him that he should try to get the plate off the car in the garage. The smoke's pretty bad but when the wind shifts a little, he's able to read it, and calls Carlyle back to run the plate.

Just as he gets off the phone he sees Lowenstein running toward him and his first thought is, *Shit, I can't deal with this guy now.* He knew Lowenstein tried to follow him from the lab, but he thought he'd lost him. Now here he is, frantically coming at him.

"They're in the basement," Lowenstein calls out.

"What?"

"They're in the basement," he says, pulling up. "You gotta get someone in there."

"Who?"

"My investigator, Ashley," he says, trying to catch his breath. "And Carolyn Dupuy." He holds up his phone to Madden. There, on the screen, is the thread of text messages with green bubbles around them. Her last one says, "In basement. Help. Door under stairs." Followed by his: "Coming."

"What the hell's she doing in there?" he asks.

But instead of waiting for an answer he sets off for the house. He goes past a firefighter who's pulling a hose and goes straight for the front door. He doesn't put his hand directly on the knob but gives it a quick touch, checking its temperature. It's warm but not burning hot, so he gives it a turn and pushes it open. "Hey, don't go in there," another firefighter shouts.

Too late. He's inside already.

The stairs leading up to the second floor are just off to the right. *Under the stairs*, he thinks. *No, behind*. Staying low, he follows a short hallway, looking for the backside of the staircase, and sure enough there's a door. He's coughing badly now, the smoke's much worse, the heat of the fire suddenly upon him. He's about to reach for the knob when a firefighter appears by his side, his face fully covered by a breathing apparatus. The firefighter starts to pull him out, but he shouts for him to open the door. "There are people in the basement."

When he opens it, Madden leads the way down the stairs and is greeted by fresher air. He goes to reach for his flashlight but the firefighter already has his out and waves it around the room, then trains it on the bizarre sight: there, in the middle of the room, is an ominous-looking metal-framed bed. And on the bed are two women, one of them stretched out at an odd horizontal angle, her hands extended all the way out, like she's being blown by the wind. Both of them have their mouths taped and are handcuffed to the bed.

Madden gets to Carolyn first and pulls the tape off her mouth, leaving the firefighter to help Ashley.

"Thank God," she says, her face covered in sweat. "Get us out of here. My leg's broken, Hank. It's broken really bad."

He looks over at her leg and notices her foot is pointed in a direction it shouldn't be. *Jesus*, he thinks. She pleads again for him to get her out of there.

He wants to, but there's the little matter of the cuffs. While they tend to use plastic wrist ties these days, he has a handcuff key on his keychain and two extra keys. But when he goes to reach for his keys in his pocket, he realizes he's left them in the ignition of his car.

"Do you know where the keys are?" he asks her.

"You don't have a fucking key? And you call yourself a cop. Shoot them off."

"You don't want me to do that."

"Look in those drawers," Ashley says, her mouth now untaped. "He got them out of those drawers."

Madden goes over to the chest and opens the top drawer, where he's a little startled to find a set of sex toys, including a giant dildo, two tubes of lubricants, and an open box of rubbers. He quickly moves on to the middle drawer, which has another set of cuffs, but still no keys. Then, finally, in the bottom drawer—bingo: in a corner is a thin wire ring with two small keys on it.

He returns to the bed, where one fireman is on his radio, requesting a set of bolt cutters. Madden gets the cuffs off, and the firefighter starts to plot their exit.

"I got a couple of windows over on this side," a second firefighter says. "But it's real tight. I don't think we're getting her out that way in her condition."

Carolyn is grimacing horribly, shouting for them to get her the fuck out of there, and for a brief moment, Madden wonders whether it wouldn't have been better to leave the tape on her mouth.

"Don't worry, ma'am," the first firefighter says. "We'll get you out."

And sure enough they do. A couple of tactical water strikes and a mad dash later, they make it outside with only a mild case of smoke inhalation. An amateur photographer snaps a series of shots of them coming out of the house, the most dramatic of which—a firefighter carrying Carolyn out in his arms, Madden resolutely by their side, his face covered in sweat, his eyes tearing—will appear on the front page of both the *Mercury* and *Chronicle* and as the lead story on the eleven-o'clock news.

Outside, Madden can't stop coughing but he keeps pushing aside the oxygen mask the paramedics insist he use. He can't wear an oxygen mask and talk on the phone at the same time.

"I need you or someone there to get on the phone to Hertz," he says to Carlyle. "I need them to track down a vehicle immediately. I don't have the plate, but it's under Marty Lowenstein's name and it was rented last Saturday. Not the one he rented today." He then breaks into another coughing fit.

"You gonna be okay there, Hank?" Carlyle asks.

"It's him, Brian. It's McGregor."

"What do you mean?"

"Forman's in the car with McGregor. He's not dead."

"Who's not dead?"

"McGregor."

"You're fucking kidding me."

"No, I'm not. Just find that car. It's got NeverLost. And that means it can always be found."

40 / A LITTLE SECRET

"HOW'D SHE FIND ME?" MCGREGOR ASKS.

"Why don't you tell me where we're going first."

"Make a left at the next light."

"Where are we going?"

"I don't know. Just make a left."

Mark looks like he's put on twenty-five pounds since Richie last saw him. Maybe more. He asks whether Ashley gave him the scratch on his face—or was it Dupuy? It looks oddly like a tattoo he'd once seen in prison, only longer.

"The girl," he answers.

"You hurt her?"

"She deserved what she got." She'd suckered him out. Rang the doorbell and said there was a package, then pretended to go away.

"Clever little tart," he says. "She would've made a good hire. So how'd she find me? What made her want to look for Anderson?"

Richie keeps scanning the road for police cars, but he doesn't see any. He heard sirens earlier. The cops must have been a minute or two behind them. Now everybody and his brother are headed toward the Anderson house. They probably think they're still inside. God, he hopes so. *Please*, he thinks. *Please, get them out.*

"Got lucky," he says, glancing over at the gun, which McGregor has propped up on his thigh and is pointing at his midsection. He's worried he'll hit a bump and McGregor will accidentally put a slug in him.

He tells McGregor about the guy at Macy's, the former coworker who gave her the tip on the address. McGregor doesn't react strongly.

"Figures," is all he says. Then: "Make a right here."

They ride in silence for a moment, Richie concentrating on making the turn. McGregor's right. It actually isn't as hard as he thought to drive in handcuffs, though he can't see himself pulling off a quick, evasive maneuver with any success. He still feels a little woozy from the head blow and his stomach's churning badly. He's also thirsty as hell.

"You kill him?" Richie asks. "Or you have someone do it for you?"

"What do you think?"

"I don't know, that's why I'm asking. What'd you do you with Hsieh?"

McGregor laughs. "A fucking prop," he says. "The guy spoke almost no English. He didn't have a clue what was going on."

Anderson did most of the talking, he says. Did it well, too. Said exactly what he was supposed to say and even spiced it up with a few added flourishes. As instructed, he played hard to get, said he would never sell, and Cahill, their Aussie investor, took the bait.

"So this was all about money?" Richie says. "Ten million bucks. That's what this was all about?" He'd argued so assuredly to Madden that money was the motive for the murder, yet now he can't quite fathom it.

"After all the monies came out of the wash, it came to more than that," McGregor says. "But to answer your question, no, it was a confluence of factors. You like that? A *confluence*," he says, enunciating the word, himself enamored of it.

"I don't understand," Richie says, shaking his head.

"What's not to understand?"

"How you could come up with something so crazy. This is fucking crazy, man. You planned this all out, didn't you?"

He smiles. "For almost two years. Ever since I met Anderson in the hospital."

Talk about serendipity, he says. There Mark was, all bent out of shape and not feeling too good about life, and he ended up in a room with another sad sack. Only Anderson was ahead of him. He'd actually tried to kill himself.

Before he ended up in the hospital, he'd been having some dark, self-destructive thoughts, Mark says. He'd taken a big hit in the 2008 crash and then things started to go south with Beth. And despite staying out of prison, he'd never been freed of the accident. It dogged him. There were people who doubted his story and a few others who came right out and said they didn't believe him. He was no longer invited to the TED Conference and other prestigious events. And one guy came up to him after he'd spoken on a panel and called him a killer. To his face.

"I killed a young woman," Mark says flatly. "A promising young woman. You didn't have to live with that. You were lucky."

"Lucky?"

How can Mark even *think* that? It's one of the dumbest things anybody has ever said to him.

"Shit," McGregor says, "we're going the wrong way. Make a left at the next light."

This, from a guy who said he didn't know where they were going.

He and Anderson resembled each other, Mark says. Same height, complexion, and eye color, and just a year apart. Anderson had a few pounds on him, but hey, that was easy enough to fix. He just had to up his calorie intake for a few months, let himself go a bit. Actors did it all the time.

"'Now there's an idea for a movie,' I thought to myself, lying there all depressed and self-loathing in that hospital room. Guy doesn't want to live anymore so he sells his life to someone else. Instead of selling an organ like those poor schmucks in South America, he'd sell his whole life."

"What was he going to do with the money once he was dead?" Richie asks.

"I don't know, maybe he had a relative or someone he wanted to hook up. Shit, if he's going to kill himself, he might as well get something for his trouble."

"And you were just the guy who was willing to provide it."

"Well, that was for the movie. In real life, you can't tell him that eventually you're going to have to kill him. That doesn't go over so well. And sadly, once people come into half a million dollars, they have a habit of wanting to live a little longer. Sometimes a lot longer."

McGregor smiles again. But this time when Richie glances over, he sees that McGregor is not only smiling, but he's staring back at him.

"Ah, man, I missed you, Richie," he says, giving him a little slap on his shoulder with his left hand—the one that isn't holding the gun. "We had a fucking good time, didn't we? Back in the day."

"Ancient history, Mark. Ancient fucking history."

"The glory days. Before women brought us down."

"Women brought us down? You're blaming women, plural? What the fuck are you talking about? You sound wasted."

"That's because I am." Then, not missing a beat: "Bear right. And follow the signs to 280."

Madden calls Carlyle back to ask for an update on the Hertz car-tracking situation. Apparently, he hasn't gotten very far.

"I don't know what to tell you, Hank. We're getting a little bit of a runaround. I've got Pastorini making calls. They've transferred him twice, put him on hold."

"Is he on the phone to corporate? Who's he calling? You need someone high-level to authorize this. Tell him to step it up."

Lowenstein comes over. He's been talking to Ashley, making sure she's all right, but he must have seen Madden talking on the phone, looking frustrated.

"Where are we at?" Lowenstein asks.

"We're working on it," Madden replies. If it were anyone else, he would leave it at that and rebuff any more intrusions. But it's Lowenstein, and Lowenstein isn't going to sit back and take his bullshit. So he adds, "But if you've got any strings you can pull with Hertz corporate, I'd encourage you to pull them."

Lowenstein nods, seeming to appreciate the gesture, then takes out his phone and makes a call.

"Hi, Elizabeth, this is Marty Lowenstein," he says. "I'm a President's Circle member and I'm about to put your exceptional service to the ultimate test."

"I haven't driven a car in over eight years," Richie says.

"Really? It's not hard. You can pick it up a little."

McGregor talks as they drive, explaining the evolution of his plans with increasingly slurred words and jerky hand gestures. Project A, as he liked to call it, became an obsession. It invigorated him, he says.

Obviously, the key to the whole thing was pulling off the body switch. He knew he'd have to disfigure Anderson, but he didn't want to go so far as to burn him, making him totally unrecognizable. He was relying on Beth to identify the body and he wanted it to look like a crime of passion, one a wife could have committed. Those were the two underlying principles he started with, and he worked backwards from there.

While he needed her to make a positive ID, he knew that in any suspicious death, the coroner's office wouldn't simply take her word. They'd start with fingerprints, move to dental, then finish with DNA. If he had the first two nailed—or three if you counted Beth's ID—he figured he'd have more wriggle room with the DNA. Over the months, he'd acquired a couple of Anderson's toothbrushes, a hairbrush, nail clippers, and a number of other personal effects he could exchange for his. While there was no escaping the fact that he would leave some of his own DNA around no matter how careful he was, as long as there was enough of Anderson's around to pick from, he'd be in decent shape.

The fingerprints and dental records were an easier fix than he thought.

"Everything is digital now," he says. "And everything digital is open game for manipulation."

For all his issues, Anderson had never been arrested. That was a big plus. Other than giving his thumbprint when he got his driver's license, he'd never been fingerprinted.

McGregor says the "thumbprint part" wasn't a huge challenge. His previous company had been awarded one of the contracts to help modernize the state's computer system and integrate a new online voter registration system. That gave him a back door into the DMV, which he'd kept in his back pocket, so to speak.

He thought the dental records would prove much trickier, but it turned out that not only did his and Anderson's dentists both use digital X-ray machines, but also the same software.

"I'm not going to lie," he says, "it was a little hairy, but it's not like you're hacking into the Pentagon. I just had to pick the right time to switch the files."

As Mark tells the story, Richie briefly forgets he has a gun pointed at him and stops caring where they're headed. In a way, it's fascinating, if not horrifying—the lengths to which McGregor has gone to extricate himself from his life, in the process completely infiltrating Anderson's.

How'd he get to Anderson? Drugs. Anderson dug painkillers and tranks: vikes, percs, oxies, benzos, z-drugs, "all that shit." But it was more than the promise of drugs that got him to the house that day. It was money, too, he says.

Anderson had been asking for another hundred grand. Usually, he met him at his shitty little apartment in Mountain View and later at the house in San Carlos. Anderson was a lazy fuck. That's why he didn't make it. His idea of a good time was sitting in his hot tub smoking a joint and then having some dude handcuff him to that bed downstairs and pound him in the ass and tell him what a fucking loser he was.

Richie wonders who McGregor's talking about, himself or Anderson? Sometimes it's hard to tell. He lets it go, though. He wants him to finish the story.

McGregor says that as a precaution, he always made sure that they both kept their cell phones off twenty minutes prior to each meeting and twenty minutes after so they couldn't be tracked. The same rule applied this time but he told Anderson to meet him much closer to his home—on the El Camino in front of the Guild Theater in downtown Menlo Park. He said he had something special for him.

When he got there, he opened the trunk of his car and showed him a briefcase with money in it, let him touch a stack to see that it was real. He said there was twenty thousand inside, which was a lie; it was five. He said he didn't have any more cash but he could take the car. It was worth seventy, maybe more. Just give him a ride home and he could take it. He'd sign over the title to him right now. And that would be that. They'd be done. For good this time.

Anderson seemed amenable to the deal. He'd always coveted that car, and was happy to take possession, though he was momentarily flummoxed over what he was going to do with his own car.

Not my problem, McGregor said. Stick it in a garage. Did he want the car or not?

Like any junkie, Anderson was focused on getting a fix. Every exchange they had seemed to end with that.

"What you got pharmaceutical-wise?" he asked.

He told him he'd left a bottle of "oxy" in the glove compartment (which Anderson promptly fished out and opened), and had another few bottles at home he could give him.

When they turned onto Robert S Drive, McGregor, in the passenger seat now, ducked down, pretending to look for something on the floor between his legs, then pressed the remote for the driveway gate, and Anderson pulled the car inside.

He had everything set up, ready to go. Distracting Anderson, he told him to check under the front seat of his other car in the garage for more pills. They should be in a little cardboard box, he said as he slipped on a pair of black golf gloves.

Anderson looked and said there was nothing there.

McGregor told him to keep looking. They were there. But they weren't, and when Anderson stood up and turned around, he never knew what hit him. McGregor struck him high across the neck and then several times in his chest and upper back. Wham, wham, wham. Anderson went down and McGregor slammed the backside of the tomahawk into his face. Once, twice, and then a third whack for good measure. It was over in less than thirty seconds.

"I was breathing hard, my heart pounding like a goddamn jackhammer. But I pulled it together. I stuck to the plan. I wrote 'Hack' in Anderson's blood on the floor with my left index finger."

Then he slipped the weapon into a garbage bag and wrapped it up tightly. Next, he removed Anderson's wallet and everything from his pockets, including his car and house keys and phone, and replaced them with his own, dropping his own moneyless wallet on the ground near the body. Last was the watch, his prized Rolex. God, he hated giving that thing up. But he wanted to create confusion. The fake robbery would look so blatantly botched it wouldn't make sense.

When he was through checking and rechecking everything, he took off his shoes and stepped into a pair of nearby sandals, careful never to touch the ground with his feet. He then took the briefcase out of the trunk and walked over to his pool house, stripped down to nothing but a T-shirt and jeans and stuffed everything else—shoes, weapon, long-sleeve shirt, and the briefcase—into a duffel bag that could be worn as a backpack. The final touch was a modest disguise:

a blond wig with a ponytail that he covered with a John Deere hat and a cheap Weed Wacker that he slung over his shoulder. He then walked out the back of his property, slipped through his neighbor's yard and emerged on the adjacent street, Corinne Lane, and headed up to Valparaiso and back to the El Camino and Anderson's car.

Everything had gone off without a hitch. "A thing of beauty," McGregor says, pausing reflectively. Then he says, "You wanna hear something fucked up?"

Richie shrugs. Like he has a choice. Like what he'd just told him already wasn't fucked up enough.

"That program I wrote for the shell company, the code Anderson sold back to us, was the best work I'd done in a long time. It was pretty spectacular. Ended up with a patent for one piece of it. It kicked the shit out of what our engineers came up with, which wasn't bad, mind you."

"If it was so good why didn't you just keep everything legit?"

"People are constantly doing beautiful work and no one gives a shit. Everything's fucking 'freemium' these days. You gotta ramp pretty fast and you're dealing with a lot of different variables. You either can't get to critical mass or you get to critical mass but you don't get the return on investment you said you would and all of sudden your optics are all off. Next thing you know you're looking through the bottom of a Coke bottle and drinking Jack, fending off the hounds. Why deal with all that stress? It's a hell of lot easier to raise the money than to actually make it. And shit, this way I didn't have to give away any of it to my vampire wife."

He had a point, Richie admits. But there's still some stuff that doesn't make sense.

"Like what?" McGregor asks.

"Like how could you count on Beth to make an ID? I mean, she had to, you know . . . she had to know your body," he says, struggling to get the remark out.

"Dude, we hadn't had sex in a year. And I put on some weight over the last few months. And shit, how long would you want to look at a body that had been hacked up like mine was? It was pretty gruesome, man. But here's the kicker. Here's the fucking brilliant part."

Using his left hand, he yanks up his shirt, then wedges his thumb in his waistband and pulls it down, exposing a patch of skin on his waist, just below the belt line. Richie glances over and sees that it's a small tattoo that looks like a snake. There are some letters underneath it that spell something he can't make out.

"I got this tattoo. Exact same one Anderson had. I made sure she noticed it. Cops ask for identifying characteristics: here it is."

Wow, Richie thinks. "What are the words? What's it say underneath?"

"Sedition 1918."

"What's that?"

"Some fucking gay rights group he was a part of in his twenties. Gay marriage and shit. I'm all for it, by the way. They thought the name was clever. He and a few of the other boys went out one night and got themselves tatted up. You know, solidarity for the movement, which must not have been much of a movement because I did a search on Google and didn't find anything. Lots on the Sedition Act of 1918, though."

Sedition Act? It rings a bell from a history class but he doesn't know exactly what it refers to.

"Hey, slow down," McGregor says. "There's highway patrol all along here. I don't want you to get a ticket."

That's exactly what Richie wants. He accelerates more, pushing the speedometer to eight-five.

"I said slow down."

"What are you going to do? Shoot me going ninety? We'll both be killed."

"Good," McGregor says, raising the gun a little. "I've got no problem with that. We can do it that way."

Richie looks at him, decides he's serious, and eases off the gas.

"Where are we going, Mark?"

"You know where we're going, Richie."

He does. He's known ever since McGregor said to get on 280 and go south. This is the route they took the night of the accident.

"You don't remember this part because you were asleep," McGregor goes on. "But you're going to remember it this time."

They drive in silence for a little bit, then McGregor says:

"I'll tell you, man, it's something to be able to see what happens after you die. All the flowers in front of the house like that, a lot of them from strangers. And all the nice things people had to say. It was really quite moving."

"You're an arrogant asshole. You always were."

"Yeah, I know. But when we were friends, you used to like that. I made you laugh."

That was true. He did make him laugh. Just then the first sign for the Sand Hill exit appears and McGregor says:

"Hey, get ready. Turnoff's coming up."

"What are we doing here, Mark?"

"I thought we'd pay our respects. What do you say?"

"And then what?"

"Then I'll let you in on another little secret."

"What kind of little secret?"

"You'll see."

They drive in silence, the question and answer session seemingly over—or entering a new phase. He glances over at McGregor, who's wearing a small, self-satisfied smile. It's all a game to him. The same psychological bullshit. With McGregor, it had always been about gaining the upper hand. He had to have it. And now he was doing it again.

What's the endgame? Richie thinks, looking ahead to what the best time to jump him will be. He's just going to have to go for it. *I'm gonna live till I die*, he says to himself, remembering one of Sinatra's famous quotes, which always struck him as something Yogi Berra would say. *I'm gonna live till I fucking die.*

He pulls off at the Sand Hill exit and then struggles a bit with the steering wheel as they go around a tight loop that leads them back over the highway.

"I was having a little trouble keeping my eyes open on the freeway," McGregor says. "But I was fine here. I remember being glad to get off."

They head down Sand Hill and Richie looks at the speedometer. They're going forty-five. He goes through the first light and passes the Rosewood Hotel on his right. Buildings with the names of venture-capital firms litter either side of the road.

"Slow down," McGregor says, staring straight ahead.

He should have done it then, should have put his hands together and taken a swing at him, but he was looking, too, mesmerized by the road ahead.

"I must have fallen asleep right here," McGregor goes on. "I never saw the red light until the last second. I was probably only out for three or four seconds. Max. Okay, pull over. By the cross."

Richie turns the wheel a little to the right, then a little left and straightens out, guiding the car into the wide bike lane, positioning the left wheels of the car just inside the line. It's not a good place to stop. A car whizzes past. Then another. They're going really fast. Like torpedoes.

"Turn off the engine," McGregor orders. "Just put it in park and hit the button."

The gear shift is between them, with Ashley's purse practically lying on top of it just in front of the radio and GPS screen. Reaching over with both hands, Richie takes the lever and gets set to put the car in park when something stops him. *Don't*, he thinks. He pushes the lever up, and he says, "Fuck, I didn't know that cross was still here," causing Mark to glance over at it. In that moment he lets the stick come back down to D. He then reaches over to the ignition button and pretends to tap it, saying, "The family maintain it?"

"I don't know," McGregor says. "But I've gotta see it every time I take fucking 280."

Richie leans back in his seat, leaving his hands in his lap front of him

"Bummer."

McGregor turns his head left, his eyes looking out the windshield toward the intersection. He stares straight at the spot where the woman died.

"Their car came out of nowhere," he says. "I opened my eyes and there it was in front of me. It just fucking appeared. There was nothing I could do. I could see it was bad right away. We'd gone right into them. That Cadillac was a tank. And then I looked over and saw you lying there. And I said, 'Richie. Richie.' And you didn't answer. And then I shook you. And nothing. You were fucking limp. And I went to feel for a pulse and I didn't get one. I didn't think you were breathing; I thought you were dead. And that's when I panicked. I thought, 'Shit, I killed this guy right before he's going to get married. I'm never going to live this down.' And that's when I decided to switch seats. I climbed over you and unhitched your belt and slid you over into the driver's seat. I had time to wipe down the steering wheel with my jacket and then I took you by the back of the shirt and slammed you up against the wheel as hard as I could to make it look like you hit the thing on impact. And I remember you slumped over to the left and all of sudden you coughed and woke up. I saw you take a breath and make a sound, and I was like, What the fuck? But by then it was too late. I heard the sirens and I just focused on making sure it looked like I was in the passenger seat. I put your hands on the wheel and you actually took it. You held on to it."

"That's your little secret," Richie says when he's through. "That's what you brought me here to tell me? That you thought you'd killed me but you then accidentally saved my life?"

"That's it," McGregor says.

"And I'm supposed to believe that?"

"You can believe what you want. That's what I'm telling you happened. That's the fucking truth."

And then they hear the sirens. At first they seem to be coming up Sand Hill in front of them. Then it sounds like they're coming from behind. And then Richie realizes they're coming from both directions at once.

"Why didn't you tell the cops that? Why didn't you just fucking tell the truth back then?"

"I always told you, man, when you do something you've gotta be committed. Totally committed. I made a choice. And you know, it was more important for me to go on. It was more important for the shareholders. I had a lot of people depending on me. I couldn't go to prison. No, strike that. I *wasn't* going to prison. It just wasn't happening. And it isn't happening now either."

"But it was okay if I did? And it was okay for you to take Beth."

"I didn't take her. She took me. Make no mistake about that."

"But you thought it was okay nevertheless."

"You never had enough spine, Forman. You were never cutthroat enough. But you sure as shit could sing. I'll give you that. You did a mean Sinatra, even back then."

The cops are upon them now. The first vehicle to reach them is an

SUV that looks familiar. It makes a left in front of them, its tires squealing, and screeches to a halt in the intersection right in front of them. A second vehicle, this one a sedan, follows in its wake and pulls in behind the SUV, forming a roadblock.

Richie looks in the rearview mirror and sees another squad car coming in behind them—it's probably highway patrol—and a car, a regular passenger vehicle, a Mercedes, coming to a stop next to them, not able to pass through the intersection. One of the cops—he thinks it's Carlyle—has his gun out and is shouting for them to get out of the car.

"What now, Mark?" he asks. "What's your exit plan?"

He's ready for McGregor to shoot him but instead he lowers the gun and sets it in his lap and smiles.

"What now?" he says. "Now you get to be in the driver's seat forever. Sorry, kid. Gotta go. It's wheels up for me."

And then McGregor lifts the gun, bringing it up to his chin as Richie slams the accelerator all the way down to the footboard, sending the car lurching forward. Richie hears the gun discharge but he can't see anything. He's slid down in his seat, his hands in front of his face. He braces for impact and wham, the car crashes into Carlyle's SUV.

When Richie opens his eyes, Carlyle has his gun pointed at him through the windshield and there's all kinds of shouting. Richie looks over and sees Carlyle yanking McGregor out of the car and dragging him to the ground. Another cop pulls Richie out and slams him up against the back of car, pushing his face down to the trunk. The cop pulls out a set of wrist ties, somehow missing the fact that Richie's already handcuffed.

"Easy, easy," Carlyle shouts. "He's okay. This is the guy. I got him." Then, turning his head toward the microphone on his shoulder. "We got him, Hank," he says. "We fucking got him. And you're not going to believe where."

Richie comes to the front of the car and sees Carlyle standing there with his boot on top of McGregor's head, pointing his gun down at him. McGregor's groaning. He's still alive. The bullet missed.

Richie takes a step forward, leans down, and kneels. He then moves close to McGregor's face and says in a quiet voice that only McGregor can hear:

"We're not even close to even, asshole. Not even fucking close."

41/ ESCAPE CLAUSE

COGAN'S THE ONE WHO ENDS UP TALKING TO BETH FIRST. SHE'S called Carolyn's cell phone, and Cogan, who's holding onto it for her, picks up when he sees her caller ID info pop up on the screen.

Richie listens as Cogan tells her that Carolyn's at Stanford Hospital in very serious condition. She's been stabilized but she has the worst kind of open fracture. She's gone into surgery, it's being performed by a friend of his, the chief of orthopedic surgery, and several other surgeons are attending. So she's in good hands, but the surgery is going to take awhile.

"I've got someone who wants to talk to you," he says, and hands the phone to Richie.

"Hey, Beth."

"Richie?"

"Where are you?" he asks.

She says she was in a class at the gym. She came out and looked up at one of the screens by the treadmills and saw a picture of Carolyn being carried out of a house by a firefighter and Madden by their side. She couldn't believe it. Then she saw his and Mark's picture up on the screen. She didn't have any headphones on and couldn't hear anything. She called Carolyn immediately.

"What the hell's going on, Richie?"

"You better get down here. We're at the hospital. I've got some things to tell you."

Fifteen minutes later she shows up, still in her gym outfit.

"I'm sorry for my appearance," she says to the group in the surgical waiting room, a little surprised by how many they are. "I didn't shower. I came right over."

Lowenstein's there, sitting next to Ashley, who's been playing it tough, insisting she's okay. Physically she is, but every so often Richie sees one of her legs start shaking and she puts her hands under her armpits and hugs herself. Richie himself has come over from the emergency room, where he received ten stitches and now has a small bandage on the right side of his head. He's been diagnosed with a Grade I concussion that has Grade II aspirations. When the doctor told him he should take it easy for the next couple of days and not drive, he agreed.

Between the two of them and Cogan, who uncharacteristically tears up at one point, it's a motley-looking bunch, so when Beth, typically stunning, apologizes for her appearance, no one's quite sure what she's talking about. Richie gets up and takes her aside, leading her out of the waiting room. They go down the hall a bit, near the elevators.

"There isn't going to be a funeral, Beth."

"There isn't?"

"You're going to need a divorce after all."

She looks at him, confused.

"Mark's alive," he says. "He's always been alive."

"What?"

She just stares at him a moment, then her knees start to buckle, and he reaches out and grabs her before she hits the floor. After the initial shock wears off, he props her up against the wall and she stands there for a few seconds, leaning against it, her hand on her forehead, partially covering her eyes.

"Where is he?" she says.

"In custody."

He then recounts the day's events, getting interrupted a few times whenever a nurse or doctor or visitor arrives in the elevator. He tells Beth how Ashley went to investigate a tip she had on Anderson's whereabouts and how he and Carolyn had gone to look for her and ended up stumbling into a much more hazardous situation than they'd anticipated. After killing Anderson, Mark took Anderson's identity, living in his house. He tells her about getting bonked on the head, then being trapped in a laundry room upstairs while Ashley and Carolyn were locked up in the basement, Carolyn with a broken leg, which he'd only heard about well after the fact. Mark had then set the house on fire with the two women in it and taken him hostage in the car.

"He had a gun," he says. "He had me drive him back to the scene of the accident. He was going to kill himself."

With each new detail, Beth seems more astonished. She feels terribly for Carolyn. Is she going to be all right? He tells her the surgeons are concerned about her developing a fat embolism, which is a frequent occurrence with such injuries. And a little of the bone had poked out through the skin, which meant they had to watch out for infection; they were pumping her full of antibiotics.

"She's looking at a very long rehabilitation, but it could have been worse," he says. "She could be charcoal. And who knows, maybe her ex-boyfriend in there will marry her. He seems pretty broken up."

Beth doesn't respond. Her eyes drift away, her thoughts elsewhere.

"Why'd he do it, Richie? It's just insane. It doesn't make sense."

He tells her Mark had bank accounts with over thirteen million dollars in them that he had access to. He was all set to leave the country but ran into a small problem: Anderson had lied to him and told him his passport was current when it wasn't. He still could have gotten out of town and figured out a way to get a new passport quickly, but he just decided he'd lay low for a few days. He seemed to take some perverse pleasure in hiding in plain sight. It was a bit of hubris, Mark told him. Things were looking pretty good from where he was sitting and he figured he'd sit back and have a cocktail or two and enjoy the show. Shit, once they cremated his body, as he'd requested in his will, he'd be home free. He joked that he might even catch some of the funeral on Saturday. It had always been a fantasy of his, since he was a kid, to watch his own funeral.

"He didn't seem to have a concrete plan for what he was going to do afterwards," he says. "He said Central and South America were the next big frontiers for the Internet. He was looking at Nicaragua. But it just didn't seem like he'd put that much thought into it. He just figured he'd somehow reinvent himself."

"So he did it for the money? I don't understand. He had the company. They were just about to launch. The product was good. I saw it."

Yeah, but he didn't think he'd ever have a shot at the big exit. Just wasn't in the cards, he told Richie. So this was it. This was his big exit. This would show everybody.

However, it wasn't just about the money, Richie says, mentioning Mark's comment about a "confluence of factors." He wanted to set her up, implicate her in the murder. While he was trying to goad her into reaching out to Richie to create some innuendo, things changed when she decided to meet with him down here in Menlo Park. He decided to modify his plan. It was too good an opportunity to pass up. And it turned out better than he thought it would.

"My arrest was a bonus," Richie says. "You were the real target."

It ended up being a mistake, though. Mark told him he regretted involving him to the degree he did. He said he was sitting there watching the news and Marty Lowenstein suddenly appeared out of the blue. He said to himself, *Shit, Marty Lowenstein, how the fuck did that happen? Where did he come from?*

"That's just crazy," she says for what seems like the tenth time. "But I don't understand, who was trying to blackmail him?"

"He was blackmailing himself."

Her jaw drops again. "You're kidding me?"

"Just a diversion," Richie says. "One of many. I've gotta ask you something, Beth. One thing's been bothering me."

"Just one?"

"Well, a lot of things. But there's one thing I've been thinking about a lot. Did you know?"

"Know what?"

"It wasn't him. I mean, how could you . . ."

As his voice trails off, she looks at him and lets out a long sigh, then looks away, down at the floor. It's unclear whether she's trying to recollect something or is carefully considering her answer.

Finally, she says, "The truth is that when I first saw him there in the garage, my initial thought was that it wasn't him. I didn't know whether it was just the shock of seeing him lying there or whether it was something in my subconscious. It wasn't anything in particular. It looked like Mark. He was dressed how he dressed. He was the same size. Same hair. And I saw his watch. But this little thing in the back of my mind said it wasn't him. But I let it go. If I had any doubt about it, it went away after they said his thumbprint matched and they found the tattoo I told them about. And I think they even had his dental records, didn't they?"

Richie nods. He tells her how Mark switched them. And then he told her about the tattoo.

"My God," she says.

"I know. But you didn't say anything? You didn't express any doubt? When you ID'd the body, why didn't you say anything?"

She shakes her head.

"They asked me whether it was him. And I said, 'Yeah, I think so.' I mean, it was horrible. You can't imagine. What Mark did to that poor person was horrible. I thought you really had to hate someone to do what he did. I thought—"

And then he knows. "You thought it was me, didn't you? You thought I killed him?"

She lowers her eyes, not able to look at him.

"I did," she says after a moment, lifting her eyes. "I thought you'd done it. This time I thought you'd done it."

"Why?"

"Because I still loved you. And I thought you still loved me." A brief pause, then, her eyes looking at him beseechingly: "You do, don't you?"

He stares back at her, not answering. Then he reaches up with his hand and takes her chin gently between his fingers.

"Love is love," he says, and just then the elevator dings, the doors open, and Bender and Madden step out.

"Just the man I wanted to see," Bender says. "Did you see the post? I made this fucking guy into a hero," he says, pointing to Madden, who's carrying a small Big 5 Sporting Goods bag in his hand. "Did you read it?"

"You didn't make me into a hero," Madden says. "You made yourself into a hero."

Richie had seen the article. Lowenstein had showed it to him. The title was, "How I Solved the McGregor Murder: The Inside Story."

"Well, that too," Bender says. "But that's true. That's a fact. We did it, huh, buddy?" he says to Richie. "We got him! I can't fucking believe it. I'll give you a little time. I'm sorry, did I walk in on something? Oh, hello, Ms. Hill. I'll give you two a little time and then you and me will sit down and I want the whole story. I want all the details. I get the first interview, understand? You're still mine for another twenty-four hours."

"No, he isn't," Lowenstein says, coming out from the waiting room with Ashley in tow. "Didn't you read the little line in the contract about what happens in the event that the charges against my client are dropped?"

Bender doesn't miss little details like that. He takes pride in not missing those kinds of things. And from the look on his face it's clear that he hasn't missed it this time either. Rather, he's dismissed it.

"Are you going to tell everyone the good news, Detective?" Lowenstein says.

"The DA's scheduled a press conference forty-five minutes from now. He's going to announce the charges against McGregor and drop the charges against Richie."

"Shit," Bender says. "What were the fucking odds of that happening?"

"Come on," Madden says to Bender. "I'm going to say hello to my old friend Cogan in there, see how he's doing. But afterwards, I'll give you a ride over to the press conference and give you an exclusive. I'm retiring."

Bender thinks about it a moment, then nods, mainly to himself. "All right. That's not bad. I can work with that. Let's do it."

Madden then hands Lowenstein the Big 5 bag.

"Thanks," Lowenstein asks.

"My pleasure."

Then he walks off into the waiting room, leaving the four of them standing there.

"This is for you, Richie—as promised," Lowenstein says, passing along the bag, which Richie can see has a mitt inside. "What do you say we go outside and play a little catch? I've got my mitt in the car. We'll come back later and see how she's doing."

"I like that idea," Richie says, pressing the button for the elevator. When it arrives, he lets Ashley in first, then Lowenstein. Then he gets in. Beth hangs back outside the elevator, looking at them.

"You coming, Beth?" Lowenstein asks.

Beth looks at Richie, not knowing what do.

"Sure she is," Richie says, taking her by the arm and pulling her in.

Once the door closes, Lowenstein says, "I know you're a Wilson man, but I think it's time you gave it up."

Richie opens the bag and looks inside. It's a tan-colored mitt and it has a ball inside the web. He thinks it's going to be a Rawlings, but it isn't.

It's a MacGregor.

ACKNOWLEDGMENTS

FIRST, A SPECIAL THANKS TO MY AGENT JOHN SILBERSACK AND ESTEEMED publisher Peter Mayer for bringing this novel to fruition, tolerating my views on ebooks and publishing, and even being willing to take my advice. While this is a work of fiction I have a number of people to thank for helping me keep it in the realm of reality. A shout out to Sergeant Tony Dixon of the Menlo Park Police Department, who graciously let me ride around with him on the mean streets of the hamlet I grew up in. Also thanks to Jim Simpson, Detective Sergeant (Ret) of the Menlo Park Police Department, for taking the time to let me bounce my scenarios off him and answer my questions. For legal counsel I turned to my friend Don Rollock, former Nassau County ADA turned criminal defense attorney, who I'd hire if I got into any trouble. And then there are the countless tech entrepreneurs who met with me over the years as part of my day job and shared their experiences. And finally, I had several folks mark up early and late versions of this work in an effort to make it better: Jerry Gross, John Falcone, Adrienne Friedberg, Mark Bloom, my father Martin, and editors Stephanie Gorton and Dan Crissman. Thanks for your time.